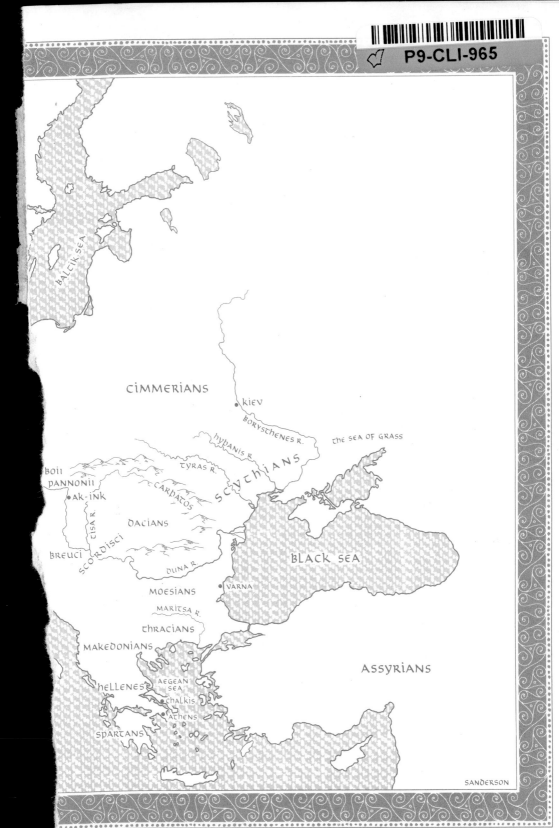

BALTIC SEA

CIMMERIANS

•kiev

BORYSTHENES R.

THE SEA OF GRASS

hypanis R.

TYRAS R.

Boii
PANNONII

•Ak-ink

CARPATOS

SCYTHIANS

TISA R.

DACIANS

BREUCI

SCORDISCI

DUNA R.

BLACK SEA

MOESIANS

•VARNA

MARITSA R.

ThRACIANS

MAKEDONIANS

ASSYRIANS

hELLENES

AEGEAN
SEA

chalkis

Athens

SPARTANS

SANDERSON

THE
HORSE GODDESS

Morgan Llywelyn

HOUGHTON MIFFLIN COMPANY   BOSTON 1982

Library of Congress Cataloging in Publication Data

Llywelyn, Morgan.
   The horse goddess.

   1. Celts — Fiction.   2. Europe — History — To 476
Fiction.   I. Title.
PS3562.L94H6   813'.54   82-6234
ISBN 0-395-32514-5   AACR2

Printed in the United States of America

D 10 9 8 7 6 5 4 3 2 1

For Charles, always,
and my two Seans

This book is dedicated
to the hope that men everywhere
may discover brotherhood,
and find freedom.

Contents

PART ONE
The Blue Mountains

Chapter 1

IT WAS NIGHT, and the spirits walked.

In the lodge of the lord of the tribe, Toutorix, the Invincible Boar, Epona waited for the representatives of the spirits to come for her. Since sunrise she had carried a knot in her belly, but she refused to give in to it. She had gone through the day as if it were any other day, pretending not to notice the jealous teasing of the other girls and the suddenly speculative glances of the boys. She had eaten her meals without tasting them and had licked her fingers afterward as if she had found the food delicious. It was important to avoid offending the spirits of the animals and plants that had been sacrificed for her nourishment.

As the sun moved across the sky the knot in her belly became a stone. The older women began preparing her for the night's ritual, and she submitted in silence as they bathed her body in three changes of cold water, and oiled her skin with perfumed oil from a silver Hellene ewer. Rigantona watched closely to be certain no drop was wasted. It was her oil and her ewer.

Epona's masses of tangled, tawny hair were pulled smooth with a bronze comb and plaited into three braids, with a copper ball knotted into the end of each to signify her status as the daughter of Rigantona, the chief's wife. Rosy-cheeked Brydda batted at the balls to make them swing, and laughed like a child, but for once her infectious gaiety did not strike an answering note in Epona.

After sundown she could no longer wear the short tunic appropriate for children, but she was not yet a woman, so her mother wrapped her in a blanket woven of soft baby goats' hair and pinned it securely with one of her own bronze brooches. "Be certain you return that brooch to me afterward," Rigantona said sharply. "Don't you dare lose it!"

Afterward. It was hard to believe there might be an Afterward, when you were going into the unknown to face the spirits. Epona looked into her mother's face and thought of all the questions she wished she could ask, but she said nothing aloud. What lay ahead was mystery. To be worthy of her blood she must face it bravely, just as any warrior went to certain death, knowing that life continued beyond. Afterward.

At night the spirits walked.

When the long purple shadows swallowed the lake the women would come for her. Epona's younger brothers and sisters sat big-eyed on their sleeping benches, waiting. The chief and his wife stood on either side of her, proud and tall, prepared for the arrival of the *gutuiters*. They heard the footsteps on the path outside. They heard the knock: three heavy blows on the wooden door.

Epona's heart was pounding, but she tossed her head back and stood very straight as the door was thrust open. Nematona, Daughter of the Trees and senior *gutuiter*, a woman as lean and vigorous as a mountain pine in spite of her many winters, strode into the room. "We have come for the girl child," she announced with the authority of her office. Two other women entered behind her, bringing with them a scent of sweet smoke and bitter herbs.

"She is not ready," Rigantona protested according to custom but without sincerity. She had waited a long time for this night, to see the child leave. She held Epona by one shoulder and Toutorix took hold of the other, ready to propel the girl forward if she should threaten to humiliate them by balking. Children did sometimes struggle at this final moment, and even those who knew her best could not always predict what Epona might do.

"Come," Nematona commanded, holding out her hand.

I do this willingly, Epona said in her mind, to her mother. *If I did not, you could not force me; you could not!* She had had many similar conversations with her mother over the seasons, not all of them silent.

She clasped Nematona's hand firmly, realizing by the warmth of the *gutuiter*'s fingers how cold her own were. It would have been clever to warm her hands by the fire before the women came for her, but of course no one had suggested it and now it was too late. What was done now must be of her own doing.

Nematona led her from the chief's house, the other two women walking beside them, holding torches aloft. Epona ached to steal one look backward, to see if her parents were watching her straight back and squared shoulders; but she heard the door pulled shut behind her, its hinges creaking. Only the lord of the tribe had the new iron hinges Goibban had recently designed. Epona heard the thud of the bolt, signifying that the child was now barred from the lodge of the mother; she might enter again only after she had passed into her nextlife.

The lodge of Toutorix occupied a central position in the village, a community of dwellings and workplaces built of timber and clinging to the western shore of a narrow, winding alpine lake. Grouped around the chief's house were the lodges of his nearest kinsmen, the nobles of the tribe, and beyond these clustered the smaller lodges of miners and craftsmen and stockmen. Arranged for convenience around the village perimeter were the workshops and carpenters' pavilion, the dome-shaped bakehouse and smoke-houses, the storage pits and holding pens for the livestock. In a place of honor, slightly set apart and surrounded by precious space, stood the forge of Goibban the smith.

The mountains rose abruptly, crowding in on the village as if to shove it from its precariously narrow perch into the cold lake. Clinging to the forested slopes above were the lodges of more miners, for many men now worked the great Salt Mountain. In the folds of the hills, above deep wooded valleys, were the old smelters and mine shafts that had supplied the tribe with copper for bronze-making for many generations. Nearby were the huts of the charcoal burners, the strange men who held themselves apart from most aspects of village life yet faithfully cut wood and tended the smoldering charcoal mounds upon which the forge and smelt-ers depended.

A timbered palisade shielded the village from view of the stony path leading up over the hills to the mountain passes. Four nights to the west, along that trail, lay the famed Amber Road leading far north to the "sea gold" of the Baltik, and south to sunny Etru-ria, where it was partially paved with stone, and causeways had been built over the frequent marshes.

Along this road were shipped copper ingots and bronze ornaments, furs and hides and cattle, casks of honey and resins, bales of wool, beeswax and tools and countless wagonloads of salt, the outpouring produce of the Blue Mountains.

Following the same road up from the south came gold and silver, wine and olive oil, faience glass beads and topaz jewelry and ivory bangles, perfumes and dyes, and tanned strangers from lands warmed by the seas of endless summer.

Aside from the trail through the mountains, which villagers called the trade road, the only other access to the community was by water, across the lake. This proved a convenient route for floating out timber and bulk shipments of salt to be moved into the descending waterways and the network of rivers to the north.

Up the steep valley at the head of the lake was the great Salt Mountain itself, dominating the thoughts of all those within its sphere of influence, providing a wealth for the tribe of the Kelti that they could neither measure nor exhaust.

For most of each day, the village lay in the shadow of the towering mountains. What little level terrain existed was long since crowded with buildings, except for the tribe's commonground, near the lodge of Toutorix. Epona and the three *gutuiters* must cross this open space on their way to the sacred grove and the house of Kernunnos, Priest of the Stag, chief priest of the Kelti.

Shapechanger.

No! Epona would not let herself think about the shapechanger. Her loathing for the man might weaken her, and she must not allow that to happen. *I will do this my way*, she said to herself. *My way*. She matched her pace to the processional stride of the *gutuiters* and pressed her lips together to keep them from quivering.

Sometime during the long day one of the women attending her, Suleva, She Who Bears Only Daughters, had broken the prohibitions to whisper a fragmented warning: "You must not show fear. An awful thing will happen if . . ." Then the woman shrank into herself and said nothing more.

The *gutuiters* began the ancient chant:

> *"Maiden to sacrifice,*
> *maiden to sacrifice.*
> *See her go.*

See her go.
Dark is the night,
cold is the wind.
See her go.
See her go.
Follow the fire,
follow the fire.
See her go!
See her go!"

They moved their upper bodies in time to the chant, bending from side to side so the torches they carried made swirling patterns of light. The swaying movements and light dizzied Epona, and it was an effort to keep her steps regular, one foot set neatly in a direct line in front of the other as was proper for mountain dwellers.

Spectators, crowding into the doorways of their lodges, took up the chant: "Maiden to sacrifice. See her go!" Their voices rang in the night air, calling the attention of the spirits to Epona.

As she came abreast of each lodge, those who watched were careful to look down, for it was considered dangerous to meet eyes with a person passing between worlds.

An evening breeze sprang up, bringing the smoke from Kernunnos' lodge to meet the little procession, and as they passed the house of the dead, the voice of the chief priest could be heard, joining in the chant with secret words from the language of the spirits. That harsh voice carried a long way.

The valley seemed to grow darker, as if the residual twilight were being sucked out of it by the smoke and the chanting. The breeze became a cold wind from mountain passes still blocked by snow, and the ice crystals it carried froze out the softer scent of the pines at the edge of the sacred grove.

Epona did not look at the trees, but she heard Nematona call to them with love, and heard the soughing of their branches in answer. There was a spirit of exceptional power in the sacred grove. To walk close to the gnarled trees was to feel its presence, like a multitude of eyes looking at you, like the humming of a vast hive of bees, like the breathing of great animals, crouched and waiting, thinking unimaginable thoughts.

The people of the village gave up the chant and went back into

7

their sturdy safe lodges, to their bright warm fires. Only Epona and the *gutuiters* remained under the open sky, where the awakening stars could see them.

The path became narrow and broken, and sharp stones pressed into Epona's bare feet. Beyond the trees stood the magic house of Kernunnos, which she had never seen, for children were forbidden to go near it. It was built of oak, like the house of the dead, instead of birch, as other lodges were. The wood of the sacred tree was used for these special buildings because having once been sanctified they must stand forever; they could not be remade.

There was another structural difference between the house of Kernunnos and those of other people. All other lodges of the living were rectangular; that of Kernunnos was built to conform to the sacred circle. Trees crowded close behind the priest's lodge, and Epona knew from whispered stories that the ravens of Kernunnos sat hunched like black spirits of doom in those trees, surely aware of her approach.

The smoke issuing from the magic house was acrid and made her cough.

The *gutuiters* stripped her of her blanket before shoving her inside the lodge. At first she could see nothing, could be aware of nothing but the smoke stinging her eyes and nostrils and the sound of the chanting reverberating through her being, making her part of itself. A beating like a drum. There was a drum; she could make out its voice, the booming of the priest drum, and it came closer. Something was coming closer. Something terrible and irresistible.

There was a shrill cry directly in front of her, and a face materialized from the smoke, a sharp-featured face like that of a fox, with yellow eyes that burned into hers. The power of those eyes made everything else fade away and she saw only the feral gaze of Kernunnos the priest.

Shapechanger!

Epona was nauseated by the visceral revulsion she always suffered when she was near the chief priest, but she struggled to fight it off. It must not interfere with the ritual.

Kernunnos was dressed in a cloak of animal skins, with dangling paws that swung limply as he circled the girl. She smelled his body; rank, musky, a wild animal's smell. His eyes stared and glittered. On his head towered the branching antler headdress that marked him as a shapechanger, the rarest of the *druii*, the most awesome member of that priesthood whose talents were passed on through the blood or, occasionally, bestowed as a sign of exceptional favor from the spirits themselves.

In one hand Kernunnos grasped a piece of horn, a prong taken from the antlers of a mighty stag sacrificed generations before. The bone had been polished and sharpened to a fine point. At its tip it bore a permanent stain, like ocher.

Kernunnos lifted the prong to the level of Epona's eyes and shook it at her. "Your time has come," he chanted in a singsong voice. "One life is over. One life begins. It is always so. Make ready for the spirit of the strong and the powerful, Epona, the strong and the powerful. Make ready for the sacrifice of the blood, for the blood is the life. Make ready for life, Epona."

"E-po-na, E-po-na," the women chanted. They began to move, dancing, bending, forming a circle around the pair in the center, holding them within its magic ring. Circling, circling.

"Epona!" they cried. "Mother to daughter to mother to daughter, open the way. Open the way!" The *gutuiters* danced faster and Kernunnos began to dance too, turning with them, always holding the sharpened prong before Epona's eyes as if he were using it to lead her. She followed him because there seemed nothing else to do. Her feet had no will of their own, moving in an ancient pattern her flesh and blood knew but her mind did not. Kernunnos understood. His hot eyes smiled at her across the antler; through the smoke. He lowered his hand and the prong touched her breast, just pressing the skin at first and then digging in hard, drawing blood. Kernunnos danced and turned and darted at her again and again, seeking out the tender parts of her body, watching with his feral eyes to see how she reacted.

He could kill her easily. He could tear open her unprotected body with that horn and kill her, and there was nothing she could do about it. Who could question a sacred ritual? Who knew what the spirits might direct him to do? Epona had walked into mystery; no one who returned from the lodge of Kernunnos ever spoke of the ceremonies performed there. It was forbidden.

With balled fists held tight to her sides, she faced the priest and waited with all the dwindling courage she possessed, aware of her bravado draining out of her like urine trickling down her legs. Never before in her life had she, eldest daughter in the lodge of the chief, been hurt; only skinned knees and stone-bruised heels, and a kick from one of Kwelon's oxen. She was unprepared for pain; hot, lancing pain. She fought to keep herself from shrinking away from the stabbing antler.

The dancing unit, with Kernunnos and the girl still held in its center, moved closer to the firepit in the middle of the lodge. The youngest and fairest of the *gutuiters*, Tena, She Who Summons Fire, took a pottery jar from the stone hearth and shook its contents over the flames, murmuring an invocation. A gout of greenish smoke belched up from the coals, filling the lodge with a smell like overripe fruit.

The smoke swirled around Epona, caressing her. It filled her lungs and her brain and permeated her being, and with it came a sort of ecstasy, a drunkenness such as affected those who drank too much wine. Nothing seemed so important anymore. Her blanket was gone, and with it her mother's precious brooch . . . so? Kernunnos whirled and gibbered and the pain came . . . but? It did not matter. It was hard to remember that she had ever been afraid. Her newly grown breasts felt heavy for the first time, and there was a heat at the bottom of her belly that had not been there before. Not so much a heat as an ache, a needing . . .

She turned and turned like a hungry child seeking the mother's nipple, and the ache went with her. She surrendered to it. She collapsed into this wonderful soft swirling sensation with its colors and odors and a faraway ringing of bells — were they the little bronze bells the women wore on their ankles? Did it matter? How delightful to be cushioned in this new way and feel a reasonless happiness glowing through her flesh. She smiled. She laughed softly to herself. She shook her head so the weight of her braids whipped around her and she was not afraid.

The hot smoky air felt good on her bare skin, and the lightning flashes of pain as the antler kissed her meant nothing; they could not hurt her. She was sweating profusely and the close air of the lodge made her wish she had more clothes to take off, take off her very skin, break free of whatever it was that was pressing in on her, pressing . . .

She was very dizzy. The drum was beating and the bells were tinkling and the *gutuiters* were singing in faraway voices. A wave of nausea shook her and she closed her eyes for a heartbeat, feel-

10

The Horse Goddess

BOOKS BY MORGAN LLYWELYN

The Wind from Hastings
Lion of Ireland:
   The Legend of Brian Boru
The Horse Goddess

ing her balance desert her as she did so. She stumbled forward, throwing out her hands, expecting the priest to break her fall, but Kernunnos was no longer there. He was behind her now, prodding cruelly between her legs, and the pain was too intense to be denied. She was on her hands and knees and he was hurting her, hurting her . . . she chewed her lips to keep from crying out. With an incredible effort she managed to stagger to her feet and face him, refusing to be savaged from behind.

The prong slashed like a knife across her breasts.

The shapechanger stared at her. His lips were drawn back from his teeth into an animal's snarl, and he was singing a high-pitched ululation that changed and became the cry of wolves on a winter night, far off in some snow-filled valley. No one who heard that cry could escape the thrill of fear that followed the wolf's passage down countless generations. The wolf sang of wisdom, of loneliness and freedom, reminding men huddled in their lodges that there were wiser spirits in the world — and better hunters.

The shapechanger looked at Epona through a wolf's face. The animal itself seemed to stand before her, marking her for its prey. To her surprise, in that desperate moment some inner prompting came to her, as clear and sharp as a human voice speaking. With a nod of understanding, Epona looked into the terrifying visage of the shapechanger and drew her own lips back from her teeth, matching him snarl for snarl.

Kernunnos laughed.

The women seized her and lowered her to the ground. One sat on her chest and the other two spread her legs wide so the priest could dance between them. The chanting became muted as Kernunnos invoked the names of the spirits of tree and stone and earth, calling on them all to witness the ritual and accept the girl's passage to the nextlife. When he sang the names of the water spirits the women wailed in chorus, spitting into the palms of their hands and rubbing the liquid on Epona's skin. When he called upon the fire Tena gave a great cry and light blazed up in the lodge.

Epona felt very far away from herself. She waited passively now, almost indifferently, as Kernunnos squatted between her spread legs and deftly guided the sacred horn to the entrance of her body. The priest closed his eyes and sang the song of the gateway; he demanded admittance for the spirit of life. As the chant rose

11

in power the women moaned and fell silent. The voice of Kernunnos shrilled upward into a final ringing note and one exquisite stab of pain lanced through Epona.

The women shouted in triumph.

The girl lay panting on the floor. They did not hold her now; they stood at a respectful distance, smiling down, and Nematona extended a hand to help her to her feet. Tena and Uiska, Voice of the Waters, came closer to caress her fondly. It hurt to move but she would not let them see her wince. Why give way to pain now, when the worst was over? She was surprised to realize the smoke had cleared away completely, and the lodge of the priest was just a warm room with a friendly fire blazing in the circular firepit.

She stood swaying, vaguely aware that the women were sponging her body with heated water. As her vision cleared, she realized the priest's lodge was far different from the luxuriously furnished home of the lord of the tribe. The dwelling of Kernunnos resembled an animal's lair.

Every bedshelf was covered, not with soft fur robes, but with whole skins bearing feet and tails. The heads had polished pebbles for eyes. The hides of larger animals, such as stag and bear, were pulled into lifelike postures by leather thongs suspended from the lodgepoles that supported the thatched roof. Dead birds, their bodies gutted and packed with salt, roosted in every crevice and spread their wings against the walls in startlingly lifelike flight. Rams' horns and stags' antlers were fastened on every available surface, creating a forest of horns. Boars' tusks and the bleached skulls of wolves were lined up around the hearthstone, crowded amid the pots and jars.

Only the priest was missing. Epona could not remember his leaving; he was just not there anymore.

The three women moved around her, kneading her flesh with melted fat, making little clucking sounds when her thighs quivered involuntarily. "You will be all right now," said Tena in her hot quick voice. "You are a woman thisnight, and from now on your spirit will guide you wisely. You passed your test very well."

It was the first time one of the priesthood had spoken to her as an adult. She tried to answer in a voice too quavery to trust, then cleared her throat and tried again.

"It wasn't bad. It didn't hurt," she told them.

The *gutuiters* exchanged glances of approval.

"You are brave," said Nematona. "You have proven fit to be the mother of warriors."

What was it Suleva had said? "You must not show fear. An awful thing will happen." Suleva, She Who Bears Only Daughters.

Epona flushed with pride, but the insatiable curiosity that was part of her nature prompted her to ask, "Why is it so important to bear warriors? We are never attacked here in the Blue Mountains."

"Not in your lifetime, no." Nematona passed her knife hand across her eyes in the classic sign of negation. But that is only because the battle reputation of Toutorix discourages other tribes from trying to capture the Salt Mountain. Yet we have fought before, and doubtless will again. We must all be capable of defending what is ours.

"But the children you bear will never have to fight for the Salt Mountain, Epona, because they will not be born here. Men will come from distant tribes of the people and give Toutorix many gifts in order to ask for you as wife. You will be highly prized, not only because you come from the chief's lodge but also because you are a strong, healthy young woman with courage to pass on to your sons — sons who will take their first meat from the tip of your husband's sword and serve as warriors in his tribe, wherever that may be."

Nematona's words reminded the girl of another cause for concern, now that the ritual of woman-making was completed. Like all women of the people, she was free to choose her own husband from among any who might ask for her, but the man she selected would make her part of his tribe in some place far from the Blue Mountains.

No, Epona said silently, stubbornly, inside herself. *Not me. It will be different for me; I have my own plans.*

It WILL *be different for me. I will make it so!*

Nematona brought her a thick fur robe and folded it around her body. Pale-haired Uiska, of the colorless eyes and snowy skin, pinned the robe closed with Rigantona's brooch, a massive bronze circle incised with a curvilinear design that drew the eye along the endless turnings of existence. It was a favorite pattern of the people, the representation of life flowing into life.

13

Redheaded Tena stroked the fur robe. "This was made from the hide of a pregnant she-bear," she told Epona. "Very strong magic. It has been saved for a long time for the daughter of Rigantona."

The robe was heavy and had a rank smell. When Epona wrinkled her nose, Tena chuckled. "Awful, isn't it? I suspect it needs airing, Epona. When the Hellene traders come after snowmelt, get some kinnamon from them and rub into the fur. Until then, you really don't have to wear it; it's just a symbol of your new status."

"By now everyone in the village knows my new status," Epona replied. "But I will wear it, in spite of the smell. It isn't as bad as the odor of the squatting pit or the dye cauldrons, and as you say, fresh air will help." She could imagine the way her sisters' eyes would shine when she came home wearing that splendid fur, and the fun they would have dressing up in it. Even Rigantona had nothing better.

Nematona opened the door of the lodge and Epona was astonished to see pearlescent dawn above the mountains. Had the night passed so quickly?

Of course — one must never forget the power of the spirits.

Mindful of the responsibilities of her profession, one of the *gutuiters* took Epona by the shoulders and faced her toward the rising sun. It was time for the final phase of her initiation into womanhood.

Uiska began it, in the solemn teaching voice all *druii* employed when giving instruction. "The sacrifice has been offered and accepted; the portents are good. You will be a fertile woman. The gateway of life has been opened within you, so you can enjoy bedsports and lifemaking with a man without fear of pain, and your children will begin with pleasure and enter thisworld smiling.

"But another gateway has been opened as well. You are now an adult member of the people, which means the spirit within you has been awakened. From now on you must always have an ear turned inward to listen for its voice, the voice that speaks without words. When it commands, you must always obey. That is wisdom.

"We do not encourage a child to listen to its spirit, because the spirit of a child, newly housed in flesh after living in the other-

14

worlds, is playful and giddy, like one who drinks too much wine for the first time. It lacks good judgment. We do not call to awaken that spirit until both it and the body have had time to mature. For you that season is at hand, and now your spirit is fully awake. You have become a free woman of the Kelti, Epona, daughter of Rigantona. Never forget!" Her voice lashed the whip of command.

She continued, "There are times when the spirit will warn you for no reason you can see, but always pay heed to such warnings. To be deaf to the voice of the spirit within is to be crippled, a burden to others for as long as you live. It is better to have been born with a physical deformity and been exposed on the mountainside so your spirit could seek better housing. But you are not crippled, Epona; you can hear the voice. Like sight and smell, touch and taste and hearing, it is a sense to guide you. Use it well."

Epona nodded. *That* was what had happened, then; in the moment when the shapechanger appeared to be a wolf and she snarled back at him, the spirit within had spoken to her, telling her to show defiance.

"But how does my spirit know these things?" she asked Nematona, who was standing to one side, watching her with a grave smile. "Where does its knowledge come from?"

"From the source of all wisdom," the senior *gutuiter* replied. "From the great fire of life that is shared by every living thing, in thisworld and in the otherworlds. The spirit within you is just one spark from that fire, but through it you are given access to the accumulated knowledge of the whole, if you will only learn to listen."

Epona frowned, trying to stretch her thoughts wide enough to embrace understanding. "Are you saying the spirit in me is kin to the spirits in the animals and plants? How can that be?"

Tena spoke up, taking her turn in the instruction. "*All* life is part of one life," she said, "and that one is sacred to all. We worship it in each of its many forms. It animates us and we share in its immortality. The spirit known in thislife as Epona will die and be reborn, slip in and out of the flesh, move from world to world, as we all shall, but it will continue to partake of life because we are all parts of the whole.

"The great spirit of life has many faces. In summer we worship

15

it in the form of the goddess, for spring and summer are the seasons of the female, the time of birth and harvest, the celebration of warmth and light and fertility, life renewing itself.

"Snowseason is the season of the male, the hunter of the autumn and the craftsman of the winter, the provider who shelters and protects. It is the time for testing, for strength and endurance, and for the death that precedes birth.

"Death is nothing to fear, for life comes after. Spring follows winter. Morning follows the night. Be joyous and unafraid, Epona, for you are part of immortal life itself, and the great fire burns in you."

Tena stretched out her hand and laid it palm down on Epona's forehead. Without conscious volition, Epona closed her eyes and crossed her hands over her heart in response. A radiance filled her; a commitment to her place in the endless cycle; a pleasure in being part of the whole.

The *gutuiters* walked back to the chief's lodge with her, not surrounding her as guards, but following one pace behind as an escort of honor. As she walked, Epona felt little twinges of pain and something warm trickled down her legs. By the time she reached her family's lodge her thighs were sticky and she could smell blood.

At the door of the house the *gutuiters* saluted her and turned away. Over her shoulder, Tena said, "Take care not to dream of a man nextnight," and the other two laughed. Nematona laughed like the rustling of leaves; Uiska's chuckle echoed the bubbling of brook water.

In accordance with the ancient custom, the older members of Epona's family had kept watch for her through the night. Toutorix had honored her by dressing for her arrival in a fresh linen tunic and new woolen cloak, Rigantona's finest weaving, in the red and green plaid of his family. Around his neck he wore the heavy gold neckring of a proven warrior chief, and massive bronze bracelets reinforced the strength of his wrists. The hair on his head had been newly bleached with lime paste, disguising the fact that it was no longer ruddy gold but streaked with silver, thick with the frost that obliges a man to measure his age in winters rather than summers. His cheeks were clean shaven, as was customary for a man of noble rank, but beneath them his mustache and beard were as luxuriant as ever. Toutorix wore an air of aggressive masculinity as easily as he wore his tartan cloak, though his broad shoulders were beginning to stoop and the muscles in his legs had grown stringy.

Married women still made approaches to him and many children in the Blue Mountains bore the stamp of the lord of the tribe on their faces: the passionate proud features and sky-colored eyes.

Over his tunic Toutorix sported a broad leather belt ornamented with bronze plates and squeezing him a bit more tightly than it had in his youth. But he was not fat; no man of the people would willingly allow himself to grow fat, to suffer the ridicule and punishment meted out to one who lost his shape and could not fasten his belt. Seen casually, he was the same powerful patriarch his family had always known, and Epona was warmed by the sight of him.

Arrayed in her best linen gown, Rigantona stood beside her husband. She was seasons younger than the chieftain, but as women did not bleach their hair it was possible to see that frost was making inroads in her yellow braids. Yet her shoulders were broad and proudly carried, and the breasts that had suckled many children were still relatively firm. When she raised her arms the muscles rippled in them as they had done when she was a girl, so skilled in the use of sword and spear that no boy her age could stand against her. No longer did she train, stripped, to fight beside her husband if needed, however; by now she was content to enjoy a degree of leisure and wear all the jewelry she possessed wrapped around her neck and stacked on her arms and fingers. The autumn of her life was a pleasant season for Rigantona.

Epona saluted the chief, then went directly to her mother to show she had returned the brooch. Rigantona examined it thoroughly before looking at her daughter's face at all.

"I am told I did well," Epona remarked, knowing better than to expect warmth or praise from her mother. Rigantona was not like other mothers. "I might have done better if I had known what to expect," the young woman added.

"The rituals are mysteries," Rigantona responded. "Tests, to see how well we face the unknown. Did you cry out?"

"No."

"Good. Toutorix was worried about you, but I told him no daughter of mine would prove a weakling." She turned away from

17

Epona and lifted the brooch to the firelight so she could admire its design once more.

Epona started to get a drink of water from the embossed bronze *hydria* on its tripod by the door, a luxury purchased from the Hellenes and now copied in every household in the village, but Alator was there ahead of her, anxious to fill her cup. His eyes glowed with pleasure at being the first to offer a drink to the new woman in the family. Epona smiled at her younger brother, remembering how she had hurried in the same way to be the first to do a service for their older brother Okelos, when he returned, pale but swaggering, from his man-making.

She longed to wash the sticky blood from her thighs and crawl onto her bedshelf, but there were still rituals to be observed, and her dry throat burned with thirst. She said the customary thanks to the spirit of the water and carefully scattered drops in the four directions before draining the cup. Then her family lined up to congratulate her, and there was a small feast.

She was exhausted, but she would not show it. *Stand tall!* urged the spirit within. *Your new life begins.*

Chapter 2

E PONA SPENT THE EARLY MORNING in fitful slumber, never deep enough to be transported into the dreamworld. Instead she wandered through a shadowed place where the real and the unreal melted together and were wrenched apart by something cruel, with an animal's face. At last she gave up the effort to sleep altogether and sat up on her bedshelf.

It was the first day of her life as a woman.

She ground her fists into her eyes to rub the mist from them. *I wonder if I look different now?* she thought. *Will Goibban like me?*

Before leaving her bedshelf she gazed contentedly at the chief's lodge in which she lived, appreciating it anew after spending the night in the magic house. Her home was a large rectangular hall, built of snugly fitted birch logs and topped with a steep thatched roof. An opening at either end, just below the ridgepole, allowed light and air. As was appropriate for the chosen leader of his people, the house of Toutorix possessed a carved rooftree, its surface covered with intertwining patterns of life, with symbols for the more powerful spirits, with mystic signs to reinforce authority and fertility. These were carved not only on the downward face of the rooftree, but all the way around, even where they were hidden by the thatch, for they were meant for other than human eyes.

The family's bedshelves, constructed of tamped and hardened clay, extended down both sides of the lodge, providing sleeping

19

space for more than a dozen people. The shelves were covered with piles of furs and served as seats during the day. Beside them were wooden chests, carved and painted by the craftsmen of the tribe, designed to hold clothing and household articles. Tools, weapons, and the two-horned staff of chiefdom that Toutorix used for refereeing games took up space in the corners. As in all lodges, a firepit occupied the center of the room, with cooking utensils on its stone hearth and a bronze cauldron suspended by iron chains above it.

In a choice location close to the fire stood Rigantona's wooden loom, towering up into the shadows. Weights hung from each of the vertical warp threads, and the frame was painted with ocher to show the honor in which the premier activity of the household was held. Rigantona herself sat behind the loom, her strong arms moving as energetically as if she had enjoyed a night's sleep. She did not look up as her daughter got off the bed, but she spoke to her.

"Now that you're a woman, Epona, you can take my turn in the bakehouse today. I want to get my weaving finished before the traders start coming; it would never do for them to see my family in the same clothes we were wearing last sunseason."

At the far end of the room Brydda, the young wife of Okelos, was sitting on her bedshelf, playing with her new baby by swinging a string of blue beads in the air above it and laughing when the infant gurgled and cooed. The action distracted Rigantona from her daughter. "Where did you get those beads, Brydda?" she demanded to know.

The girl hesitated. "Okelos gave them to me."

Rigantona pushed herself away from the loom and stood up. "They look like mine," she said.

Brydda shifted on her seatbones. "Okelos gave them to me," she repeated. "I give you my word." She met Rigantona's eyes with her own.

Rigantona stopped her advance on the young woman. No one of the people would question the sworn word of another; as everyone knew, words had more magic than weapons. "Very well," she said, with obvious disappointment. She sighed and turned back to her loom.

During the exchange between the two women Epona sat on her heels beside her bedshelf and opened her clothing chest.

When she raised the lid she stared in astonishment. The brief, coarsely woven tunics of childhood were gone, and in their place, carefully folded, were ankle-length robes she had never seen before. Even in the shadows of the lodge they glowed with bright colors. New clothes. Women's clothes, of dyed wool and linen instead of the plain undyed fabrics used for children. Rigantona must have put them there while her daughter was in the priest's lodge.

Epona lifted out a soft red gown and held it up, recalling when that lot of wool had been dyed. "I like a warmer red than this," Rigantona had remarked, rejecting the material for her own wardrobe. Now Epona gladly slipped the gown over her head and buckled her leather girdle around her waist. Beside her bedshelf were shoes of chewed leather, shoes that remembered the shape of her feet. Shoes she had worn the day before, when she was a child. Would they still know her feet, now those toes belonged to a woman? She slipped into them and smiled to herself; they were the same friends they had always been. Good. She bound them snugly around her ankles with leather thongs so the mud left by melting snow would not suck them off.

Epona possessed only the jewelry appropriate for children, bracelets and anklets of bronze and wood, but she found a new circlet of beautifully engraved copper waiting in the chest, beneath the colored wool. She glanced toward Rigantona, but her mother was once more preoccupied with her loom. Perhaps this ornament had been too small to go around the wrist of the chief's wife.

She slipped it on and started for the door.

Brydda called, "Wouldn't you like something to eat? The little children left broth in the pot and here is some of the cheese you like."

"No, your spirit is generous, but I'm not hungry yet. I just want to go outside for a little while before I go to the bakehouse."

Brydda nodded. Epona was an adult now. She was responsible for caring for herself and getting her own work done; the others would supervise her no longer. From now on it would be a point of honor with her to see that she completed her share of the labor.

The outside air was so sharp it knifed into Epona's throat and left the brittle taste of ice on her tongue. She drew breath all the way to the bottom of her lungs and held it, letting it burn, because it would feel so good when she finally exhaled.

Aaahhh.

After the atmosphere of the lodge, thick with the smells of people and food and sleep, a breath of the pine-scented wind was like a drink of honeyed water.

Epona stretched, reaching her arms high and twisting with animal sensuality. The long gown she wore felt strange, bulky. It would seem odd to have her legs covered all the time by skirts.

A pale candescence of light shouldered the mountains as the morning sun finally cleared them. Forested peaks soared skyward, beautiful and free as birdsong, patterned with constantly changing light and shadow and fragrant with conifers. The lake sparkled below, brilliant points of white light rippling on its surface as a breeze moved across it.

I wonder if I look different? Epona asked herself again. She could have gone back to the lodge and borrowed Rigantona's polished bronze mirror, but that might start an argument. Fortunately there was a substitute close at hand — the clear dark lake, an intense blue-green in the morning light.

She started across the commonground, headed toward the water.

Drifting smoke carried cooking smells from the lodges, from meat boiling in bronze cauldrons and barley simmering in water heated by stones from the firepit. Children ran through the village, yelling with the ceaseless energy that characterized all the people. Dogs barked, birds sang overhead, half-wild pigs rooted between the lodges.

Most of the miners had already left for the Salt Mountain, dividing themselves into crews for cutting the rock salt and for felling and placing the timbers to support the galleries within the mine. Few worked in the old copper mine anymore; the salt was more profitable. The last contingent of stragglers was just setting out, the unmarried men who had no wives to urge them off their bedshelves or handclasp them at the doorway. Six or seven of them came across the commonground on a line destined to intersect with Epona's, their casual banter changing to something else as they approached the girl.

The men of the Kelti were much taller and more powerfully built than the Etruscan and Hellene traders who came to barter for their salt. Fair of skin, they bleached the hair on their heads with lime paste and combed it stiffly back from their foreheads. Their eyes were the color of sky and water, and each man sported a beard of yellow or reddish gold and a heavy, drooping mustache, proud symbol of virility.

The miners were dressed in thick wool tunics, their legs wrapped in fur leggings bound by leather thongs. Mittens of leather and sheepskin caps protected them from the numbing chill within the Salt Mountain. On their backs were leather knapsacks fastened to wooden frames, containing bundles of pine twigs to be burned for illumination within the mine. The chunks of salt from the day's labor would be carried home through the twilight in those same backpacks.

Each man had a tally stick thrust through his belt, notched to show the number of loads of salt he had brought out of the mine during that moon period. A man of the Kelti could make up a splendid fiction about his sexual prowess — if no quick-tongued woman was nearby to contradict him — or he might invent an astonishing tale of impossible feats on the sports field. But he would not falsify the number of notches on his tally stick, for that represented his sworn word as to the exact share of the trade goods he was entitled to receive for his efforts. A man who tried to cheat the others of the tribe by claiming more than his due was sent to the spirits in the otherworlds to apologize.

As they drew near Epona the miners' walk became a swagger, with shoulders thrown back and strong white teeth glinting through their mustaches. They strutted, they grinned, they nudged each other aside in an effort to attract the attention of the newest woman in the valley.

For the first time in her life, Epona saw men looking at her as they did not look at children.

"Hai, Epona!" one of them called. "Sunshine on your head!"

"A day without shadows," she responded, feeling a flutter of excitement at the base of her throat. At last, the real beginning of her adult life! The men fell into step beside her, crowding close, saying flattering things, patting or pinching her or touching her braided hair. "Now you are a woman, eh? And what a woman! You will steal the light from your mother."

"That Rigantona was magnificent in her youth," one of the other miners remarked. "I've heard them tell tales of her . . ." He smacked his lips and his friends laughed. Epona laughed too, a little nervously but enjoying herself. Shyly at first but with growing confidence she responded to their teasing. How delightful this was! A swing entered her walk as if her slim hips had already spread for motherhood. She bounced on the balls of her feet and her laughter rippled across the commonground.

Soon the miners reluctantly turned aside to follow the steep trail to the Salt Mountain. Epona watched them go with regret. Then a vestige of childhood broke through and she burst out in giggles.

Grown men! Flattering me!

There was a bit of swagger in her own walk as she proceeded down to the lake.

To catch a glimpse of her reflection she had to wade into the icy water far enough to clear the weeds at the shore. She took off her shoes and gathered her skirts in her hands before easing into the shallows, a favorite sport of all the children in warm weather. The weather was not yet that warm, but she did not have to be brave; no one was watching. She gasped and her face twisted as the bitter cold gripped her feet and ankles.

When the worst of it had passed, leaving her lower legs numb, she looked down into the water, waiting for the surface to calm. A blurred image of her own face looked back at her. To her disappointment, it was the same face she had always known: wide-set blue eyes beneath level brows, straight nose heavily sprinkled with freckles, curving lips, and a willful little chin. Only her heavy braids looked unfamiliar.

She stooped to peer more closely, hoping to see what the miners admired.

"Epona! Epona, wait for me!"

Her best friend, Mahka, came running down the slope toward her. Mahka, daughter of Sirona, who was married to the chief's brother Taranis, was a sturdy girl, taller and heavier than Epona, but she had not yet begun the moon-bleeding and her chest was as flat as a boy's. The time had not come for Mahka's woman-making.

Epona waded back to shore, feeling the wind chapping her legs. She welcomed the long skirt now. She sat down and began using it to rub her legs and feet.

24

Mahka flopped down beside her on the damp mud. "I'm wait-ing. Are you going to tell me about it?"

Epona bent over her reddened feet, massaging them. They felt as if they were being bitten by hundreds of ants. "Tell you about what?"

Mahka laughed. She did not have the deep voice of Taranis, but her voice was low for a woman's, and always sounded a little hoarse. "You know what I mean — the woman-making. We promised each other long ago that the first one to be made a woman would come back and tell the other what it was like."

"Oh." Epona inspected her toes carefully before pulling on her shoes. Mahka squirmed beside her, radiating impatience.

At last Epona said, "I would tell you if I could, but I don't know how." She felt deliciously superior.

"Just start at the beginning. Or at the end; beginnings and ends are all the same, they say."

"I couldn't explain it in a way you would understand. Woman-making isn't like anything you know, Mahka. You'll just have to wait until your own time comes."

Mahka doubled her fist and pummeled Epona's shoulder, hard enough to raise a bruise. Not many of the boys were still willing to fight with Mahka these days; she liked to do damage. "You said you'd tell me. You said! Now you talk just like an adult."

"I am a woman."

"You look the same to me," Mahka told her scornfully. "Except for those braids. They make you look like Rigantona."

"I will never be like Rigantona; I'm just myself," Epona de-clared.

"You're not my Epona anymore," Mahka said. "I know how it will be. You won't play with me anymore, you'll be sitting at a loom, or talking all the time about lodgefires and linen. We'll never race again, you and I."

"I don't have to do anything I don't want to," Epona responded hotly. "I can still race you if I want; I'm a free woman of the Kelti."

"Then race with me now!" Mahka leaped to her feet. "We'll get Alator and some of the others and race all the way around the village."

How Epona longed to do just that! To run with thudding feet

and laughing lips along the narrow pathway kept smooth for the footraces of the men.

But that would mean giving in; it would mean that Mahka had won and talked her out of her new glory.

She passed her knife hand over her eyes. "No, I will not," she told the other girl. "I'm going to the bakehouse."

"Is that what you want to do?"

Epona scrambled to her feet, trying to look eager. "Yes. Just think, Mahka — I'll get the first bite of the new bread. And maybe I'll race with you later. If I feel like it." She squared her shoulders and started up the slope toward the bakehouse, trying to convince herself that this was, indeed, what she wanted.

She had not expected the transition from one life to another to be so difficult. So must the dead feel, gone to the next existence but still looking over their shoulders toward the world they had left.

She walked with firm tread through the village, reminding herself how eagerly she had anticipated thisday. Then the glow from Goibban's forge caught her eye and she remembered the real reason she had longed to become a woman.

Goibban. The peerless smith of the Kelti.

She turned away from the direction of the bakehouse.

The smith's forge, constructed to his own design, had a floor and workbenches of hardened clay and a timber framework to support thatched walls and roof. If a random spark ignited the thatch, it was more easily replaced than solid timbers.

A gifted craftsman with copper and bronze, Goibban, while still a very young man, had developed a technique for working star metal. The material had once been available only in small amounts, tiny pure chunks of iron said to have come from the stars themselves. Such precious metal was used for jewelry. Then miners discovered it could be found in many of the territories of the people, in ore like copper or tin. Smiths tried without success to extract the exceptionally strong metal in sufficient quantities and with a workable spirit so it might be used for tools and weapons.

Goibban was intrigued by the problem. The old copper smelters he knew could not attain sufficient heat to melt iron from its ore, so he devised a series of stone-lined pits in which he alternated layers of charcoal with layers of crushed ore, forcing air through the furnaces with a bellows until he had enough heat to melt the ore and squeeze out the spirit of the star metal in its truest form. The spongy mass must then be kept hot and beaten repeatedly to drive out impurities, the lesser spirits that could cause the iron to lose its courage. The end product was a bar of malleable wrought iron, ready for the anvil.

Goibban had trained apprentices to do the actual smelting, handling the raw ore and working the goatskin bellows and blowpipe that controlled the heat of the fire. This freed Goibban to work with hammer and chisel, creating unbreakable tools and weapons to replace the old bronze ones, and inventing new uses for the iron.

Already his fame had spread beyond the Blue Mountains.

There was usually a cluster of admiring children gathered around the forge, crowding each other for a vantage point to watch the smith at his anvil. When the great hammer crashed down and the sparks flew they oohed and aahed in unison. There was no rival for the drama of watching Goibban turn a bar of iron, glowing at white heat, into an axe head or an axle. Only Kernunnos inspired greater awe. But Kernunnos was a frightening figure to children, while Goibban was patient with them, and kind, so long as they did not get in the way of his work. Goibban was immensely popular with everyone in the village — and as yet unmarried.

There were those who whispered he had given his spirit in marriage to the spirit of the star metal and would never take a wife to be its rival. Goibban himself had said — a saying repeated now around many fires — "Gold is precious, copper is flexible. But the star metal, iron! Hot, it is as soft and graceful as a woman; cold, it becomes as hard and strong as a warrior. Nothing is more worthy of a man's devotion than iron."

In spite of this, or perhaps because of it, many women attempted to compete with the iron for the smith's attention. If a married woman showed interest in Goibban her husband usually encouraged her, for such a lifemaking could bring honor to the family and perhaps a child with the smith's gift.

On this bright spring morning Goibban was shaping axles for the wagons of Kwelon the oxkeeper. The work was going slowly. Sweat beaded his broad forehead and ran down his nose, dripping like a melting icicle. The new apprentice had not succeeded in clearing this batch of iron of impurities, and Goibban would have sent it back to the fire if Kwelon had not been so anxious to have the axles. Soon the passes would be cleared of snow; soon wagons must be on their way south, piled high with salt.

Goibban wore little more than a leather apron around his waist because of the heat of forge. His powerfully muscled torso and arms were bare, gleaming with perspiration, as the hammer rose and fell. His whole concentration was on the job at hand, so he was not aware of his customary audience. He did not notice when the cluster of children parted to make way for a new arrival.

He did not even hear Epona the first time she spoke his name. She called again, louder, and he glanced up to see one of his special favorites among the children, a girl who was content to sit quietly for hours, watching him work without interrupting. In return he had made toys and trinkets for her and given her more than one bright blob of metal to play with, metal that should have gone into something more valuable.

She kept his gifts at the bottom of her chest of belongings: special treasures, hidden away and shared with no one. For several seasons she had spun her dreams around them; they had come to represent more than Goibban suspected. When the other children teased her and called her Goibban's pet she no longer fought them with her fists, but blushed and hid her face, secretly pleased.

Seeing her now, Goibban gave her the little wink that he reserved just for her, and asked quickly, so as not to lose time from work, "What is it, child?"

Epona smiled shyly at him, willing him to see her as the miners had seen her, not as a gawky youngster with freckles like butter forming in the milk.

His eyes took in Epona's braided hair and long gown, but his mind did not register the fact because it was not pertinent to the forging of the iron. His arm rose and fell, rose and fell, and the sparks showered from the anvil like runaway stars.

Epona tried to think of something womanly and charming to say but the spirit within betrayed her; there was only silence in her head. "Epona, what do you want?" he asked again.

Defeated, she passed her knife hand in front of her eyes in negation. "Nothing. I only . . . I came to wish you sunshine on your head," she offered lamely.

"And a day without shadows to you," he responded kindly, the flicker of a smile crossing his mouth above his golden beard. These children! Then he caught sight of a heavy smear of carbon in the

28

iron, indicative of an unevenness in strength, and he forgot all about Epona.

The girl shoved through the circle of spectators and walked slowly away from the forge, face turned downward, studying her feet.

Something alerted Goibban and he glanced up once more, watching her slender back as she walked away. A long gown? She had been to her woman-making, then? But only yestersun . . . Perhaps she had come for something important after all. But no, if she had anything to say she would have said it; women of the people always spoke their minds. He shrugged and attacked the iron.

As Epona slouched across the commonground the fragrance of baking bread floated to meet her. Her mouth filled with saliva and she was thankful to remember her day's task. At least she had a woman's job, now; not just the incessant woodgathering that any child could handle.

A woman's job, but not the recognition she sought to go with it.

The radiant morning had lured another from the chief's lodge. Rigantona had grown impatient with the walls crowding in on her, and as soon as the men and the children had gone their separate ways she was anxious to seek the sun. But first she must dress.

Rigantona never left the lodge without preparing herself to appear as the wife of a great chieftain. The village of the Kelti had become a major stopover on the trading routes since the discovery, many generations ago, of the Salt Mountain, and important visitors could be expected at almost any time; sometimes even before the passes were clear enough to allow traders' wagons. Representatives from other tribes of the people came in search of prosperous Kelti wives and joined with wily Illyrian and Hellene merchants and temperamental Etruscan businessmen in bartering for furs and craftwork and salt.

Always, the salt.

The sunseason was at hand; soon strangers would come and be impressed by the sight of the chief's wife. But like all the Kelti, Rigantona also dressed to please herself, relishing fine fabrics and jewelry, adoring brilliant colors and soft furs. As every grown woman did, she wore a dagger, almost a shortsword, thrust through her belt, convenient to her knife hand, and she was skilled in its use. As Toutorix's wife she was entitled to more jewelry than any other woman of the tribe and she liked to array herself in every piece of it: dangling gold earrings, bracelets of bronze and amber, a neckpiece inlaid with coral from Massalia, rings of ivory and copper and star metal, bronze anklets and massive brooches. She braided her hair into a coil atop her head and fastened it in place with a handful of little silver pins. The Kelti believed art central to life, rather than peripheral, and Rigantona took great pride in the fact that every article in her household, no matter how utilitarian, was meticulously crafted and beautifully ornamented, even the smallest hairpin.

She had just finished her toilet when she caught Brydda watching her with undisguised envy.

I earned it all, Brydda, she thought complacently. *I earned it all.*

"Mind the fire," she instructed the other woman. "I leave its life in your hands. I am going out." She slung a cloak of blue wool and fox fur across her shoulders and left the lodge.

The clear light dazzled her and she squinted a little. Even after all these seasons, the lambent quality of mountain light surprised her almost as much as it had when she first came to this place from the northern riverlands, to be wife to the chief of the Salt Mountain. Then she had thought she would have everything; a home amid soaring, easily defended peaks in a village famed for its wealth, and a husband described as the Invincible Boar.

She had not realized then that Toutorix, already a grizzled warrior, had far too many responsibilities as lord of the tribe to pay much attention to a woman, aside from lifemaking, and that every aspect of his person must be shared with the rest of the tribe.

That was the sort of thing a woman discovered too late.

Rigantona noticed her oldest daughter headed for the bakehouse and set off in that direction herself, sniffing the air. At least the pleasures of food never failed one, and it had been a long time since her breakfast of cheese and salted venison with goats' milk pudding.

She intercepted Epona at the doorway of the earthwalled bakehouse. "Get us a loaf of hot bread to share right now," she ordered the girl, "and walk with me. My back aches and my eyes are burning."

"I was just coming to begin our baking . . ." Epona started to explain, but Rigantona waved her hand. "Later. Yestersun was the last of your childhood, and now I suppose I must talk to you as my mother talked to me. After my own woman-making." She did not sound enthusiastic about the prospect.

Epona entered the bakehouse and asked Sirona for one of her loaves of bread, fresh from the oven. "My mother requests it," she explained when Sirona raised her eyebrows. No one refused a direct request from the chief's wife, even Sirona, whose feud with Rigantona entertained the entire tribe.

When Epona brought the loaf she and her mother strolled through the village, dividing the bread between them, their teeth crunching the grains embedded in the chewy dough. At last they sat together on a boulder near the log palisade. Rigantona stared into space, licking her fingers, trying to recall the words her mother had used on a similar occasion. But that was many summers ago and the memory had turned to smoke and fog.

"About men," she began, and stopped. Epona waited, digging with one forefinger at bits of grain caught in her teeth.

Rigantona tried again. "Do you know what men expect of women?"

"Certainly. To protect the lodgefire so it only needs to be rekindled at the start of each new year, to fight as warriors if needed, to cook and weave and sew and salt meat and dry herbs and . . ."

Rigantona cut off the flow of words. "What about bedsports? What do you know about that?"

The girl's cheeks were bright pink. Like all the people, she caught fire easily. "I know everything about bedsports. Our family shares one lodge; I've seen men and women together all my life."

"Seeing something done and experiencing it yourself are not the same thing, Epona. You can watch me eat the thigh of a pig and if you had never eaten meat you would not know what I was tasting. Until a man enters you the first time you know nothing about bedsports — or men, either."

Epona resented her mother's patronizing tone, but the topic was causing an inexplicable wave of shyness to wash over her, turning her skin hot from the inside. She asked in a voice barely above a whisper, "Then what is it like? Tell me."

"That depends on the man. Some are like pigs, rutting; others have all the artistry of a bard playing the lyre. If you learn bedsports with a skillful husband you will come to enjoy his body and your own; if not, it is your right according to our custom to find someone who pleases you better, just as soon as you have given your husband one living son."

Epona gazed at her mother earnestly, a frown creasing her sunny freckles. "How can I be certain of having a good husband?"

"Foolish girl! You are of the family of Toutorix; you will have your pick of the most outstanding men from every tribe of the people within thirty nights of the Blue Mountains."

Epona looked away, across the commonground. "And suppose I don't want a man from some other tribe? Suppose I choose to stay here, married to one of the Kelti?"

Rigantona's jaw sagged with shock. "You can't! Our men always bring their wives from beyond the mountains, and our women always go to other tribes to form alliances for us. That is part of the pattern, Epona. About that, you have no choice."

Yes, I have, Epona said within herself, setting her jaw. She watched with unseeing eyes as some women removed grain from a storage pit, while others stacked firewood on the north side of their lodges. A work crew moved around the outside of the baking house, patching holes in the earthen wall. Suleva was combing her goats in one of the livestock pens; Kwelon and two of the smith's apprentices struggled to fit a red-hot iron tire to the rim of a cartwheel made of mountain ash. Above the bustle of everyday activity could be heard the voice of the *drui* bard, or history singer, Poel, accompanying himself on his lyre as he taught a collection of children the tales of their ancestors.

Epona's eyes followed her people about their tasks but did not actually see them; her thoughts were only on herself.

"Why can't I do things differently if I want to?" she wanted to know. "Women of the Kelti are free, are they not? As free as their men? How can we be free if we are enslaved by some pattern?"

Rigantona was accustomed to her daughter's outbursts of rebellion, recognizing in them something of herself. But of course they were not to be tolerated. "The pattern protects, as you know, Epona," she reminded the girl. "It does not enslave. The pattern governs all that we do, and the *druii* interpret it for us, since they are more sensitive to its limits than the rest of us. It can sometimes be tugged into a new shape, but that is strictly *druii* business and not for us to attempt. The important thing is to keep the

32

pattern intact; it must never be broken. Never! The *druii* tell us that would make us vulnerable to forces beyond even their control.

"But what makes you even suggest such a thing, girl? Is there some Kelti man who has drawn your eye?"

"Goibban," Epona whispered, keeping her eyes lowered.

"The smith, is it? Hai! Your choice does you credit. But of course it's impossible, a childish notion. Just remember your high standards when the time comes to choose from among those who offer us gifts for you. A woman of the people must never give herself to any man but the best.

"That's another thing we must discuss. I almost forgot it, and it's very important. By our custom, a girl must wait until her marriage bed before her first lifemaking, but later, if she does have reason to share bedsports with another man, she must be certain he is at least of her husband's rank. Listen to me, Epona!

"Give yourself only to the bravest and most gifted. The children you bear must bring honor to your husband's family. The history singer must never say of you that you engaged in bedsports with a man of lower status than your husband, for that would be an unforgivable insult to the man you have married." Her mouth twisted. "Of course, that might limit you to your husband's brothers, if they have no women of their own and ask for you. But perhaps you will be lucky."

Epona heard herself asking the question that had haunted her since she was a small child. "Did you think it was lucky to go with Kernunnos?"

Rigantona drew back and stared at her. "How could you remember that? You were so little!" The woman was surprised to find the memory still caused a crawling in her vitals, even after so many seasons. *He took me dry,* she recalled, shuddering, *and his hands were like talons, ripping my flesh. The things he did . . . he always enjoyed it most when I screamed.*

Epona saw her mother's face turn as white as the memory of snow, and the slippage of Rigantona's controlled mask shocked her. "I followed you once," she related, "when you went into the trees with him. I always thought he looked so . . . frightening . . . and I suppose I was worried about you, even if I was very little. Then I heard you scream and I ran away."

Rigantona's face seemed to have turned to stone. "I quit going with the priest long ago," she said in a remote voice. "Once I thought it would be a great honor to share bedsports with him; I thought a shapechanger would do things that other men could not." She curled her lip in disgust. "I was right about that, I suppose, but now I wish it had never happened. It is not a memory I cherish, and I don't want to talk about it with you.

"But I did learn a valuable lesson, and that I will pass on to you. Bedsports, though they may be pleasurable, can cause you great pain. There are more satisfactory pleasures than a man's body, Epona."

"What are they?"

"When you have borne as many children as I have, you learn to appreciate those things that are quiet and make no demands. Gold and amber and ivory, those are the real pleasures, believe me. I enjoy the way they look and feel and the way they make me feel. That delight never fades. They do not cause pain, nor do they turn away and leave a woman cold in her bed. They never stink of stale wine in the morning.

"Don't expect too much of men, Epona, and do not waste time sighing for creatures you cannot have, like Goibban the smith. He is probably not as good as you might imagine anyway. Give your affection instead to things you can count and carry, Epona, for they will never disappoint you and they are all that lasts."

She sighed, a long, drawn-out sigh. "Things you can count and carry."

Rigantona was silent for a long time. Epona was reluctant to break into her thoughts; she spat on her finger tips and gathered the last breadcrumbs on her damp skin. When the silence had become intolerable, Rigantona summoned one last piece of advice.

"Have as many children as you can, to increase the strength of your husband's tribe," she told her daughter. "Whoever he is, he will reward you well for that. And keep your teeth in your head as long as you can. They start falling out when you start having babies. You will have to seek aid from the *gutuiters* of your new tribe if you want to keep them. When you accept a husband, be sure you look at his teeth first and don't take a man with bad ones. His breath will stink in bed. Toutorix at least has strong teeth."

She could think of nothing else to say. Life was to be learned

34

by living it, and each person had to make his own discoveries. She was not fearful for her daughter's future; she was not even very interested in it. Not all trails through a forest reach the same destination.

Her duty discharged, Rigantona stood up. "You can go to the bakehouse now," she said. "I just saw Sirona leave, so her oven will still be hot. Think about what I told you and do some more growing; there is not enough flesh on your bones yet to interest a man anyway."

She strode away, back to her loom and her own life. Epona watched her go, trying to sort through tangled thoughts and feelings. Rigantona was right, she was bony still, like a yearling calf; another summer and winter might turn her into someone Goibban would really notice. Surely an exception to the pattern would be made for someone as important as the smith of the Kelti, if he wanted to marry a woman of his own tribe.

It had to be that way. Throughout the long, dark winter, had she not walked with Goibban in the dreamworld?

The bakehouse waited for her. The village rang with the voices of the women, the noises of the livestock, the clear hard striking of the anvil. Across the commonground, Mahka and Alator and some others were racing in a furious game of stick and ball, slamming into each other and shouting with laughter.

Epona cast one look at the bakehouse, then gathered her long skirts in her hands and ran to join them. "Hai!" she cried. "I challenge you all to a race! I can run faster than any of you!"

Chapter 3

WITH THE ADVANCE OF SUNSEASON there was more light for longer days of work. Goibban the smith lay sleepless on his bedshelf at night, his mind whirling with ideas, his large hands unconsciously shaping designs atop his blanket. The iron was an endless source of inspiration. To work it was a sacred act of creation: bending, beating, capturing a thought and making it tangible with the melted essence of the ore.

As a child, Goibban had loitered around the copper smelters on the long blue evenings when the smoke rose high above the mountains. He loved watching as the miners raked out the smelting pits, banking fires at the lode faces of the mine galleries so their heat would split free the ore to be mined the following day. He dreamed of the time he would work with metal; he never wanted to do anything else.

But copper and bronze did not satisfy him, and gold was too easy. It did not offer any resistance to his great strength, but formed itself to his desire like an overwilling woman, without spirit. If he forgot himself and did not work with the utmost delicacy he could destroy the shape he sought to create.

The old master smith died and Goibban, his chief apprentice, took over his lodge and forge in the days of Toutorix, the Invincible Boar. There was always plenty of work to be done but it did not exhaust his vast reservoirs of energy. He fell into the habit of making little toys in the evenings, models of weapons and household goods for the children to play with, and soon he had a crowd of youngsters around the forge whenever he worked. He would glance up occasionally and reward them with a fond, if distracted, smile.

Then Toutorix had taken a load of iron ore in return for a few casks of salt, and Goibban had found a challenge worthy of his ability. He lost interest in copper and bronze. He wanted only to pit himself against the most unyielding opponent he had ever found, the star metal. Something in the integrity of the material appealed to something deep inside himself. Properly handled and correctly judged as to its temperature and tensile strength, iron could be made obedient. But the slightest mistake could turn it brittle and useless. It became a competition between the man and the iron, and it was the competition Goibban loved. For years now, he had thought of little else.

When Toutorix called on him for an inventory of work in progress, Goibban announced with pride, "We have enough extra tools to offer some more in trade this season."

"Beyond our own needs?"

"Yes, and we still have raw ore from that lot you got from Mobiorix last sunseason. Fine quality, that. I'm putting together a few items I think the Etruscans and Illyrians might find especially desirable: tweezers, shears, household knives, even a couple of iron plowshares I've made according to my own design."

"Last season the Hellene traders asked if we had any iron weapons," Toutorix remarked, avoiding an outright inquiry.

Goibban stroked his mustache. "We have scythes and chisels, and I've been experimenting with some files for sharpening and a kind of toothed knife for cutting wood."

Toutorix gazed around the forge, considering. Once he had enjoyed the intricacies of arranging trade based on the bounty of the Salt Mountain, and his dealings with such distant tribes as the Boii, the Belgae, and the Treveri had earned him fame among all the people. This in turn had drawn new traders from the east and the south, the music-obsessed Thracians and the dainty Etruscans with their language like birds twittering. Wagonloads of luxury goods had given the Kelti a taste for gold ornaments and red wine, expensive merchandise they would soon be importing from as far away as the land of the Hellenes.

But that was long ago, when Toutorix was rightly called the

Invincible Boar. His strength was fading now, though he admitted it to no one. There were times when his mind seemed to have lost its agility and he found himself fumbling through a negotiation, unable to get the best of an opponent. He now preferred to barter with old acquaintances still respectful of his reputation.

Like the Hellenes who wanted iron weapons.

"How is your supply of daggers?" he asked Goibban.

"Enough to last for a generation."

"And swords like the one you made for me, with the metal folded back upon itself and layered in the blade? Thin as it is, it is the strongest I've ever used, and it keeps its edge. Have you made more of those?"

A light came into Goibban's face as when a mother is asked about her favorite son. "There has never been anything to equal that one, except those I've made since. With one slash they can bite through a bronze shield."

"The Hellenes would pay dearly for them, then," Toutorix said. "The warriors of Sparta are reported to be invading Messenia; they will have use for good weapons."

Goibban scowled. "Would you sell iron blades to those not of the people? I don't think that's so wise . . ."

Toutorix threw back his head and looked down his nose at the smith. "You have been overpraised, Goibban; it has given you the idea that you are a thinker. I am the thinker. I am the warrior, and I am the best judge of such matters, until the tribe elects someone to replace me because I am no longer competent. When that day comes my replacement will be a warrior's son, not a craftsman. Remember that."

The two men eyed each other. The lord of the tribe was old, and felt every night of his life in his bones. Goibban was bigger, and younger, with no sag to his skin. His eyes were a hot blue, like the flame of his forge.

Discretion had begun to replace reckless courage on Toutorix's list of survival skills; he throttled his temper and added, in a more placating voice, "Just prepare some weapons for me to show, in case there is a market for them. You will be amply rewarded, and you can trust me to see they are not put into the hands of potential enemies.

"Besides, the Hellenes already have some iron weapons, you know; the material is not unheard of among them."

38

Goibban snorted. "They have brittle metal, an inferior product they get from the Assyrians or some such people. It is nothing compared to ours; they do not have the secret."

"We will keep the secret and the best weapons for ourselves, always," Toutorix assured him. "Am I not the lord of the tribe?"

Meanwhile, Epona was practicing the new arts of womanhood, finding her place in the interlocked pattern of life. There were moments when she felt the pride of her sex and race flooding through her and she walked with new dignity, but then a change of mood would overtake her as patches of brilliant sunlight and purple shadow followed each other across the face of the mountains, and she thought herself nothing more than a child, pretending.

She listened hungrily for the voice of the spirit within, and was relieved each time it spoke to her, not with words but with an intuition in the blood, commands direct to the muscle and bone. She heard without ears the voice older than time.

Go this way, not that way. Bow down before this stone. Do not eat that. Turn your bowl over and smooth its base with your hand to honor the craftsman who made it; his spirit watches and will be pleased.

I guide, the spirit within told her. *You listen and follow. I tell you how to live thislife.*

It was well past midday, and her share of the work was done. She spent the morning helping Brydda wash wool for dyeing, feeling the strain in her back and shoulders, though she did not complain. A woman of the people should not complain of physical discomfort; it was a point of honor. Men might make a big show of small injuries on the sports field or in the mines, but women bore pain in silence. That was their strength.

Now, with the afternoon before her to spend as she chose, she decided to go to the livestock pens. She never tired of being with the animals; she always felt most comfortable when in their company. Their natures, unlike those of humankind, were constant and comprehensible. She even enjoyed the smell of the pens, the combined odor of fodder and churned earth mixed with dung.

Grazing animals were herded long distances to steep upland meadows, but some animals were always in the pens, for convenience or special care. There were usually working oxen and the stocky draft ponies purchased from the Cimmerians to pull carts, which were also modeled on the Cimmerian design. Light passenger carts, elaborately carved, more suitable for display than for hard usage. The oxen pulled the big wagons filled with salt.

In one corner was the pair of little horses that had grown old pulling the chief's cart on ceremonial occasions. They stood together companionably, head to tail, dozing as the sun crept westward to warm their aging bones. They were good friends of Epona's. The young woman climbed up on the fence and hooked her elbows across the top so she could enjoy a leisurely chat with them. At her call, her favorite, the bay with the crooked blaze across its face, lifted its head and came toward her. It was a shaggy, broad-shouldered animal, with big-boned legs but a meager rump. What beauty it possessed glowed in its brown eyes.

"Sunshine on your head," Epona offered fondly. The bay met her eyes and their two spirits greeted one another. The pony lifted its face to hers and exhaled a warm, grassy breath. She blew her own gently back into its nostrils. Understanding flowed between herself and the animal. They were intensely aware of each other, their communication unhampered by the awkward construction of human words. They belonged to dissimilar races but shared the common experiences of life and death, and each enriched the other by existing.

The bay pony stood quietly, absorbing the tension from the girl and giving back a sense of tranquillity. *Smell the air. Feel the sun. Be, just be,* it seemed to tell her.

She let her eyes smile at the little horse, for it would not perceive bared teeth as a friendly gesture. "Yes," she agreed, acknowledging its wisdom. "You are right. I have nothing to worry about. Goibban will . . ." her voice trailed away, not finishing the thought, but there was no need to finish it. Not with the horse; the horse understood.

Epona dangled one hand over the fence and twisted her fingers in the pony's shaggy mane. The two stood for a time in peace and understanding, sharing existence.

Gradually Epona became aware of something through her sense of touch; an awareness as strong as the voice of the spirit within. She closed her eyes, concentrating. Her inner self merged with that of the horse and she realized that the bay was old, and tired. Flies were annoying his soft underbelly and he lacked the energy to dislodge them. Dry skin itched around his withers and along

his level spine, and the flesh sagged from the bone, seeking re-
union with the earth mother. The cartpony was a weary creature
who had endured too many harsh winters and would not last
through another. He and his companion had finished their lives.

"I'll speak to the *druii* about releasing your spirits soon," she
promised them. "You won't have to be old much longer. At Samhain, the start of the new year, when the great bonfire is built,
we will let you go. Before the worst of the winter. Just enjoy this
one more sunseason first."

"You can talk with the animals, Epona?" said a voice just behind her, startling her. She slid down from the fence and turned
to face Kernunnos. The priest was standing very close, his pointed
canine teeth showing through his thin lips. His voice was sibilant,
the whisper of snakes' bellies over stone.

She tried to edge away without being rude, but her back was
against the fence and he moved with her, like a shadow.

"I like animals," she said as politely as possible, giving him
nothing. His proximity repelled her.

"Do you like men, too?" Kernunnos asked. His voice contained
the insinuation that something so natural was somehow twisted
and ugly, with hidden meanings. She had the distinct impression
that to answer him truthfully would give him a sort of power over
her.

"I like animals," she said firmly, tossing her head to show him
her spirit was hers alone.

The priest's mouth gaped open, showing a red and pointed
tongue. "Hai! Have you ever seen . . . through the eyes of an
animal? Can you do that?" He grabbed her wrist, clutching it
tightly, his hot eyes attempting to bore into her secret self. "Tell
me, girl: Have you ever had dreams in which spirits came to you
and offered you gifts? Do you see things others cannot?"

She tugged but he would not let go. He rocked back and forth
on his heels without loosening his grip, humming to himself. His
slitted eyes closed, then flared open. "I feel it in you!" he cried.
"There is a strength . . . you are the first woman of the Kelti in
my lifetime to have such a gift . . ." His face closed and became
cunning, greedy. "I could speak to Toutorix and offer to instruct
you myself; it would be an honor. There are things I could teach
you that you cannot imagine, Epona. You are sensitive to the
world beyond the eyes and ears; I could show you so much, girl.

41

So much." His voice was not overtly threatening, it had become more dangerous than that. It was seductive, soft as smoke, filled with promises of things unseen. Things she did not want to see.

She raised her wrist with an abrupt gesture and twisted it out of his grasp. "I don't want you to teach me anything," she told him, rubbing her arm where his nails had bitten into the soft flesh.

"I could make something very special of you," he insisted, moving toward her again. "I have always suspected it . . ."

"My life is my own, no part of it is yours, shapechanger," she told him emphatically, fighting back an emotion very like fear.

Kernunnos smiled with his mouth but his eyes were flat and cold. "You are mistaken. Whatever gifts you have been given belong to the tribe. If you refuse to share them you will suffer. Look!" He stretched one long arm in the direction of the trading road. "Men are coming even now, but not merchants. These are men of the people from a tribe on a muddy river, and they are bringing gifts for the parents of marriageable girls. You will find one of these men very desirable, Epona. But if you go with him you will live a hard life and have a painful transition, dying with blood in your mouth beside a muddy river. Yet you will not be able to resist going. It is your punishment for refusing me, and you will suffer. You will suffer!"

His voice was the singsong of *druii* prophecy. It turned Epona's bones cold. Spinning away from the priest, she hurried toward the chief's lodge and the protection of four strong walls. Kernunnos' voice followed her. "One or the other, Epona! He who comes will take you, or I will! You cannot escape."

"I can," she whispered under her breath, running.

She had no doubt that the men he had foreseen were coming, but she did not intend to be available when they arrived. As the oldest daughter in the chief's lodge she should be on hand to offer food and wine to travelers, but if she left the village before they arrived there was a chance she could change the pattern; it need not happen as Kernunnos had prophesied.

The lodge was temporarily empty except for Brydda's baby slumbering in its fur-lined bedbox. Okelos had returned early from the Salt Mountain, as he so often did, and he and Brydda had gone someplace together. Rigantona, angered at being left alone to mind the baby, had gone after them, but she would not leave the hearth untended for long.

The warm clothes Okelos wore in the mine lay carelessly tossed on his bedshelf, his leather knapsack of pine twigs beside them. Without stopping to think, Epona pulled her brother's tunic over her head, though it was much too large for her, and belted it as tightly as she could. She snatched up the mittens and knapsack and eased out the door. The rest of the miners were just reaching the village, and there were shouts of welcome, suddenly interrupted by the strong clear voice of Vallanos the sentry, announcing that someone was coming along the trade road. At such a time, no one noticed Epona as she slipped from her family's lodge.

The trail to the Salt Mountain was steep and unfamiliar, for children were forbidden to use it. Epona felt certain no one would seek her there. She could take care of herself easily, she thought, sheltering in the mine and feeding herself from berries and the small animals she knew how to snare, until the visitors had arranged marriages with other women and gone on their way.

She would have an adventure, such as boys had on the first hunt of their manhood.

Above the village stretched the narrow valley for which the tribe was named, the valley of the Kelti, sloping steeply upward toward the high peaks. Here Poel came at each change of the moon to recite the occurrences of the community to the spirits of the ancestors, and to take back any messages they might send to that part of the tribe currently in the world of the living.

Beyond lay the entrance to the Salt Mountain. It appeared innocuous enough for a gateway to unlimited wealth, just a gaping hole braced with timbers and leading down into darkness. The core of rock salt stretched for an unknown distance beneath the valley; no man had explored its farthest reaches.

Epona hesitated. The blue of the sky had melted into the lake, and a bank of soft clouds, indistinguishable from mist, was moving up the valley toward her, swallowing the light. Mountain rain could be sudden and hard.

Better get inside; the clouds were sweeping closer and Epona could smell the rain now. From the leather knapsack she took pine twigs to make a torch and a pair of firestones given to Okelos by Tena. She struck the stones together, calling on the fire spirit, but nothing happened.

43

A gust of cold wind hit her. It would be much more comfortable inside the mountain, in the tunnel that now seemed inviting compared to the approaching storm. She struggled with the fire-stones and at last ignited a spark and lit her torch. Holding it aloft, feeling confident once more, she went down into the Salt Mountain.

No, it is not safe, the spirit within warned, but she chose not to listen.

At first there was nothing but a dark tunnel burrowing into the earth, its walls hacked out with bronze axes and shored up with timbers. There was no sign of the salt, though the air had a salty tang, a dry, nose-tickling feel to it. The tunnel narrowed as it dropped, and where the slant became steeper sections of tree trunks had been jammed horizontally into the earth to provide crude steps. Soon it was impossible to see back to the tunnel mouth. The darkness closed around Epona, and her torchlight seemed feeble by contrast.

Go back, urged the spirit within.

No! she told it. *I am not afraid. I am safe here, my lord Toutorix is chief of the Salt Mountain, and I can go where I please.*

Besides, I'm here now. I want to see the salt.

A blast of cold air whistled down the tunnel, making her shiver.

After an interminable time, her torchlight caused something to sparkle ahead of her and her heartbeat quickened. The tunnel branched into galleries and there was the salt. All around her, above, beside, beneath, was a world of crystalline beauty. It crunched under her feet. The torchlight reflected as from walls of ice, but when she pulled off her mitten and ran her hand over the surface it was not cold, just rough and grainy. She licked her fingers, tasting the salt.

She had entered a magic world, and she wandered through it with delight, her worries temporarily forgotten as she went down one tunnel after another, lured on by new beauties of light and color as the torch illumined the changing surfaces of the rock salt.

She did not know how deep she was, but all at once she became aware of the mass of the mountain above her, and herself beneath it, so small. So fragile by comparison.

Now she could hear the spirit within with dreadful clarity, telling her she had done a stupid thing, urging her feet to leave the Salt Mountain. She looked around uncertainly. Which way had

44

she come? All the tunnels were so similar. She had not noticed the identifying marks notched in the salt, nor would she have known how to use them to find her way.

She was very far underground and she was lost.

She started to run. The salt crunched and slid beneath her and she heard an ominous rumble behind her. Looking back, she saw that her movements had dislodged a small slide, like a rockslide, and a heap of salt had fallen into the tunnel, partially blocking it. She ran back, fearful the tunnel would be blocked altogether, trapping her. She scrambled over the slide and went on more slowly, her breath rasping in her throat.

A turn and then a turn again . . . surely she had come this way. Was it familiar? Did it look like this? No, all the tunnels seemed the same, nothing but gleaming rock salt. All alike, all alike . . . she was too panicked now to listen for the spirit within, to trust it to guide her feet. She came to another salt slide, much larger than the first, big enough to trap a man beneath and kill him. She knew then that she had not come this way before. She retraced her steps, watching for any slight rise in the footing that might indicate she was going toward the surface. The air was thick and hard to breathe; her heart hammered in her chest. She was so intent on the lift of the salt underfoot she did not notice the largest slide of all until it came rumbling down on her.

Chapter 4

Esus, the Silver Bull, chief of the Marcomanni, had accompanied his sons and the sons of his kinsmen to the territory of the Kelti in search of wives. "If you are ready for women to tend your wifefires, be sure you choose them from among the daughters of the Salt Mountain," he had counseled them. "We will arrive just after snowmelt, so as to have the pick of the ripening women, but don't be too particular. The important thing here is to establish more alliances with Toutorix and the Kelti and get a better trading arrangement than we have had. If you find Kelti women of lifemaking age who are willing to marry, take them."

The Marcomanni arrived in the village driving richly carved carts of polished wood and leading pack animals laden with gifts. No mention would be made of wives, not at first; their gifts were merely unworthy tokens of the respect in which Toutorix was held by their tribe.

A banquet of hospitality was quickly arranged and Tena built a great fire in the feasting pit at the edge of the commonground. Soon dusk would fall, and more meat was needed to supply the guests; Toutorix went to the magic house to speak to Kernunnos, and hunters were dispatched around the perimeter of the lake. Meanwhile, the women of the village prepared to serve the available food; Rigantona contributing a haunch of venison roasted with honey that she had intended for her husband's meal.

Toutorix's eyes followed the departing treat with mild regret; it was truly a chieftain's portion, and he had not intended to share it.

"We don't want the Marcomanni to think we are poor," Rigantona reminded him.

"Poor! They will hardly think that. Just look at our people. They're so weighted down by jewelry they clank when they walk, and as for you, I could support a whole tribe by bartering off your collection of ornaments."

Rigantona's eyes flashed. "It's mine, not yours to barter! If I were widowed it would go with me, as much of it came with me."

"Not that bronze buckle with the blue stones," Toutorix commented. "For one example. I seem to remember your getting that in exchange for honey gathered in my hills."

"Honey gathered from my bees."

"Honey the children gathered for you from wild bees; you did not risk any stings to get it."

"Those bees are not wild," she told him, unwilling to let any point escape her. "I can command them as the shapechanger commands the game."

"There is a fine distinction there, but for once I'm not in the mood to fight over it. These Marcomanni have brought a lot of gifts to exchange for the privilege of courting wives, and I want them to have a look at our Epona. Where is she?"

Rigantona glanced around the lodge. Three small boys played by the firepit, three little girls played by the loom. Of the older children, Alator and Okelos were working together on cutting up a leather hide, but Epona was nowhere to be seen.

Rigantona shrugged. "Out, I suppose."

"Don't you know?"

"I haven't had time to watch her all day, no! She is a woman now; she comes and goes as she pleases."

"I expected to see her on the commonground, staring at the strangers, for the girl is usually as curious as a raven, but she was not there," Toutorix said. "And now she is not here. She should be at the guest lodge right now, serving red wine to the Marcomanni and heating cauldrons of water for their bathing. When another tribe of the people visits, our hospitality must be beyond any they could offer us in their own village."

He opened the door of the lodge and gazed out, watching the

women scurrying to prepare for the feast. Perhaps they would have to eat in the lodges; the sky was already darker than it should be, the wind had turned colder, and the clouds were beginning to pelt the earth with stinging particles of ice. "Where is that girl?" Toutorix muttered. The spirit within had an uneasy feeling.

He went for the second time that day to the magic house. The black birds in the pine trees made derisive noises as he approached; the air was thick with blue smoke. He found the priest stretched naked on his bedshelf, forearm across his eyes. Toutorix wrinkled his nose at the smell of the lodge but said nothing; it was shapechangers' business, after all.

"The hunting is going well?" he asked to open the conversation.

"A great stag appeared and led a whole herd of deer to the lake," Kernunnos reported with satisfaction. "There is more than enough meat now to feed your guests for many nights, and when they leave, the women will have meat to salt."

"Surely we haven't killed more than we need?" Toutorix asked with concern. Waste offended the spirits. To kill game unnecessarily would result in famine, the animals disappearing just when they were most needed.

"Of course not," Kernunnos replied, insulted. He sat up, looking at the chief through slitted eyes. "You are worried, but not about meat. You know we do not overkill."

Toutorix held his face immobile. It was unseemly for a chief of the Kelti to express excessive concern over one daughter, but Epona was his special favorite. He empathized with her reckless spirit and was touched by her occasional bouts of doelike shyness. Rigantona was all muscle and hard edges; Epona was the blaze of the fire and the soft sound of rain on thatch.

"My eldest daughter does not seem to be in the village, and I have asked everyone," he said. "A storm is coming. And the Marcomanni are looking for wives."

"Ah. Epona." Kernunnos rolled off his bedshelf and walked, still naked, to the open door of his lodge. The wind was blowing harder now and raised the hackles on his skin; the cold shriveled his scrotum but he paid no notice. He stared out, his eyes filmed over.

The priest was already exhausted from his exertions in a way

48

that only a shapechanger could understand, but his life belonged to his tribe. When his art was needed, there could be no hesitation, no limit to the giving. His obligations had been set forth many generations ago by the great *druii* who had first come to understand the ordered rhythms of life, death, and rebirth.

All forms of existence were subject to complex, immutable laws, even in the otherworlds. Everything was maintained in a delicate state of balance requiring absolute harmony. There were things that could not be changed; actions that, once taken, must always bring certain reactions. The *druii* were the gifted ones, born with a greater innate understanding of these laws than the rest of the people. With that understanding came the ability to manipulate some of the lesser forces of nature, but those powers must always be used for the benefit of the people.

Power misused made the practitioner vulnerable to the rage of the great fire of life and could mean the fragmentation of his own small spark from that fire. His individuality might be torn apart and scattered on the winds between the worlds, left to howl in baffled hunger in the darkness, never to be whole again.

"The girl is not in the village," Kernunnos said at last. "I can feel her . . . far off. Very far," he added, surprised. He turned back to Toutorix. "And something is wrong."

"Find her!" roared the chief of the Kelti.

"Leave me," said Kernunnos. "When I know, I will come and tell you."

Toutorix returned, halfheartedly, to his guests and the preparations for feasting. Already the boasts and the contests had begun. Soon Bellenos, the most aggressive of Esus' men, would be wrestling Okelos — or Goibban, if the smith could be talked into taking part — for the hero's portion of first meat served. A boisterous gaiety had replaced the energetic industry of the community, and kin-fights were breaking out, wagers were being placed, dogs were barking, women were laughing. The first festival of the new sunseason had begun, ignoring the last icy blast of winter driving down from the peaks.

Alone in his lodge, Kernunnos crouched beside the firepit, speaking in the spirit language. He rocked back and forth on his haunches, reaching outward with his mind, exploring his psychic surround with invisible fingers. At last he nodded to himself and got to his feet. From his collection of animal hides he selected one of the most powerful and drew it over his shoulders as he began the song of incantation.

Epona woke in absolute darkness. She knew a moment of disoriented terror, thinking she had gone blind. The darkness was so solid it was tangible, and she was alone in it with a monster that gasped and panted. Her head cleared a little and she recognized the sound as her own labored breathing.

She was alive, then; somewhere under the Salt Mountain.

She felt a tremendous weight pressing down upon her and tried to shift beneath it, only to be rewarded with a stab of pain. She gasped, inhaling air thick with particles of salt that made her choke and cough. Fire was running up her arm. Surely its light should enable her to see something . . . ? No. It was not fire, but pain. The salt-fall had long since extinguished her torch, and she was partly buried under the slide, one badly injured arm pinned beneath her body, her legs numbed by the weight of the salt.

She forced herself to go limp, trying to rest and gather strength. All her life she had heard stories of mine disasters resulting from some thoughtless insult paid to the earth mother, but she had never thought to apply such risks to herself. Now those memories rushed back, larger than life.

More than one man had carried his pick and mallet into the mine and never returned.

It was unthinkable that she meet the same fate. She would not just lie there and die meekly. She moved her body in various directions by infinitesimal degrees, trying to learn just how she was trapped. The wrong move could bring more salt down on her, burying her completely and ending any chance for escape. It took all her will power to lie calmly and try to think, as she should have thought earlier, before any of this happened. She wanted to scream and struggle, but that would mean a sure death.

If she wriggled one muscle at a time, like a snake shedding its skin, she was able to ease the weight on her torso slightly and begin to worm her way out from under the salt-fall. The worst part of the process was in trying to move her injured arm. The darkness was a kindness, for it kept her from seeing just how badly the bone was broken.

She was shocked at her lack of strength. The smallest movements left her breathless and exhausted. Once she got free of the salt-fall itself, how could she ever find her way to the surface when she had been unable to do so while uninjured?

Better not think about that, urged the spirit within. *Get free first. One step, then one more.* Now she listened.

There was a distant sound. Epona froze, trying to lift her head and hear better. Was someone else in the mine with her? Usually all the miners returned home well before dark, and it must be night by now — or morning. How could she tell? She tried to call out but broke off in another fit of coughing. The salt-fall rumbled, threatening to move again.

Something was coming toward her through the tunnels. She could hear it clearly now. But there was no sound of human voices. Something seemed to be shuffling . . . or maybe that was the roaring in her own ears that was rising, drowning out all other sounds. Her head spun dizzily, and she faded in and out of consciousness.

She seemed to see a strange blue light moving through the heart of the Salt Mountain. It glowed through the crystalline walls. A giant, shambling shape moved darkly at its center. Down one gallery and then another, turning as if in search of something, a shaggy beast prowled through the mine, its heavy head swinging from side to side. Sometimes it walked on all fours, but where there was room it reared erect, gesturing with immense clawed paws, then dropped down again and continued its prowling.

Epona awakened with a jolt. She could see; the blue glow was in the corridor with her, outlining a huge bear that stood not six paces from her. Her mouth was as dry as sand. There was no way she could escape the beast, which must have been driven into the caves by the storm without and its own hunger within. She lay immobilized, staring up at it, expecting to die but still not resigned.

Never resigned.

She groped with her free, uninjured hand and found a chunk of salt the size of a *kaman* ball. If the bear came toward her she would throw the chunk and try to hurt his sensitive nose. There was little chance it would discourage him, but she had to try, she had to do something . . .

The big head turned from side to side and she caught a glimpse of glinting yellow eyes. Narrow, slitted, yellow eyes. The bear ambled closer, grunting, its hot breath swirling around her and becoming one with the pain and the thick salty air.

Darkness closed over her.

Kernunnos came to the feast, dressed in one of his ceremonial robes. Recognizing a shapechanger, even the rowdiest of the Marcomanni fell silent and concentrated on their food while the priest summoned Toutorix aside.

"The girl is trapped in the salt mine," Kernunnos said simply.

"One of my family is lost in the mountains," Toutorix cried to the feasters, his arms lifted in the sign of command. "Brave heroes that you are, prove your courage now. The priest tells me we must bring her back without waiting for the end of the storm or the daylight, or she will die. Come, warriors. Come, strong men. Show us your courage!"

The wind swirled and roared over the lake, making the last statement of snowseason, reminding puny man that the elements were not subdued, they chose to have a voice in his affairs. The men of the people, Kelti and Marcomanni together, equipped themselves with weapons and torches and prepared to search for Epona. The slopes were slippery with ice and the way was treacherous; the interior of the Salt Mountain was unknown territory to the Marcomanni, fabled but forbidding. Still, what member of the people could resist such a challenge to prove his valor?

Toutorix would lead the way. He had spent most of his life in the mines; there was not a corridor he did not know, a gallery he had not worked at one time. He almost jigged with impatience, waiting for the rest of them to get ready. It was not a job for one man alone, not in this weather.

Wrapped in furs, the three *gutuiters* accompanied the search party as far as the valley of the Kelti and waited there to care for the girl if she was brought, injured, out of the mine.

Below, in the magic house, Kernunnos once more retired to

his bedshelf. His ribs stood up like lodgetimbers, pushing through his flesh, and he could see the hammering of his own heart beneath the taut skin. It would take him a long time to recover. He closed his eyes and sank wearily into the dreamworld, where nothing was demanded of him.

The Kelti led the way into the mine with their lit torches, calling out to one another at frequent intervals. The priest had not been able to identify the exact corridor where Epona lay but had described its general size and shape, the turnings that led to it, and the approximate distance to the surface. Three or four areas might answer to those specifications, so Toutorix ordered the men to divide into groups and he took the most promising direction himself. He was not walking cautiously, as men learned to do underground, but trotting as if he ran in open air, careless of where he put his feet. "Epona!" he called again and again. "Answer me, girl. Where are you?"

His voice and the others, calling, echoed eerily through the salt caverns, distorting sound itself. Soon it was impossible to tell who was where.

Toutorix headed for the lowest level of the mine. His party could feel the oppressive weight of the mountain over them. The Marcomanni began to hang back, physically uncomfortable and emotionally uneasy. It seemed to them that they had entered a monster's belly and the open mouth might close behind them, swallowing them up. If this was the price for working the Salt Mountain, let the Kelti pay it! Brave warriors though they were, the Marcomanni were out of their element now, and their thoughts yearned back toward light and air. The girl seemed unimportant, even if she was of the chief's family. Proving themselves was less necessary than it had been. This was one of the otherworlds, and they liked no part of it.

"Come on, you!" Toutorix thundered at them. "Are you cowards? Hurry and we will find her soon."

The accusation of cowardice, the epithet no man of the people would willingly suffer, forced them on, but they were muttering among themselves and making extravagant secret promises to their tribal spirits.

Suddenly Toutorix stopped, holding up his hand. "I thought I heard something."

53

The men with him listened, but they heard only the blood roaring in their own ears and the faint crunching underfoot as they shifted weight on the salt.

"I hear nothing," said Bellenos of the Marcomanni. "It may be we have come too deep and missed her; I think she is somewhere above us, if she is here at all."

Toutorix gritted his teeth. "She is here. Follow me." He plunged on ahead.

This time he was certain he heard a faint moan, a little animal whimper of pain in one of the dark tunnels off to the side. He had to stoop to enter, for it was lower than the central corridor, and his torch smoked against the salt. Without hesitation he made his way down the tunnel until his light revealed a salt-fall as white as a hill of snow blocking his way, crystals sparkling in the flickering light of the burning pine twig torches.

Epona had crawled out from under the mound before her strength deserted her, and now she lay on the far side, hidden from sight. But she heard his voice and managed to call his name.

Toutorix thrust his torch at the nearest man behind him and began scrambling up the salt-fall. He burrowed into it like an animal, tearing it away with his hands until a cloud of crystals filled the air. The other men fell back. They heard his voice and then hers, then his again, crowing in triumph. The experienced miners crowded forward then, each fighting to be the first to use his tools in the narrow space to free the chieftain and the girl. The light was uncertain and the confusion total, but at last Toutorix, his beard white with salt, staggered back into the main gallery, Epona cradled in his arms.

"Is she alive?" "Let me see!" "How badly is she hurt?"

Ignoring them all, he pushed past them and headed for the surface. He insisted on carrying the girl himself; he would let no one take her from his arms, even the powerful Goibban, who had been leading one of the other rescue teams. Epona's eyes flickered open briefly and she caught a glimpse of Goibban's concerned face in the torchlight, but before she could even smile at him she was carried past and he disappeared from her range of vision.

Toutorix plodded upward, flexing his legs deeply at the knee as he had learned to do in his boyhood, his first trip into the mines. The girl in his arms was no heavier than many a load of salt he had carried out; yet she seemed to weigh more with every step he took. Something ached in his chest, but he ignored it.

The pain branched out into his cup-hand arm, hurting like a tooth gone bad.

The *gutuiters* met them with furs to wrap around the girl. They ran their expert fingers over her body quickly, lightly. "The bone of the arm is broken and has come through the skin," the Daughter of the Trees said. "I will prepare healing herbs and Uiska will make the bone-paste. Get her back to the village quickly."

Toutorix was comforted by Nematona's words. Fortunate were the Kelti, possessed of such knowledge as the *gutuiters* had brought into thisworld, embedded in their wise, old spirits. There were few ailments for which Nematona could not make a healing medication out of plant or tree. Tea of foxglove could strengthen a faltering heart, essence of willow bark could relieve an agonizing headache. Even the deadly burning growth could be checked and shrunk away if detected in time and treated with Nematona's brew from the sacred mistletoe. Most revered of trees was the oak, which harbored the mistletoe.

They started back for the village, Tena walking close beside the girl, chanting the song of the fire to keep her blood warm. Crowding against Toutorix's shoulder, Bellenos of the Marcomanni looked at the face of Rigantona's daughter and thought how fair she was. Her skin was the color of milk; her matted hair, with salt crystals caught in it like stars, resembled the gold of ripe grain. But of course she was badly damaged now; that arm looked nasty. She would not do for a wife, not this season. If she lived, she might be permanently crippled, quite unacceptable for life-making. When some of the men took the girl from Toutorix and carried her the rest of the way in a hammock made of blankets, Bellenos fell back and did not help them.

In the lodge of Toutorix the *gutuiters* worked over Epona. The smaller children had been sent to their bedshelves, and Rigantona and Brydda busied themselves carrying out the instructions of the *druii* women. Uiska brought a silver bowl from her own lodge, a ewer of water with a living spirit in it, and a bag of powdered bone. Nematona prepared a compress from the herb *samolus*, plucked, as always, with the cup hand. So urges the spirit within.

Voice of the Waters made a paste of the ground bone, bone

55

that had been burned in a magic fire to cleanse it of malign influences. As Okelos held his sister still, Uiska took hold of the broken arm and forced the bone ends back into place, shaping the thick paste around them and fitting the skin over the wound. Half-conscious though she was, Epona chewed her tongue bloody to keep from crying out and disgracing her family. *I will never do anything foolish again*, she promised herself. *Never, never . . . aah! It hurts!*

When the arm was repaired, Nematona bound it in one of her compresses and neatly splinted the limb with two sections of polished wood from a healing-tree.

"Will the arm be crippled?" Rigantona asked then. She did not need to ask if her daughter would live; the *druii* had made no preparations for the transition of a spirit.

"She is strong," Nematona answered. "We will wait and see. If she develops the fire that eats the flesh, send for Uiska; other than that, just keep her quiet. She has been very fortunate, if you ask my opinion."

There was no more feasting that night. The Marcomanni slept heavily in the guest lodge, snoring from the effects of too much wine, and Toutorix lay wide-eyed on his own bedshelf, thinking of Epona and trying to ignore the pain that came and went in his chest and burned like a steady flame in his throat. He had not mentioned it to the *gutuiters;* he wanted them to concentrate their skills on Epona. He was the lord of the tribe, above pain and illness, and he did not want his people to think him otherwise.

Chapter 5

THE MARCOMANNI HAD GONE. Shouting exultantly to one another, their young men had driven away with fine strong women of the Kelti beside them in their carts.

Sirona, who had sent Mahka's oldest sister with them, was wearing a new necklace of amber beads as big as birds' eggs, and Rigantona scowled every time she saw it.

Epona was thoroughly miserable, but it was not the pain of her broken arm that upset her. She had disregarded the spirit within; she had acted heedlessly, like a child, and damaged the body housing her spirit. Her mother was right to be angry with her.

At least that was what she thought sometimes. At other times she felt a rising anger against Rigantona for seeming to care more about the marriage gifts the girl could bring the family than about the girl herself. Rigantona made a great point of mentioning, at least once a day, that they would probably have to wait a whole year, a whole cycle of the seasons, before men would offer gifts to the lodge of Toutorix in return for the privilege of wooing Epona.

Rigantona's only concern was for the things you can count and carry. *But I am a person,* Epona told herself fiercely. *I am part of the whole, more important than a mere bracelet or neckring.*

"No man may want to marry you at all," Rigantona commented when Nematona came to change the dressing on the arm and the thin, bruised flesh was briefly visible. "That arm looks to me as if it's going to heal crooked. You will be disfigured, and then what are we to do with you? Feed you all your days?"

It was useless to point out to Rigantona that there was always enough for the tribe to eat, as long as they showed the proper reverence to the spirits.

Nursing her injury and her grievance, Epona thought of the young women who had gone off with the Marcomanni. At the next major seasonal feast of the people, in honor of the great fire of life itself, late in the sunseason, all the tribes would take part in games and celebrate marriages to ensure an outpouring of strength and fertility sufficient to carry them through the approaching winter. At that festival, in the territory of the Marcomanni, the women of the Kelti would marry their warriors in a ceremony as old as the history of the people, and the tribe's history singer would memorize their names for future generations to know.

You could have taken part, the spirit within reminded her. *You could have been an honored wife. Will Goibban be willing to break the pattern for you now that you are damaged? What have you done to yourself?*

Every few days another band of traders arrived with wagons loaded with *amphorae* of wine and crates of fine cloth and luxury items. Soon Rigantona was flaunting — particularly in front of Sirona — a set of bracelets made of blue and green faience beads, strung with silver spacers. Cups made of glass and said to have come originally from the storied Sea People were another new acquisition, and drew many admirers. The translucent glass was frozen magic.

Toutorix and his family lounged around their firepit in the evenings and speculated on the lives people must live in lands where such objects were commonplace.

"Illyricum fascinates me," Rigantona said. "That trader with the bad teeth was telling me, in that outlandish accent of his, that Illyrian women are wearing gowns of a fabric from the east called silk, a wonderful cloth woven of some sort of spiders' webs. Imagine having a chest full of such garments! He gave me some silk thread, and it is the lightest, softest material I've ever seen. I plan to embroider a gown with it."

"The Illyrians say that everyone in their land wears silk," Okelos remarked.

58

Toutorix cleared his throat, a sound like water pouring over gravel. "I wouldn't run downhill to believe the word of an Illyrian if I were you," he advised Okelos. "They are said to be of Dorian stock, and in all the years I've dealt with Hellenes, I've found the Dorians to be slowest to meet my eyes. Their honor is ice in the sun and the truth melts away from them. I doubt seriously if everyone wears silk in Illyricum.

"More than once I have had some Dorian try to tell me that many generations ago they were members of the people, our people, but I have never accepted that tale. They are not to be trusted."

"Those who claim Dorian blood are famed warriors, and they look more like us than other southerners," Okelos pointed out.

Toutorix replied, "That only shows they once pleased some powerful spirit and were rewarded with long bones and fair hair instead of being short and swarthy like other Hellenes. I am not persuaded they are our kin; they are outsiders and I give them no concessions. No matter what lies they tell for their own advantage, I never forget I am a Kelt of the Salt Mountain, and my spirit within can see the truth. I keep a grain of salt on my tongue to remind me not to be fooled by such as the Dorians."

As he spoke, Toutorix absent-mindedly rubbed his chest under the armpit, on the side of the cup hand. Epona, sitting at his feet with her back propped against his knees, was aware of the gesture and strangely troubled by it. She looked up at him and the Invincible Boar glanced down long enough to rumple her hair fondly, but his thoughts were elsewhere.

Okelos had moved the conversation farther south than Illyricum, to the cities of the Ionians: Chalkis, Eretria, Athens, where it was said every luxury and vice could be bought or sold. "How could enough people to inhabit ten villages stand to live all crowded together in one place?" he wanted to know. "It reminds me of a huge hive of bees, easily smoked and robbed of their honey. Why would people choose to live packed together like sheep unless they are weak and vulnerable? Why would a man build a house attached to his neighbor's house unless he was afraid his own walls were not strong enough by themselves?

"When Bellenos of the Marcomanni was here, we talked, and he suggested we build two-wheeled carts, for men and weapons rather than merchandise, and follow the traders back to their cities. They claim to be so wealthy, yet they only bring a portion of their riches into the Blue Mountains. Why shouldn't we go and get more of it?"

Rigantona was nodding agreement.

Toutorix passed his knife hand over his eyes. "We have no need for more wealth. The Salt Mountain has made us as rich as any Hellene or Etruscan, and we will be richer still if the trade in iron develops as I think it will. Why go chasing after something we do not need? Isn't that like hunting when you need no meat, a dangerous disharmony?"

"Don't you ever long to put on your bronze war helmet again?" Okelos asked him.

"I put on that helmet many times in my youth," Toutorix replied, his eyes misting with memories. "Yes, it was good to carry the sword and shield into battle, but now I am surfeited with it. It is like eating too much pork. If you survive, there comes a time when you do not want any more."

Okelos hunched forward, his elbows on his knees and his freckled face hungry. "You won all the battles, Toutorix; now no tribe of the people challenges us anymore. How can I prove myself to be a warrior with no one to fight? There are only the games to play, and that is not the same.

"Besides, I have spent my life walled in by these mountains. I want to see what lies beyond them. I want to know the lands of long summer, where mountain shadows do not fall across my path for half of every day. I want to watch the Sea People come riding over the Tyrrhenian Sea in their painted ships, with sails like eagles' wings." His face glowed with more than the reflection of the firelight.

Listening to him, Epona, too, felt the first siren summons of faraway places. Painted ships, with sails like eagles' wings.

"You have been out of the mountains," Toutorix reminded Okelos. "You took a wagon full of gifts all the way to Mobiorix of the Vindelici when you wanted a wife."

"That was nothing."

"When you came back you talked about it till everyone yawned."

Okelos shrugged. "They are just another tribe of the people. They are too much like us to be really interesting. They were generous with me because of you, you know; Mobiorix told me how he had come as a young man to try to take over the Salt Mountain and the two of you fought for seven days and feasted for seven nights."

Toutorix hid a smile in his beard. "Almost seven days and nights," he amended.

"It makes no difference now. But none of Mobiorix's women would come into the Blue Mountains with me. Even when they knew I was of your lodge. I had to settle for Brydda, who was only the daughter of the chief's sister, and I came back without even bloodying my sword. It was not much of an adventure for a hero.

"Do you not understand, Toutorix? I want to test *my* strength against famous warriors, as you have done. I want to win riches on my own, so my family will honor me as your family honors you."

"If you want your family's respect, why don't you spend more time in the Salt Mountain?" Toutorix asked him with a trace of irritability. "I served my time in those dark tunnels. That is honorable work and good for a man; it takes a warrior to fight the cold and the dark and his own fears, and bring out the salt. But you are too good to be a miner, is that it? Okelos of the white hands. You would rather carry a sword than a pick. All you offer your wife and child is boastful talk. You fart with your mouth."

Leaving the sound of sarcasm hanging on the air like bitter smoke, Toutorix left the fire and stretched out on his bedshelf, his back turned toward his son.

Okelos moved over to sit closer to his wife. In a low voice, he told Brydda, "Toutorix has grown old. The elders of the council should be thinking about a new chief."

Overhearing him, Epona asked, "Who would that be; you, Okelos? You are not to be compared to Toutorix!"

"I am his close kin, his blood," Okelos reminded her. "The choice will be among his sons and his brothers, the noble warrior blood, so why not me?" He raised his voice to be sure Toutorix heard him, but the older man gave no sign.

Rigantona looked at her son with suddenly calculating eyes. It would be nice, now that she thought of it, to be the mother of the new lord of the tribe. Otherwise the title might well go to her husband's brother Taranis, who had his own coterie of followers, and Rigantona would not fare so well with him. Sirona would see to that.

"This is not a matter to be decided here," she said to Okelos. "Toutorix is still our chief. All our loyalty goes to him now, do not forget that." In a slightly lower tone she added, placatingly, "When your day comes, my son, you will want that same loyalty."

Okelos' eyes were bright. "You hear?" he said to Epona. "Rigantona agrees with me; she says my day will come."

Epona was not ready to imagine her brother as lord of the tribe; to imagine anyone other than Toutorix holding the staff of authority, protecting and guiding them all.

Rigantona was taking a second look at Okelos meanwhile; rethinking. How would the tribe fare under such a leader? She knew her son; as Epona had said, he was not to be compared with Toutorix. Still, she and her husband could anticipate many more seasons of health, could they not? There would be no election of a chieftain soon; there was nothing to worry about.

Rigantona stood up and stretched before preparing for the bedshelf. *How nice it would be*, she thought, *if any unpleasant eventualities could be put off like debts, to be paid in the nextworld instead of this one.*

In the morning Toutorix seemed as hearty and energetic as ever and Epona thought she must have been wrong to worry about him. But she could not help noticing the sidelong glances Okelos shot at the old chief, and she overheard one of the women tell Brydda that the salt miners were grumbling about some of the recent trading deals the lord of the tribe had arranged for their salt.

The men went off to the mines, the women tended the lodges and livestock, and Epona scratched at her arm and wished the healing time was over.

The alpine summer settled over the blue-green lake and the forested slopes, bringing with it a hum of bees and a fleeting lush indolence. Without the snap of ice in the air, men walked a little more slowly. Women sang more softly as they did their chores, moving languidly like plants reaching for the sun. Even the ceaseless preoccupation with woodgathering lessened.

Epona was mightily bored.

The advance of sunseason brought the summer games, replacing the winter contests that kept the hunting and fighting skills of the people at a peak during the long period of cold, when game was scarce and indoor activity occupied much of their time. In snowseason, grappling, knife throwing, and tossball were popular. In sunseason, men and boys gathered on the commonground to cast a series of graduated stone weights or to be selected for teams of *kamanaht*, the stick-and-ball game using the *kaman*, or bent stick. ·

During the snowbound time of winter, while adult women were weaving and sewing, little girls had done their own very important work. They braided basketfuls of patiently collected animal hair into the hard round balls that would be sent slashing across the commonground by the swiftly running competitors of sunseason.

From snowmelt until first frost the village rang in the evenings with the shouts of the players. The game began as soon as the first crew of miners returned and exchanged their heavy clothing for nothing more than battle aprons and war jewelry. It often continued until the moon was high in the sky, which made it so difficult to determine the winning side that the contest then disintegrated into a rousing kin-fight, cheered on and sometimes joined by the women.

After first frost, those same *kaman* would be employed for beating through upland meadow grass to start and strike small game for the salting house, putting to practical use the coordination of hand and eye perfected on the sports field.

Epona enjoyed the games, though she did not enter into them as wholeheartedly as Mahka, who dreamed of playing on a team with the men. Once Epona had shouted and cheered for Taranis and Okelos, but more recently she had gone only to watch Goibban, to see his rippling muscles gleam with sweat and admire the white teeth laughing through his golden beard as he raced across the commonground, warding off the opposition with a backhand slam to the throat or a crack over the head from his *kaman*.

Unfortunately, Goibban never paid any attention to Epona during *kamanaht*, though she waved shyly whenever his face was

63

turned her way. She sometimes saw older, married women sidle up to him and murmur suggestions, and sometimes it hurt so much she could not watch at all.

On a day of soft clouds and gentle breezes she turned her back on the games entirely and went off to visit a more reliable love, the spotted hound bitch who was Taranis' favorite hunting dog. The hound had a litter of puppies nestled with her in a shallow depression she had dug for herself under the edge of Taranis' lodge. As Epona approached, the bitch raised her head and wagged her tail in welcome.

Playing with the puppies was a gentle joy. Their eyes were not yet open, but they were already curious and bold beyond their physical limitations, clambering over one another to investigate the scent of the newcomer with their uneducated little noses; pressing their milky-scented bodies close to hers. Epona lay down on her side at the edge of the nest and she and the hound exchanged amused glances, enjoying the young together.

One little dog, more precocious than his siblings, wriggled his fat body out of the hollow and found his way into the open space between lodges. The bitch whined anxiously. Epona scrambled to her feet to retrieve him before he strayed too far and was killed by one of the half-wild pigs that wandered loose in the village, rooting for food and awaiting the spear.

As she grabbed the puppy she saw Brydda come out of the chief's lodge with her baby slung on her hip and hurry toward the crowd of spectators watching *kamanaht*. The game was a particularly noisy one, and Okelos was leading the winning team. Brydda had found she could not bear to stay in the lodge, tending the fire, for one more moment, while the crowd was cheering her man.

But someone should be tending the fire; it should never be left for more than a very short time. When a woman was newly married and entered her husband's house for the first time, a *gutuiter* kindled the sacred lodgefire for her and expected her to keep it alive for the entire cycle of seasons. It must never be allowed to go out. It was an insult to the spirit of fire — the benevolent and dangerous spirit — to leave a lodgefire unwatched for longer than it took to go to the squatting pit. One of a woman's most important duties was to care for and feed the bright power that warmed and fed her family in return.

64

With Brydda's arrival in her household, Rigantona had at last been freed, to some extent, of that constant duty, and now she could turn it over to the younger woman whenever she wished to leave the lodge for something important, such as watching Toutorix referee *kamanaht*. Unmarried Epona was of course not allowed to tend a wifefire. But for Brydda it was a sacred trust.

The hound bitch barked, recalling Epona's attention. Surely Brydda would watch the game for only a little while and then return to the lodge. Epona carried the venturesome puppy back to his mother, the incident already forgotten, and settled down to enjoy the company of her friends.

Clouds eventually cloaked the setting sun. The sky turned dark. Night ran toward the village on swift feet. The sounds from the commonground told Epona the game was over and the brawling had begun, and soon the men would return to their lodges for food and drink and bedsports. Her own stomach was growling as she gave the bitch a last pat on the head and scrambled to her feet, headed for home.

The interior of the lodge, the haven that had glowed an unfailing welcome in every season, was black. The door was a yawning mouth, opening on darkness. Rigantona had just arrived and stood within the doorway; as Epona hurried up she raised her voice in an eerie wail. "The fire has died! The spirit has starved under my own roof! Our family will be punished!" The tall woman bent double in the gloom, moaning with grief.

Darkness lived in the lodge. The dark of the night beyond the rim of firelight, the night of the wolf and the bear; the dark of millennia past, pushed back and held at bay only by the spirit of the fire.

Epona shrank back, unwilling to enter. She felt her near-kin crowding behind her and heard their exclamations of shock and disapproval. Then Brydda's voice, crying out, "What's happened? Why don't you go in . . . The fire! What's happened to the fire?"

Rigantona controlled herself and straightened up, her eyes as cold as lake water. She came out of the lodge and grabbed Brydda by the elbow. "You should know," Rigantona hissed. "You let it die. In my memory, no wife in this tribe has let a lodgefire die. You are an enemy now."

Brydda cowered before the upraised fist of the older woman. "I didn't mean . . ."

"You didn't mean!" Rigantona roared in anger. "You let the fire spirit starve to death and you didn't mean! What if we had no *gutuiter* to rekindle it for us? What if we were alone and without fire stones? We would die, and our unborn children within us would die; many might be lost to the tribe because of your carelessness." Her voice was shaking. "You are an enemy, Brydda," she accused again. "Epona, go to the commonground and bring Toutorix here at once; then summon Tena."

Ignoring the throbbing in her arm when she ran, Epona raced over the footpounded earth in search of Toutorix. Once she would have found him in the center of a joyous battle, but now he stood to one side with his arm around his brother Taranis, shouting encouragement as Goibban trounced two of the miners simultaneously. When Epona tugged at his sleeve he looked down with annoyance, but even in the twilight he could see the trouble in her face. He followed her without hesitation.

His family was huddled together outside the lodge. Within the lodge was nothingness; anything could happen to a person in that darkness.

Epona left Toutorix with Rigantona and the now-sobbing Brydda and went to bring Tena, She Who Summons Fire.

The matter was very serious. A tribal council must be convened immediately, with all the *druii* in attendance, since the spirits were involved; but before anything else the chief's lodgefire must be relit. To leave the lord of the tribe in darkness might bring a similar darkness on all his people. The tribe crowded around outside as Tena, already chanting incantations, entered the lodge alone. Other families had joined Rigantona and her children and jostled one another for vantage points, peering inside, anxious to see the expected birth. Toutorix stood off to one side, holding Brydda's arm in a relentless grip. Okelos had come at the run, angry at first but then as shocked as the others, and now he stood as far away from his wife as possible. If she had brought the fury of the spirits down upon them, it was better not to call attention to the fact that she was his wife.

The damage Brydda had done was already evident. The sky, in sympathy with the spirit of the fire, was showing no stars. Black clouds had piled up over the lake and a distant flicker of starfire warned of a coming storm. The Kelti murmured uneasily; the angered spirits might call down the starfire to attack their lodges and burn them. Such things had been known to happen; starfire had struck and killed people where they stood.

A tiny spark, a faint glow, flared into life within the lodge, and then flame blossomed. The watchers sighed in unison. Crowding close to the doorway, those in front could see Tena's face, golden above the firepit, as she sang to the newborn flame and nurtured it.

Now it was safe for the chief's family to re-enter, but Brydda was not allowed through the doorway. Wrapped in blankets, she spent the night huddled outside the lodge, and Rigantona brought the child to her for nursing without speaking to her.

As dawn broke over the mountains, the elders of the tribe and the members of the *druii* met together in solemn council to discuss the fate of the unfortunate young woman. She was the mother of a living child, which weighed in her favor, though her firstborn was a girl and that was a negative sign. She might never bear warriors.

Poel spoke for the *druii*. "The spirits make existence possible for us; they provide us with fire and water and meat; they guide every step of our lives. If one of the people insults a spirit, all of the people are held responsible. We must act for the good of the tribe."

"For the good of the tribe," echoed the council.

Toutorix stood and held aloft the staff of authority that had been used just the evening before to referee *kamanaht*. Now it must serve a more serious function. Struck three times upon the ground as urged by the spirit within, it would make his word law that no member of the tribe dared break.

"The woman Brydda has insulted the spirit of the fire," he intoned. "She must go to the land of the spirits and apologize on behalf of all of us."

The council voted in unanimous assent. Okelos, waiting outside the council ring, heard the words of the lord of the tribe and saw the others raise their hands in agreement. He thought then of Brydda as she had been when he first brought her from the riverlands, a merry girl, laughing at everything he said, taking nothing seriously, bursting with life like a sapling tree. When she submitted to him he had felt like the strongest man alive.

67

I chose a foolish woman to be the mother of my children, he thought now, with regret. He wanted to smash his fist into something: the wall of the lodge or the face of an enemy.

The women set to work immediately to build a huge wicker basket. Kernunnos oversaw the work. "It must be in the shape of a flame," he told them, "large at the bottom and narrow at the top. It will become the flame, in token of the sacrifice."

Building the wicker basket took a full day. Meanwhile, Brydda crouched outside the lodge of the chief and no one spoke to her. No one met her eyes. She was given food and water but nothing else. Sirona, wife of Taranis, came to take her baby away, though there was an argument over that.

"We can raise the infant in our lodge or expose it, if that is what my son wishes," Rigantona told Sirona. "This child is part of our family."

"If you keep it, you have no human milk to give it," Sirona pointed out.

"I might soon."

Sirona raised her feathery dark eyebrows. Her hair was a pale silvery white, which had earned her the name of Star, but her brows were dark clouds over smoke-gray eyes. Epona had always thought her very beautiful, though she never said so within her mother's hearing. "You will not have milk," Sirona told Rigantona now. "You measure your age in winters, your breasts will not fill again. But look! I have plenty." She pushed down the neck of her gown and lifted one plump breast for inspection, squeezing it so a few rich drops dribbled out. She was haughty in her triumph.

"Let her have it." Okelos sighed wearily. He did not want the baby of a foolish woman. "Just don't let Brydda see you taking it away."

Rigantona gave up; she had not really looked forward to raising another infant anyway. "The child is yours, then," she told Sirona. "By the time she is grown enough to be worth the gifts of young men I will probably be safely in the nextworld; I would get no benefit from her."

When the wicker basket was finished the *druii* began their work. Throughout the night they burned fires and chanted. They danced the ancient patterns and sang the ancient songs. Their voices carried across the village and many a woman lay awake in the night, glancing at her own wifefire occasionally to be certain the coals were still glowing.

At dawn the full tribe assembled except for the women who guarded the fires. On this day of all days, no fire would die for lack of attention.

The sun rose through a hazy sky. "It is a bad omen," Kernunnos commented to Poel. "We must hurry, before something happens."

The wicker cage was set up in the center of the commonground. It was lashed together with leather thongs and constructed in the unmistakable shape of a flame. One side was left open so Brydda could enter.

Kernunnos, dressed in a feathered cloak and wearing an eagle headdress, circled the cage nine times to the knife hand, whispering in the spirit language. Tena stood beside the cage, her coppery hair glinting in the sunrise, her arms lifted above her head.

A naked woman was led forward with a strong warrior on either side to hold her up if her strength failed. Okelos found it difficult to watch; he expected Brydda to embarrass him further. But from some unguessed reservoir of strength she managed to walk forward steadily, though she was very pale. Death was not to be feared, but the prospect of pain terrified her. As everyone knew and Rigantona had never let her forget, she had screamed during childbirth.

When she saw the wicker basket she closed her eyes and swayed on her feet.

They put her in the cage and lashed it closed. The head of each family of the Kelti came forward in turn, to lay one piece of wood at the base of the wicker as that family's offering to the fire spirit.

Brydda crouched in the cage, though it had been built high enough to allow her to stand proudly upright. Her arms were wrapped protectively around her body.

Kernunnos began playing the priest drum. One single beat, repeated again and again in a gradually increasing tempo.

Tena bent over and laid her hands on the wood, open palms downward. She moved slowly around the cage, touching every log or branch she could reach. Then she stepped back and waited, eyes closed, arms outstretched, calling on the spirit of the fire.

Tiny red eyes began to wink deep within the pyre. A spiral of smoke twisted upward. Something crackled, like ice breaking up at the edge of the lake, but no flames showed yet.

Brydda moaned.

The *druii*, chanting, commanded her to speak to the spirits in the otherworlds on behalf of all the tribe, to beg forgiveness and ask that no harm come to the Kelti, no fire consume their lodges, no fever burn their flesh. The people joined in the chant, leaning toward the fire and the cage in its center, willing the woman to be strong for her journey.

The fire came alive and leaped upward. It twined like ivy around the wicker bars, outlining them in red and gold. Brydda drew back with a gasp but there was no place to go beyond their reach, not in thisworld. The *gutuiters* had instructed her to swallow the smoke, that she might be freed more quickly, but she was now too panicked to remember. She threw herself back and forth in the cage, thrusting out her white arms, the heat crisping the gold hairs on them.

"Okelos, where are you? Help me; I'm afraid!"

Okelos turned his head away. He met the eyes of the lord of the tribe; commanding eyes. He made himself turn back and watch.

Brydda screamed. The smoke billowed and the air stank of burning flesh.

The people of the Kelti waited.

When at last the wicker burned through and collapsed, a great shower of sparks shot into the sky and the massed spectators sighed, one deep groan of relief.

It was time to get on with the tasks of the living.

Chapter 6

A GUARD WITH A TORCH was posted at the smoldering pyre that night to keep the dogs and pigs away until the ashes were thoroughly cooled and the *gutuiters* could collect them.

Brydda had not undergone the ritual of the house of the dead before her burning, and therefore her ashes would not be stored in an urn and buried with the ancestors. She had gone directly to the spirits; her ashes had much power. They would be saved until next sunseason and then worked into the earth, to whisper to new growing things of the warm sun waiting for them.

It was the first such sacrifice Epona had witnessed — a member of her own lodge, burning. Esus of the Marcomanni, the Silver Bull, believed that sacrifices should be hung in trees, having been taught this ritual by his tribe's *druii*, but Toutorix was known for his use of the wicker basket.

"Fire liberates the spirit sooner," he explained, "and the shape of the basket helps keep it mindful of its purpose in being sent to the otherworlds. If we were not blessed with a shapechanger, we would attempt to communicate directly with the spirits of the game by building baskets to resemble the bear and the stag."

After the burning, Epona returned to the lodge in a pensive mood. She knew Brydda was gone, body and spirit, and yet she could not quite believe it. Was it possible that laughing face would not toss her a wink across the cooking pots anymore? How could it be that no Brydda would share little jokes or giggle over gossip with her? Who would be Epona's ally in the silent tugging of the personalities within the family of the chief?

The atmosphere in the lodge was tense. Okelos was sullen; Toutorix was quiet and withdrawn. He was rubbing his chest again and he had no appetite. Rigantona had already appropriated Brydda's possessions and was railing at Okelos for having married a girl who was not only irresponsible, but possessed little property.

"You went to the Vindelici with plenty of gifts," she reminded her son. "You should have brought back one of the women from the lodge of Mobiorix."

Okelos thrust out his lower lip. "I told you before, I did the best I could."

"I hope you do better next time," Rigantona said with a sniff.

Thinking of next time — and his cold bedshelf — Okelos approached Toutorix. "I should go for a new wife before first frost," he said, "or I'll have to wait all through snowseason."

Toutorix lay on his bed with his arms folded across his chest. He stared up at the carved rooftree. "We can't spare you now," he replied. "Traders are coming constantly, every man is needed in the mines — though you do little enough. But even your small contribution would make a difference."

"But that means I won't have a wife for a whole year, until the next feast of the great fire!" Okelos protested. "What am I to do?"

"There are plenty of women in the village who smile at you or put their hands on you," Toutorix remarked. "Share bedsports with them."

"They are other men's wives. I want my own; I want to possess the woman I sleep with."

"A wife isn't a possession," Toutorix reminded him. With a weary sigh, he sat up. His hair was matted and his face was ashen in the light of the lodgefire. "A wife is a free woman of the people, belonging only to herself. Only her children are yours until they marry. Why do you think you have to own everything?"

Okelos would not answer. He turned away from the lord of the tribe and went to his stacked weapons, his sword and his spear, his little collection of knives. He squatted beside them, for a warrior must always sit so he could rise quickly — only women sat crosslegged. He ran his thumb along the edge of the sword, testing it, and there was a faraway look in his eyes. "This place is too small for me," he said to no one in particular.

Rigantona went to him. "Be patient," she advised. "If you will only make an effort, you may be chief some day."

"Can you promise me that? What about Taranis? What about the council?" A sly look crept into his face. "If I were chief, things would be different. Better. For you, too; I would see to it. Sirona would get no more ornaments to flaunt in your face.

"You could help me, Mother. You could go to the chief priest and ask him to use his influence . . ."

"No," Rigantona said sharply.

"Why not? He might do it for you. His eyes still follow you; I've watched."

"I don't want to ask Kernunnos for anything," Rigantona said firmly.

"Not even for me?" Okelos presented his most charming face to his mother, stroking her arm, winding her hair around his fingers. A sweet, calculating smile shone through his sandy beard. "As lord of the tribe, I would be very generous to you."

On his bedshelf, Toutorix began to snore.

Epona was not paying much attention to the rest of her family. Alator, Banba, and the younger children, overexcited by the events of the day, soon fell asleep, and the bickering of the adults made Epona uncomfortable. Only Brydda had never argued. She had shrugged off the bad moods of the others and taken nothing very seriously.

Yet this was a serious world, and she had misjudged it. Poor Brydda . . .

Had she found her way into the nextlife by now? Had her spirit gotten over its dying and made a comfortable transition? Was Brydda happy in the otherworld?

Epona longed to know. It was painful to think of Brydda as being unhappy, or lost, or grieving for the world she had left behind.

The spirit within was speaking, making a suggestion.

Epona went to her bedshelf and stretched out with her head to the north, the direction the *druii* believed was most sensitive to the otherworlds. She closed her eyes and pictured Brydda's face.

Traveling into and out of the otherworlds was an ability the

73

druii alone claimed. They knew the way; they knew how to lower the barriers between. Epona had always taken it for granted that only the priesthood could do this, but now she had a new thought: *If the* DRUII *can do it, then it can be done. It is not impossible. Maybe I can do it, just for a heartbeat, just long enough to see Brydda and assure myself she is all right.*

It might be dangerous; strange tales were whispered of the otherworlds, and the *druii* were known to take elaborate precautions before venturing into them. But Epona did not think any area where gentle laughing Brydda was could be dangerous. And she would only try to gain entry for a moment, just to see . . .

She waited on her bedshelf, concentrating on her near-sister's face. For a while nothing happened. She strained, reaching, and then began the first soft sensation of blur and slide. She submitted to it willingly. The walls of the lodge seemed to recede. *Concentrate. Reach out.*

In the distance she heard a beating like the priest drum and it was as if that sound were in some way connected to the heart thudding in her chest, the two merging into one as she moved . . . floated . . . drifted . . . spun . . .

Down and through darkness. The stomach queasy; a sense of separation that violated the integrity of one's being.

Gray mist swirling. Light. Light far off, the gray mist close. Shadows moving in the mist. Her body on its bedshelf began to shake but she did not know it. She was already somewhere else, but not in the nebulous, fleeting dreamworld she had romped through in childhood. This was a different place and had a reality unlike any other.

One of the shadowy forms drew closer to her and she tried to speak to it, but it was not her voice she used. Words came out of her head in thoughts and were answered in kind. The shape hovering near her was not Brydda, did not know Brydda, she must seek elsewhere. It reached out imploringly to her, wanting something indefinable from her, and she shrank away, frightened by the implicit hunger in its demands. She fled from it toward that lovely glimpsed light. There was warmth and brilliance; there was surely Brydda, who had gone to the spirit of the fire.

Moving was different here; not walking. It was a matter of will, and she was aware in some subtle way of a kind of attachment trailing behind her like a weightless rope, linking her with herself on the bed in the lodge. She knew from the spirit within that the linkage must not be broken if she ever hoped to return; that was one of the laws of this place.

She moved and sought. She felt without seeing; she saw without understanding. She became aware of something very familiar, close by; an infectious laughter, merry and childlike.

"Brydda?" She tried to move closer and found she was passing through apparently solid objects as if they were water. And then she was under the stars — stars not arranged in any pattern she knew. Brydda was there; with but not part of that lovely, luring light . . . she wanted to touch Brydda, to offer at least a hug in parting, but the knowledge came into her that such communication was not needed here. It had already taken place . . . in another season . . . except there were no seasons . . . no now, no then, only directions, and one could go forward or back . . . or stay, or become lost among those strange stars . . .

It would be so easy to surrender to the tempting bodiless freedom, but something hard and stubborn within Epona resisted. Brydda was all right . . . was content . . . was continuing, and that was all she had wanted to know. Epona was not ready to know more. She wanted to be home, on her solid bedshelf, housed in her familiar skin . . .

She shuddered violently, feeling as if she had fallen through the bed, her stomach swooping sickeningly. Her eyes flew open and saw the glow of the lodgefire on the log walls. She heard Rigantona raising the bronze cauldron, the iron chain creaking.

Reassured, she closed her eyes again and sank into dreamless sleep.

Okelos was still in a dark mood in the morning. He made no effort to go to the mine. Instead he prowled about the lodge, snatching food from the pot and drinking wheat-beer and honey even before the sun cleared the mountains. He was plainly miserable but would talk to no one. His younger brothers and sisters fled the lodge.

Epona felt sorry for him. He had cared very much for Brydda, and he seemed to be suffering now. She remembered times when he had played with her, or done things for her; she thought of how proud she had often been of him after *kamanaht*.

When Okelos growled inaudibly in response to some harmless remark of hers, Rigantona lost her temper with him. She was in a bad mood herself. Without Brydda she must stay close to the lodge and tend the fire and the smaller children, while beyond the door was a radiant mountain morning, with air as sweet as wine in the blood. Brydda should have been sacrificed by the Marcomanni, not the Kelti. She should have been hung in the trees to die slowly and suffer long. She deserved it.

"Why don't you get out of my way?" Rigantona asked her son angrily. "How can I do anything around here with a grown man lolling about? Toutorix, get him out of here; I'm sick of his face this morning."

Toutorix, who was taking an uncommonly long time about washing and dressing himself, further disrupting household routine, cast a stern look at his oldest son. "Go to the salt mine," he said peremptorily. It was an order, not a request. With Brydda's death, everything had changed. Okelos had lost status. He was no longer a married man but a dependent on his mother's cooking once more. If he angered Toutorix he could be sent out of the lodge to live in a hut with no wifefire, without any luxury other than that he earned himself, and the lodge of Toutorix would eventually belong to Alator instead.

Okelos pulled on his mining clothes and left the lodge, but he did not go far. He stopped outside, staring across the common-ground at the blackened spot where the pyre had been. Epona, coming outside, saw him there and was pained by the misery in his eyes.

She wanted to give him something.

She came close to his side and said, in a low voice, "Brydda's all right, Okelos. She's happy again, and laughing."

He glanced down, startled. "What are you talking about?"

"Brydda. I saw her lastnight. I went into the otherworlds and . . . and she was there. I was with her."

"You couldn't have done that!"

Epona's spine stiffened and a hard line showed through the soft flesh of her jaw. "I did. I give you my word." Otherwise, how was he to believe her and be comforted?

Okelos caught her upper arm in his knife hand and squeezed. "You really saw her? You can go into the otherworlds?"

The immensity of her claim was beginning to dawn on her. She was reluctant to say more, but his grip was demanding. "Yes," she told him, lowering her eyes. "At least, I could lastnight. I don't know if I will ever be able to do it again, and I have no reason to try. It was not . . . pleasant."

Okelos' voice vibrated with excitement. "You must be *drui* and we never knew!"

She pulled back. "But I'm not. The abilities of the *druii* make themselves known in childhood . . ."

"You're late, that's all. But you have the gift, Epona! Think what you can do with that!"

"I don't want to do anything with it," she told him. "I want to forget about it; I certainly don't want to live my life in the priesthood. I have other plans."

"You are little more than a child, you don't know what's best for you. How can you have plans already?"

She lifted her chin. "I know exactly what's best for me. I want to stay right here in the Blue Mountains all my life."

"You see! As a *drui* you can do that; you will not be sent off as a wife, you will be too precious to the tribe.

"*Gutuiters* don't marry at all, so there will be no infants in their wombs to distract them from the voices of the spirits. You will stay right here, and help us, and . . ."

She glared at him. "I'm sorry I ever told you anything. You don't understand. I have no intention of giving up marriage to stay in a lodge with other women. I have plans I can't talk about with you, and I beg you not to tell anyone else about the otherworlds. Forget I ever said it. It was a mistake, a dream, nothing more."

Okelos narrowed his eyes. "Ah, no, sister. You gave your word."

Okelos went on to the salt mine, but he returned early. He watched for an opportunity to speak to Rigantona when the lodge was temporarily empty of any who might overhear. Then he went to her with a present.

"This is fine enough only for Rigantona," he said, holding it out for her to admire.

The woman's face lit with pleasure. She seized the object and turned it over and over in her hands. It was a perfect model, in miniature, of the chieftain's cart in which she had first seen Toutorix, tall and proud in all his finery. Even the wheels turned, and little leather traces waited for impossibly small ponies.

"Who made this beautiful thing?"

"Goibban."

"This is no child's toy; it is a jewel made of bronze."

"And silver, see the designs on the sides? And the axles and wheels are iron."

"Magnificent," she breathed. "But . . . why are you giving this to me? You must have paid the smith a high price for it. What do you want in return?"

"What makes you think I want something in return?"

Rigantona was sitting at her loom, a plaid of coppery red and bright green wool before her. Now she set the bronze cart down on her lap — carefully — and leaned back, bracing her arms on her bedshelf. She surveyed Okelos with amusement. "I carried you in my body," she reminded him. "My blood knows your blood. You would never make such a sacrifice unless you expected to gain a great advantage."

Okelos was not embarrassed; he was flattered his mother recognized what he thought of as shrewdness. He would be a splendid trade-arranger, better even than Toutorix.

"There is a trade involved," he admitted. "Something for everyone. I give you this, and you influence Kernunnos to support me as lord of the tribe when the time comes."

"I said I would not go to the shapechanger, even for you."

"You don't have to. You will send Epona."

Rigantona stared at him. "Epona?"

Okelos nodded. "She is *drui*. She is still unmarried; you can give her to the priesthood."

"She's not *drui*, she's just an ordinary girl. The priest would have no use for her; he must confine his lifemaking to married women of the tribe."

Okelos' voice was urgent. "I tell you, she is *drui*. She can travel into the otherworlds; she did it after Brydda's sacrifice. She told me about it and gave me her word it was true."

78

Rigantona was dazzled. Her own daughter. Could it be possible . . . ? She quickly recognized the possibilities, the prestige and benefits that would accrue to her as the mother of a *drui*.

Watching her eyes, Okelos smiled. "If you offer Epona to Kernunnos, he will have to give you a gift in kind. You can then ask him to support me as new lord of the tribe. Toutorix grows old; surely you see that."

Rigantona was running her fingers over the little bronze cart again. "The priest would give anything I asked in return for a new *drui*," she said, bemused. "They are found so rarely. Anything I ask . . ."

"Yes!" urged Okelos.

Meanwhile, Epona was wandering through her day distracted. She regretted having mentioned the otherworlds to Okelos, but it was too late now. And nothing could be changed. She performed her chores without really being aware of them. The swirling mists of the otherworld she had seen were always in her mind, part of its landscape now, drawing and seducing her, frightening her with glimpses of things she was not prepared to encounter. It was too much; she was overcome by the experience and desperate to shake off its effects. *Never again*, she promised herself. *Never again!*

She had spent most of the day with Sirona and some of the younger women, caring for the livestock in the animal pens. Four young bull calves had been castrated to supply new oxen for Kwelon's wagons, and Nematona was on hand to spread their wounds with a healing paste and attend to the details of the sacrifice of the amputated testicles.

The women, sweating and straining, had caught and thrown the little bulls and held them down for the operation, cheering one another on with bawdy comparisons between the size of the severed testicles and the equipment of their own men.

Epona's injured arm kept her from the more physical efforts, and she had to be content with sitting beside each animal in turn, stroking it and keeping it calm while Nematona's skillful hands repaired the insulted flesh.

Rigantona found her there and beckoned to her. Sirona noticed her marriage-sister and could not resist a jibe: "Come and help us, Rigantona who was once so strong. Let's see if you can hold this squirming beast — or has the snow in your hair quenched the fire in your bosom?"

Rigantona scowled at her rival. Sirona was younger, more agile, and from the shape of her body she was quickening with new life. Taranis was virile; Sirona went to no other men. She had already bragged openly to other women that Taranis would someday be lord of the tribe.

Without deigning to reply to Sirona, Rigantona led her daughter away from the animal pens. She looked closely at the girl's arm. It seemed to her to be taking a long time to heal; she had every reason to believe it would be crooked, ugly. Such things happened. Then what man would offer gifts for Epona? The girl might remain on their hands always, unmarried, unwanted, eating good food, allotted a share of everything the family earned . . .

"I have been thinking about your future," Rigantona began. "And just this day I was told by your brother that you have the *drui* gift. I think that is a wonderful solution for our problem. I will offer you to the chief priest to be initiated; what do you think of that?"

Epona stared unbelievingly at her mother. "But I don't want to!"

"Of course you do, what a foolish thing to say. It's a very great honor, Epona; surely you realize that?"

"I don't want that kind of honor. I want the respect a married woman is entitled to receive from the tribe; I want the honor of bearing children, of creating a house for another spirit."

"You're too young to make such choices for yourself. Not long ago you were rebelling against the pattern, which proves you are still too new to thislife to make your own decisions. Someday you will thank me for sending you to the magic house."

The magic house. Condemned to a life of swirling mists and chanting. Instead of Goibban's manly grace to companion all the days of thislife, there would be only Kernunnos . . . The image of the wolf's face flashed before her eyes again, recalling the intense dislike she had felt for the shapechanger as far back as she could remember.

"Don't do that to me. I would hate it!"

Rigantona's face was set and unyielding. "You are being very foolish; you are lucky we still have authority over you in this matter. To be *drui* is to be granted access to the secrets of the earth, Epona; it is more power than you would ever have otherwise. I would have given up a husband and children myself, gladly, for such an opportunity."

"But I want a husband more than anything else in thisworld."

"I assure you, you will be happier without one. The *gutuiters* are spared all that, spared the discomfort and inconvenience of childbearing and raising so they may give their full attention to the spirits, and I think they are better for it. Look at Tena, or Uiska. Their breasts are still high, they look seasons younger than they are. I've always secretly suspected they use their magic to keep themselves strong and beautiful past a woman's usual time; wouldn't you like that?"

"No! I just want the life I've always expected to have."

"No one gets the life they expect," Rigantona told her with a trace of bitterness in her voice. "That is why we barter with the spirits to try to get the best deal we can." She looked pointedly at the girl's bandaged arm. "What man will want you now? The people do not take disfigured wives."

"I won't be disfigured."

"How can you tell?"

"I just . . . know."

"Hai," said Rigantona. "Is that another gift you have, the gift of healing? Can you heal yourself?"

"No. I don't have any gifts, I tell you. I don't have them and I don't want them." Epona backed away from her mother.

"You don't seem to realize I'm doing this for your own good, Epona," Rigantona insisted, following her. "You have no say in this; it's not like accepting or rejecting a particular man as husband. Quit sulking and try to appreciate your good fortune. We will have such a ceremony, such games and feasting . . ."

As Epona was listening horrified to her mother's glowing plans, Toutorix was receiving his own bad news. For the first time, his position as lord of the tribe was being seriously questioned by the tribal council. Even his younger brother Taranis, who had always been his strongest supporter and warrior-of-the-shoulder, came forward to testify he felt the reign of the Invincible Boar was nearing its end.

In his abnormally deep voice, Taranis said to his brother,

"Lately you have been giving away our wealth to the traders in return for shoddy merchandise and inequitable terms." The members of the council nodded agreement. "This season you have not demanded the highest price as you did in the past. You have let their oiled tongues beguile you into accepting their sixth or seventh offer instead of really bargaining. Your skills are failing you, Toutorix."

The chieftain turned on his brother in white-lipped anger. "How can you say these things to me? Since I became lord of the tribe, have I not expanded our trade until we now live here as luxuriously as the princes live in Etruria? Who else could have done that?"

"You speak the truth. You have been sunshine driving out cold shadows, Toutorix, but your light is dimming now. Your evening has come. If there were a battle to be fought, I do not think you would be able to manage your sword and shield."

Okelos was standing just outside the council ring, his eyes shining hotly. Toutorix, glancing up, saw the expression on his face and was reminded of young wolves, waiting to bring down an old stag. Life passes on to life; so says the spirit within.

Toutorix got to his feet, forcing himself to rise as if there were still some spring in his legs, but the effort cost him. He had aged mightily this sunseason and he knew it; he had spent more of himself than he could spare. "There may be some wisdom in what you say," he acknowledged, "but I will have to think on it. Perhaps in the snowseason, when there is time for long conversation and deliberation, we will consider choosing a new chief. But in the meantime I am still strong enough to care for my people!" He slammed his staff against the earth for emphasis and strode away from the circle.

Once out of their sight, however, his shoulders slumped with fatigue. He realized there was little time left. The tusks of the Invincible Boar were drawn. With or without his acquiescence a new chief must be chosen all too soon, and his spirit would have nothing left to do in thisworld.

He made his way back toward his lodge, feeling neither the wind at his back nor the earth mother beneath his feet. He did not even see Epona until she flung herself on him, throwing her arms around him and shouting, "Stop her, stop her! Don't let my mother ruin my life!"

He staggered under the weight of her assault. "Do what? What are you yelling about?"

"Rigantona means to give me to the *druii* to be trained as a *gutuiter*, even though I don't want to do it. I would much rather burn in a cage and escape thisworld," Epona cried, her words tumbling over one another in their eagerness to escape her mouth. She flung her arms wide, then clutched Toutorix again; she expressed all her youthful horror and indignation almost incoherently, but gradually Toutorix understood. Rigantona had found a way to be sure of getting something for the girl now, instead of waiting and gambling on her desirability as a wife.

He gently disentangled himself from Epona, surprised that her embrace had caused such numbness in his arms. "Rigantona can be greedy," he said, "but you need not worry. I am still lord of the tribe — for a little while — and I can command. I will tell your mother that you are not to be forced into the priesthood. You wait here; it will be all right." He patted her hand.

Rigantona was striding toward him, hot on her daughter's heels. Seeing her, Toutorix set his face in the stern, implacable mask of his warrior days. He called her name in an angry voice. Rigantona hesitated.

Watching the two of them, Epona clenched her fists by her sides and hated her feeling of helplessness. *I have a right to shape my own life*, she thought, not for the first time.

Toutorix faltered. Six paces away from him, Rigantona saw his face take on a strange bluish color and his eyes widen. He opened his mouth as if to say something but no word came out, only a croak like that of a trampled frog. His cup arm clamped convulsively against his side and his knife arm made a wild circle in the air, then canted forward with the rest of his body, falling like a toppled tree, out of the world of now.

Chapter 7

E PONA WAS THE FIRST to reach him. As soon as he stumbled she darted forward, and by the time he hit the ground she was already calling for help. She threw herself to her knees beside the fallen chieftain and cradled his head in her arms, willing him to open his eyes and look at her. But the eyes remained closed, buried in deep purple shadows. The face of Toutorix looked like a skull, the skin as pallid and lifeless as beeswax.

Rigantona bent over them. "What happened? Is he all right? Get up, Toutorix; don't lie there on the ground making a fool of me."

Epona tried to shut out her mother's words. She needed to concentrate on Toutorix in this very special moment, for she needed no *gutuiter* to tell her his spirit was leaving his body. She looked up at her mother imploringly and pursed her lips to ask for silence.

Rigantona understood at last. She knelt on his other side, her face almost as pale as his. Both women heard the death rattle in his throat as his spirit forced its way upward, and watched in silence as his lips gaped open to release it.

People were forming a circle around them now, jostling and asking questions, but their voices died away as soon as they realized what was happening. One must be silent during the passing of a spirit. They had been silent after Brydda's last wild shriek.

Poel pushed his way through the crowd and knelt next to Epona.

She glanced up quickly, grateful for the swift arrival of a *drui* at the moment of transition. Poel laid his fingers against the side of Toutorix's neck, feeling for the throb of lifeblood, but there was no response. He waited long enough to be certain, then passed his hand over his eyes, signaling Rigantona that her husband's life was over.

Still they waited. Life, and the end of life, has its own rhythm.

In the silence they heard the faintest sigh. It might have been wind in the pine trees but it was not. The crowd fell back so as not to impede the passing of the spirit. Epona felt the weight in her arms grow heavier.

"Gone," she said softly. Her eyes and her throat were burning.

All lesser matters must be set aside now. The lord of the tribe was dead, and no other business could be conducted until the ceremonies of his transition were completed. Vallanos and some of the nobles went to the passes to intercept approaching traders and demand they make camp until Toutorix rested with the ancestors.

Toutorix had had the bad timing to die before a new chieftain could be chosen to whom he would hand his staff; therefore, it became the property of his widow until the council elected his successor. But such an election could not be held until the funeral rites were completed, and until that time, Rigantona held the staff of the chieftain and none could dispute her authority.

With considerable satisfaction, she propped the staff against her loom where all who came into the lodge could see it. She then sent her children from the lodge and summoned the elders of the tribe, as well as the five *druii*.

She made a big show of offering her guests red wine and honeycakes, but they all knew they had been invited for a serious purpose. Rigantona began explaining almost at once.

"Toutorix was an exceptional chieftain," she reminded them, as if there was any chance his prestige might already be tarnishing while his body was still cooling in the house of the dead. "Perhaps the greatest leader in the history of our people. Under his guidance, the Kelti developed a trade network that crosses the earth like rivers and streams. Because of his reputation, Kelti daughters have married into every important tribe of the people; our blood is everywhere. We have more friends than enemies. Who else can make such a claim?"

85

The elders nodded their heads. Rigantona had begun the meeting as the late Toutorix had always opened negotiations with traders, by talking on subjects where there was agreement and getting them accustomed to assent before the hard bargaining began.

"I have stood at my husband's back," she went on, "and listened to the strangers who come here from other lands. I have heard how the dead are honored elsewhere, among the Makedonians and the fierce warriors of Sparta, among the Lydians and Phrygians and the Etruscans of Etruria. Especially among the Etruscans. The funeral they give their dead princes would do honor to the dying sun itself. Our paltry rituals are insulting by comparison, and the spirits we send into the otherworld must be embarrassed when they meet the spirits of the Etruscans.

"Need I remind you, no member of the Kelti likes to be embarrassed? And Toutorix least of all?"

She addressed Nematona directly. "You are senior *gutuiter;* you preside over birth into thisworld as the priests preside over birth into the next. We honor your wisdom. Tell me, Daughter of the Trees, is it not true that the *druii* adapt each funeral ritual, its songs, its sacrifices, to the person in transition? Must not one's way of death fit, even as clothes fit the body?"

"You speak truly," Nematona agreed.

"Then should not a very special celebration be prepared for my very special husband, one that would cause his name to be remembered for all the generations to come?"

Nematona paused before answering, trying to feel the thoughts of the other *druii,* but the lodge was filled with so many tensions she could not separate them from the general atmosphere.

"What you say has merit," Nematona replied at last, cautiously. Better not make a commitment until she could see where all this was leading and confer with her colleagues.

Rigantona, however, smiled with satisfaction. It was enough agreement to begin the serious bartering; she had learned much, standing at her husband's back. "Hai. Then I would like to have Toutorix buried unburned, as the princes of Etruria are buried, with enough symbols of wealth and prestige beside him to impress anyone he may meet in the otherworlds. And when I make my own transition, I want my body put with his, to share in all he has as I have done in thisworld."

86

There was a frozen hush in the lodge. Even the fire seemed to hold its breath, its omnipresent cheerful crackling muted to a hiss.

The *druii* and elders looked at Rigantona incredulously; they were shocked by her suggestion. She gazed back at them with all the authority she could summon, determined not to be intimidated by the protests sure to come.

Rigantona had been badly frightened recently. Although she had seen sacrifices before, Brydda's death haunted her, filling her thoughts with fire and screaming, making her suddenly nervous of consigning her own body to the flames. Formerly she had given little thought to transition; the high, sweet air of the Blue Mountains did not foster the diseases that ravaged the riverlands from time to time, and death seemed far away, something that happened only to the old. Rigantona had never thought of herself as old. She felt the same inside as she always had. When she looked in her polished bronze mirror, she thought she saw the face she had seen when she and Toutorix were first married.

She would grow old sometime, of course, but not yet. She would leave her flesh and her jewelry, her clothes and scented oils, sometime. When she and Toutorix were feeble and tired of their bodies. Many seasons from now.

Then all at once Toutorix was gone, and when Rigantona looked in her mirror she saw a face she hardly recognized, an aging face with the sap dried out of it. She had nothing left but her wealth . . .

She must hurry to make provisions to take it, all of it, with her, to enjoy in the otherworlds. And there was a way it could be done. Other peoples knew of it, practiced it, believed in it. She would, too.

Old Dunatis cleared his throat and stood up. Everyone turned respectfully to watch him. Many seasons ago, when Dunatis was still a young miner without even a shortsword and throwing spear, his wife had borne two children by the old history singer of the tribe, Maponos. Both of those offspring had subsequently proved to be *druii;* the first was Poel, and later, Tena. Now Dunatis was revered by the Kelti, enriched by gifts given to him in honor of his offspring. He had built himself a lodge high on a steep slope where none but the eagle could approach him, and it was said the spirit of the mountain herself guarded him because he had been so favored.

87

"We have burned the bodies for many generations, and we have prospered for many generations," old Dunatis said in his phlegmy voice, fixing Rigantona with the stern eye of tradition.

She replied, "Toutorix and I sometimes discussed this, as a man and woman discuss things on their bedshelf." *Or we might have,* she thought to herself, *if he had ever had time or inclination.* "Does not the history singer tell us that in the morning of our race we lived far to the east on a great plain, and buried our dead unburned, in barrows in the earth?"

The *druii* and the elders rolled their eyes toward Poel and the bard nodded assent.

There was precedent, then.

Rigantona's eyes sparkled, as she sensed triumph. "I only ask that we consider a return to this good way of sending our dead to their nextlives. It is not appropriate for a lord of the tribe Kelti to have his discarded flesh burned and the ashes poured into a miserable urn better designed for storing melted fat, a few trinkets dropped in beside him like child's toys. No! We can carry our debts over and pay them in the nextworld, so why not carry our wealth with us as well? As others do? Are we not at least as wise as the Etruscans?

"Are we not wise enough to consider a ritual the chief himself desired?" She flung that last statement at them like a lump of gold thrown into the trade, knowing no one could contradict it. Who could guess what the lord of the tribe had said to his wife on their bedshelf?

It was a shrewd ploy. The councilors were reminded of the chief who might be watching them at this very moment from the otherworlds, assessing their reactions. It would be a foolhardy thing to anger the spirit of a man like Toutorix. In his youth, he had been the strongest warrior of the people, and once freed from his worn-out body he might be that strong again. It was well known that he never forgot an insult or set aside a grudge. If this new ritual was truly what he wanted . . .

Dunatis stroked his scanty white beard. "There may be something to consider here," he told Rigantona, watching as she closed her fingers around her husband's staff and ran her hand up and down it, slowly, drawing all eyes, bringing the power of Toutorix to life once more in the lodge. The staff of ultimate authority.

"The council cannot take responsibility for making such a decision," Dunatis told her. "We can only advise. It is *druii* business, this making or changing of ritual."

"But you would not oppose it?"

Dunatis looked around the room at the other elders, carrying on a quick consultation with his eyes. "No," he said, turning back to Rigantona, "we would not oppose it if the *druii* say it can be allowed."

Rigantona turned to the five *druii*, sitting shoulder to shoulder. "How say the members of the priesthood?"

Uiska murmured in her soft voice but no words could be understood. Her restless hands moved in her lap, her fingers rippling like water. Tena sat with the firelight burning in her red hair and said nothing. Nematona stared into some leafy distance no one else could see. Poel covered his face with his hands, lost in contemplation.

Kernunnos stood, facing the wife of the dead chief. "You propose a very serious undertaking, Rigantona," he told her sternly. "This would be a major change in the pattern and I am not certain it would be of benefit to the tribe.

"Spirits enter thisworld naked and appropriate bodies to inhabit while they are here — human, animal, plant — we do not know the reason why a spark from the great fire of life chooses one body over another. Some return to take human form again and again; others do not. But when it has exhausted the possibilities of a body the spirit moves on, because life is always on the move, seeking.

"Would a spirit, therefore, have any real need to carry a great weight of possessions from thisworld to the next? Why should it be so burdened when it did not come here that way? Is it not better to set the spirit free on wings of flame, to go forward with its existence unimpeded?"

Tena threw back her head and looked up at Kernunnos with a bright hot smile.

Rigantona set her jaw. This would be a fight and she had no intention of losing.

"I only want to do what is best for my husband and the tribe," she said. "As I have the consent of the council, I think we can allow them to return to their lodges and I will discuss this matter privately with the *druii*."

If a struggle for power beyond death was to take place between the chief's wife and the priesthood, the elders unanimously preferred to stay clear of it. Without hesitation they handclasped Rigantona, one by one in the order of their rank, and filed out of the lodge.

When she was alone with the five *druii*, Rigantona put her ultimate weight on the scales of trade.

"I realize that I am asking you to make a great effort and take certain risks," she said, "and I understand that a comparable sacrifice is demanded. I am prepared to offer one. Nothing can be asked without a gift being given, and there is such a gift for you: my daughter Epona."

They looked at her in surprise. "For what purpose?" asked Poel, knitting his brows together.

"Epona is *drui*," Rigantona told them proudly.

The *gutuiters* and Poel exchanged astonished glances. Kernunnos narrowed his eyes and leaned forward slightly, saying nothing, as Rigantona related in detail — enlarged by her own imagination — the incident of Epona's visit to the otherworlds. "It is true," she finished triumphantly. "She gave her word to my son Okelos; you have only to ask him."

Kernunnos drew his lips back from his teeth. "That is not necessary. You speak truly; the girl is *drui*. I have known it for a long time. But she was resistant when I tried to discuss it with her, and I thought she would marry soon and leave us, her talent dormant within her like sap in a winter tree."

"She has a damaged arm," Rigantona pointed out. "It makes a difference to those who come seeking wives, but am I right in assuming it makes no difference to the priesthood?"

Nematona nodded. "Even if it heals crooked — though I believe it will be straight, in time — that would not affect her ability to use the powers she has been given, whatever they may be. She is a strong woman, and young; many seasons younger than any of us. We need her and she would be welcome. We have been concerned that too many seasons would pass before we found someone to pass on our knowledge to. But the creation of a different ritual of transition . . . a major change in the pattern . . ."

She pretended to be unsure, though no one had any doubt of the outcome now. A new *drui* was beyond price. But there must be a certain amount of hesitation and urging, of offers and demurrals. The exchange of gifts was hedged with formalities and could not be accomplished simply, for that would make the gift itself seem to be worth little effort.

When Rigantona was at last assured the funeral ritual would be created as she wished, a wave of relief swept over her and she felt a certain fondness for her oldest daughter. Because of Epona her own prestige was greatly enhanced, and when she went to the otherworlds . . .

Then she remembered. The gift of Epona to the *druii* was to have been for Okelos, to get support for his chiefdom.

She had an obligation to mention it. "The council will have to choose a new lord of the tribe," she said. "My son Okelos is a grown man of noble warrior lineage; he is as eligible as my husband's brothers. In consideration of my daughter Epona, will you support him with the elders?"

Kernunnos twitched his thin lips. "We are *druii*, pledged to do only that which is beneficial to the people. I do not think there would be any advantage in having Okelos hold the staff of authority. He is like a hound puppy, lazy and quick to bite. When he is older, perhaps . . ." He let the thought drag to a stop of its own weight.

Rigantona did not pursue it. She had what she wanted; her future was assured whether Okelos became lord of the tribe or not. She could tell him she had tried; what more could she do?

Imagine the expression on Sirona's face when she learned Rigantona's daughter was *drui!*

Kernunnos returned to the magic house in a state of elation. The girl Epona could move into the minds of animals already, he was certain of it. Perhaps she even had the ability to become a shapechanger. The benefit to the tribe of having two shapechangers at once could be incalculable.

The future seemed bright with promise.

Throughout that night and the next day, while the body of Toutorix lay on its oak trestle in the house of the dead, the *druii* communed with the spirits. The people in the lodges could smell the smoke of Tena's fires: scented smoke, sometimes nauseating, sometimes hauntingly sweet. They could hear the voice of Nematona mingling with that of the trees in the sacred grove. At the lake's edge, Uiska knelt and importuned the spirit of the water, while in the valley of the Kelti Poel sang to the ancestors. In the magic house, Kernunnos read the portents and felt with his mind into the otherworlds, searching for positive or negative influences.

He was pleased with the results. He could detect no resistance to this new ritual; in fact, it was very favorably received. The return of the whole body to the earth mother established a pleasing harmony within the pattern.

As he performed the various invocations and ceremonies, Kernunnos felt himself surrounded by benign influences. If one was highly sensitive to the things that could not be seen, as he was, one need make no mistakes and offend no life forms. Sometimes Kernunnos felt that he was exceptionally favored; that every step he took was planned for him in advance by an unseen guardian, so he moved through life under invisible guidance as the ships of the Sea People were blown by the invisible wind.

The great ceremony to celebrate the transition of Toutorix from now to the otherworlds was scheduled to begin at the next sunrise. A matron from a warrior's lodge was dispatched to watch Rigantona's fire for her, as she and her children prepared to follow the funeral procession.

When the sky paled above the mountains to the east, the chief's old cartponies were harnessed for the last time. Their trappings were decorated with fine bronze studding, and embossed plates and red plumes were thrust through their bridles. Goibban himself would lead the ponies, for they would have no driver. Toutorix rode in his cart with closed eyes and a pebble in his mouth to keep the departed spirit from re-entering.

Epona noticed how strong and splendid Goibban appeared as he marched at the front of the procession, following the *druii*. He had spoken formally to Rigantona, but he paid little attention to Epona, which darkened the clouds in her sky. There was a preoccupied expression on his face and only the iron was in his thoughts. The funeral would take most of the day; probably no work would get done at the forge until nextday, and he was jealous of every lost moment.

The cart bearing the chief's body was followed by his family and then the tribal council. Next came the representatives of each family in the tribe, smiling, to show that this was indeed a happy occasion. Birth was a cause for mourning on behalf of the newly arrived spirit, for thislife could be hard. Death was a time for celebration; new opportunities awaited the spirit as it moved on.

They left the village and climbed upward through the silvery light to the valley of the ancestors. This was a most sacred place. Here were the buried urns of the dead; here the spirits of the mountains came together and talked among themselves in voices the ignorant might mistake for wind.

It was a place of power.

A special tomb, dug into the earth and lined with timbers, had been prepared for the chief's body. A fill of stones and rubble had been dumped between the wooden walls and the surrounding soil. With more time the tomb could have been better prepared, but even in the high cool air of the mountains the body of a man would not keep indefinitely. Soon it would begin to smell and draw malign spirits carrying sickness. And if they had taken more time, to empty the flesh and fill it with salt and hair as Kernunnos did his birds, they would have had to delay the election of a new chief. In the future, the ritual could be refined.

Each of Rigantona's children brought some possession of the old chieftain's: his hunting horn, his drinking cup, his throwing spear. Epona proudly bore his shield, and Okelos carried the magnificent sword and decorated sheath Goibban had made. The young man hated having to leave that incomparable weapon in the tomb, but when he became lord of the tribe he would have one even better. That was a comforting thought.

Every member of the Kelti wore something red. Red was the color of death, signifying the return of the spirit to the great fire of life from which it came. Red was the color of life, and blood, and rebirth.

Every family presented gifts to accompany Toutorix to the otherworlds and to remind him to speak well of them. Taranis brought an enormous cauldron of bronze, polished to a gleam and decorated all around its rim with symbols of life and harmony. Others contributed jewelry, imported pottery and ornaments, their best

93

household goods, embroidered cloth, small figures representing accomplishments on the battlefield or at *kamanaht*, weapons and tools and whatever they had that was deemed worthy of the lord of the tribe.

Six strong warriors lifted the discarded body and carried it into the tomb, where it was stretched on a wooden platform, the head toward the rising sun to encourage rebirth. The gifts were arranged around the corpse. "Remember that we gave you these," the donors chanted, mindful of the obligation incurred by the receiving of gifts. When everyone else had made an offering, Rigantona stepped forward and laid on her husband's chest the small bronze cart Goibban had crafted.

She looked at Toutorix for the last time with an expression of infinite regret, then turned away.

Seeing Rigantona's gift, Kernunnos regretted that they had not prepared the tomb to hold the real cart and ponies as well. Next time, perhaps. Now, they built a pyre around the cart just beyond the mouth of the tomb. Goibban held the team by their bridles as Uiska approached, carrying a bronze basin. She was followed by the chief priest, wearing a dappled horsehide and with his hair freshly bleached and stiffened by lime paste.

Kernunnos stood in front of the cartponies and began the chant of sacrifice, praying to the spirits of the animals to agree to the sacrifice as a hunter prayed to the spirit of the game he sought to show his respect for the value of the gift it would give him.

As Kernunnos raised his knife to the first pony's throat, Goibban's eyes happened to meet Epona's.

In that moment the young woman was experiencing the sacrifice with her whole being: the sharp edge of the knife, the hot rush of life flowing out. It was as if a haze obscured her vision. Only when the haze cleared and the two animals lay peacefully on the earth mother, their generous red blood collected and their entrails cut out for divination, did she realize Goibban was staring at her as if he had never seen her before.

He felt that he had not. Now he saw that she had become a young woman indeed, with braided hair and swelling breasts. She was pleasing to look at; her proportions were in perfect harmony, like a fine design. Too bad she was of his tribe, his blood . . . He shrugged away the thought. There were women in plenty when he wanted them.

Still, none of them had the same quality as Epona, standing a dozen paces from him, looking up now, looking at him . . . there was something intense about her, something akin to the heat that softened iron . . .

Then men stepped between them to pile wood around the bodies of the ponies and Goibban turned away, his part in the ceremony finished. The forge was waiting.

Rigantona stood at the entrance to the unroofed tomb, mentally calculating the treasure accumulated within. All this she would share with Toutorix in the otherworlds. He had always been generous, at least.

"We have honored the lord of the tribe as he deserved," she announced, and at her signal Poel came forward to begin singing the first of the praise songs even as workmen started roofing the chamber and piling it with a mound of earth and stones.

The people of the Kelti returned to their village, Rigantona among them. The *druii* remained with the workmen at the tomb, waiting for the ashes of the sacrifice to cool.

Epona remained also. The pain and then the exultation she had experienced when the ponies died had shaken her, and the memory of Goibban's eyes, meeting hers, had confused her, making it difficult for her to clarify her impressions. For a little longer, she wanted to stay close to the tomb in which the chief's body lay, looking as it had in life. She envied Toutorix the peace she had seen mirrored on his face.

Kernunnos watched out of the corner of his eye as she loitered around the tomb, stooping to examine a flower in the grass, gazing upward at the cloud formations. Perhaps the girl remained because she was drawn to *druii* ritual. Had her mother spoken to her yet? Did she know she was promised?

This might be a good time to persuade her to join them willingly. Her gift could not be forced, but her body could; being unmarried, she was still her parents' property. If she felt resentment it would take much longer to shape her mind and develop her arts. Perhaps he had been too strong with her before, Kernunnos told himself. It might be better to be gentle, as when wooing a young doe.

He sat down on the grass to make himself smaller, less ominous. He stretched his body full length. He looked up at the clouds she was watching. She did not seem to be aware of his

95

presence until he spoke. "Do you know it is possible to control the clouds, to herd them like animals?" he asked in a conversational tone.

Epona started. The smell of the burned horseflesh and the entombed presence of Toutorix had been holding her attention; now she turned to see the priest lying on the ground like a wounded animal. He was too far away to be threatening.

"I have to go now," Epona said. "My mother will need me to help serve the funeral feast."

"Not yet. Stay here a little longer," Kernunnos urged. "We can talk, you and I. We have never talked, but we have more in common than you know, Epona." His voice was kind and not so different from any other man's voice. She looked at him, appraising him. He was a male Kelt, lean, older than she but younger than Toutorix had been. There was nothing unusual about the face of the chief priest, seen at this distance in the clear daylight. It was merely human.

No, he is not merely human, said the spirit within sharply. *That is a mask he can assume like any other.*

Shapechanger.

"I must go right now!" she insisted, starting off down the valley at a pace just short of a trot. The priest sat up and watched her go.

"It will be different when I have you in the magic house," he promised under his breath.

Tena came over to him. "What did you say to her?"

"I just wanted to talk to her but she took fright. She will need some taming, that one."

"Perhaps she's frightened of her own abilities," Tena remarked. "Having the power can be an unsettling experience, especially when you are young and do not fully understand what it means. I was gathering wood as a small child when I discovered, quite by accident, that I could summon fire without using firestones. It scared me so badly I hid in the lodge for days and told no one."

"You are not afraid now."

"No, but that is because I've learned how to control my gift and use it for the good of the tribe. I can draw heat the way a single pine tree can draw starfire; can you imagine how terrifying that ability would be to someone who had no *drui* to explain it to her?"

"There is nothing frightening about Epona's gift," Kernunnos said. "She is of the animals, as I am."

"Maybe it is you she fears," Tena replied.

Kernunnos did not answer, but gazed off down the valley after Epona. His lips drew back from his teeth, revealing the pointed canines, and even Tena felt uneasy. The shapechanger was like no one else.

Nematona, who as a newly initiated *gutuiter* had presided at Kernunnos' birth, had confided the details to Tena one long winter night in their lodge. "His mother died when he was born," Nematona had said.

"Sometimes women die in childbirth in spite of all we can do; it is part of the pattern."

"Yes, but not like this. I never saw a woman as badly torn as the mother of Kernunnos was," Nematona replied. "It looked as if she had been ripped to pieces deliberately, from the inside.

"When Kernunnos was older and his gifts had been recognized, we all knew he would someday be the chief priest, but when he reached manhood and the time came for him to kill the old priest and take his place, do you recall how he did it?"

Tena looked down at her clasped hands. "I remember," she said, almost in a whisper. "Each night the chief priest came back from the dreamworld with a new mutilation, until at last he died of them. And Kernunnos took his place."

"According to tradition the ritual death is to be done swiftly, with a sharp knife or painless poison," Nematona said. "But Kernunnos would not have enjoyed that as much."

Remembering this conversation, Tena, who was never cold, shivered.

Chapter 8

EPONA RETURNED TO THE VILLAGE thinking, not of the dead chief who would be honored at the evening's feast, but of Goibban. He had noticed her at last; she was certain of it. He had looked at her as a man looks at a woman he wants. Now everything would be all right; she need not fear the shapechanger or Rigantona's threat to send her to the magic house. *Perhaps,* she thought, *the spirit of Toutorix was with me at that moment, watching over me, directing Goibban's eyes.*

The world had seemed dark; all at once it was bright again, the sunshine returned.

When she reached the lodge she found Rigantona also thinking of something other than her dead husband — or so it appeared.

Toutorix had been absent more than he had been with her; Rigantona was accustomed to that. What she found difficult to accept was the fact that he would never be with her again. She had grown used to having him at the back of her mind, available to be blamed for all the large and small annoyances of her life. Each evening he would enter the lodge, braced and ready for the tirade she would deliver. Toutorix was stone, nothing could hurt him, but that daily recounting of her frustrations had always made Rigantona feel better.

Now he was gone. It was not his body on the bedshelf she would miss as much as that patient face, absorbing her venom and turning it away from herself. In some way her disappointments had been, every one of them, her husband's fault, and now he had escaped her, taking his culpability with him. Whom could she blame after thisday?

With the grim determination of the born survivor, Rigantona immediately began searching for new concerns to crowd out the old.

As Epona entered the lodge, she saw her mother standing beside the firepit, holding a piece of woven wool to the light. "Look at this," she commanded her daughter without bothering with a greeting. "I just noticed the effect the firelight gives through a rather loose weave; it blurs the colors, do you see? Beautiful. I wonder if there is some way to create that effect in the weaving process itself; what do you think?"

"How can you be thinking about your loom at a time like this? You should be preparing the funeral feast for the lord of the tribe!" Epona told her angrily. Her anger was increased by the guilty knowledge that she, too, had been thinking of something other than Toutorix, on thisnight which should be his alone.

She brushed past her mother and began the work herself, adding wood to the fire, heating a cauldron of water with hot stones, selecting foods for the feast. It was good to be busy; better than good. At a time like this it was imperative.

Young and preoccupied with herself, she did not think that perhaps Rigantona felt the same need.

The completed feast was a splendid success, roisterously shared by the kin, near-kin, and marriage-kin of the dead chief. Everyone agreed Toutorix had been granted a good death, quick and painless, second in desirability only to a hero's death in battle. It was a sign of favor from the spirits, and the departed chieftain was envied.

Toasts were being drunk to him in all the lodges. Even the charcoal burners in the hills, squatting beside their smoky ricks, red-eyed with lack of sleep lest the entire mound blaze up and be wasted, invoked the name of Toutorix and drank a cup of wheat-beer in his honor. "Share the feast with us, Toutorix," they called out. "Eat red meat and drink red wine in your new place, and sing the songs of the brave!"

Epona ate her food thoughtfully, chewing each bit almost as if it were the first time she had tasted roast pork, or smoked fish packed with cheese curds, or onions baked in bread. The meal

99

was delicious. The death being commemorated made all the feasters more aware of and appreciative of life.

As Epona remembered from other funeral feasts, many would share bedsports thisnight when the eating was over; a night of transition was best celebrated by lifemaking.

Noticing his sister sitting withdrawn, a faraway look in her eyes, Okelos teased, "Where is our Epona? Not with us; look at her. Are you getting ready to go to the otherworlds again, sister, and search for Toutorix? Will you salute him for me?" Okelos had already drunk many cups of red wine.

Epona whirled on her brother in anger. "I do not go to the otherworlds. Why are you saying that? Stop it, Okelos!"

Okelos sat back with a smug expression. "You did go; you gave me your word you had done it."

Rigantona looked up from the suckling pig she was systematically demolishing. Was the girl trying to get out of it by denying her gift? It would not succeed; the chief priest had already verified the fact that Epona was, indeed, *drui*. And now was an excellent time to let all the kin know it, to say the words aloud and see the expression on Sirona's face.

"Of course you can travel to the otherworlds, my child," Rigantona said sweetly. "Kernunnos himself has affirmed that you were born *drui;* you have a great future ahead of you." Cutting her eyes to the side, she saw that Sirona was staring with a gaping mouth. Lovely!

"Everyone is mistaken," Epona argued desperately, feeling the eaten food curdle in her stomach. Doors seemed to be standing open in her mind, and swirling mists poured through them, circling around her, summoning her . . . No! It never happened. "I imagined it," she told them. "I was wrong to brag to Okelos, but it is all a mistake, you must understand."

Rigantona's eyes blazed. "How dare you deny such a gift! Are you trying to embarrass me in front of the nobles of the Kelti? What will Kernunnos say to such a lie after he has accepted you in return for the chief's funeral ritual?"

Okelos was aghast. He leaped to his feet and faced his mother, forgetful of the faces watching both, forgetful of everything but the betrayal just uncovered.

"What about the election of the chief?" he demanded to know. "Epona was to go to the *druii* in return for their support for me, not just so you could lie unburned in a tomb with all your jewelry piled around you!"

Epona was equally upset. She tried to get Okelos' attention. "You traded me for the staff of authority?" she asked him. "Without even discussing it with me, as if I had no rights as a free woman?" But Okelos did not hear her; it was his mother's answer he wanted to hear.

Rigantona checked her words before they gave anything more away. The future was held in delicate balance right now; it was best not to incur her son's anger until the council had made its decision. Kernunnos was right, Okelos would not be the best choice for lord of the tribe, but who could say what influences might affect the outcome of the election? Okelos could yet be chief . . . then she would have him for a son and a *drui* daughter. Everything would be hers, at last.

"I asked Kernunnos to support you as part of the exchange," she assured Okelos. That much was true. A late request, tied on at the end like the unimportant tail of the goat, but she need not tell him that.

"Mother!" Epona cried, feeling hope shrivel inside her. Their dialogue had told her the bad news already; she had not only been offered, but obviously accepted. She threw herself down beside Rigantona, wrapping her arms around the woman's waist in the supplicating gesture of a small child. "Please listen, I don't want to spend my life practicing magic with the shapechanger. I can't stand being near him. Surely you, of all people, understand that."

Rigantona firmly disengaged herself from her daughter's embrace. "It isn't as if you had to share bedsports with him, Epona. He is forbidden to use you for that, the *gutuiters* do no lifemaking. Besides, he . . ."

"It isn't bedsports that concern me," Epona interrupted before Rigantona could complete her explanation. "I don't want to have anything to do with Kernunnos, not ever, not in any way. He repels me; he has since I was a little child. And I have no desire to practice magic, either. It makes me feel . . . strange. I want a different kind of life; we have talked of this, don't you remember? Don't you understand?" She stared at her mother with her whole spirit naked in her eyes.

Rigantona looked away, displeased that this argument was taking place before her assembled kin. They would think the girl had been taught no obedience. "It is done," she said decisively.

"But I have been to my woman-making; I'm an adult now. You should have pledged me when I was still a child if you meant to do this awful thing . . ."

"Awful thing! You should be grateful to all the spirits that your gift was discovered at all, even if so late. I am still your parent until you marry, so we are both fortunate that I have time to make up for my oversight in not realizing your abilities sooner." Trying to silence the girl, she turned to Sirona. "Am I not lucky, marriage-sister? And is Epona not lucky also? Tell her for me, will you?"

Sirona's eyes shot daggers but they glanced off the impenetrable hide of Rigantona.

"Toutorix said I didn't have to do this!" Epona cried to the assembled kin.

"Toutorix is dead," Rigantona said complacently. "I am the only person with authority over you now. Besides, he never told me any such thing." She raised her cup hand. The Hellene goblet she held was brimming with wine. "Let us stop this squabbling on a feast night and join in happy memories of Toutorix, shall we? It is unseemly to behave this way on his night."

The feasting continued until the morning star rose in the sky. Okelos enjoyed every moment of it, having convinced himself that Rigantona had truly arranged his election. She was his mother, after all; she would be loyal. And it was not too much to ask, even in addition to the new ritual.

What a funeral he, Okelos, would have someday, after many long and splendid seasons as lord of the tribe. What piles of treasure he would take into the otherworlds· with him! He should be grateful to Rigantona for assuring such an opportunity. When the feasting ended he fell into a drunken sleep on his bedshelf, still smiling to himself.

After leaving the funeral feast for the privacy of their own lodges, the various other contenders for the vacant chiefdom discussed, with their wives and supporters, the unfair advantage Rigantona had taken. Offering her daughter to the *druii* in return for their support! The woman needed to be taught a lesson.

After many heated arguments and more than one blow being exchanged, an agreement of sorts was reached. Taranis was the most likely successor to Toutorix; the others would throw their support behind him, and urge the council of elders to do likewise. Rigantona and that worthless son of hers would be thwarted.

Taranis raised one last objection. "But if the spirits themselves desire Okelos to be lord of the tribe, what can we do?"

It was Sirona who answered him. "Nothing. But I do not believe that is what the spirits want. Were you not listening tonight, husband? Rigantona traded the girl for the funeral, and, unless I am mistaken, support for Okelos was secondary. At no time did I hear that the *druii* had pledged it. Go to the members of the tribal council one at a time and talk to them, remind them of your abilities and the weaknesses of Okelos. Remind them that Rigantona tried to barter for the chiefdom. We will see who wins."

While these discussions were going on, Epona was also without sleep. She lay curled in a tight ball on her bedshelf, trying not to hear the sibilant voice of Kernunnos, whispering, cajoling, demanding.

He and Rigantona and Okelos had worked together to weave their threads around her life like the web of some giant spider, capturing and devouring its prey. If they had their way she would not be Epona anymore, she would be something else, someone she did not kmow.

She clenched her fists, holding on to herself, determined not to let go. *Goibban will save me*, she promised herself.

The tribe could wait no longer to let traders back into the village. Supplies of barley and wheat were running low, and the women were complaining of a shortage of flax. The chief, lord of the tribe, negotiator with outsiders, must be chosen immediately. Already carpenters were preparing a ceremonial rooftree to be installed in the lodge of whoever was elected.

The next day the elders convened and, after due deliberation, announced the election by unanimous vote of Taranis to be chief of the Kelti. Taranis of the deep voice. Taranis the Thunderer.

"You failed me!" Okelos, in a rage, accused Rigantona. "I should have known you would do everything for your own benefit. You got what you wanted but made no effort for me."

"I did what I could," she assured him. "You are still young, and Taranis is much older. He will not live forever. Your time will come . . ."

103

He shook his head. "You've cheated me out of what was mine, Rigantona. I will never forgive you."

"I'm not any happier about it than you are. The new lord of the tribe will be inaugurated at midday and I will have to surrender the staff of authority to Taranis, while that wife of his watches and laughs out of the side of her mouth. Do you think I like that?"

"I think it's exactly what you deserve," Okelos told her bitterly.

The tribe assembled on the commonground to witness the inauguration of the new chieftain. Everyone who was able was expected to attend, a tradition that did not please Okelos. He dressed for the occasion in a battle apron and stiffened his hair with lime paste so it stood to a ferocious height. "They will regret not choosing me," he muttered to himself, several times.

Epona managed to be out of the lodge early so she did not have to accompany her mother to the ceremony. She did not want to be with Rigantona at all. She hovered instead on the fringes of the crowd, impressed in spite of herself by the splendor of the occasion, the first such inauguration in her lifetime. All the people wore their best clothing, their most ostentatious ornaments. Nematona had ordered swags of greenery draped around the stone, the bone of the mother where Taranis would stand to receive the acclaim of his people. Sacred fires had been lit around the perimeter of the commonground, and the people were chanting the song of thanksgiving; a new lord would protect the tribe.

While Epona's attention was fixed on the festivities, Kernunnos sidled up behind her. He grabbed her elbow before she was even aware of him and whispered, "Your training will begin at the next full moon, Epona. We will send for you. Or you can come to us on your own feet. But you will come."

He was gone like smoke, before she had time to do more than shudder.

She saw her friend Mahka standing with Alator and went over to her. Mahka seemed so solid, so self-confident, and Epona now felt unsubstantial and vulnerable. She was being blown by a shifting wind; she longed to be sturdy and sure, like Mahka.

In this one sunseason Mahka had grown half a head taller. She looked like a woman now, with powerful shoulders and a strong-boned face. But the familiar childish grin broke through when she saw Epona.

"Sunshine on your head! Come and stand with us for the ceremony, will you? It's about to begin; soon Taranis will walk naked from our lodge, and Poel will bathe him and wrap him in the chieftain's cloak. You can see the whole thing from right here."

There were congratulations to offer; Mahka now was a member of the family of the chief. But the other girl shrugged off Epona's sincerely felt happiness for her. "What difference does it matter if ours is the chief's lodge or not? I don't care about that."

"You certainly should," Alator told her. "Taranis will distribute the trade goods now, and that means your family will get first choice of the best things. You can have almost anything you want in return for his taking responsibility for us all."

Mahka's gray eyes glinted. "All I want is to be a warrior. I want to learn to drive a war cart, like the two-wheeled ones painted on the Hellene pottery. I would swing my sword and lead hundreds of men in battle; I would die a hero's death."

Epona was used to Mahka's dreams. Once she had entered into them gladly, wrestling and fighting with stick swords, playing army to Mahka's general, but now these seemed childish amusements. Mahka would soon be a woman; she would forget such things.

"There are no battles to be fought here," she reminded her friend.

"Haven't you been listening to your own brother? Okelos has been talking to some of the other young men of taking an expeditionary force into the lands of the Hellenes. There's a lot of interest in it beyond the council fires. Men speak of the shortage of women and land, they say they will have to go outside anyway to find enough space to raise more families. You must admit the village has grown very crowded. With a band of warriors, Okelos claims he could establish new settlements and offer everyone better lives."

"Okelos just wants to go and rob the Hellenes," Epona told her.

Mahka made a negligent gesture. "If he is strong enough to take their treasures in battle, why shouldn't he? The strongest man should always have the best, so he can support his family well and raise more and stronger children. How else is the tribe to prosper?

105

"As for myself, I intend to persuade them to take me along. I can fight as well as any of them; you know that, Epona. I can do much more for the tribe by winning new lands than I can by marrying some stupid farmer in another tribe and raising a litter of puking children."

"Have your parents given consent?" Epona asked.

"They will. And if they don't, I'll run away and do it anyway."

"You would disobey them like that?"

"Of course. I've heard them say that you are pledged to the *druii* by Rigantona, and that you don't want to go. You should run away too, Epona. You have to fight for yourself in this life."

How easy it is for Mahka to say that, Epona thought. Her body and her family were intact, her future was certain. Too many unsettling things had happened to Epona in too short a span of nights. She felt she stood on shifting salt instead of solid earth, and without that firm base it was not so easy to talk of fighting back.

But there was Goibban. At least she had that, and that was all she needed. With the remaining shreds of her childhood's faith she believed Goibban would be willing to marry her.

"I'm not going to go to the magic house," she told Mahka. "You'll see; you'll all be very surprised." She smiled a secret smile and turned back to watch Taranis become the new lord of the tribe.

Once he was bathed and properly attired in the cloak of a chieftain, with all the colors of all the families mingled in its weaving, Taranis followed the *druii* to the sacred stone. He watched impassively as the spirits of fire and water, earth and air, were offered their due sacrifice, and he promised them his people would continue to work in harmony with nature, that the bounty of the land might never be diminished nor its essential spirits insulted.

At the high point of the ritual Rigantona came pacing slowly through the massed crowd, the staff of authority in her hand. She gave it to Poel, who in turn offered it to Taranis.

Tall, heavily bearded, with a neck like a bull's and a voice like thunder, Taranis cried out three times to the assembled tribe, "I challenge any man who is stronger to take this from me!" At his first call Okelos made a slight movement as if he would step forward and everyone turned to look at him, but then he subsided, face red with angry fire.

When no one answered the challenge, Poel pressed the staff into the hands of Taranis. The *drui* then turned to face the Kelti, his arms flung wide. "All that lives, dies and lives again! So the old lord of the tribe goes on to new life. Now is come the season of Taranis the Thunderer, and all our loyalty belongs to him. As long as he leads us we shall share in his strength and his prosperity, for he is ours, and that which is his is ours. Sing with me the song of the people. Sing of all that is good and harmonious and life sustaining."

They sang, full throated and joyous. They belonged to the new chieftain and he to them, joined together in the splendid totality of the Kelti, each person an integral part of the whole. Part of something magnificent.

The traders waiting encamped beyond the palisade could hear the tremendous roar of unrestrained joy that rolled through the Blue Mountains.

At sundown, Epona stood in the doorway of her mother's lodge, anxiously awaiting the appearance of the moon. It came as a silver crescent above the peaks, a thumbnail slice of white in a lavender sky. There was time, then; many nights to go before she was expected in the magic house. She would speak to Goibban immediately.

But in the morning her courage failed her, and she put it off until the next day, and then the next. The right words were somehow never on her tongue; the spirit within did not offer them. But there was time, the moon was not yet full.

The traders came and Taranis sat in the trading circle with them, listening to their offers and examining their goods with pursed lips and narrowed eyes. He drove hard bargains, and his deep voice and unfamiliarity seemed to intimidate some of the merchants. Men began to say, around their lodgefires, "Taranis is going to make a fine chief. Hai, let's drink another cup of wine to the Thunderer."

The *druii* began seeking Epona out to have little conversations, each in turn, except for Kernunnos, who waited.

Nematona came into the lodge where she was working on the embroidered skirt of a gown. Daughter of the Trees sat beside her and pointed one long, tapering finger at the design Epona was struggling to master. The younger woman was gnawing on her lips and occasionally pushing damp hair off her forehead with

107

the back of her wrist; embroidery was not one of her talents. "Be careful how you place each thread, Epona," the *gutuiter* instructed. "It must conform to the pattern. Pattern is the structure that underlies all life, you know. The priesthood is not just a tribe within a tribe, assembled so that some might live off the efforts of others in return for offering sacrifices and dealing with spirits. No. The *druii* are those who are aware of and understand the pattern composed of all living things, beings which must act in harmony with one another in order to survive. The pattern is older than the people, and knowledge of it has been handed down through more generations than there are threads on the loom. The pattern is the magic of the stones — alas, we have forgotten most of that now! — and the song of the trees. All things must conform to the pattern or be broken."

Conform to the pattern or be broken.

Epona thought of Kernunnos, waiting with his slitted yellow eyes in the magic house. She thought of living with scented smoke and chanting, going each night into otherworlds where mist swirled and things were not what they seemed.

Then she thought of the Blue Mountains and the sweet fresh open air, and the pattern of light and dark across the slopes she had loved all of thislife. She thought of Goibban, and the laughter of his children, clustered around her knees.

Uiska intercepted her while she was carrying water to refill the *hydria* in the family's lodge. "Are you looking forward to the day you join us, Epona?"

Epona gave her a truthful answer. "I hope that day never comes."

Uiska's face wore the ghost of a smile. "All days come. And pass. Never fear one, because it is already part of the past and behind you."

Epona set down her heavy leather bucket. "What does that mean?"

"Only that the past and future are one, and both exist now, thisday, as real and solid as the links of an iron chain. The present is the link that holds them all together.

"When you are initiated into the priesthood you will learn to move along that chain at will, because you will be fully aware of the solidity of the other links."

108

"How can that be?" Unwillingly, Epona was intrigued.

Uiska instructed, "Stand still, Epona. Close your eyes. Feel. Reach out with your mind. Open the pores of your skin. Can you feel the village around you, and the mountains beyond the village? Feel those mountains. Feel their weight and substance. You can do it if you concentrate. Ah, yes, I see it in your face, just a little. Hai!

"If you are able to do that much, you can learn to feel the past and the future in much the same way, because they are as real as those mountains. As you could walk from this village up those slopes, so you can walk from thisday into lastday. It is no harder than visiting otherworlds."

"Then why do you not do it more often? I've hardly ever heard of such a thing," Epona said.

"It is frustrating," Uiska told her, "to visit the past, for we can go as spectators only; we cannot change it. We move through it as ghosts; we see but do not touch."

"And the future? What about the future? That is what I would like to change."

The pale smile on Uiska's face melted like snow. "The future can only be changed in the present, Epona. And it is even less wise to walk in that direction. It takes much courage to look into the future, and some of the things to be seen there would scorch your eyes. Better not to know, believe me. Learning to resist that temptation is part of the discipline of the *druii*. To know the future is to try to change it in the present, and that throws everything out of harmony."

"I do not understand."

The smile returned as Uiska told her, "That is the beginning of wisdom: to admit that you do not understand. You will. You will learn and grow, for that is the purpose of all living."

She drifted away, insubstantial as fog, leaving Epona tantalized. So much to learn, so many questions she could ask . . . but that would mean making a commitment to Kernunnos and the magic house, and she would not.

Would not, would not, would not!

Shortly after sunrise the next day, Vallanos the sentry blew a long blast on his ram's horn and then ran down into the village, breathless with excitement.

109

"Strangers are coming," he announced as the people of the Kelti crowded around him. "They are not like anything I have seen before."

Taranis ran his fingers through the mingled bronze and copper hairs of his beard. "What's so different about them? Are they warriors of some sort?"

"That's the trouble, I don't know what they are." Poor Vallanos was obviously distressed. "They are not men like us at all. I only caught a glimpse of them from a distance and then I came straight here to tell you, so you can prepare for their arrival. If there is any way to prepare for such things, I mean."

"What are they?" many voices demanded to know.

"They do not appear to be human. From what I could see they are half man and half horse; men's bodies growing from horses' backs. They are the monsters the Hellenes call *kentaurs!*"

Chapter 9

SHOVING AND ELBOWING each other, the men and women of the Kelti ran toward the palisade and the road beyond. The fleet-footed young, Epona and Mahka among them, were among the first to arrive at the trail's edge, where they halted in astonishment.

Four creatures were coming up the road: sinewy, long-legged beasts with very low withers and finely shaped hindquarters, nothing like the blocky little ponies used for draft animals or the asses and onagers the traders sometimes brought. Their stride was different, too. Instead of a choppy, short gait, suitable for pulling weight, they moved with long and fluid strides that gave an impression of effortlessness, like red deer trotting. "How beautiful," Epona murmured to herself.

Then she looked at the human figures rising from their backs.

The creatures approaching were not *kentaurs* at all; they were horses straddled by separate human beings, with separate legs and feet, who nevertheless moved with their mounts as one.

"Imagine sitting on *top* a horse and floating along like that," Mahka commented. "How much better that must be than jolting around in a cart!"

As the horses drew nearer, it was easier to make out the details of their riders, towering above the earthbound Kelti. The horsemen were heavily bearded, with deep-set eyes and unkempt long hair beneath snug peaked helmets made of felt. They wore felt tunics, loose across the chest but narrow in the sleeves, and below that a peculiar form of split skirt that wrapped around each leg individually and was then gathered into soft leather boots.

How sensible for a man who straddles a horse, the Kelti commented to one another admiringly.

The clothing of the strangers was dyed in intense shades of blue and red and yellow, faded and worn but still gaudy. The apparent leader of the band wore a short cape of an unfamiliar spotted fur, and all of them sported massive gold necklets half-hidden by their tangled beards. The horses' bridles gleamed with intricately worked ornaments of silver and bronze.

The men of the Kelti began pointing out to one another the weapons the horsemen carried. Each rider had an unusual case strapped to his hip on the cup hand side, obviously designed to hold both a curved bow and a supply of arrows with deadly three-edged heads. A leather sheath tied to the knife hand thigh contained a bronze-hilted shortsword, and a lethal assortment of knives was thrust through the belt. In addition, three of the four had large packs tied on behind them that could surely contain other weapons.

The fourth, the leader, rode a prancing gray horse with a bristling upright mane that swayed in rhythm to its gait. As they neared the staring crowd, this man kicked his mount and galloped forward boldly, one hand hovering above his sword hilt.

"Demand travelers' rights!" he cried. He spoke their language with a guttural accent, difficult to understand, but his words followed the traditional formula for requesting hospitality that no member of the people could refuse. Old Dunatis responded with "Come and be fed!" and the four horsemen rode down on the village of the Kelti like thunder from the mountains.

Vallanos was sent at the run to summon the miners home. This was obviously not a familiar trading delegation; Taranis wanted all the able-bodied men of warrior status in the village, just in case.

Meanwhile, the villagers crowded around the horsemen, who remained seated on their animals. A few hands reached out hesitantly to pat a steaming haunch or examine a bobbed tail. The spectators, eyeing the bows in their cases, quickly decided among themselves that these horse riders had cut off their horses' tails and manes to avoid interference with their shooting. They must be very serious archers, very fine hunters.

Or warriors.

"Who is chief here?" the man on the gray wanted to know. His eyes swept over the crowd but he looked directly at no one.

Such dark, dark eyes, Epona thought. *He has the face of a hawk that cannot be tamed.*

Taranis stepped forward. "I am lord of this tribe." He carried his unsheathed sword in his hand.

The horsemen did not seem to feel threatened. "Good. We come to talk trade."

Nothing about the four horsemen resembled the stream of merchantmen familiar in the Blue Mountains. "You want salt?" Taranis inquired, not bothering to conceal his surprise.

With an easy gesture the horseman swung one leg across his mount's neck and slid to the ground. His eyes glanced at the sword the chief held. Within his heavy brown beard a line of white teeth flashed.

Strong teeth, without gaps, something said at the back of Epona's mind.

"Not salt," the stranger told Taranis. "You have iron, is it so? You have special good smith? People talk, east, of your smith, your iron. We want swords, we give gold. Is it so?"

There was an exchange of meaningful looks among the elders. At the edge of the crowd the soot-smeared face of Goibban himself appeared, marking this occasion as one momentous enough to draw even the smith from his work.

The stranger was standing directly in front of Taranis now, holding out his knife hand to show that it was empty of weapons. After a moment's hesitation, Taranis sheathed his own sword. The horseman gave a slight nod of his head, as if prepared to bow in greeting, but when Taranis did not respond in kind he quickly abandoned the gesture.

"This is Kazhak, son of Kolaxais, Prince of Horses," he announced in a strong voice. Taranis responded with his own name, and the two men handclasped their weaponless knife hands.

Epona was standing close enough to them to be aware of a strong male odor emanating from Kazhak's body. It was not acrid and musky like the shapechanger's; merely the powerful smell of sweat and horses. But in the mountains where water was plentiful the Kelti had become addicted to frequent bathing; they had come to find the smell of unwashed flesh offensive, and routinely greeted

113

all guests with bathing water. Yet Kazhak's odor did not seem unpleasant to Epona. It was more that of a horse than a human.

Kazhak was surveying the crowd with a haughty stare, as if he still towered above them on his horse. The men of the Kelti were generally much taller than he, but he looked at them as though from a vast distance, with eyes used to seeing across endless expanses.

Now that names had been exchanged, it was proper for Taranis to ask the stranger his tribe. The horseman's answer stunned the listeners into momentary silence.

"Kazhak is Scyth," the newcomer announced with ringing pride.

A Scythian! The wild nomads of the distant steppes, the fearsome warriors who had rolled, windblown, across so many lands to the east, driving out the legitimate landholders with a callous disregard for the traditions of generations of settlements and cultivation. The Scythians had even dispossessed the Cimmerians, doughty warriors themselves, forcing them from their homelands and scattering them through the mountains and river valleys formerly occupied only by various tribes of the people.

Even in the heart of the Blue Mountains the reputation of the Scythians was known, and men talked around their lodgefires of the marauders from the Black Sea region, the savages who had introduced a new style of warfare to Galicia and Thrace and even Anatolia. The Scythians were reputed to be sometime allies to the Assyrians, having taught them their skills with horse and bow, and occasionally sending detachments of mercenaries to the Assyrian armies. These nomads had come galloping from the birthplace of the sun to terrorize much of the known world with random violence.

Now a Scythian was standing calmly beside his horse in an alpine village, requesting iron.

The Kelti gaped at him in astonishment.

Epona was one of the first to recover. She had grown up in the lodge of the chief; she knew how to behave toward strangers, no matter how odd they might seem. Besides, she just had to get a closer look at that gray horse. It appeared to be a stallion; the other three were gelded, like oxen. She edged past Taranis and put her hand on the gray's neck, feeling the silky texture of the hair. How different it was from the coarse hides of the ponies!

The saddle, also, was worthy of investigation. It consisted of

114

two small pillows she would later learn were stuffed with deer hair and then sewn together, to cushion the rider's thighs. In addition there was a saddlecloth, a woolen girth, and a leather strap passing under the horse's tail and helping to hold the saddle in place. The entire rig was decorated with cutouts of colored felt depicting wild animals fighting, the details highlighted in colored thread and pieces of precious metals. From the saddle itself hung leather pendants similarly decorated and edged by bands of fur, and woolen tassels swung against the stallion's flanks.

Nothing like it had ever been seen in the Blue Mountains.

Epona stroked the stallion's neck again, and as she did so, Kazhak turned around and looked at her. His brown eyes unwittingly met and locked with hers, then he scowled and turned away.

Those are not the eyes of a savage, she thought.

Becoming aware of Epona's convenient presence, Taranis said, "Epona, perhaps you would show these strangers to the guest house? You and your men are welcome to the best we have to offer, Scythian, poor though that may be, as long as you care to stay in peace and trade with us. This woman will see that you have everything you need to make you comfortable while we prepare a feast in your honor. Then we will talk trade."

Taranis was relieved that Epona was available for this traditional duty of a chief's daughter. Mahka would have probably refused outright, embarrassing him in front of the Scythians, as she had already refused to be instructed in the other traditional duties of her new station. Fortunately, Epona seemed happy to oblige.

While she took the strangers to the lodge set aside for guests, Taranis wanted to meet with the tribal council and discuss this new development. The way he handled these Scythians would be the first major test of his new chiefdom, and he intended to make no mistakes.

Kazhak had been listening to his words intently, his curving dark brows drawn together as he strove to follow the language of the Kelti, his eyes watching the chief's lips. When Taranis abruptly concluded the conversation by bringing forward the yellow-haired woman Kazhak was startled, but he did not allow himself to show it. Then the woman spoke to him — *spoke* to him! What sort of people were these Kelti, who let their women come in contact with strangers and actually say words to them?

She indicated that he was to follow her. He glanced around but saw no overt menace, aside from the rows of staring and fascinated Kelti. Many of them carried weapons — even the *women*, as he now noticed — but they had made no effort to use them for intimidation. He signaled to his men to dismount and follow him. No one must question the courage of the Scyth.

The guest house was a spacious lodge, permanently fitted out with the best the tribe had to offer. The four Scythians followed Epona, leading their horses, and a great number of Kelti trooped at their heels. Epona walked with her head high and her step light, hoping the spirit of Toutorix was watching. He had trained her well.

At the door of the lodge she turned to her guests and smiled, puzzled that none of them would meet her eyes. Eye contact was a ritual among the people, for it was often said, "Eyes that meet yours cannot keep the secrets of the spirit from you." Yet these Scythians looked at one's nose or mouth or hair. It made her feel awkward.

"Please make this your home for as long as you stay with us, oh Kazhak," she said solemnly. "I will see that you are immediately served red wine, and heated water for bathing."

"Bathing? You mean wash? In *water?*" He recoiled, appalled by the suggestion.

"But of course. We will have a cauldron heated for you at once, and after you are purified the . . ."

"No wash!" Kazhak announced with finality. "Kazhak is Scyth. Not pollute water with body."

It was a delicate moment. The people of the Kelti looked at one another with bafflement. It was important not to offend the prohibitions of others, but what sort of folk did not wash?

Kazhak was not insensitive; his ability to detect nuances was part of his survival equipment. He shot a quick glance at his men, warning them to be silent, then addressed the yellow-haired woman, enunciating very carefully so there would be no misunderstanding.

"Steam make man clean," he explained to her. "Clay make woman smooth. Keep water clean for drinking only, is it so?" Fixing his eyes on her forehead, he offered a pleasant smile.

His nostrils curved like the lines of Rigantona's favorite brooch. His hair was a very dark brown and his skin was tanned to leather by sun and wind, though around the eyelids, in the furrows of squint lines, it was as white as Epona's. Kazhak's eyes were as warm and dark as those of his horse, and a keen intelligence burned in them.

At that moment Kernunnos joined them, his presence creating a distraction that rescued Epona from an awkward situation. The chief priest had dressed himself to impress the strangers. A mantle of wolfskins enveloped his lean body, the heads and tails dangling, the empty eye sockets outlined with red paint. Bracelets of shells from the distant sea of King Aegeus testified to the reach of his arm. From his temples branched the antlers of a great stag.

In other regions people bowed to their shamans, but apparently no Kelti bowed to another, so Kazhak stood erect also, pleased to observe the local custom. Here was a personage of real importance, and a male. He was finding it disconcerting to be talking to a woman who was not his, but apparently that was another of the local customs. Incredibly, these Kelti women seemed to think they had some sort of status of their own.

Kazhak turned gratefully to Kernunnos. "There was offer of wine?" he remarked, man to man.

Kernunnos could not answer immediately. First protocol required he offer the welcome of the spirits, setting forth his own credentials as their representative and introducing the Scythians to the unseen powers whose realm they had entered. Kazhak waited patiently; his three companions busied themselves with hobbling their horses. Such formalities were boring, and they were glad to let Kazhak bear the burden alone.

When Kernunnos finished his speech he went to the door of the guest house and rang a bronze bell, to alert spirits within. Then he stepped aside, expecting the Scythians to enter.

Kazhak balked. His three men stood at his back, also unmoving. The spectators shifted their feet and whispered among themselves.

If a visitor refused to enter the guest lodge it was a mighty insult; Toutorix had always stressed this to his family. Epona still carried his honor on her shoulders. She moved directly in front of Kazhak and put her face so close to his he could not help meeting her eyes. She felt his intense embarrassment and it puzzled her, but she tried to reassure him with a gentle smile and a calm, firm voice. "We offer the best we have," she said. "Let us give to you."

Kazhak's eyes were filled with doubt. "It is not wise to go into box with strangers," he told her, rather than Kernunnos or the other men standing around them. His hand was very close to his sword hilt.

"This is not a trap," Epona said. "It is a house."

"Dead people are put in houses made of wood," Kazhak told her. "Living men should be under open sky, is it so?"

It was getting easier for her to understand his words. He spoke slowly, his tongue giving strange music to the familiar Kelti words, but her ear had found the rhythm of his speech and she tried to answer him in kind.

"Among our people living men sleep safely in wooden houses, and are not afraid," she said. "We harm no guests in our houses. The guest is honored here."

It was like trying to win the confidence of an animal; a magnificent wild animal. The Scythian was as muscular as any Kelt, except perhaps for Goibban, and his clothes could not disguise his natural grace. He walked on the balls of his feet, moving like a mountain cat, and even standing still he gave an impression of strength and agility.

Still he hesitated. Without thinking, without any prompting from the spirit within, Epona reached out and put her hand on his arm. For the third time their eyes locked.

With a great show of bravado the Scythian threw back his shoulders and stalked into the lodge.

His men followed him as far as the doorway, unwilling to trust themselves to the containment of the walls but hoping for a share of the wine.

Kazhak moved suspiciously around the room, eyeing everything and touching nothing. Epona made certain there was fresh drinking water in the bronze *hydria* and sent a woman to bring a torch bearing wifefire from the lodge of the chief. Soon the interior of the house was golden and glowing with warmth, and women were arriving with baskets of bread and bowls of cheese.

Still, Kazhak seemed uncomfortable. He had not seated himself on a bedshelf, preferring to stand close enough to the open door to see his men outside. When Sirona carried in a large *krater* brimming with wine, Kazhak indicated that he wanted the other Scythians to sample the beverage first. Only then did he drink.

"Is good," he told Epona approvingly. It was his first recognition of her efforts at hospitality, and she felt she had won a small victory. He still would not meet eyes with anyone else.

Epona did not mention bathing again.

The Scythians were like birds who will not nest, but only perch on the rim, ready to fly. There was no point in waiting until they made themselves comfortable, as they seemed to have no intention of doing so. Therefore Kernunnos and Poel moved ahead to the next step of tradition by leading a deputation of elders and heads of families into the lodge to share wine and introductions. Epona persuaded Kazhak to sit next to the hearth and drink with them, though he went through the motions like a wary horse, ready to spook.

Kernunnos seated himself at the Scythian's cup hand; Taranis at the other side. The chief's brief consultation with the elders had not been reassuring; they had no special suggestions for ways to handle these strangers. "Watch and listen," was the best they could advise.

Epona, Sirona, and other women of the noble families moved around the lodge, serving food and taking part in the conversation of the men. Kazhak turned to Taranis. "Chief has many wives?" he suggested, nodding toward the bustle of women; big, fair, blue-eyed women.

"No, just one," Taranis answered.

Surprised, Kazhak turned to Kernunnos. "Just one wife?" he asked, as if he could not believe such a thing.

The priest smiled. Kernunnos had a trick of smiling with his lips without ever letting the expression reach his eyes. Kazhak disliked the effect. He was reminded of the lions and spotted cats that roamed his native grasslands, sometimes freezing their prey with the terrible power of their gaze.

"A man has one head, one wife, one lodge," the priest replied.

"Is it so?" Kazhak looked at the furs piled on the bedshelves, the carved wooden chests and handsome household pottery that were part of the furnishings of the guest house. He noted that both men and women wore many bronze ornaments and there was an occasional gleam of gold or electrum.

"Much wealth," he commented. "And only one wife." He turned his head to look toward Epona, who was standing behind him. "You enough wife for him?" His eyes sparkled with good humor.

Epona felt a blush burning upward from her throat. "I am not

119

the chief's wife," she replied. "I am of his brother's family." To cover a sudden fit of shyness she offered Kazhak a loaf of bread, but instead of taking it he reached out and seized one of her long braids, pulling it forward so it gleamed in the firelight.

"The wealth of the Kelti," Kazhak announced to the room at large, holding up the hair for all to see. "Kelti gold! Is it so?"

There was a shout of laughter. As awed by the horsemen as they would have been by a manifestation of unfamiliar spirits, the Kelti had been uncertain how to react to these exotic strangers, but Kazhak's compliment won them. They were soon drinking to him and his horses, gulping the good Hellene wine, and the atmosphere in the lodge became decidedly convivial. An *amphora* of wine was carried outside for the other Scythians so they could join in the festivities in the way they found most comfortable, under the open sky.

The miners returning from the Salt Mountain heard the laughter and shouting issuing from the guest lodge as soon as they reached the outskirts of the village. They had come on the run, leaving their axes and mallets forgotten in the galleries. The first strange sight to greet their eyes was the four saddle horses, hobbled with rawhide thongs and encircled by admirers.

In front of the guest house was another crowd surrounding three strangers who were seated crosslegged on the earth like women, drinking red wine and singing loud songs no one could understand.

Miners and horsemen stared at each other.

The seated Scythians looked up at blond or redbearded giants whose eyes were like alpine lakes and shoulders were mountain broad, warmly dressed in leather coats and tunics of woven wool. The miners saw sinewy men with legs curved by lives spent on horseback, and fair skins darkened to swarthiness by the harsh climate of the steppes. Their snarled hair and beards were varying shades of brown, from near-black to light, and their eyes were also brown, though the fairest had gray eyes and a high-bridged, arrogant nose. In spite of the variations in coloring all their faces bore a similar stamp, sculptured into sternness, slightly softened now by wine. But they exuded an air of vitality; the same passion for living animated Kelti and Scythians alike. And to add to their attractiveness, the horsemen were glad to share their wine with the miners.

After several drinks strangers became friends, making rough jokes that required no subtleties of language to be understood. They found enough words and gestures in common to carry on rudimentary conversation, and discovered that both parties frowned on the Hellene custom of weakening good wine with water.

Meanwhile, within the guest lodge, Taranis had begun questioning Kazhak about his homeland. The way of life the horseman described soon had his hosts listening enthralled.

Kazhak explained the unfettered existence of the nomad. "We build no house where enemies can find us. We follow no roads. Horse carry us anywhere, fast. Fold tent, pack wagon, go. We find something we want, take and go. Find woman we want, take and go. Man live on horse, woman live in wagon or tent, do work, keep quiet," he added meaningfully, though no one noticed.

Listening to this paean to masculine freedom had even the oldest men leaning forward, eyes alight with interest. Kernunnos noticed their seeming approval and scowled. "But how do you support your tribe?" he wanted to know.

"We have horses, sheep, cattle. Man with many wives goes where grass is good, plenty meat and cheese, good milk from mares for children. Herds move easy."

"Do your women ride on horses, too?" Taranis asked, trying to imagine his beautiful broad-hipped Sirona straddling a horse.

"No," Kazhak said shortly, in a tone that indicated he was not interested in any further discussion of women. He had said all there was to be said about them already.

Old Dunatis wanted to know, "Do you plant any crops?"

Kazhak looked insulted. "Dig in dirt? No. Let others dig in dirt. We take their grain, we go."

Okelos was sitting across the firepit from the Scythian, and at these words he nodded in approval, elbowing the young man sitting next to him.

Taranis remarked, "We heard last sunseason that there were a few Scyths in the valleys of the Boii, farming."

Kazhak's voice dripped scorn. "Is lie. Real Scyths are horse men only, like Kazhak."

Kernunnos leaned forward, trying unsuccessfully to spear the man with his eyes. "And what of your spirits? What holy places do you have for worshiping the powers, if you just 'take and go'?"

Kazhak grinned. "God you cannot take with you is no good, is it so? We have no holy places, take gods with us everywhere, is much better. How can *place* be holy?"

Kernunnos felt a creeping alarm. "Tell us of your . . . gods," he said, feigning benign interest.

Kazhak was not fooled. "You would not like. Better you tell Kazhak about your gods. Could be, they stronger, then Kazhak make sacrifice to them."

In his best rhetorical voice Poel recited the names and descriptions of the spirits of fire and water, of mountains and rivers, of rocks and trees, of field and grain, of the animals of the forest. Kazhak listened impassively to the long pantheon of influences pertaining to every human interaction with nature. It was only when Poel spoke of the deity to whom Kernunnos himself was dedicated that Kazhak reacted.

"Stag, yes!" he cried, slamming his fist against his thigh. "Stag great animal, Kazhak respect stag. Hunting stag is good for man, make him fast, make him smart.

"But stag is no god, is just animal. Meat."

Kernunnos, Priest of the Stag, glared at the Scythian with barely controlled fury. To deny the power of another tribe's deity was an insult of the most contemptible kind. There were countless spirits with which mankind must retain good relations; spirits as different from one another as the races of humans that worshiped them, but every person who was not weak-minded respected the power of all gods and strove to offend none, since all life depended on their mercy.

"You are ignorant!" Kernunnos said loudly, unable to control his tongue.

Taranis almost choked on the wine he was swallowing at that moment. Before he could recover himself and try to undo the harm, Kazhak smoothed matters over on his own.

The Scythian had taken no offense. His broad smile grew even broader, to include everyone in the lodge. He held up one forefinger and shook it at them like a parent reproving naughty children. "No no, Kazhak wise. Spend long nights on back, looking at stars. Stars make man very wise. Man has much time to think, looking at stars."

"Your words will drive the deer from these mountains and there will be no more venison for our cauldrons," Sirona said, wringing her hands.

"Kazhak not make stag angry," the Scythian replied. "There be plenty deer here; this season, next season. Kazhak take bow and arrows, get you stag tomorrow, prove spirit not angry. Is it so?"

There was a tense silence in the lodge. Confident and unperturbed, the Scythian continued to beam at the Kelti, and something of his own conviction began to infect his listeners. Okelos was the first to let the anger drain from his face and be replaced by an answering smile.

Kernunnos hated his people for being so easily impressed.

"You do not understand the nature of the animal spirits," he told Kazhak in a frosty voice. "Perhaps your race has no shape-changer to speak to them in the tongue of the creatures. I pity you your poverty. Tell us, traveler: What do your kind worship that is of more importance to you than the very animals that nourish us?"

"Three gods," said Kazhak, holding up three fingers. "Three only. Easy. Not so many to make angry. Tabiti, Papaeus, Api. Fire, Father, Earth."

"You hold nothing else sacred?"

"Sacred." Kazhak puzzled over the word, his lips moving silently. "Stronger than man, is that your meaning? The horse, that is stronger than man. War is stronger than man. So is friendship. Many men cannot destroy one friendship."

Kazhak paused to drain his cup and Kernunnos considered his words as the room buzzed with repetitions of them, one person to another, with varying degrees of outrage or amusement or undisguised interest. These Scythians were more ignorant than the chief priest had realized, but perhaps less dangerous than he had feared. They had no true knowledge of the realm of the spirits and therefore could not fight from there. The few gods they professed were familiar faces with new names, less than a handful among the countless aspects of the great fire of life whose rituals must be observed in order to maintain man's precarious place in the balance of nature. With so little understanding the Scythians were no threat.

Yet there were two objects of reverence named by Kazhak that disturbed the priest. Not tangibles one could influence or be in-

fluenced by, but abstractions, as insubstantial as smoke, as difficult to grasp as the art of the shapechanger.

War.

Friendship.

What spirits were involved? How could they be dealt with?
How could they be controlled?

Kernunnos retreated into the dark places behind his yellow eyes
and thought about these things.

Chapter 10

A WOMAN CAME TO THE DOOR to announce that the feast promised the Scythians was ready on the commonground. She intoned the familiar summons: "Soon the shadows of night will swallow the day, so let us build up our fires to hold back the darkness, let us sing songs with our friends, let us share our meat and our wine . . ."

"We go, eat meat, drink more wine." Kazhak joined in with enthusiasm, jumping to his feet. He left the guest house much more willingly than he had entered it.

Kernunnos regretted the change of locale. In the unrestrained atmosphere of a big outdoor banquet — the only way it was possible to accommodate everyone who wanted to take part — the Scythians would doubtless drink enough red wine to keep them harmless until nextday, but it would not be possible to talk to them on any meaningful level. And there was much Kernunnos wanted to find out about the horsemen.

This Kazhak was the representative of strange customs and troubling influences. Kernunnos was already certain his presence among the Kelti was a disruptive factor that might have far-reaching consequences. He had arrived too soon after the transition of a powerful chieftain and the introduction of a new ritual; the pattern had been strained and would take time to heal.

But there would be no time for healing. Kazhak was in the village now, and it was obvious the men of the Kelti were already mightily impressed with his saddle horses, his ornaments and weapons, the practicality of the garment he called "trousers," the amount of gold he and his men possessed but undoubtedly had not earned through peaceful trade. Take and go. Kazhak's description of his rapacious way of life had excited many of the young men, walled in by their eternal mountains.

Kernunnos thought it would be prudent to learn as much as possible about the intruders and make magic to counteract their influence before it became too strong, perhaps permanently damaging the pattern.

The center of the village was lit by the orange glow of a great feasting fire. The smell of roasting flesh and crisping fat hung on the air. The people came laughing from their lodges, dressed in their best linen tunics and robes, warm woolen cloaks in bright colors slung across their shoulders. It was proving to be a fine season for feasting.

Swaggering, brawny, boasting men, miners and craftsmen and stockmen, endowed with an enormous capacity for enjoyment and a boundless delight in the music of their own words, the men of the tribe milled around the fire exchanging anecdotes. Every adult male was a hero, at least in his own lodge, and had his personal following of half-bearded youths, jealous of their kinsman's standing in the community. Their hands twitched above their knife hilts in hopes of a whispered insult that could give birth to a joyous brawl.

Framed by golden beards and flowing mustaches, the lips of the Kelti men shaped tales in a constant attempt to best one another. No man could let a good story go unchallenged by a better one; no fist could escape comparison with a larger one. Prowess with timber axe or miner's pick was as much a source for bragging as skill with sword or sex, and the size and stamina of a man's physical equipment was the subject of many a rowdy dialogue.

Laughing and winking, swaying their hips and arching their backs, the women moved freely among their men, as richly dressed as their mates, taking full part in the by-play and equally quick with tongue or fist. There were pinches and pattings; eyes that dared and teased.

The stories being told grew longer and more imaginative. The Kelti said of themselves that they did not lie, but they sometimes took a very long way around in getting to the truth, with frequent stops at interesting spots along the way. A straight road and a simply told story held no interest for them. They were mountain people, used to twisting, turning trails.

It was a splendid evening. Any excuse would do for a feast, and any festival was cause for celebrating all the pleasures of life. The air around them sparked with the outpouring of their energy, their exuberance, their matchless enthusiasm for living that was balanced by their utter disregard for death.

Kelti.

The Scythians blended easily into such a group. Like men finding lost brothers, they discovered a common thread of character that spanned the difference between their cultures. Both were passionate people, equally given to joy and melancholy, the one spicing the other.

A certain mistrust lingered, for these were not men to abandon the habit of wariness, but the occasion had a magic of its own that lowered barriers. The horsemen even began to accept the shocking sight of women taking part in a social occasion; their eyes followed the graceful figures admiringly, if furtively.

A brawny young Scythian called Dasadas, who had impressed everyone around him by drinking a truly phenomenal amount of wine, found himself explaining by gesture the Scythian rite of brotherhood. Demonstration seemed to be the only road to clarity, so Dasadas and a willing salt miner cut their arms and mingled their blood in wine, drinking it off to the cheers of the crowd.

It was the kind of dramatic gesture the Kelti loved.

Soon each Scythian had his own circle around him, fingering his clothing, admiring the unfamiliar animalistic forms represented in his jewelry, eager to know the details of life lived at the gallop.

Kernunnos was visibly upset.

He went to Taranis. "I like nothing about these horsemen," he said darkly. "They are dangerous."

"How can they be dangerous? There are only four of them."

"Four of them that we can see, here, but where are the rest? Surely four men alone would never have traveled all the way from the Black Sea region. Suppose they have an army at their backs, hiding in the mountains to come down on us when we least expect them?"

"Have you felt such an army?"

"No," Kernunnos was forced to admit, "but these people are very strange to me; I have difficulty sorting out any clear impressions of them as yet. I know only that they should not be here."

Taranis had already helped himself to the wine *krater* many times and was feeling more like a genial host than a newly elected chieftain still secretly unsure of himself. He was by nature an affable man, not given to mistrust. The thunder of his voice was a bluff that gave the impression of a more belligerent disposition than he possessed. He was beginning to like these Scythians; they were good companions around a feasting fire. He defended them by saying, "Kazhak tells me there were originally more of them, but only four are left. They have come across many territories, after all, and through the current holdings of the Cimmerians, who hate them.

"If they had warriors waiting in the hills, don't you think they would try to take what they want, given their natures, rather than bartering gold for it? I believe Kazhak when he says they have traveled this long way as men of his tribe frequently do, looking for new pastureland or opportunities."

"Pastureland . . . in the Blue Mountains?" Kernunnos was scornful of the suggestion. "They are not such fools as that, Taranis. They came for new opportunities, I agree with that much: opportunities to rob us and harm us."

"Kazhak tells me they want only to trade for Goibban's iron; he says its fame has spread like the rising sun, and as soon as they learned of it they abandoned their other goals and headed straight here."

"If they had more men, they would have come prepared to kill us for it," Kernunnos muttered. "Why do you believe everything this Kazhak tells you, Taranis? Do you see the truth in his eyes?"

Taranis hesitated. "No . . . I could not look him in the eyes, he always turned away, but there is a reason according to the custom of his race. Kazhak says no one among the Scythians looks into the eyes of another unless they are brothers. Near-kin or bloodkin, I suppose he means."

"Kazhak says, Kazhak says!" The chief priest was swept by a cold fury. "I tell you what Kernunnos says: You should drive those horse riders out of here now, thisnight!"

"They have come for trade," Taranis repeated stubbornly. "What will happen to the carefully developed reputation of the Kelti if we refuse to trade? Have you seen all the gold jewelry they carry? Magnificent pieces looted from wealthy Thracians and Hellenes. They have been displaying them freely and the people already lust for them; how can I send the Scythians away now?"

"Toutorix would do it. He was a strong chief," Kernunnos said pointedly. Taranis clenched his jaw but the shapechanger continued by saying, "Toutorix knew there are more important things than trade."

Taranis had grown to manhood in a family made prosperous by trade, in a wealthy village whose existence depended on the goods brought in to them from the outside world, not only the luxury goods but the grains and foodstuffs they could not grow in the Blue Mountains. Taranis could not remember a time when the tribe had to make do with less. Even more than Toutorix before him, he loved hearing the creaking wheels of the traders' wagons coming up the road.

"You would have us starve then, priest?" he asked Kernunnos with scarcely veiled sarcasm.

The Priest of the Stag was insulted. "The tribe will never starve. I bring the game, always!"

Taranis backed down. This was a bad way to begin, antagonizing the most powerful of the spirit-traders. "Yes, of course you do, I realize my words were poorly chosen."

"Very poorly. Beware of offending those you cannot see, Taranis. Your grip on the staff is not as strong as you think." Kernunnos narrowed his eyes and stared fixedly at the chieftain, and Taranis found he had a strong desire to propitiate the chief priest. "What would you have me do? Should our warriors really drive them out?"

Kernunnos considered. "That would damage the pattern; we do not openly break the traditions of hospitality, and right now we must be particularly careful of keeping things in the proper balance.

"I will give a demonstration, very soon, at the feasting fire, to show these Scythians the power of the Kelti and convince them that they cannot stand against us. That is the best way; intimidation. When they are cowed by the sight of my magic, you will find them easy to barter with and quick to leave after, and I do not think they will urge others of their kind to come to us here.

Let them go out from the Blue Mountains and tell strange tales of the Kelti to their savage kin."

Satisfied, Taranis returned to the feast and Kernunnos withdrew to the magic house to prepare.

Aware of the night of the full moon drawing closer with every breath she took, Epona glanced often at the sky as she served the tribe's guests. There was so little time left. She saw Goibban on the other side of the great firepit and tried once more to shape just the right words to approach him with, but then Taranis bellowed for more wine and her thread of thought came unraveled.

Mahka was not taking part in the feast at all. She had gone off with some of the boys approaching the time for their man-making and was taking part in a mock battle with real injuries, having a wonderful time. Taranis was embarrassed by her defection. He had hoped to use this occasion to show his people how admirably suited his family was to their new station — "Every bit as good as Rigantona and those brats of hers" was the way Sirona put it — but now he had no senior daughter to sit behind his cup hand. Sirona sat behind his knife hand, in her proper place, and beside her there was a glaring emptiness.

"Sit here," Taranis ordered Epona. "A man must show that he has strong women at his back."

Kazhak glanced up when the yellow-haired woman was placed among the feasters in the area of honor. He saw her sit down and then look up at the night sky, as he so often did himself. When the feasting cup was next passed his eyes happened to meet hers again, and to his own surprise he smiled at her, as he would have smiled at a blood brother.

Though her thoughts were far away at the moment, Epona was caught and held in that smile like a netted bird. She returned the Scythian's gaze. Those dark, dark eyes, and that beguiling grin. There was a kind of magic involved there . . . she was not thinking about Goibban; she was not even thinking about Kernunnos. She sat in confusion, looking at Kazhak. *Somebody I know is looking at me out of this stranger's face!* she said to herself.

When the ceremonial feasting cup made its next round, Taranis rose and presented it to Kazhak. It was an extravagant gesture, worthy of a Kelt. The cup was of Hellene olivewood mounted in silver and ornamented with colored stones, and had cost Toutorix a cartload of furs.

Suddenly Kazhak sprang to his feet and ran from the circle of firelight. In a moment he was back, brandishing a damp felt bag.

"You give Kazhak silver cup," he said. "Now Kazhak give gift in return." Obviously delighted with his idea, he plunged his hand into the bag and pulled out a human head.

He held it up by the blood-matted hair so everyone could see it. The drained face was ashen in the firelight, the scummy eyeballs rolled back in the head, the tongue lolling from its mouth. A sword stroke had decapitated the man but left a tag end of bone and gristle protruding from the stump of the neck. He had been dead for many nights.

The indrawn breaths of the Kelti sounded like a rush of wind above the crackling of the feasting fire.

"This mighty warrior!" the Scythian announced to his shocked audience. "Kazhak collect many heads, tie around horse's neck in battle to frighten enemies, but this best one yet. This man fight *beautiful*, kill many my brothers. Much smart man in here, almost beat Kazhak." He tapped his knuckles on the pallid forehead. "Now Kazhak give this head to his friend Taranis. Cut off top, line with gold, make fine drinking cup, is it so?"

Taranis saw the elders rolling their eyes in his direction. He could expect no help from them at this unprecedented turn of events; everything was up to him. He tried surreptitiously to locate Kernunnos in the crowd, hoping against hope that the chief priest had returned from the magic house, but saw no sign of him. He must handle it alone, then.

He got to his feet a little unsteadily, regretting the last five or six cups of wine. "It is . . . a splendid gift," he said to Kazhak. "An extraordinary gift. I . . . umm . . . I think no chief of the people has ever been given such a gift."

Kazhak grinned, pleased, and there was a smattering of relieved handclapping. People were beginning to breathe normally again, but many still could not take their eyes off the Scythian's gory trophy.

Kazhak slammed his open palm across Taranis' back, almost knocking the wind out of the other man. The Scythian beamed his big smile and shook the head, sending droplets of congealed blood flying. "Power is in the head, is it so? Head is where man lives. You take, you possess now." With that he thrust his present into his host's face.

It took the experience of generations of warrior blood for Taranis to stand his ground and not step back, but in spite of himself his hands came up defensively — and Kazhak deposited the head in them.

"Now you have all power this mighty warrior. Kazhak give to you. If you want, hang head on your wood house, nobody bother you. Head warn them off. Protect you, protect all yours.

"We friends now; Taranis, Kazhak. Taranis have special good swords for his friend Kazhak, Kazhak give his friend Taranis much gold. All happy, is it so?" He flung his arms around the shoulders of the Thunderer and gave the startled lord of the tribe a bone-wrenching hug.

Taranis sat back down, carefully placing the head on the ground beside him. Sirona suddenly decided she was needed to carry another tray of bread to those beyond the first rank of feasters, but Epona did not move away. She looked at the dreadful thing and recalled the instruction of the *druii*. The head was only an empty shell, after all; the spirit had long since made its transition. There was nothing in that rotting flesh to fear except its very ability to inspire fear. Epona was tired of being frightened. She glared at the severed head and kept her place.

There was singing and storytelling, and one carcass after another was stripped to the bone by the hungry feasters. Roast venison and boiled mutton and stewed coney with littleberries; bread and cakes and cheese and wheat-beer; clotted cream atop dripping sections of honeycomb; onions stuffed with herbs and wrapped with strips of bacon; lumps of fat rolled in spices and pine nuts; wild strawberries simmered in clover tea; lambs' livers on a silver dish.

And wine, wine, wine. It was a grand feast.

The sky was dark and the stars wheeled overhead and the power of the fire overrode the power of the night. At last, when all the songs were sung and the children lay curled asleep at their mothers' feet, Poel stepped to the place of honor and began a long story-song, reciting the relationship of the tribe with the birds and animals of the forest. Sometimes he danced out a segment; sometimes he stood still, eyes closed, and chanted in the *drui* voice, its eerie music echoing from the surrounding peaks as if the mountains joined him.

The eyelids of the listeners grew heavy, as their bellies were heavy with food. The fire was warm, the night was old, the laughter and shouting had been replaced by a murmur of voices and the clatter of pots and bowls.

Then that too fell silent, as Poel finished his song and walked away from the fire.

The time had come for the art of the shapechanger.

Tena came walking through the circle of feasters. She was dressed in a thin gown of bleached linen, silhouetting her body against the firelight. The watching Scythians sat up a little straighter. She went to the edge of the firepit and threw a powder onto the glowing coals. Flame flashed; red smoke billowed out over the crowd, making some of them cough.

The smoke thinned into tatters and drifted away and Tena was gone with it. One of the Scythians, the darkest, who was called Basl, uttered a startled exclamation.

On the other side of the feasting fire something moved, swirled, drew light and color from the flames themselves and coalesced into a figure that might have been a man in a cloak of feathers. Arms extended and became wings. A hoarse cawing issued from the apparition. It moved back and forth with a curious hopping gait, calling out the name of first one person and then another, and those called answered in hushed tones, crouching low on the earth mother as the winged thing danced toward them and then flitted away.

The feathered figure was turning and turning, faster and faster, folding its arms about itself and becoming more compact until it seemed on the verge of dwindling away altogether. And then Tena was beside the fire again, tossing another powder into the flames, and the bird thing disappeared in a great gout of smoke.

From everywhere and nowhere came the voice of Kernunnos, solemnly chanting the names of the bird spirits.

Two more women joined Tena beside the fire. The *gutuiters* danced, weaving back and forth in an intricate pattern. They were as graceful as flickering flames, swaying, skipping, spinning in the firelight. Three women . . .

Or was it four?

Sometimes it looked like four. Yes . . . no . . . Kazhak leaned forward. There were definitely four figures involved in the dance

133

now, but one of them did not seem to be human. It was tall, wraith-thin, glimmering as pale as frost, moving its boneless body as sinuously as a weasel.

A white weasel.

It turned and looked out at them with a weasel's cunning face, its vicious teeth bared, the little ears flat against its head.

Kazhak fumbled for his knife hilt.

The women closed around the figure and the name of the weasel spirit was chanted in high, inhuman voices.

The *gutuiters* whirled away and the weasel was gone. In its place was a solitary figure, as broad as it was tall, a furred shape with glinting yellow eyes and sharply pointed ears. It darted forward on slender legs and snapped savagely at one of Taranis' hounds, which had wandered too close to the feasting fire, its dim mind fixed on meat.

The dog yipped and tumbled onto its back in the classic posture of canine submission, but the thing bearing down on it did not acknowledge the gesture. Too late, the dog realized its mistake and scrambled to its feet, trying to run. The giant silver wolf seized it before it had gone more than a few steps and slung it to the ground. The dog screamed but there was no help for it; before any of the spectators could move the wolf had torn its throat open and was lapping at the blood with feverish thirst.

Taranis jumped to his feet, but the wolf raised its head and looked at him, and he sat back down. The huge animal very deliberately finished its meal of the hot, pulsing life leaving the dog's body, then turned from its victim and trotted back into the billowing smoke.

A fog was closing over the village. The air glistened mistily. Shapes became blurred, sounds muffled. Kazhak regretted having left his battle sword in the guest lodge as a bow to protocol. He looked around for his men but could not pick them out of the crowd.

Something came dancing toward him through the mist and the smoke, a tall, quasi-human figure, and the face of Kernunnos flickered briefly before his eyes. The Scythian shook his head to clear it. There was no one in front of him, only the fire.

The voices of the Kelti were joining in the chant the *druii* had begun, calling on the birds of the air and the fish in the waters, praising the fruit of the trees and the grain in the fields. The people rocked their bodies back and forth as they chanted, moving with one rhythm, one will, following the pattern, linked in ecstasy. Kelti. Part of the whole.

The smoke roiled and billowed around them and shapes swirled within it, shapes only dimly defined. The thing that might have been Kernunnos moved among them, assuming one form and then another. He had fur, he had feathers, he had the liquid eyes of the doe and the broad flat snout of the badger.

Kazhak became aware of the beating of a drum that seemed to lead his own heartbeat as it led the dancers, slowing down, speeding up. The music of the lyre, the thin piping of the reeds. Bronze rattles. Kazhak had heard rattles before, the shamans of the horse people used them. This was not reality then, but magic? Or was the magic reality? It was hard to think, with the chanting and the smoke.

The bronze rattles sounded continually, their monotonous undertone of menace rising and falling with the rhythms of the dance. A wolf howled. A cat screamed. A fox barked. A tall man with burning eyes and blood on his lips danced and chanted, and the spirits looked out of his face.

Shapechanger.

Chapter 11

SOMETIME DURING THE NIGHT, in the smoke, as part of the dancing, Kernunnos had stood for a moment at Epona's shoulder. She had not seen him but it was not necessary. His voice, cold as the voice of an insect using human words, reverberated through her skull.

"Nextnight the moon will be almost full," it reminded her. "The night after that you enter the magic house, Epona. Once something has been given to me it is mine. It would have been better for you if you had come to me of your own free will, but either way, you will come at the appointed time. To the magic house, Epona."

She sat walled in by horror but no one noticed. All around her were free people; the Kelti who prided themselves on their freedom and would surrender it to no man; the Scythians who rode the wind and shaped their lives as they chose. But she would be trapped in the magic house, her individuality stripped from her and made subservient to the will of the spirits. The time would come when she would dance at the feasting fire with the *gutuiters*, or . . . something voiceless was speaking to her, telling her. She crossed her arms over her diaphragm and leaned forward, listening.

He will make you a shapechanger, said the silent voice of the spirit within.

Some would have welcomed the opportunity, but Epona rejected it with every fiber of her being. She got to her feet unnoticed by the feasters and left the banquet. The red eyes of the fire watched her go but told no one. The white eyes of the stars saw her leave but did not care.

Epona walked as far as the edge of the sacred grove and stood alone, listening to the trees breathing. Untrained though she was, she made an effort to reach out with her spirit and feel the pattern as it applied to her, hoping to find a tear in it she might slip through.

When the feasting fire was only a bed of glowing coals, and the last feasters, exhausted by too much wine and food and emotion, had staggered off to their own lodges, Kazhak lay beneath the stars, in front of the guest house. He rested his head on the neck of his gray stallion and tried to untangle his thoughts. The memory of smoke clouded them, reminding him of the fumes of the hemp burned on the Sea of Grass. There were times when it was pleasant to float on such fumes, but not here, in the land of the Kelti, where any loss of the sharp edges of reality might be dangerous. These people were not what they seemed.

The Kelti eluded understanding. They were reputed to be great warriors, which a Scythian could understand very well, but now that he had walked in their tracks and eaten their food he realized that was only one aspect of their nature. They seemed to live in several worlds at once, the here and now and some other places, other worlds only dimly glimpsed. On the Sea of Grass the shamans claimed such places were the haunts of demons, realms to be feared, the dark and terrifying other face of life to which all were ultimately doomed. Yet the Kelti spoke familiarly of the dead as of temporarily absent friends; he had heard them do it around the feasting fire, casually inviting the spirits of their ancestors to enjoy the feast.

The shamans claimed that only their own powers protected the living from the uniform malevolence of the dead. The Kelti did not consider death to have any reality at all, and certainly gave no impression of fearing it. Sitting at the banquet, Kazhak had listened with growing bafflement to the conversations of those around him, the conversations that so often included allusions to forces more complex and powerful than any recognized by the shamans of the steppes. He had seen the shapechanger work his magic — if it was magic — and he had noticed how the people included aspects of an incredibly rich and unseen spirit world in every facet of their own lives.

Yet aside from those called *druii*, they were not priests, but ordinary men and women, flesh and blood. Men and women who seemed to know something that he, Kazhak, did not, something that allowed them to gaze on the horrifying shapechanger, one face melting into another, with calm acceptance.

Their reality was like none Kazhak knew. They appeared to have powers beyond his understanding, and even as he scoffed at them he was deeply impressed, and equally wary of the Kelti. They carried their dreams in their eyes — like that yellow-haired girl. He did not know how to deal with such people.

As a Scythian, Kazhak was accustomed to moving through life with an indifference to the natural order. The rootless wanderers on the Sea of Grass strove for no balance and searched for no harmony with their environment. When one resource was exhausted, they simply moved elsewhere. Only headlong motion and acquisition interested them. Their raped and pillaged victims had no claim on them and ceased to exist for them as they receded on the horizon. The land itself was not part of them, merely the surface they galloped upon. They did not care if its power was greater than theirs; they would ignore it until the tribute was exacted, and then they would go down without regret, into the wooden houses in the earth.

Such a way of life had proved stronger than those who stood against it. Farmers, villagers, townspeople, bound to their place and their possessions, had been helpless when attacked by warriors who had no respect for either. Life for the Scythians was brutal and easy.

But these Kelti were different from the various peoples the nomads had previously encountered. Even in his befuddled state, Kazhak felt the differences. They had something beyond property, something that could not be slung across a horse and carried away, to serve as a brief entertainment and then be tossed aside when something newer was found. It would be interesting to take a piece of that — whatever it was — back to the Sea of Grass; take the valuable part that gave the Kelti their strength and prosperity, and leave behind the inexplicable, the swirling mists, and the man who turned into an animal.

It would be like taking the head of a good warrior and leaving his dangerous sword arm behind. But could the two be separated, in the case of the Kelti?

Kazhak wrestled with his thoughts, trying to pin them down, striving to see what was real and obtainable and what was illusion, or menace. Reality slipped like fog through his fingers, and he fell asleep at last to endure fitful dreams seen through clouds of smoke, distorting things that were distorted enough already. In his dreams he caught glimpses of the eyes of the shapechanger, watching him, and he heard the priest drum and the incessant bronze rattles.

The next morning all the Scythians were edgy. His men made it plain to Kazhak that they were more than ready to leave. Their numbers were too few to take the iron swords by force; they would, indeed, have to leave all the gold for them, and that would need to be explained in the future. But accounting was many days away. For now . . .

"Just make trade and go," urged Dasadas.

But Kazhak had an unfulfilled commitment. He had observed that these Kelti were obsessed with honor and the keeping of their pledges, and perhaps that was one source of their good fortune. An oath taken on one's father's hearth was binding to the death among his own people. He felt obligated to show these Kelti that the Scythians had an honor to equal theirs. He could not match their shapechanger with his magic, but he could show the men of the Kelti a different kind of power, that of the superior hunter. Were not the bows and arrows of the Scythians more deadly even than the spears of the Assyrians?

"Kazhak promised you stag, Kazhak bring you stag," he announced to Taranis when the chief appeared with his council at the trading circle, ready to discuss the exchange of gold.

Taranis had spent a difficult night. He had taken the decapitated head back to his lodge to avoid offending his guest, but Sirona had refused to share his bedshelf as long as the thing was under their rooftree. "Put it in a box," she told him, "or give it to your hounds, but get it out of my house."

"I can't do that. What kind of man dishonors the gift of another? Besides, who knows what strength the thing may have? It is said the Scythians are invincible in battle; heads like this may be their secret, talismans of great power. It would be foolish to discard something like that."

Sirona folded her arms across her breasts. "That head or me," she told him.

On his way to the trading circle in the morning, Kazhak noticed the head fastened on a peg beside the chief's door — on the outside of his lodge.

When Kazhak announced at the trading circle that he would hunt and kill a stag for his hosts, a cheer was raised. This was another of those splendid gestures that could be told and retold later, around the lodgefires. Poel might make a song about it.

Taranis, however, was taken aback. He had come prepared to do serious trading. Hunting was not a priority just then; there was plenty of meat still, in spite of the feast. He was upset to see that Kazhak seemed disinterested in trade. He urged the Scythian to return his thoughts to the matter at hand. "We will hunt later," he said, dismissing the subject.

Kazhak did not dismiss it in his own thoughts.

At the request of the chieftain, Goibban and his apprentices brought a selection of swords wrapped in oiled wool, and Taranis proudly displayed these to the Scythians, ignoring Goibban's scowl of disapproval over the transaction.

Kazhak picked up a sword, hefted it in his hands, passed it to Dasadas for examination, and said, "Good. Kazhak go get stag now, then we give you gold and go, is it so?"

It was the most casual trading deal Taranis had ever heard, and he was scandalized. He was all prepared for serious negotiations, equipped with his little bronze Hellene scale and his shrewd business sense. Now none of that seemed necessary.

Goibban was insulted. Though he disliked selling weapons to outsiders, he was angered at the Scythians for treating his work so lightly. His best efforts lay at their feet; splendid blades, already honed to a sharp edge, set in heavy bronze hilts lacking only the ivory inlay to be as fine as that buried with Toutorix. And those savages barely glanced at them! Only the one called

Aksinya, a bandy-legged, slightly potbellied man with eyes like polished stones, even bothered to hold one of the swords long enough to brandish it a few times. Then Kazhak said something to him in their own language and he dropped the sword in the dirt.

"Do not appear so eager," Kazhak had told him sternly. "They will think we have not seen weapons as good as this before." They had not, but it was better if the Kelti did not know this.

Kazhak turned to Taranis. "You go with Kazhak now, hunt stag?" he asked, one friend to another. He was looking forward to hunting with the chief of the Kelti, so an impression of Scythian strength might be left behind when they departed.

"I have to consult with the elders of the tribe," Taranis told him. He loved hunting, but he was not anxious to go on an unplanned expedition with the Scythian. What if he got no deer himself; how would that look? He motioned to Dunatis and a few others and they formed their own small circle, discussing this latest development.

Kernunnos joined them. His eyes were glinting with malice. "Those Scythians plan tricks," he warned. "They are not Kelti; not honorable. They will get you away from the village and kill you, perhaps, then attack us when we are without a chief."

The elders agreed to the wisdom of his words. Licking his thin lips, Kernunnos suggested, "Send someone else with him, Taranis. Send . . . Okelos, son of Rigantona. He is your near-kin; let him represent you."

"I do not want to lose face with the Scythians," Taranis said, uncertainly.

"You will not lose face, I give you my word. But it is imperative we teach those horse riders a lesson so they will have too much respect — too much *fear* — of our abilities, to ever come here again and attack us in strength. Hear me, Taranis: This is more important than trading a few swords for a bag of gold."

"What about the swords?" Goibban interjected, having a considerable stake in this.

"Perhaps the Scythians will be too upset to think about the swords. They might even leave all that heavy gold behind them so they can travel faster; I expect they will soon be in a great hurry to leave this valley."

Taranis shook his head. "We could not let them abandon their gold to us without giving them a fair exchange. That is theft, and we do not steal."

"It does not matter, I tell you!" Kernunnos cried, his voice rising. "Gold and swords are not important; they only have value for a brief time, in thisworld. The important thing here is to intimidate the horse riders. If something happened to their leader, for example, do you not think that would make them fearful and anxious to leave?"

Taranis lowered his deep voice still further. "I do not like what you suggest, shapechanger. Do you propose to do harm to Kazhak, a *guest*? That goes against our most cherished traditions. The guest in the house is sacred."

Kernunnos replied, "I will not touch Kazhak or any of his men, either with my hand or with weapons. I give you my word."

There were other ways to do harm, especially if you were *drui*, and Taranis was very much aware of them. Still, if the Scythians could be frightened into departing without their gold — a richer hoard than any Toutorix had recently acquired — and the Kelti could truthfully say no man had raised his hand against them . . . Taranis ran his fingers through his beard and thought.

"We must be very careful how we act here," he told the priest. "If there is any suspicion of deliberate malice on our part, those who have traded with us before might begin avoiding the Blue Mountains. Then what would we do for flax and wheat . . . and wine?"

Someone had gone to fetch Okelos, whose name Kernunnos had interjected into the discussion. He arrived in time to hear only the last few words, but he already had an opinion to voice. "If we had horses that would allow us to sit on them, and were as fast as the Scythian animals, we could go and get what we need. We would no longer be dependent on the goods others bring in to us. With our swords and horses for riding we could go anywhere, take anything. For the good of the tribe," he added hastily, aware of the eyes of the elders upon him.

Kernunnos addressed Taranis directly, chief priest to lord of the tribe. This was a solemn moment; many issues hung in the balance. If the influence of these Scythians was not destroyed now, soon it would infect all the tribe, not just the young hotheads like Okelos. Expendable Okelos. The pattern would be changed forever, pulled into a new shape even Kernunnos could not manage.

"I speak to you from the spirits," Kernunnos intoned, his voice seeming to echo from some deep cavern. The Kelti tensed, recognizing *drui* magic. "Do as I say now, Taranis. Send the leader of the Scythians after the stag; tell him of the mighty one living in the highest patch of meadowland, at the end of the trail to the sheep pasturage.

"Okelos, you are to guide him and hunt with him, but be sure the stag is his, do you understand? After the hunt, when you come back to the village, tell us — all of us — everything you have seen. Is that clear?"

Okelos nodded, glowing with pride. It was the first time the chief priest had paid any attention to him since his man-making, and he interpreted it as a sign that Kernunnos recognized his mistake in not influencing the election of the chief. *He sees now that I am strong and have good ideas*, Okelos told himself. *If I acquit myself well thisday, who can say what might happen?*

The hunt was quickly arranged. Kazhak was disappointed that Taranis could not accompany him personally, due to the press of certain urgent tribal business that had just arisen, but he accepted Okelos good-naturedly. "You help Kazhak, Kazhak share stag's liver with you," he offered with customary generosity to a hunting companion.

Okelos hurried back to his lodge for his hunting spear, in case there was some lesser game worthy of his effort. He could think of no great stag living in the place described, which puzzled him, but of course the shapechanger would know better about such things. He looked forward to the hunt with keen anticipation.

Meanwhile, Epona had found it impossible to stay away from the Scythian horses. They fascinated her. They had an elegance of line, a harmony of proportion that made their use as riding animals seem inevitable; there was even a gentle curve to their backs, inviting one to sit. While the Scythians were occupied with Taranis and the elders, Epona pulled grass to feed their horses by hand and talked patiently to the animals, trying to make friends with their spirits.

It was another way of distracting herself from the coming full moon.

She saw Goibban return from the trading ring and almost immediately afterward she noticed Kernunnos, running low to the earth, dart between two lodges and head for the nearest stand of pines above the village. Beyond those pines lay the trail to the high pastures.

When the priest was out of the area Epona felt as if she could breathe more deeply. The anxiety that had floated over her all day like a gray cloud was lifted and she felt a surge of confidence.

There would never be a better opportunity.

She smoothed her hair and gown; she bit her lips to redden them; she thrust her shoulders back to lift her full breasts.

Now was the time, if the time was ever to be.

She headed for the forge, walking slowly, eager to know what Goibban would say and simultaneously putting off facing him as long as possible, just in case.

As she neared the forge she heard the rhythmic clang of metal on metal. In turns as patterned as those of a ritual dance, the apprentices were striking the orange-hot blade of a sword with their hammers, pounding the iron into its final shape. As each hammer struck the next was falling and the third was lifting away. Goibban held the blade with a pair of tongs, his gaze intent upon the work. He did not look up when Epona approached.

"Goibban . . ." she began.

"Wait, girl," he muttered. "It is time for the quenching. We must be quiet while the spirit of the sword is tested . . . *now!*"

He lifted the glowing blade from the anvil and plunged it into a long trough of cold liquid. Clouds of sizzling steam obscured the interior of the forge. The apprentices held their breath in the urgency of the moment. Star metal was surrendering to the will of man.

The steam faded away. The blade lay quiet in its bath. With a reverent expression on his face, Goibban lifted it very gently. The apprentices leaned forward. Goibban examined the blade, stroking its surface with his burned and calloused thumb.

"Yes," he said at last.

The apprentices broke into relieved grins and clapped one another on the back. Even Epona felt the relaxation of tension and the joy of accomplishment; it permeated the smoky forge with the sweetness of a job well done.

Goibban turned to his visitor.

"I need to talk to you alone," she said baldly.

Women — wives — had made that request before, but of course Epona must have some other reason. There was a pleading in her face. The girl was in some kind of trouble needing a strong man's aid, or required a particular kind of work that only a smith could do. And who better than Goibban?

He smiled and wiped his hands on his leather apron. "Come to my lodge with me," he invited. "There is no one there but my mother, and old Grania never puts her fingers in another's bowl. Anything you have to say, you can say in front of her."

He gave crisp instructions to his assistants and strode toward his lodge, Epona trotting at his heels like one of the hound puppies. Too late, she realized she should have walked at his shoulder, a woman and an equal, and she hurried to catch up. Her heart was beating very hard.

In Goibban's lodge, Grania sat on the far side of the firepit, busy with some sewing. She greeted Epona politely with beer and bread, then forgot the girl was there, as people must do who share a lodge with others.

"What is it you need, Epona?" Goibban wanted to know. "I don't make jewelry anymore, if you're bringing an order from Rigantona. I'm training Vindos the White to work with soft metals, and . . ."

"I don't want to order jewelry," Epona interrupted, the words leaping out of her mouth before she had them properly arranged in her head. "I want you to marry me." Then she stared aghast at him, astonished by her own audacity.

Goibban shook his head as if he had gotten water in his ears while swimming in the lake. "What did you say, Epona? I didn't understand you."

Having gone so far there was no turning back. Perhaps that was why she had blurted out the words so quickly. In a voice lowered by embarrassment, she said, "My mother has pledged me to Kernunnos to be trained as a *gutuiter*. I am unmarried. I am still hers and live in her lodge, though I've been to my woman-making. I have to go into the magic house at the next full moon unless some man asks for me as wife in the meantime. There are no wifeseekers here now, but if you were to ask for me, Goibban . . ."

The smith had been sitting on the edge of his bedshelf, hands dangling relaxed between his knees, but when he realized what Epona was suggesting he stood up abruptly. "I can't marry you, Epona. You are of my own tribe!"

It was a credit to old Grania that the woman did not look up, but continued with her sewing. If the hand that held the bone needle trembled, it may have been due to her age.

"Don't you like me?" Epona asked.

"Of course I like you, I like all the children, but that doesn't mean . . ."

"I'm not a child any longer, I'm a woman," she insisted, and for the second time he became aware of the intensity that smoldered in her like a banked fire.

He looked away in confusion. "Yes . . . I know, I mean, I can see you are a woman. But that makes no difference. Even if I wanted you . . ."

"Is it because of my broken arm, is that it? I've looked under the bandages, I know it's going to heal all right, it will be straight. Goibban, I'm not going to be disfigured . . ."

"It isn't that, Epona. You know it isn't that."

She caught one of his big hands in both of hers and held it tightly. "You are as important to the tribe as the Salt Mountain is," she told him. "Taranis would order almost anything done to keep you content, I know it. If you tell him I am the price for your continuing to work the star metal, he will let us marry. He will!"

Goibban pulled his hand away from her as gently as he could. "I could not say that to the chief, Epona. It would be dishonest. I am content now, I need no bribe to keep me working the iron. I already have everything I want. I have my work to do, a good mother to cook my food and keep my fire, and the respect of the tribe. Whenever I want a woman I can almost have my choice; I'm in no hurry to seek a wife.

"No matter how much I like you, asking for you would complicate my life more than I care to do."

"Are you afraid to do something that's never been done before? Is that it?"

He seemed to swell like a frog filling itself with air to impress a rival. "I have done many things that were never done before, and I am not afraid of anything but starfire and earthquake," he told her. "But I respect the pattern, the laws we live by, for what is man but his laws and his tribe? I will not break one and lose the respect of the other.

"If you have a chance to be *drui*, take it, Epona; that is my advice to you. Go to the magic house and be happy, as I am."

She was shaking as if with a chill. "You're a coward!" she flung at him. It was the ultimate insult and the anger in his eyes warned her she had gone too far, but she no longer cared. Goibban had been her secret safety; until this moment she had truly, deeply, believed he would take her, he would want her as much as she wanted him. She had been as confident of him as she was once confident of her parents and her place in the tribe. But now Goibban had refused her. Toutorix had gone to the otherworlds when she needed him most; Okelos had betrayed her, and Rigantona had traded her away like barter goods. The foundation stones of her life had crumbled beneath her feet, and all she had left was herself.

So be it, said the spirit within, speaking at last.

"You are a coward," she repeated through clenched teeth, and saw Goibban unthinkingly double his fists. "Hit me," she challenged him, putting her own hand on the hilt of the knife in her belt. "Just hit me, smith, and see what happens. I'm not afraid, like you. Hit me!"

Goibban let his hands fall open at his sides. He became aware that his mother was staring at him across the firepit.

"You had better leave, Epona," he told the girl.

"Neither fire nor water would make me stay," she answered, nursing her rage for the strength it gave her. She stalked past him and out of the lodge.

In the open air her situation hit her in the face like a reflection of sun on lake water, temporarily blinding her. Goibban had refused to stretch out his hand to her. All that awaited her now was the full moon, and the magic house.

And the shapechanger.

She drew a deep breath. "No," she said to no one but the spirit within. "They can't make me do it." She began walking slowly through the village, unaware of direction, letting her feet pick the way.

Beyond the village, Kazhak and Okelos sought the great stag. Once past the palisade the two men had begun a steady upward climb, zigzagging along trails that were mere threads haphazardly strung across the mountain as if tossed by a petulant hand. Armies of pine marched upward with them in dense ranks. The alpine silence was so deep it pressed on the ears; the altitude made Kazhak yawn repeatedly.

Several times Okelos hesitated and looked back, a puzzled frown on his face. "What is?" Kazhak asked each time, but Okelos only shook his head and trudged on. At last he stopped absolutely still, frozen like a wild animal at the sight of the hunter, and signaled Kazhak to do likewise.

The two men stood in a silence broken only by the thudding of their own hearts. The trail behind them was empty; no twig snapped, no branch moved. Yet Okelos was certain now that they were being followed. Then, like a trick of light, a face peered out of the trees for just the bat of an eyelid and disappeared again before Kazhak noticed it.

Kernunnos.

Druii business.

Okelos started to say something to Kazhak, but the spirit within stopped him. Whatever reason had brought the priest on their trail did not concern Okelos. He wanted no part of it. There were currents and undercurrents in everything involved with these Scythians; let Kernunnos take care of it.

"I thought I heard something, but I was wrong," he told Kazhak. "Follow me; the place we seek is not far away now."

They were moving along the edge of a cliff where part of the mountain had been torn away by heavy snow, forming a treacherous rock slide. The two men were forced to walk single file, their weapons in their hands. Above the narrow trail the slope was steep and heavily forested; below yawned the devastated ruin left by the avalanche.

Kazhak was following Okelos closely. Suddenly he drew a sharp intake of breath and whispered, "Deer!"

Okelos peered ahead but saw nothing. He looked up the slope into the dark trees but there was no flash of a red hide.

"Where?" he asked the Scythian.

"There, there!" Kazhak pointed straight ahead. "Big stag. Biggest stag Kazhak ever see."

148

Okelos looked along the trail in bafflement. Shortly ahead of them it lifted and rounded a curve, disappearing from their vision as it climbed upward to a hidden strip of meadow. As far as Okelos could see, there was no deer.

By now Kazhak was burning with the lust of the hunter. Deftly fitting an arrow to his bow, he shouldered Okelos aside and hurried up the path, oblivious to everything but the giant stag. No mountain man would have been so careless of his footing, but Kazhak was not a mountain man.

Then Okelos saw it, just where the trail turned from sight: a brown shadow and a magnificent rack of antlers, proudly lifted. With a thrill of horror he realized it was no normal deer that waited there, on the very edge of the precipice, luring Kazhak on.

Kazhak saw a stag. A huge stag. A stag to boast of for the rest of one's life. He grinned in total joy and released his first arrow, only to see the animal flicker from sight and vanish around the bend. How could he have missed at such a distance? Grabbing the next arrow from his case he ran forward, exulting in the moment, obsessed with the kill. On the narrow trail the animal could not possibly escape him.

There it was again, just ahead. Not running away but standing squarely, challengingly, the equal of any hunter, a creature of pride and passion like himself. The thought came to him that he and the stag had each been shaped for this one glorious confrontation, the ultimate expression of their malehood.

The stag lowered its head and brandished its many-branched antlers to threaten him, and with a laugh Kazhak sprang toward it, forgetting his bow, forgetting the mountain, seized with the idea of meeting the creature in hand-to-hand combat — this splendid beast who would not run, but stood to fight. He would grab it by its antlers and wrestle it to the earth with his bare hands; he would cut its throat and spill its blood onto the mountain soil.

That would be a tale to tell!

Okelos started to yell a warning but his words dried in his throat and he watched in silence, unable to change what was about to happen, while Kazhak hurled himself at the thing he thought was a deer.

The stag's eyes, huge and liquid and brown, were fixed on the

Scythian, and then they changed and Kazhak realized they were not the eyes of a deer. In the final moment left him, after he had already committed himself to the forward momentum of a powerful leap, the eyes became yellow and piercing and . . . human.

Kazhak struggled desperately to check himself and regain his balance, but he had been lured too far. His feet hit the crumbling shale at the edge of the slide and the earth dropped away beneath him. Okelos, close on his heels, had to spring backward to avoid being trapped by its sudden collapse as the shale tumbled downward.

Kazhak waved his arms wildly, overbalanced for an eternal moment, then cartwheeled out into space.

Down, down, a sickening drop through stinging stones and choking dirt, the cruel fingers of exposed roots gouging him as he clawed for handholds he could not catch. The side of the mountain seemed to lean toward him and then pull away. He slid into and through a gully running vertically down the face of the slope; he had the impression of being caught between two cliffs, like the molars of a giant carnivore, chewing, closing on him, and then opening just before he would have been crushed.

His body hit a stony outcropping with an impact that knocked all the air from his lungs in an agonized whoosh and slowed his downward plunge but did not stop it. He tumbled on again, picking up speed, the scree falling away from him. He endured a forever of falling.

Then his head struck something solid and his skull filled with exploding stars.

Chapter 12

OKELOS GOT TO KAZHAK as quickly as he could, sliding down the mountain himself, cursing and badly frightened. He had almost fallen to his death with the Scythian, and the footing was still treacherous. But honor demanded he recover his guest's body, even at the risk of his own life.

Okelos now regretted having come on the hunt. Some honors were better declined, and this was one of them. Tardily he realized he might have been intended to go over the precipice too; had Taranis and Kernunnos arranged it between them, to end any challenge Okelos might someday make for the chief's staff? *Yes*, said the spirit within.

At last, breathless and bruised, he reached the Scythian's crumpled body. It was badly abraded on face and hands, and a thin stream of blood was running from one nostril, but to Okelos' astonishment, the dark eyes opened as he bent over the supposedly dead man and Kazhak muttered something.

Okelos squatted beside him. "What did you say?"

The Scythian stifled a groan and made himself grin instead. "No . . . stag. Fool Kazhak. Big . . . joke on Kazhak, is it so?" His eyes closed and he lay still.

He was breathing steadily, however, and gave every indication that he intended to go on breathing. He would have to be taken to the village immediately; by the time Okelos could bring help back some wild animal might find him and accomplish what the shapechanger had failed to do.

Okelos was strongly moved at this moment to thwart the shape-changer.

He struggled with the unconscious body, trying to find the best way to carry it, and at last got it hoisted across his back and shoulders and began picking his way diagonally down the slope, trying to find safe footing so that both men would reach the village alive.

The children were the first to notice his arrival. Approaching from the pasture trail he was not seen by a sentry, and had almost reached the center of the village, with a pack of youngsters crowding at his heels asking questions, before any of the adults was aware of Okelos and his burden and ran to help him.

The village was thrown into uproar. Kazhak's men were soon roaring like bulls, demanding explanations. The *gutuiters* were trying to get to the injured man to tend his wounds; the embarrassed lord of the tribe, horrified — or appearing to be — at the accident that had befallen his guest, was getting in everyone's way.

The commotion attracted even Epona's attention. The crowd was moving toward the guest lodge, where the *gutuiters* meant to care for Kazhak, and Epona's feet carried her with the crowd as her ears caught snatches of conversation. Some people who knew nothing were trying to explain everything to others who knew less.

"It was a hunting accident."

"Was he mauled by a bear?"

"Fell down the mountain."

"How could he fall down the mountain? Wasn't there a guide with him?"

"No, he wandered off by himself."

"Yes, Okelos, son of Rigantona, was with him and let him fall."

"That explains it. Okelos has always been careless, just like that wife of his. But how is this going to look to the Scythians? Will they want revenge?"

"Is the trading arrangement jeopardized?" This from someone older, wiser; a contemporary of Toutorix.

Epona was not surprised to hear the accident blamed on her brother. He would not have made a good lord of the tribe. Once more, the wisdom of the council of elders was proven. How fortunate the Kelti were to have so many old heads!

But an old head could not help her now; if she went to one of the elders for advice in her own dilemma, they would only side wih Rigantona. The promise had been given, after all. She had been exchanged, like something you can count and carry.

The only advice she had been given that might be any good to her was Mahka's: *You should run away, Epona. You have to fight for yourself in thislife.*

She was standing to one side, watching the people crowd around the guest lodge, glancing from time to time at the angry faces of Kazhak's three men as they stood nearest the door, and it was then the idea came to her. A wild idea, a reckless idea, exactly the sort of thing that always occurred to Epona; an idea that could not be credited to the spirit within.

Nematona emerged from the lodge and Epona hurried to intercept her. "Will the Scythian be all right?" she wanted to know.

Nematona smiled. "I doubt if he could be killed with an axe. They breed strong men on that Sea of Grass he talks about. He is cut and bruised and some of his ribs may be injured, but he never winced when I bound them and now he says he is ready to ride. We were able to convince him to take one night's rest — he is somewhat weakened — but I suspect he and his men will leave at dawn nextday. They are all extremely anxious to go."

Anxious to go, thought Epona. *So am I; anxious to go.*

"Have you seen Kernunnos?" she asked Nematona.

"He was away for a while, but now I believe he is in the chief's lodge. Do you want to see him?"

"No," said Epona firmly. "I never, ever, want to see Kernunnos."

Nematona patted her shoulder. "The shapechanger upsets you, doesn't he? He is difficult to like, I realize, but you will find he is very wise and a skillful teacher. When he finishes his share of your instruction in the arts of the priesthood you will know as much as anyone can while living in thisworld. I almost envy you, Epona, having so many secrets opened to you for the first time."

You could not argue with one of the *druii.* They were so snugly interwoven with the physical aspects of the earth and the unseen powers of the otherworlds that they could no longer understand the reluctance of someone like Epona, who found the thought of giving her entire life to the priesthood unbearable. The *druii* were convinced theirs was the ideal existence; the kind of freedom Epona required was no more necessary for them than rain was necessary for rocks.

Freedom, Epona thought, hungrily. Passionately. *Freedom such as the horsemen must know, sitting on those beautiful animals as they run across the . . . what was it called? The Sea of Grass?*

Imagine a sea of grass. Not sailing ships but galloping horses, and a horizon unlimited by mountain peaks.

The Scythians will return to their sea of grass and I am supposed to go to the magic house.

"Nematona, are you certain the Scythians will leave nextday?"

Nematona's lips twitched. "I can give you my word on it. I think Kernunnos would carry them all out of the village in his arms if necessary, to get rid of them. Right now he is not too happy with your brother, either, Epona. You would be wise to suggest to Okelos that he stay out of the shapechanger's way for a while."

Nematona headed for the lodge the *gutuiters* shared; a tall, stately woman in a rough brown robe like the bark of a tree. Epona knew if she narrowed her eyes Nematona would melt away into the forest surrounding the village, her graceful figure one with the pines and the ferns, moving in eternal softness among the green and living things, part of them forever.

Daughter of the Trees.

I am just Epona, the girl told herself, standing with her head held high. *And I will remain Epona.*

She sat down in a comfortable spot where she could keep an eye on the guest lodge.

Kernunnos had returned to the village to find that nothing had gone as he expected. The Scythian had somehow survived his dreadful fall and was not even crippled. The Kelti were more impressed than ever with his hardiness; they chattered among themselves about the strength and endurance these horsemen must possess.

Some of the men were saying to others, "Perhaps the secret is

154

in the heads of their enemies; there may be something to that. Suppose we were to nail heads to our lodges? Suppose we have our women make us some of those trousers — that looks like an excellent garment, warm and practical for mining, as well as for riding. We could learn a lot from these Scythians."

Kernunnos was furious. He blew into the chief's lodge like a cold north wind. "We have underestimated these horse people," he told Taranis.

"We? It was your idea to send him on the hunt. Can it be that he is stronger than you, Kernunnos?"

The shapechanger's lips writhed back from his teeth. "Impossible. He should never have survived that fall. A mistake must have been made . . ."

"*I* have made no mistakes," Taranis said pointedly. "I gave the Scythians hospitality, I exchanged gifts, I even arranged a very satisfactory trade. Whatever trouble there has been you have caused, Kernunnos. Kazhak has told his men we injured him with some sort of trick, and they are understandably very angry. They may well leave without bothering to conclude the trade at all."

"This is not just a trading matter! I tell you, the whole future of the people is involved; I have seen it. If we do not destroy the influence these strangers have, in another generation you might not even recognize the Kelti."

He spoke with the voice of prophecy. The eyes of the chief priest were clouded, and hooded by their long lids, but for once Taranis was too upset to be intimidated by the powers of the *drui*. The villagers had seen the Scythian gold; if it was taken away again, they would blame him, and their all-important loyalty to him might be weakened. A brash young man like Okelos, who promised them more . . .

"I am going to do my best to see that the trade is completed before the Scythians leave, Kernunnos," he said. "Then they will go and be forgotten, you will see."

"They will not be forgotten! And they may well come back, with more of their kind!"

"If they do, we will enlarge our trading arrangements with them to everyone's advantage," Taranis told him, "and in the future I will ask you to let me handle dealings with outsiders, for that is the function of the lord of the tribe. I see now that this is no business of the *druii*. And if by some chance they return with warriors, meaning us harm, we will defeat them with our own warriors and Goibban's iron. No one can successfully attack us here; that has been proved many times."

Kernunnos felt his guts twisting. How arrogant Taranis was! Like all the Kelti, he put too much faith in his courage and his physical strength, and there would come a time when those allies would be insufficient.

The continuation of the tribe as a strong, spiritually intact unit was the responsibility of the chief priest, and Kernunnos was not going to be allowed to fulfill that responsibility. Since the coming of the Scythians his position had already been eroded.

Nursing his resentment, he left the chief's lodge and headed for the magic house to consult the spirits. He caught sight of Rigantona's daughter outside the guest lodge, sitting on the earth close to the hobbled horses of the Scythians, and stopped abruptly.

It was a sign, a good omen at last. When he most needed help, there would be another *drui* to add strength to the magic that held the pattern intact and the people of the Kelti safe.

He approached her on cat's feet. "Epona," he said, his voice caressing. "Epona."

She whirled around to meet his eyes. She would no longer give him the satisfaction of seeing her pull away. "It is not yet the night of the full moon," she told him.

"I was hoping you could be persuaded to join us early," the priest said. "You are needed now."

"The promise was for the night of the full moon," she reminded him, standing her ground.

"There is a threat to the tribe and I must call on the combined strength of the *druii* to counter it," Kernunnos said. "Your help will be invaluable." His voice repelled Epona. It reminded her of globules of grease floating on the surface of the water in the *hydria*.

"I am not trained," she said.

"Not yet, but you have a force in you, Epona; a greater force than you realize. I know how to harness that force. There is nothing to fear, it does not hurt."

She was haughty. "You know I'm not afraid of pain."

"Then come with me now and help me, daughter of Rigantona. Working together, you and I will do such magic as the first *druii* did many generations ago. We can make the pattern stronger than ever. We can keep the Kelti here, in the Blue Mountains, safe and prosperous, able to resist whatever forces of change might try to destroy their unity. There are other people of strength rising even now, Epona, I can feel it, and they will threaten us in future generations. But we can make the Kelti more cohesive, put new weapons in their minds rather than in their hands. Hai! When you give your life to the tribe . . ."

"I don't want to give my life to the tribe. I want to live it for myself." Why would no one listen?

"Would you forget your obligation to your tribe?"

She could sense the desperation in him and it surprised her. "I will never forget I am Kelti," she said. "But I will not come to you before nextnight." She was not lying when she said it, merely walking around the truth.

"Very well, girl." He was angry, but he would not push her; he could not afford to make her more hostile. "But when the full moon rises I will see you. Do not forget."

He left her alone then, with the horses.

"Oh, please," she whispered, not knowing which spirit to address in this instance and so addressing the all in one. "Please!"

The sun moved across the sky and the shadows grew tall from the west. At last Taranis and the elders approached with tense faces, carrying the selection of weapons the Scythians had seen earlier. As they neared the lodge Kazhak's men, Basl, Aksinya, and Dasadas, stepped forward to guard the door. Epona noticed that both parties kept their hands close to their weapons.

"We have come, Kazhak," called Taranis in his booming voice, "to ask the health of our friend."

There was silence within the lodge. The Kelti waited.

"I wish you sunshine on your head in the name of the tribe of the Kelti, and of Taranis the Thunderer!" the chieftain cried more loudly.

No answer. The Kelti shifted their feet and looked at one another; the Scythians fingered their sword hilts.

Uiska appeared in the doorway carrying a basin, and then Kazhak stood behind her, a new pallor underlying his swarthiness. Addressing Taranis, he said, "Kelti have good wishes for Ka-

157

zhak?" There was no mistaking the sarcasm in his voice. It cut through his thick accent like a blade made of star metal.

"Of course we do," Taranis assured him. "Your unfortunate accident on the mountain grieves us . . ."

"Accident." Kazhak considered the word, chewing it as if it were meat. Then his lips curled; he did not like the taste. "No accident. Kelti broke own law of hospitality. Try to kill Kazhak."

The members of the council all began speaking at once, each disclaiming such a possibility. They built one elaborate statement atop another in an attempt to convince the Scythian the Kelti had never hurt a guest in the history of the people.

Kazhak folded his arms across his chest — carefully, for his tightly bound ribs were sore — and listened to them impassively. His dark eyes gazed beyond to some distant horizon. When their speech ran down of its own weight, he turned as if to go back into the lodge.

Taranis held out his hand. "Wait!"

"Why wait? Kazhak rest tonight, ride tomorrow. You not want us here, we go."

"But what about the swords?"

Kazhak waved his hand in a gesture of dismissal. "Swords not matter. Friends matter. Kazhak and Taranis were friends. No more. Kazhak will tell wherever he rides, Taranis of the Kelti cannot be trusted."

Taranis was dismayed. The whole affair had been bungled. His reputation would be permanently damaged if the nomadic Scythians spread stories about him throughout the lands beyond the Blue Mountains, lands crisscrossed by the traders.

"Wait, listen, I will prove that you are wrong," he pleaded. He turned to the man at his shoulder. "Go quickly to Goibban's forge and bring back the best of whatever he has; swords, spearheads, knives. Bring it here right now."

He turned back to the leader of the Scythians. "We will prove our good faith by giving you much more than we originally agreed upon. Is that not a sign of friendship? I give you my word, no further harm will come to you or your men in the territory of the Kelti, and when you leave your horses will stagger beneath our gifts."

Kazhak's face gave away nothing. "At dawn, we go."

Taranis became effusive. "Certainly, certainly, if that is what you wish. We will have the iron ready for you whenever you want to leave. In the meantime, we will prepare another feast, a feast for friends, and we will . . . ah . . . hold games to entertain you and your men. As we do for friends," he emphasized.

"Your priest will be there?" Kazhak's voice was harsh.

"No. No! Kernunnos will not join us thisnight." Taranis had no intention of feasting with the shapechanger, not after thisday's disaster.

Goibban, tight lipped and red faced, came from the forge with two apprentices. They carried finely crafted daggers, iron spearheads, and the sword Goibban had been preparing for the new chief, its polished bronze hilt inlaid with coral and amber. It pleased Taranis to see how beautiful the sword was; at least he could offer the best the tribe possessed.

At his direction, the apprentices laid the iron weapons at Kazhak's feet. "The Kelti request you take these as a small token of apology," Taranis said.

Goibban, who could expect no additional gold for this assortment of his best work, made a noise deep in his throat, and old Dunatis coughed to cover it up.

Kazhak examined the weapons by pushing them around with his foot. "Good things," he commented. "Better than first ones, is it so?"

Insulted again, Goibban answered haughtily, "All my work is equally good. The hilts of these are more decorated only because they are for the nobles of our tribe."

"Kazhak is noble of his tribe," the Scythian replied. "These knives, this sword, almost good enough for Kazhak. Almost," he added, and deliberately spat in the dirt.

Another silence ensued. Everyone waited while Kazhak considered. Then he permitted a very small smile on his lips only, in the manner of the shapechanger.

"Kazhak accepts," he said. "We take weapons, leave gold. But tomorrow we go." There was a guarded quality that had not been in his voice before. From it, Taranis knew that in spite of Kazhak's acceptance of the trade, things were irrevocably changed. The Scythians might feast with them, and, if he was very fortunate, they might not accuse him elsewhere of having attempted to kill their leader. But whatever tentative bonds had been forged between the two peoples were broken.

The council would be sure to point out to him that Toutorix, in his prime, would have handled the matter very differently.

From the Scythian gold hoard, Taranis carried a special piece back to his lodge as a gift for Sirona. It was a cat of solid gold, pinned to be worn as a brooch, exquisitely graceful and lifelike as it clawed at its own tail.

Sirona fingered the heavy piece. "It is strange that these savage men choose to take such beautiful things from the people they rob. I would not have expected them to have an eye for beauty."

"The Scythian Dasadas told me his people ordered that made as they have much goldwork made to their own requirements, by Hellene craftsmen. Gold has great significance to them."

"But where do they get the raw gold?"

"Ah, I suspect that begins as other articles they have stolen, and is melted down and reshaped. But you are right; they have quite a taste for craftsmanship in spite of their wild ways."

"Is it possible they are a people of many layers, like the Kelti?" Sirona suggested.

"No one is like the Kelti," Taranis said.

At the order of the tribe, games would be played during the remainder of the long summer twilight, in an effort to improve the Scythians' humor. Areas were quickly staked out for wrestling, a course was marked for a foot race, and targets were set up for spear and bow. The best athletes among the Kelti drew lots to determine which would compete with the Scythians.

Taranis himself was to fight with sword and shield as part of a team competition: he and two others against Kazhak's three men. The winner was to be the first side to draw a drop of blood from the other.

Sirona brought her husband his weapons, chanting in the traditional way as she presented them: "Your sword is sharp; your shield is polished. With my own teeth and the sweat from my breasts I have softened the leather of the shield strap. When you fight, fight well. If you die, die laughing."

The first race was run, seven laps around the commonground, and Vallanos won it handily, beating his Scythian opponent, Basl, by an impressive distance.

Watching from the sidelines, Kazhak commented, "Boy has legs like deer."

Epona was standing close to Taranis and the Scythians once

again, both in her capacity as hostess and because she did not intend to let Kazhak out of her sight before he left the village. Now she told him, "Living in the mountains makes us agile."

"Agile?" Kazhak stumbled over the word.

"Graceful," she simplified.

For the first time since his accident, Kazhak summoned a genuine smile. "Graceful, yes! Like Kelt girl, is it so? Move like running water?"

He chuckled. Epona blushed, pleased.

The games progressed to mock battles. Taranis and his three men fought the Scythians, and under the order of the chief, Kwelon allowed Aksinya to nick his arm and draw first blood. It was skillfully done, for the Kelti would never have forgiven a chief who took their victory from them, but even so the Scythians were suspicious. Kazhak's dark eyes flashed. "Do not make easy for Kazhak's men," he warned Taranis. "No more tricks."

"No tricks!" Taranis assured him. What was it about these Scythians that kept forcing him into dishonorable positions? Kernunnos was right after all; they were a menace.

But soon they would be gone, and trouble with them.

As the games progressed in difficulty the villagers crowded around, cheering their favorites, making extravagant wagers as men took turns lifting boulders or hurling large stones and comparing the distances. The Scyths did indeed hold their own, and Taranis granted them no further concessions. None could come close to them in the competition with bow and arrow, where their skills were awesome. The yelling of the crowd rose in volume as the contest produced an increasing rivalry in the participants, and soon there were injuries and lost tempers on both sides.

The brawny, pale-eyed Scythian named Dasadas proved to be exceptional at wrestling, putting down three mountain men in quick succession. This exceeded the bounds the Kelti were willing to concede, even to guests; and there were angry words and the beginning of a sullen undertone in the voice of the crowd.

The elders approached Taranis. "The wrestling victory is always ours," they reminded him. "If these strangers win it we are disgraced."

"Send for Goibban," Taranis said.

The smith was not in the mood to have further advantage taken of him, but he did not resist the authority of his chief. He approached the contest area naked, save for his brief plaid battle apron, and even in the gathering twilight the muscles were clearly visible beneath his smooth skin.

Epona looked at him coldly. She would not allow herself to think him beautiful, now.

The smith stepped to the center of the wrestling area to stand with Dasadas and Taranis. As referee, Taranis set forth the few rules governing the final contest of the day. He was determined to be fair beyond question, hoping to regain his reputation in some small measure before the Scythians rode away, carrying tales.

"Because Dasadas has already had three fights and the smith is fresh, I order that a handicap be placed upon Goibban," Taranis announced. "He will fight with one hand only; the other shall be belted to his side, and should he free it, he will at once be declared the loser."

Kazhak nodded. "Is fair. But do not bind the man, let him fight free. Dasadas can beat Kelt anyway, is it so?"

It was an act of courtesy matched by an act of courtesy, and the people applauded Kazhak. Only Goibban did not. He stood with his golden head down, quietly waiting for the signal to begin, and when he stepped forward to meet Dasadas he held his knife hand arm fixed against his side as if it were tied there.

Chapter 13

THE TWO MEN went into a fighting crouch, circling one another with bent knees, eyes staring, each waiting for that moment of hesitation or acquiescence in the other which would signal an opening. Dasadas saw it — or thought he saw it — in Goibban's face, and hurled himself onto his opponent like a lion leaping off a rock onto the back of a deer.

Goibban merely shrugged him off with an incredible heave of his body and stepped away. The smith turned, coming back into his crouch, arm still held against his side, weaving back and forth on the balls of his feet, waiting for the Scythian.

Dasadas grunted and leaped at him again.

Again the smith tossed him aside.

"Hunh," commented Kazhak, not smiling now. He stood next to Taranis; he had been offered a bench in deference to his injuries and refused it with scorn. His thumbs were hooked in his belt and he watched the wrestlers through his heavy black eyelashes. Epona glanced at him, but he was not thinking of her now.

Dasadas had learned his lesson; he attempted no third leap. This time he ducked his head and ran forward like a butting ram, intending to slam into the smith's belly and knock the wind out of him. Goibban did not move aside.

Sirona gave a little squeak and closed her eyes, then watched through parted fingers.

The army of pines marching up the mountainside beyond the palisade watched darkly, whispering.

The Scythian's head butted into Goibban's stomach with terrific force — and nothing happened. The smith did not even grunt.

Surprised, Dasadas forgot himself and straightened up, staring at his opponent.

Goibban's cup hand arm seized him.

It was all over in a few blinks of the eye. Goibban whirled his opponent around in spite of the mighty efforts Dasadas made to resist him, then hooked his cup hand arm behind the Scythian's chin and squeezed until the man's eyes bugged from their sockets. The other struggled to reach behind himself and grab the smith in some way, but his hands kept slipping off Goibban's sweaty skin. The crowd was yelling now, "Goibban! Goibban!" and the smith arched his back and flung the Scythian away from him. Dasadas hit the ground hard, too winded to roll and break his fall, and even as he gathered himself to get up he felt the foot of his opponent come down hard on his neck.

Looking toward Taranis, Goibban lifted his unused knife hand aloft in a clenched fist and the crowd went wild.

"Good fight," Kazhak admitted grudgingly.

Epona felt a thrill of pride for the Kelti. Everyone had been so obsessed by these horse riders they had forgotten the grandeur of their own people, but now Goibban had reminded them. And Kazhak was applauding with the rest. Epona looked from man to man, wondering.

Kazhak turned away from the wrestling area and saw her eyes on him. He smiled at her then, not the quick habitual grin intended to disarm strangers, but the slow smile reserved for brothers, for intimates of the spirit.

It felt to both of them as if they had reached out and touched.

Disconcerted, Kazhak moved off and lost himself in the press of men around him, trying to push away an inner disturbance unlike anything he had experienced before. The fast, hard life of The Horse, a man's life, beneath sun and stars, in clean wind, the tempo of the gallop, the slash of the sword, the sweet high singing of the arrow in pursuit of its prey — these things he understood. But to meet a woman's eyes again and again, and feel as if she had walked inside his head . . . it was an invasion and he resented it.

164

It was a unique experience and it tantalized him.

As the sky darkened the feasting fire was built up again, and the Kelti assembled to honor their guests once more. Kazhak would have preferred to be sleeping already, pillowed on his horse's neck, but first he must finish what he had begun. He gave a signal to Basl and the swarthy Scythian hurried away, soon to return with a bulky object wrapped in a blanket.

Kazhak had him drop it at the feet of Taranis. "The Scyth understand honor," he said. "Kazhak promise you feast on stag; now you feast on stag."

Basl stooped and unfolded the blanket, revealing the antlered deer that lay within, its heart stopped by his arrow. It was not a big buck, nothing like the stag Kazhak had thought to kill on the side of the mountain that morning. But it was sufficient to fulfill his pledge, and the Kelti appreciated the symmetry of the gesture.

If Kernunnos had been among them at that moment, he would have realized the pattern was wrenched irrevocably out of shape.

"Taranis and Kazhak even, is it so?" the Scythian inquired.

Taranis was sitting in the chief's place, dressed in his finest tartan and wearing a massive gold armband from the Scythian treasure. He smiled broadly at Kazhak, once more playing the genial host. "Yes, we are even," he affirmed. "Epona, bring us the feasting cup."

It was a long night. Sometime during it, after the feasting cup had gone around many times, Kazhak left the fire and sought his horse. His eyes were blurry with fatigue. He did not see that Epona had gotten there ahead of him, and was curled up in a ball a little distance away, sleeping with her face turned toward the horses and her bearskin robe for a blanket. The Scythians could not leave without her knowing it.

The next morning, Rigantona awoke with a sense of having drunk too much wine and having endured a bad night. She could still see all that gold gleaming on Sirona and Taranis. Her mouth tasted the way feet smelled. The flesh of her face felt thick. She swung her legs off the bedshelf and looked around the lodge. The carefully banked fire was still alive; the younger children were still sleeping on their beds. Both Okelos and Epona were missing.

Alator yawned and began the long journey toward being awake.

"Where is everybody?" she asked him, jerking him abruptly into thisday.

The little boy sat up, digging his fists into his eyes. "I heard Okelos go out a while ago. I don't know about Epona; I didn't see her come in lastnight at all. Maybe she went to watch the Scythians; everyone does."

Rigantona sniffed. She wanted the girl's help in the lodge this morning. She dressed and went out to find her. The first person she encountered was Sirona, still sporting the Scythian gold and a belly swelling with the son or daughter who would soon enlarge the chief's family.

"I hope you give birth to weasels," Rigantona murmured to her in passing.

"I wouldn't want to have children who looked so much like you," Sirona answered mockingly.

Epona was probably with the Scythians, as Alator had suggested. Playing hostess. The thought pleased Rigantona. Sirona, with her pretty face and her fertile belly, did not possess an unmarried daughter who was willing and trained in the arts of making the stranger welcome. And it was that same daughter who would join the *druii*, vastly increasing the prestige of her family. There was nothing Taranis and his vinegar-mouthed wife could do to prevent it. Hai!

Rigantona lost interest in retrieving her daughter. Let her stay with the Scythians; Rigantona was relieved that she herself no longer had to waste time and energy serving strangers. She would go to the squatting pit and then have a leisurely meal with her younger children. Perhaps even Okelos would stay busy elsewhere and not spoil the morning with his malcontent and tedious schemes. Perhaps this headache would go away if she could just lie down for a while.

As Rigantona was returning to her lodge, the Scythians were preparing to leave the village. Epona had been watching them since first light, hoping to get a chance to speak with Kazhak, but almost immediately a deputation composed of Taranis and the elders had arrived to make effusive farewells and supervise the packing of the iron onto the Scythian horses.

Kazhak was anxious to leave. He did not care to waste any precious daylight listening to these talkative people drone on and on. Hoping they would take the hint, he thrust his new sword — the

166

sword that would have belonged to Taranis — through his belt
and unhobbled his horse.

According to the tradition, *druii* came to wish the travelers safe
journey, but Kernunnos was not among them. Uiska shyly presented Kazhak and his men with filled waterskins, and Poel informed them he would sing a song about them to the children.

"You tell stories to small people?" Kazhak asked in surprise.

"Of course. It is the responsibility of the *druii* to instruct the
young in all those things they need to know and remember," Poel
explained. "Knowledge must be passed on. Do you not have
teachers for your children?"

Kazhak looked puzzled. "They watch. They learn, or they die,
is it not so?"

Poel was shocked. "All animals teach their young; our children
are our future! They must be properly shaped."

The Scythian argued, "They grow strong, ride well, fight good.
Is enough."

He was tired of dealing with these complicated Kelti. He hun-
gered for starry skies and open plains. Heedless of the pain in his
ribs he vaulted onto his horse and spun the animal on its haunches,
scattering loose dirt. "We go now!" he sang out, and joy made his
voice beautiful.

The gray stallion leaped forward, headed for the opening in the
palisade and the road beyond. The other Scythians followed gladly.

Epona began running then. If she was very quick, she could
intercept Kazhak where the trail almost doubled back on itself
along a pine spur. She was sure the Scythians would be heading
east, around the lake, rather than west to the Amber Road. The
horsemen would be going home.

Thisnight the moon would be full.

She ran harder than she ever had in her life, skimming over
the earth mother with the speed born of desperation. No one paid
any attention to her. The young were always running somewhere.

She took a short cut long familiar to the children, following a
narrow path past a solitary tree bent into the shape of a hump-
backed man by its own deformed spirit. Nematona had taught the
children to hang strips of bright cloth on the lower limbs of the

grotesque tree to encourage it to feel beautiful, so its spirit within might be reshaped. As Epona ran past she saw her own contribution of last sunseason, a wide strip of blue wool now faded by the elements.

Bow down! commanded the spirit within suddenly, breaking a long silence, but she would not take time to obey. She ran on.

The path wound through a scattering of boulders, the ribs of the earth mother thrusting through her flesh, and then Epona came out on a little knob of soil overlooking the trail and there were the Scythians, riding toward her.

She scrambled down the slope and stepped into the road, blocking their way. She had to act quickly, without thinking, or she might lose her nerve.

Kazhak held up his hand to signal a halt. His dark brows were drawn into a line across his forehead; he was not smiling.

"What is?" he asked suspiciously.

"I want you to take me with you," she told him, coming to stand at his knee.

Kazhak's brows swooped upward toward his peaked felt helmet. There seemed no end to the astonishment of these Kelti! "Is joke?" he asked uncertainly.

"I am not making a joke; I am very serious. Please, take me with you. I want to leave this village; I want to get as far away as I can before dark. There is nothing for me here anymore."

The Scythian shifted on his horse. His face revealed nothing. Unlike her people, he kept everything hidden behind those dark eyes.

"Why should Kazhak take you? You any good to Kazhak?"

At least he was considering the possibility. She recalled his comment about the Scythians' finding a woman they liked: "take and go." Her eyes sparkled, and she lifted one of her heavy braids for him to see. "The gold of the Kelti," she said. "It is yours if you take me with you."

To her surprise the Scythian laughed aloud. "You are not like other women," he told her. He turned to his companions and said something in their own tongue. It sounded very harsh to Epona's ears. The other men looked at her dubiously.

She listened for the spirit within, expecting it to tell her she was making a mistake, but it seemed to be silent. Or perhaps she could not hear it over the beating of her own heart.

168

After an exchange of conversation among the Scythians, Kazhak addressed her again. "We must go now," he said. "Not like this place. Too strange. Too . . ." At a loss for words he waved his hands in the air in a complex design, and Epona understood. "We go," he repeated. His eyes swept her body, from her head to her feet and back again. His legs clamped the stallion and it skittered on the stony trail.

"May be you be some good," Kazhak decided. He leaned forward and extended his hand toward her. "You come?"

She swallowed hard. "I come."

The strong hand clamped on her wrist and she felt herself jerked forward. There was a heave, a struggle, and then she was lying across the horse's withers in front of Kazhak, face down, her nose pressed against the stallion's shoulder. Kazhak kicked his mount, and the Scythians galloped away from the village of the Kelti.

They left behind a village buzzing like a disturbed hive of bees. Taranis was deeply concerned about the implications of Kazhak's threat, and even Sirona's loving reassurances could not convince him the Scythians would not blacken his reputation among the outsiders.

Some of the elders, harkening back to former times of invasion and battle, had begun to imagine hordes of Scythians riding into the Blue Mountains, raping and pillaging now that they had seen the wealth of the tribe with their own eyes.

The *druii*, under the guidance of Kernunnos, were striving to formulate rituals to protect the tribe from dangers only the chief priest could foresee.

Kernunnos stayed in the magic house, nursing his grievances. He knew Taranis blamed him for all that had gone wrong, and in his turn he blamed Taranis for shortsightedness and greed.

The weight and shape of the tribe was ever present in the consciousness of the chief priest. Waking or sleeping he was aware of it; he was an integral part of the whole, a finger to the hand. It moved around him, corporeal, and through him, incorporeal, and he had no life of his own that was not bound in service to the Kelti. The mood of the tribe was his. He vibrated with its ceaseless energy; he ached with pains tribespeople had felt in the past and would experience in the future. At times the massed emotions of the Kelti would override everything else and he would stand transfixed, listening to inner voices and striving to pick his

169

way through contradictory vibrations. Closing his eyes, lost to now, he existed in past and future.

On thisday he existed in agony, feeling what was to come.

"Everything is changing," he groaned aloud, his red-rimmed eyes glassy. "All that truly matters will be lost. Now we know so much; our place in thislife is secure, and we are in total harmony with the spirits. But we will rush to the new; we will abandon the pattern and lose our way. Aaaiii! for the people of the Kelti!"

Without feeling pain, he thrust his hands into his lodgefire and lifted out hot ashes to rub into his scalp and face, moaning in grief.

When the sun reached its midpoint in the heavens and Epona still had not returned, Rigantona got tired of waiting for her. But a casual inquiry could not locate her. Rigantona's temper soured.

The day passed and the night of the full moon approached. If Epona did not appear and go willingly to the *druii*, they would come for her. And how was Rigantona to explain?

At last, with a dry mouth and a painful drumbeat in her temples that she could not ask the *gutuiters* to cure, Rigantona went to the magic house herself to face what must be faced. She was Kelti, after all.

Acrid smoke issued from the priest's lodge. The black birds hooted at her. From the magic house came a rattling sound, like gourds filled with pebbles, and she could hear the *druii* chanting.

It took an act of will to force herself to enter.

The atmosphere was close and stifling hot from the big fire raging in the firepit. The air stank. For some reason, she recalled the words Epona had related, the words of the Scythian leader: "Living men should be under open sky."

Why was she thinking of that now?

A chant ended; the *druii* paused to sip water from the *hydria* and bring more wood for the fire. Kernunnos came to Rigantona, who was standing close to the door.

"Have you brought your daughter?" he asked, his voice hissing through his teeth.

There was no lying to one of the *druii*. "I cannot find her. No one has seen her in the village since early this morning, and I am very worried about her."

Kernunnos thrust his face into hers. "She has run away again, is that what you are telling me? That girl exhausts my patience, Rigantona. She is reckless and impulsive and I fear she squanders her gifts. She will be difficult to train to the priesthood because you have failed as a mother; you have not raised her to be sufficiently obedient."

Rigantona bristled. "I raised her to be strong and brave and unafraid of hard work. I did not know she was *drui* and would need other qualities."

"You should have realized there was always the possibility, woman! You are a fool, and I blame you for letting her slip through your fingers now. But she cannot go so far that I will be unable to find her, Rigantona." He smiled unpleasantly.

"I will leave you to it, then," the woman said, anxious to be out of the lodge.

His fingers closed on her shoulder, clawing the flesh. "Why so soon? Perhaps you could contribute to the magic, since your daughter is not available to us."

She went rigid. "My children are waiting for me, Kernunnos. I am needed elsewhere . . ."

"Your children are taking care of themselves. No *man* is waiting for you, Rigantona. Your bedshelf is cold.

"You have grown old and stringy, woman. You would be good food for a bear, but I think that is the only embrace that would welcome you now. Would you be willing to go as sacrifice to the Shaggy Man, Rigantona? With such a sacrifice I could make very strong magic." He leered at her, enjoying the fear in her eyes.

She pulled free of him and stumbled through the doorway. She heard his laugh behind her, blending into the cawing of the black birds.

When Rigantona had gone Kernunnos seemed to shrink within himself. Epona's defection was just one more bad omen. Could it be the spirits were displeased with him and he had failed to perceive it?

No, it could not be. A shapechanger must never begin to doubt himself, or his abilities would melt away like snow in spring. Everything could still be mended; he would find Epona and bring her back; he would counteract the influence of the horse people; he would care for the tribe.

At his order the chanting began anew.

Kernunnos crouched beside the lodgefire and reached out with his mind, searching for the essence of Epona. He thought he caught a thread of her, a glimpse, a sniff, and then she was gone, moving away from him with astonishing speed, moving even beyond the reach of hand and arm. Beyond the reach of everything but magic.

The shapechanger's lips curled back from his pointed eyeteeth. "I will bring her back," he vowed. "We cannot afford to lose her. What was promised me is mine."

PART TWO

The Sea of Grass

Chapter 14

THE HOOVES OF THE SCYTHIAN HORSES pounded the stony earth the way Goibban's hammer pounded the star metal. At first Epona merely lay like a sack of meal across the gray stallion's withers, content to be carried away, pleased to have taken charge of her own life.

That pleasure lasted only as long as she could ignore the increasing discomfort of her position. Each step the horse took jolted the breath out of her. Its bony withers threatened to slice through her torso and her midsection quickly became one vast bruise. She squirmed, seeking relief, but Kazhak's hand slammed down on her back.

"Be still," he commanded. "You bother horse."

He might put her down and leave her in the road, humiliatingly rejected again, her last chance at escaping the magic house lost due to her own weakness. She clenched her teeth and resolved to endure.

The horses followed the narrow trail single file, their feet occasionally slipping on the stones. In spite of her intentions, Epona could not help trying to make small adjustments to spare herself the increasing agony of her position. She managed to support some of her weight on her doubled arms but Kazhak immediately slapped her back a second time. "Listen, woman," he told her. "No move! We go fast, get clear of bad place."

175

She had thought she was as anxious to leave as the Scythians, yet she resented hearing her birthland dismissed as a "bad place." The thriving village, the beautiful Blue Mountains . . . not long ago she had thought she would never leave at all. How could this ignorant savage malign them so? She tried to twist around and look up at him, but this time his doubled fist clipped her smartly on the jaw and the earth spun away into some otherworld.

When she recovered consciousness the horses were no longer galloping as fast as possible on the mountainous footing, but had dropped back to a trot, an unbearably rough and jolting gait in which the gray stallion took the full concussion of his weight on his front legs, right up through his shoulders and into Epona's body.

She gasped in pain. She was being jarred until her bones threatened to come through her flesh; surely she already had a skull full of jelly and a belly full of blood. Even breathing was agony. How could the horses appear to float along so airily and yet feel like this?

She raised her head to snatch a quick glimpse of the passing landscape and realized she must have been unconscious for at least a rainbow's lifespan, for they were already quite a distance from the village. A groan was wrung from her at almost every step the horse took and Kazhak signaled to his men to pull up. He allowed Epona to slide limply down the horse's shoulder and onto the ground, where she vomited.

The Scythian dismounted and squatted beside her. He watched in silence as she retched, cuddling her bruised body with her arms, then he got up and walked a few paces away. He squatted to urinate in the manner of men accustomed to open plains.

His men waited on their horses, paying no attention to Epona. She had nothing to do with them, she was less to them than a burr in a horse's tail. She was a woman.

When she could draw a deep, shaky breath again, Kazhak came back for her. "We go now," he said. "It gets better," he added as a small comfort. He vaulted easily onto the gray stallion in spite of his injury and then moved one leg forward, indicating to Epona that she could swing up behind him and ride astride, holding onto him.

It would surely be more comfortable. It also seemed physically impossible to her at that moment.

She stood, half bent over, her arms around her midsection. "How?" she asked him.

He looked impatient, his mouth quirking in his dark beard. "Jump. Or stay."

She jumped.

The first time she got no higher than Kazhak's knee and her clutching fingers slipped helplessly off the haunches of the gray. Kazhak snorted with contempt. "Jump!" he commanded once more.

This time she succeeded in catching hold of Kazhak's belt, next to his bow and arrow case. Her legs kicked wildly and she heaved her weight upward, trying to ignore her bruises. Kazhak made no effort to help her. If she could not get on the horse he would take that as a sign that he was making a mistake and he would leave her.

After a frantic, painful struggle she found herself straddling the horse's haunches. The gray moved forward abruptly and she clamped her arms around Kazhak's middle — and his injured ribs. The Scythian uttered an angry epithet in his own language, but she understood what he meant well enough. She released him quickly and hooked her fingers in his belt instead.

Kazhak kicked the horse and it lifted into an easy canter.

Sitting upright was a little easier, though the gray's rump sloped beneath her and every stride made Epona feel she was in danger of sliding off. Kazhak let her squirm around without comment, allowing her to find her own way to ride now. Only once did he caution her: "Do not kick horse," when her legs inadvertently clamped on the stallion's sensitive flanks and the horse responded with a leap that nearly unseated her.

There was a rhythm to the canter. Up, forward, down; up, forward, down. It soon became pleasant. The broad warm rump felt good beneath her. The pounding was diminished, cushioned by the horse's muscles and the springiness of his hindquarter joints, but Epona still had an aching belly and a sore jaw where Kazhak had hit her.

Her discomfort seemed unimportant as she realized the distance they had already come. The ridden horse was a marvel, diminishing space.

The sun was high overhead, flooding the mountains with clear light.

177

They rode on and on. Time passed; she could tell by the angle of the sun and the way the shadows changed. Still they rode; climbing, descending, making their way through steep terrain. The light became less clear, more golden. It seemed they had been riding forever. Usually the horses were forced to walk, with occasional opportunities for an ambling trot. There were few stretches where the footing was safe enough for canter, and the canter never speeded up into a gallop. They had only galloped until they were clear of the vicinity of the village. The changes in pace refreshed Epona briefly, as they did the horses, but eventually she passed the point of exhaustion and still the Scythians rode on. And on and on.

The light melted into blue shadows. Surely, she thought, the men would stop soon and make camp. She was desperately thirsty and began thinking of the filled waterbags. "When will we camp?" she asked Kazhak. "If not soon, can we stop for a drink now anyway?"

"You want water already?" he asked in surprise.

"We haven't had any all day," she protested. Her voice was a dry whisper blowing on the wind.

"Is so," he agreed, and rode on.

"I am thirsty!"

"Gets better," he commented over his shoulder, but he did not reach for a waterbag.

The horses speeded up their trot on a stretch of trail between two peaks. Epona was bouncing as well as miserable with thirst. Beside her, the other men rode with impassive faces turned toward the east.

"Aren't you ever going to stop?" she gasped into Kazhak's shoulder. "Don't you get tired? Don't you get thirsty?"

"Kazhak is Scyth. Is foolish drink too much; you will learn. Wasteful."

"But there is plenty of water all around us, you wouldn't be wasting it. We can refill the waterskins anywhere. See, over there?" She risked her precarious balance to remove one hand from Kazhak's belt and point to a narrow waterfall tumbling down the face of dark rocks, a silver thread sparkling and inviting.

Kazhak and his men trotted their horses past the water, oblivious.

"Ignore thirst," he advised Epona. "Then it loses power over

178

you. On Sea of Grass is many times long distance to water, you drink only what you need. You learn: need and want not the same."

She could not believe he was serious. What sort of people would deny themselves water when it was readily available? Water was all around them, cascading off the rocks, squeezed from the earth by the pressure of its own weight. It collected in moss-rimmed pools, it rushed down to the rivers, it beckoned and tantalized everywhere. More water than anyone could ever drink. And the Scythians insisted on saving it.

Moisture her body could not spare was leaking out of her eyes and nose. She sniffled. Hearing her, Kazhak growled, "Kazhak heard Kelti had much courage. But you weak as milk. Kazhak give you away, sell you as slave to the Thracians."

From the same well that held her tears, anger rose. It held her sore bones together and lifted her aching chin. "I won't drink until you do," she told him, forcing the words out of her dry mouth. "I won't drink until *after* you do."

Kazhak chuckled. "Is so. You woman; women drink after horses, after men. You drink last."

They rode on.

A cold wind sprang up in the wake of the setting sun and Epona was thankful for her bearskin cloak. She had layered her favorite clothing on her body; that was all the property she brought with her. Behind her she left the riches of the Kelti, the things you can count and carry.

The rising moon was an artisan, sheathing the rock surfaces with silver. The main trail turned southward and the Scythians abandoned it, continuing to travel east, picking their way along a narrow thread of animal tracks, walking their horses in the gathering darkness.

Epona looked up. *Night of the full moon.*

There would be chanting in the magic house thisnight, and blue smoke would hang heavy on the air. Kernunnos would be angry, but the horses, the wonderful horses, had saved her from him. The lovely swift horses had surely taken her beyond even the shapechanger's reach by now.

She rode in a daze, no longer concentrating on her pain, not thinking about her parched and thickened tongue. There was only the horse and the night and the moon, the warmth beneath her

179

buttocks, the hard leather of Kazhak's belt, the rhythm of the animal. The rhythm . . .

It stopped. She felt irrational anger. As long as nothing changed she was learning to endure, to float free, somehow separate from her physical discomfort, but the slightest change restored her to a sore and aching body.

"Camp here," Kazhak announced. "Get off."

She tried, but her body refused to obey her. Her legs had been pulled apart for a whole day with the horse between them, and they were in revolt. It took more strength than she had known she possessed to slide one of them back, over the horse's tail. When she relinquished her hold on Kazhak she tumbled to the earth. Her feet did not feel the solid ground; her legs were nerveless and buckled beneath her. She found herself sitting in a heap almost under the gray stallion, who turned his head and looked at her with visible surprise.

Kazhak laughed, a warm rich sound rumbling up from his belly. "First time ride," he commented, vastly amused. He did not offer to help her up, just left her to scramble to her feet as best she could while keeping a wary eye on the stallion. The horse flared his nostrils and blew softly at her but did not offer to kick, and her gratitude went out to him.

The Scythians had chosen a small grove of pines for a campsite. The earth was deeply cushioned with fragrant needles, and the area was well back from the minimal trail they had been following. But the Scythians did not appear to be concerned about roads and trails; they consulted together, pointing to the stars, and seemed satisfied with their location and progress.

Before doing anything else they removed their saddles and packs from the horses, and the animals immediately lay down and rolled, scratching their backs with grunts of satisfaction, legs flailing in the air. Then Dasadas gave each horse a drink from one of the waterskins before passing the container to the other Scythians.

Epona crouched alone, wrapped in her bearskin and her exhaustion, watching them through dull eyes.

When all of the men had drunk — sparingly — they relinquished the waterskin to her. It seemed she had not even taken enough to dampen her parched throat before Kazhak took it away from her. He said sternly, "Do not bloat belly with too much water at one time."

She hated him.

They built no fire. Aksinya took dried meat from his pack and apportioned it among the men. They ate, talking together in monosyllables and ignoring Epona. When they had had all they wanted, Kazhak held up a piece of stringy-looking dark meat and motioned to Epona. "You eat now, is it so?"

She glared at him. She could not imagine being hungry. Her entire body was one big bruise, much too sore for such a complicated muscular effort as chewing and swallowing. But she knew she had to eat; she would need the strength. She tried to stand up and walk over to him. To her embarrassment, she could only walk spraddle-legged, like a newborn calf, and he laughed again.

The other men paid no attention to her, and for once she was glad.

The meat was dry and tasteless. She chewed it with a mouth devoid of saliva and almost choked when she tried to swallow, but she managed to choke some of the stuff down.

Surely nextday would be better.

Their scant meal completed, the Scythians prepared to sleep. Watching them, Epona expected they would make good use of the abundant pine needles to cushion their beds, and perhaps unpack additional blankets for warmth. In the village of the Kelti it was customary to have comfortable sleeping arrangements.

The Scythians felt no such need. When they were ready to sleep they signaled their horses and the animals simply lay down where they stood. Each man stretched himself beside his animal, pillowed his head on its neck, and closed his eyes. With neither cushion nor extra covering the Scythians were soon snoring, except for Basl, who took the first watch.

Epona had at least expected Kazhak would make some suggestion as to where and how she should sleep, under the circumstances, but he was the first one to put his head on his horse and the first one to snore. It had been a long day for an injured man.

She sat alone on the bare ground and wondered what to do. Aching in every bone and muscle, at last she crawled around on hands and knees and accumulated a pile of pine needles to make a bed for herself. Burrowing into them, she pulled the bearskin cloak over her and fell into a sleep so sodden and heavy nothing could break through it.

Before dawn she gradually became aware of voices, sounds, demands, intruding on her rest, but she pushed them away and sank back into the enveloping blackness.

Then Kazhak was nudging her with his toe, and the sky beyond him was gray with the advance of first light. "We go," he told her.

The second day was a repetition of the first. If it had been hard to get on the horse the first time, it was impossible now. Epona could not bring her knees together and her pelvic bones seemed to have punched through her skin. Kazhak, already mounted, looked down at her from the gray stallion. "Jump."

"Yes," she said as firmly as she could, and forced herself to her maximum effort. Kazhak caught her by the shoulder and heaved. Her body felt as if it were being wrenched apart, and her bones threatened to pull free from her flesh; then she was high enough to swing her leg over the horse. If she could swing her leg at all.

Somehow she did it, biting her lip to keep from crying out. She would not let him see her defeated.

The horses moved out at a smart trot.

Now Epona was certain she would die, and prayed to whatever spirits might be listening to make it happen soon, before the stallion took another step. She was not in favor with the spirits, however. She lived, and the stallion kept on trotting.

At first the day was warm and sunny, and if she had not been so uncomfortable she might have enjoyed watching the landscape change as they moved eastward through the mountains. The peaks had unfamiliar profiles; the vegetation took on a different aspect, with shapes and hues she had not seen before. But Epona could not look at scenery; her misery required all her attention.

Sometime late in the morning the weather changed and gray clouds gathered, reflecting the girl's frame of mind. Upon awakening, the Scythians had eaten a scanty meal of their tasteless meat and drunk a few sips of water before allowing Epona to do the same, and thirst had soon returned to haunt her. In addition, there was a gnawing in her stomach that might have been hunger or a revolt against the almost inedible meat with which she had broken her fast — she could not tell and did not care. She just felt awful.

The Scythians splashed through a stream, pausing to allow the horses to drink but taking no water themselves, then cantered up a steep slope. Epona felt the gray's haunches working beneath her like a bellows. As they topped the rise the sun broke through a bank of cloud, gilding a small stand of birch trees, and somewhere a bird sang.

For the first time in what seemed an eternity, Epona's attention was drawn to something beyond herself. She saw the beauty of the glade through which they rode; she let herself enjoy the sweet, tender piping of the bird. The horses slowed to a walk, and she realized with surprise that some of the soreness had worked itself out of her body. She drew a deep breath and sat up a little straighter. Her buttocks still hurt dreadfully, but the lessening of pain was a pleasure in itself.

If it does not get worse than this, she thought, *I can stand it. I will stand it. I chose to do this.*

The day passed uneventfully. The Scythians rode without rest, pausing only rarely to relieve themselves, and seemed to be avoiding any inhabited areas.

When the sun was a dull red, low in the western sky, they spotted a pair of hawks circling above them and Aksinya reached for his bow.

"Those are hawks!" Epona protested.

"Those are meat," Kazhak corrected her.

"But no one eats hawks."

"We do. People who will not eat this, will not eat that, those people go hungry sometime. Scyth not go hungry."

At least that meant they would build a fire, and she would have the familiar company of the fire spirit while they cooked the fresh meat. She began to imagine hot, tender food, though a hawk was unlikely to be tender. Aksinya brought one down with one shot and slung it from a thong tied to his saddle. Looking at the rumpled, floppy body, Epona found it hard to equate with the sharp pure lines of the hawk in flight. How empty the flesh seemed when the spirit within had fled.

She wondered if Aksinya had made proper petition to the hawk's spirit before shooting.

Looking ahead to a hot meal, she rode dreamily, letting her thoughts wander. Then, quick as a flash of starfire, something cut across the vision in her mind's eye and was gone again. It happened so fast she did not get a good look at it, but she felt uneasy. It was like an object glimpsed over one's shoulder, or just disappearing around a corner.

183

There it was again! Superimposed over the landscape around her, clear and yet enveloped in blue haze, was a face . . . a narrow face, with . . . yellow eyes . . .

She jerked upright, her fingers closing convulsively on Kazhak's belt.

"What is?" asked the Scythian.

"I thought . . . nothing. It's nothing."

I was dreaming, she told herself. *Because I am so tired.*

But after that she forced her eyes to stay open and looked very hard at the reassuring solidity of rocks and trees.

When they stopped for the night it was in a forest clearing, surrounded by deciduous trees unfamiliar to Epona. Aksinya used firestones to make a fire, sloppily built from a tangle of twigs. There was no chant to invoke the spirit. Then he ran a branch through the hawk and roasted it over the fire. He only halfway plucked the bird first, and the singeing feathers smelled terrible. Epona lost what appetite she had.

The men tore the bird in half with their hands and ate it like hungry dogs. When Kazhak had finished he passed his share of the carcass to her. It smelled rank. She turned her face away from it.

Kazhak was insulted. "Kazhak left liver," he pointed out. "You eat."

The liver was always a choice morsel; leaving it for her was a gesture of generosity she could hardly refuse. She picked the meat out of the body cavity and ate it. It was almost raw, but it tasted of blood and life, and after she swallowed it she dug some more shreds of meat from the small carcass and ate them, too.

Kazhak grinned. "You see? Gets better, is it so?"

That night Kazhak took the first watch. A few coals still glowed in the remains of the fire, casting a feeble light, though no one had bothered to bank the fire to provide warmth for the night. Standing beside it Kazhak stripped the clothes from his upper body and examined the binding around his ribs.

Epona watched him through her eyelashes. When he took off his tunic his body was covered with pictures.

She gasped aloud.

He turned toward her. "What is?"

She pointed at his torso. A wavy black line . . . a realistic snake! . . . curled around his shoulder and vanished into the grimy bandages on his chest. On his other arm a horned sheep pranced.

Kazhak looked down at himself, smiling. "Is tattoo," he explained. "Is beautiful, is it so?" He began pulling away the bandages, exposing a mat of curly dark hair on his chest, the nest from which the painted snake emerged.

"How can you do that to your body? You have to live in that body!" Epona said in a shocked voice.

"Kazhak *is* this body," he answered. "Tattoo make body stronger and better." He pulled away more wrapping, turning as he did so to give her a view of his back, where parts of horses and cats and winged creatures melted into one another as the shapechanger . . .

No! She would not let herself think of the shapechanger.

She leaned forward to get a better look at the tattoos.

"How do they do that?" she asked, intrigued in spite of herself.

Her interest pleased Kazhak. "Horse people have artists, make man beautiful. Prick skin, rub in soot. Is very fine art."

Perhaps it is, she thought, *according to the Scythian concept of beauty.* It was a person's obligation to take the best possible care of the body housing the spirit, but there was probably nothing wrong with ornamenting that body, as Goibban ornamented the hilts of the weapons he made. It was not the abuse of self that eating unhealthy food was, chewing diseased meat or vegetables picked so long ago the essential spirit had departed.

Kazhak scratched his liberated body; those strips of cloth had caused a mighty itching. He had worn them long enough, he thought. His gaze fell on Epona's arm, similarly wrapped. "You take off too?" he inquired.

She had almost forgotten. Was the bone healed? The *gutuiters* would have come to her at the right time, removed the braced rods and wrappings, offered the small sacrifice . . . but there were no *gutuiters* here.

She slowly unwrapped the bandages herself. Kazhak came to stand beside her, peering down with interest. When the arm was free she held it up and they both looked at it. The flesh was shrunken from its long confinement, but the limb was straight.

"Is good," Kazhak commented.

He threw back his head and drank the air like sweet water. "Aaahhh . . ." He looked at Epona again, with a new expression in his eyes. "You sleep?"

"Yes. I'm very tired." She began searching for dry leaves to make a bed for herself, but Kazhak's hand closed on her wrist. "Kazhak share," he said.

He whistled to his horse and the obedient stallion knelt on the ground, then stretched flat on its side. Kazhak indicated the silvery neck with a sweep of his hand.

She understood. He was offering to let her pillow her head on his horse, with him. She did not realize what an unusual offer this represented until she heard Dasadas mutter something in a clearly incredulous tone to Basl.

Kazhak's voice lashed out at them, and they fell silent, their backs turned toward their leader and the girl.

Epona looked at the recumbent horse.

She had been so reckless she had not allowed herself to think things through to their ultimate consequence. All she had thought of was escaping Kernunnos, the family that had let her down, the smith who had not wanted her enough. She saw now, with painful clarity, just what she had done.

She had offered a trade to Kazhak and he was ready to claim his share of the exchange.

Chapter 15

THE GRAY STALLION lay on its side, waiting. Its long neck was stretched on the earth. She took a half step toward it and it rolled its eye at her but did not move.

"Is good," Kazhak prompted. "Warm to sleep."

Still she hesitated.

"Kazhak come when Dasadas takes second watch," the Scythian told her. "You sleep now, wake later."

She had a brief reprieve, then; the Scythian would not lie with her until Dasadas took his turn at guard duty. Gathering her cloak around her, Epona knelt down by the stallion's head. The smell of the bear fur made the horse snort and she jumped up again, expecting the animal to scramble to its feet.

Kazhak spoke to the horse in the Scythian language with something like love in his voice; a tenderness she had not heard before. It surprised the girl and pleased her. He must feel as she did about the animals, though he did not show it openly. They were not all as hard as they seemed, these Scythians.

The obedient stallion lay immobile and Epona lay down beside it. She curled herself into as small a ball as her stiff, sore body would permit and rested her head on the horse's neck.

It was warm, silky haired, and comfortable.

That was the last thing she knew until she felt Kazhak's heavy body settle itself beside her. He slapped her haunch as if she were one of the horses.

"Wake up," he commanded. She opened her eyes, almost expecting morning, but it was not morning. It was a dark night; clouds blanketed the stars and wrapped the cold moon in gray fleece, diffusing her light.

Kazhak's hand moved over Epona's body, seeking openings in her clothing.

You are Kelti, the spirit within reminded her. *You made a bargain.*

She did not move, hoping he would think she was still asleep. Then she realized that would make no difference to the Scythian. He was thinking of himself, not her. His body was ready. She could feel his erect penis digging into her thigh as his fingers worked their way to her bare flesh.

His hands were icy cold on her naked skin, and when they touched her she jumped. Without meaning to, she slammed one elbow into his ribs, hard. The Scythian grunted in pain. He pulled away from her and sat up, hugging himself. He said nothing, however, and she curled up beneath her bearskin and wondered what he would do to her.

When the stab of pain eased he looked down at her. All he could see of her face was a small, pale oval, lost in dark shadows. He had been thinking of her as a woman but now he was reminded that she was little more than a child, in spite of the tall stature of the Kelti. She had hurt him, but he did not think she had done it intentionally. Perhaps she was frightened. She had seemed frightened when she stopped them on the road. Women were always afraid of something. They were timid and weak, like antelope. None of them would have the effrontery to deliberately hurt a man.

But his ribs were hurting him and it was uncomfortable to draw a deep breath. He moved around a little, testing his limits, then made a decision. The woman would wait; she would be available whenever he wanted her. She was his now and until he tired of her, so there was no hurry. Better to get some sleep and let his body finish healing, because they still had a long way to ride. A very long way.

Saying nothing to Epona, because there was no reason to discuss any of this with her — a woman, only — he turned over and tried to find a comfortable position in which to spend what remained of the night.

188

Epona lay wide-eyed on the horse's neck and waited for the dawn. She had never felt so alone.

Some time after Dasadas surrendered the watch to Basl, she reached out with tentative fingers and stroked the stallion's neck, scratching that itchy place common to all horses, just behind the jaw. The stallion came instantly awake; she could feel it. But he did not move. She caressed the soft flesh between his jawbones and then smoothed her palm across his broad, flat jowl.

The stallion sighed with pleasure.

Epona closed her eyes and when she opened them again it was morning and the Scythians were breaking camp.

The dawn was pink and blue and gold, the air so sharp it sliced down the throat and burned into the chest. The stillness rang in their ears like bells. The horses' breath formed small clouds, and Epona blew her own in front of her so she could watch her essence smoking on the air, briefly tangible.

Kazhak said nothing about the events of the night. He said nothing at all to her except, "We go."

Looking down as they rode, Epona noticed the color of the soil was different here, darker. The air smelled and tasted different, too, and the birdsongs she heard were not birdsongs she knew. The trees through which they rode felt as if they contained unfamiliar spirits. Not necessarily unfriendly, just . . . different. Days passed, and the mountains diminished.

They moved into a range of rounded hills, leaving the thrust of the high peaks behind them. The land opened out into a broad valley of lush grass. On the far side of the valley was the unmistakable dark slash of a road.

Kazhak and his men drew rein, sitting silently on their horses while they gazed up and down the road. They advanced toward it cautiously and dismounted. They squatted together to examine the wagon tracks and hoof prints on the earth.

As they talked, Epona made out the name of one of the tribes of the people, the Boii, and saw Kazhak frown briefly. Then he grinned and mounted the stallion again.

They followed the road for a time without seeing anyone, although twice Epona glimpsed distant spirals of smoke that must have come from lodgefires. The land beside the road settled itself into occasional hollows and low-lying areas, and a few clumps of willow were visible, their soft green darkening now as sunseason drew to a close. The breeze from the southeast carried the smell of water, and Epona and the stallion sniffed it at the same time, noses wrinkling.

"River," Kazhak commented.

It was indeed a river. All her life Epona had heard of the rivers to the north of the Blue Mountains, and imagined them as larger versions of mountain streams, boisterous and tumbling, but this was a serene, winding waterway, fringed with reeds.

"I never imagined rivers were this big," she said aloud.

Kazhak chuckled. "Is not big river. We follow, Kazhak show you big river, father river. Is it so?"

Big river. If not like this, what must a big river be like? A moving lake? She wished Mahka were with her, to talk about it.

The Scythians followed the riverbank now, preferring it to the more open and vulnerable roadway. They paused once to shoot a roebuck that bolted from the undergrowth quite near them, and Basl skillfully gutted the animal and slung it across his horse's shoulders.

"Better than hawk," Kazhak promised Epona.

The hilly pastures and rolling meadows of this new region were silty-soiled and fertile. Fields of grain under cultivation nodded their harvest-ready seedheads only a few paces beyond the riverbank. The land here had a gentler look than in the Blue Mountains; it had long been tamed to the will of man.

Successive generations had worked the soil to the point of exhaustion and moved on, leaving the earth mother to restore her own fertility through the growth of weed and tree. New settlers had slashed and burned these woods and planted their crops in the freshened earth, re-establishing the partnership. Since before the memory of man, this region had been rich in fruit and grain.

The river swung almost due south in a wide arc and the Scythians followed it, seeming more relaxed than they had in the high mountains. This was more familiar territory to them. On the eastern shore of the river the land sloped upward, forming a raised bank. They pointed out to one another the hill fort crowning the promontory and surrounded by a log palisade.

Kazhak motioned his men to a halt.

"Who lives there?" Epona asked him.

They were in natural cover, a copse of young birch trees that effectively screened them from the view of anyone across the river.

Just downstream they could see a shallow area, suitable for fording.

"Whose fort is that?" Epona repeated to Kazhak. "Are they
Boii?"

The gate in the palisade was open. Beyond the fort stretched a
golden band where fields of grain were ripening on a gentle slope,
and Kazhak's keen eyes saw men moving through the grain, their
arms swinging. Not all the figures were male; some of them had
the rounded contours of women.

The village was unprotected, then, all its able-bodied adults
busy with an early harvest.

Epona strained to follow his gaze but saw only dark specks in
the distant fields. She could not tell if they were of the people,
and Kazhak did not seem inclined to identify them by tribe.

"Stupid," he commented. "Build big wall to guard place against
warriors, but warriors no come. They forget. Go out, leave gate
open. Stupid, these people. We teach."

He grinned in his dark beard, though she could not see it.
"Hold on," he advised, and kicked the horse.

The Scythians splashed through the shallows and galloped up
the incline to the temptingly open gates of the log palisade.

There was one sentry, a tousled fellow in a blue tunic who had
been occupying himself by playing on a reed pipe as he sat on a
log bench in the sun. When he saw the horsemen starting across
the river he stood up to shout a warning, but even before his
words could ride the wind Kazhak had launched one of his deadly
arrows with its three-edged head. The projectile sang through the
air as surely as if it had eyes to see the way, finding its bed in the
sentry's throat and silencing him in mid-cry.

The horses raced up the slope and through the open gate.

Everything happened so fast Epona had only a blurred impression of the action. The village did belong to a tribe of the people,
that was obvious, but they were not Boii. Their clothes were dyed
with shades the Boii did not use and they wore their hair in a
subtly different style. The fortified village sheltered only a few
families. Epona noticed, pityingly, that they did not even possess
a forge.

The handful of folk remaining within the palisade were tall and
fair, and very frightened at the approach of the Scythians. Old-
sters and children, the best resistance they could offer was a fee-

ble one. Led by Kazhak, the riders pounded through the community and drew rein before the largest lodge. Basl and Aksinya leaped from their animals and ran inside. There were screams and the sounds of struggle, then the two men emerged carrying a copper pot into which they had thrown the riches of the household. An elderly woman ran after them, helpless and outraged.

Basl held up the pot so Kazhak could take his pick of the ornaments within it, mostly bits of copper and bronze, with a few pieces of silver jewelry and a long string of Baltik amber beads. Kazhak took the beads and waved the rest aside. His three men quickly divided the loot among themselves, fending off the villagers almost good-naturedly.

The Scythians swung aboard their horses and galloped for the gate, leaving little damage behind them aside from the looting and the wounded pride — and the dead sentry, his pipe still clutched in his hand.

Kazhak was laughing. "We teach good," he told Epona.

They galloped toward the grainfield.

Epona was uncertain how she felt about the raid. One of the people had been killed — as a man would want to die, in battle, of a sort — so he would probably receive a reward in his nextlife. Aside from that no harm had been done. And it had been exciting. Very exciting.

The red, angry faces of the villagers, their futile gestures, the way Kazhak laughed when he tossed the string of amber beads over his shoulder to Epona, trusting her to catch them . . .

Epona grinned like the Scythian, feeling the wind of their passage dry her bared teeth.

Then the raid took on a new coloration.

They galloped down on the unsuspecting farmers in their field, loosing a rain of arrows ahead of them. Many fell; Epona saw them drop and die. Yellow-haired, red-haired; members of the people. They were not warriors, they had no weapons available but the tools for harvesting, and the death they met was not a warrior's death. They shrieked in pain and died in blood and it was an ugly transition.

Epona closed her eyes and buried her face against Kazhak's shoulder blades, wondering what she should do. Get off and fight with her people? But the Scythians were her people now — and besides, they would undoubtedly kill her if she tried such a thing, and it would be a sacrifice to no purpose. She would have thrown away thislife in defense of the right to exist of persons she did not even know.

It is better to die fighting for freedom than to live without it, commented the spirit within, but it did not insist she get off the horse.

The defenders were trying to regroup, making what weapons they could of their scythes and the knives in their belts. Hunting knives, not battle swords. *Perhaps Kazhak is right,* Epona thought briefly. *They need teaching; even the Kelti, safe in their mountains, always keep swords close to hand. It is a dangerous world, thisworld, and a person dishonors himself by neglecting to guard his spark of life.*

The farmers came at them now, waving their pitiful weapons and screaming a warcry. To Epona's surprise, the Scythians appeared intimidated. They whirled their horses and galloped away, and she thought the uneven contest was over; she thought the horsemen were unwilling to fight such poorly armed men. But then the Scythians strung arrows to their bows and turned in the saddle, shooting back over their horses' rumps with deadly accuracy, and the farmers fell and died, writhing in pain.

The Scythians continued to gallop eastward, no longer looking back, but Epona looked back, and saw.

"Why did you kill them?" she shouted in Kazhak's ear. "You didn't even rob them!"

"Nothing worth taking," he told her. "Farmers and women, even heads no good to us."

"Then why?"

"Why not?"

The horses thundered on.

Epona held to the back of his belt with white-knuckled hands, and the vision of the dead people lying in the midst of their bountiful harvest, the fruit of their labors they thought would keep them safe through the coming winter, haunted her. When she closed her eyes it was on the inside of her eyelids; she could not keep from seeing it.

My people, she thought. *I should have done something.*

193

The horses worked their way ever eastward, following river valleys through varying gradations of mountains and hills, and Epona rode silently, feeling guilty. It was a new and unpleasant experience for her.

When they camped for the night she fell into an exhausted sleep immediately, her head pillowed on the stallion's neck. As before, Kazhak took the first watch — the Scythians were wary and always expected trouble — but this time when he came to rest he did not attempt to awaken her. He was embarrassed that his full strength had not returned since his injury; he did not want to lose face again by having the woman hit him and temporarily incapacitate him during their struggles — if she struggled. Hard to know. Strange Kelti woman.

He would take her later, when the injury no longer bothered him.

He sat on the ground during his watch and looked with brooding eyes at the stars. He thought of the dead brothers who had begun this trip westward with him with such great expectations, full of life and the lust for adventure, the hunger to see new grasslands and take new loot, only to fall to the swords and spears of men who were fighting for their own toehold on place and prosperity.

He must be careful to return his remaining comrades alive to the Sea of Grass. It would be a shameful thing for a Prince of the Horse to lose all his men at one time; the other men might say he was not a good warrior.

He thought about these things, not about the yellow-haired girl who lay sleeping behind him.

Epona's sleep, heavy at first, gradually fragmented into dreams. Dreams of smoke swirling, and . . . unnamed menace, accompanied by chanting . . . dreams of slaughter in a golden field.

She awoke without feeling rested. Her eyes were full of grit.

They ate a scanty meal and were riding again before the sun had cleared the rim of the world.

There was a new scent on the wind, wet and muddy, heavier than that of a clear, fast-running stream. The soil beneath the horses' hooves changed again, growing deeper, and Epona could feel the gray stallion tiring from the greater effort required to pull his feet out of mucky earth.

"Too many riders on horse," Kazhak said. "You walk now."

Feeling lessened in status, she paced resentfully at the horse's shoulder. He, too, was flaring his nostrils at the changed smell of the wind.

"Father river ahead," Kazhak said. Epona did not answer; she was in no mood to talk to the Scythian, not after the events of lastday, though his amber beads still hung round her neck, forgotten. She had no wish to make pleasant conversation with a man who had killed her people unnecessarily, with no respect for their spirits and no dignity allowed to their dying.

The surface of a wide river glinted ahead of them like a band of polished metal. Father river. Epona looked toward it with interest. How Uiska would have enjoyed this sight, the chance to commune with such a powerful spirit! The river dominated the landscape as they approached, winding serenely through banks of rich brown soil, embraced fondly by crowding vegetation.

The river was too mighty to go unrecognized. "What is the name of the father river?" Epona was forced to ask Kazhak.

"Is called Duna. Is said to rise in territory of your race."

Duna. In the language of the people, Danuba. Rigantona had been born on the upper reaches of the Danuba. Epona experienced a vivid flash of the sights and scents of home, the lodgefire glowing golden on the log walls, her mother's loom in its corner, symbol of stability. The back of her throat ached with sudden pain.

"Duna flows through many lands," Kazhak was explaining. "Better than road. Man follow Duna, can go anywhere worth going. That way, some days, is big settlement and trading center of your people, they call it Ak-Ink." He waved his hand in a broad arc that might have indicated any direction.

"Abundant water," Epona translated.

"Is so," Kazhak affirmed. "Much water everywhere Duna flows. People build little boats, build settlements, dig in dirt. Too many people. We go around, not see."

Epona was disappointed at missing the opportunity to visit Ak-Ink, well known as far as the Blue Mountains, but she was thankful the community would be spared the attentions of the Scythians.

Slaughterers of my people she thought, *and not in fair battle. Yet these are my people too, now.*

The lesser river they had been following flowed into the Danuba, Kazhak's Duna, and was swallowed up as a little child disappears in the embrace of a mighty parent. The party of horsemen followed the bank for a long distance before they found a place safe for fording.

As Kazhak had explained, the Scythians used rivers for roadways as confidently as the people of the Kelti used trails with notched trees for directional markers. The Duna wound its way down toward the lowlands, its banks usually offering easy riding. As the footing firmed again Epona was allowed to ride and walk alternately. She wondered why Kazhak had not made her walk in the mountains, where the way was so difficult for horses — except speed had been all important then.

Escaping the shapechanger.

Epona intended to maintain an angry silence indefinitely as a tribute to the dead, but she was of the Kelti, and used to the sound of conversation. The close-mouthed Scythians were starving her ears, so at last she asked Kazhak, "Where does the Danuba . . . the Duna . . . go? What is its outlet?"

"The sea of Kazhak's people, the Black Sea," the Scythian replied. He spoke proudly, as the Hellenes boasted of the great seas at the center of the world, the famed blue waters that embraced their own lands. "Duna flows east, then south, but then east again, to the sea. Father river very wise; returns to the rising sun. Kelti not know about Duna? Stupid. Duna most important river anywhere."

Epona's anger returned fullblown. This savage, this wanton killer who had unhoused the spirits of her people for no good reason, *dared* to call the Kelti stupid! She balled her fists and choked back furious words, stalking beside the stallion in a rage so palpable the horse rolled his eyes and edged away from her.

Kazhak was aware of her mood too, but he ignored it. She was only a woman.

After riding for a long time in silence, however, it was the Scythian leader who missed the sound of a voice. He realized he had enjoyed showing off his knowledge of the regions through which they rode. Why deny himself that pleasure? It was the proper function of females to provide an admiring audience for the male.

He cleared his throat as a prelude to speech and waved one

hand vaguely southward. "That way, long ride, is land of Illyricum," he informed any listening ear.

Illyricum. Epona instantly recalled her mother's fascination with
the tales of Illyricum, the silks and splendors, the treasures
brought to the cities from the corners of the earth. For her mother's sake she should question the Scythian about Illyricum, but
that was Rigantona's interest, after all, and not her own. *What did
my mother ever do for me?* she thought. *I will never see her again
to tell her what I might learn, anyway, and I am glad I will not.*

Mother.

Kazhak went on talking. "Much of Illyricum is mountains," he
said. "People tough as best leather. But as you ride south, they
get softer. Town people." He spat in contempt, being careful to
avoid Epona. She did not notice the small courtesy.

"Ride southeast many days more," Kazhak said, "see lands of
Moesians; Thracians. Interesting places. Grasslands, swamps, red
flower called poppy makes men fall asleep quick, river of
roses . . ."

"A river of roses?" Epona asked in spite of herself.

Kazhak shook his head in the gesture she had already learned
was a sign of assent among the Scythians, as a nod was the sign
of negation. "Maritsa, river of roses. Is valley of roses, flowers
everywhere, people pressing oil from petals, singing about roses,
oil, sun, war, food . . . sing about everything they see and do,
those Thracians. Noisy people."

He sounded amused. He did not look down to see if Epona was
paying attention. She was not talking so she must be listening;
women did one or the other. Being female, they could not simply
be quiet and think.

"When Kazhak boy," he said, "go with Kolaxais and brothers
to get Thracian stallions for our herds. Wonderful fast horses, but
with big heads, like ox. Good women there, too; pretty." He
smiled to himself at some memory. "But southern women spoil
early, like eggs in sun," he added, the smile fading.

Epona would not give him the satisfaction of a response.

Glancing down at her, Kazhak noticed the angry set of her jaw.
"Much copper in lands of Thracians," he continued blandly. "Men
mine copper in valley of Duna for more generations than number
of hairs on your head. Build towns, make bronze. Work some

197

iron, too — horse bits, few weapons, but not great swords like swords of Kelti. No one works iron good as Kelti. Your smith, your tribe, very smart. Very strong. Good heads."

Was he now offering her people some clumsy compliment with his cup hand? It would not soften her. She grated her teeth together and kept her eyes on the land before them, watching the hills give way to a distant plain spread like the lap of the earth mother.

Could that be the Sea of Grass? Surely not; the journey had already seemed interminable, but her own knowledge, gleaned from traders' talk in her village, told her they must still be in the territory of the Pannonii or the Boii; perhaps the Kotini or the northern branch of the Taurisci. But she would not ask.

Kazhak continued his monologue, trusting her to listen, expecting her to appreciate the effort he was making. Men did not have to discuss anything with women; she should feel honored that he spent time talking to her.

"In Thrace many different tribes, no one like any of the others," he said. "Stay all separate. Mountain people, plains people, swamp people. Each tribe proud, think other tribes" — he hunted for the word — "inferior, is it so?

"But land is southland, gets warm, gets too much sun, Kazhak thinks. Makes people do funny things. Very funny," he reiterated.

Against her will, she was interested. "What do you mean by funny things?" Silence had become an intolerable burden, its supporting edges nibbled away by her curiosity.

"Some tribes in land of Thracians eat no meat," Kazhak explained. "No flesh food, not even sheep and goats. Live on roots, milk, cheese, honey. Act like women. Do not train warriors, never have good fight. Talk about peace, peace, while muscles go limp and flabby. Grow roses, sing songs. Weak people, those people. Strong wind will come someday and blow them away."

"It sounds like a happy existence," Epona commented.

"Happy! What good is happy? Children will be slaughtered, or starve; they do not know how to fight. All must know how to fight. Fight for life or die. All things know that, but funny Thracians think they can make it not true." His voice rang with contempt.

"There are many gentle things that never fight . . ." Epona

began to argue, but Kazhak waved her suggestion aside with a flourish of his hand.

"All fight. Little birds fight, for food, for territory. You watch. Rabbit, small rabbit, soft, gentle, is it so? Rabbits fight, kick, tear each other over female. Strong one gets her, has strong babies. Is good. Is good way. Strong live, weak die."

He is right, said the spirit within.

"In herds of horse, we let young stallions fight. Keep winners to breed, geld losers," Kazhak went on. "Horses get stronger. You will see."

"You were telling me about the funny customs of the tribes in Thrace," she reminded him, anxious to hear more.

"Yes, is so. Some tribes — smarter tribes, tribes with warriors and weapons — they want send message to one of their gods. Take some nobleman and toss onto points of spears. If man die, they say god liked him, listened to him. If man live, they say he failure, bad person, is no longer nobleman. Loses face. Man no win either way. Too much warm weather make people think funny like that."

Epona bit her lip and did not laugh.

The Scythian said, "One man has many wives, good custom. Among Scyth, too; good custom. But when Thracian man die, wives fight. What woman did dead man like best? Relatives take sides. Big fights; war, almost. Very funny. One woman win, she most honored, pleased with self. Her relatives kill her, bury her with dead husband. All other wives jealous. They cry, hoo-hoo-hoo!" Kazhak broke spontaneously into an excellent mimicry of a woman crying, screwing up his face and rubbing one fist into his eyes, making a noise that caused the horses to flatten their ears against their heads. The other Scythians roared with laughter.

Epona laughed too; she could no longer help it. The spectacle was irresistible: the merciless warrior, turning himself into a wailing woman and then back again to Kazhak, smiling broadly, pleased with his performance.

Having laughed, Epona could not revert to sulking. Toutorix had been famed for carrying a grudge tucked into his beard until the hair fell out, but that had never been Epona's way. Bad feelings could sour inside like milk, and she preferred to set them aside when their first heat had passed.

They traveled on. Having discussed the Thracians at great

length, for a Scyth, Kazhak fell silent. Epona walked and trotted at the stallion's side, keeping pace.

A person afoot could not hope to match the walking strides of the Scythian horses indefinitely, though it had been easy to keep up with the short paces of the draft ponies of the Kelti. Epona was now thankful for the fleetness of foot all children of her tribe learned early and practiced often.

Her tribe. Her tribe.

Something burned behind her eyelids and her throat felt thick.

The Scythians rode, saying little to one another, their eyes fixed on the eastern horizon. Kazhak, the most voluble of the horsemen, seemed to have exhausted his fund of conversation and gradually sank into a dark and darker mood, with a scowl on his face and a set to his shoulders that warned the others to leave him alone. At such times his temper could flare up like a spark from one of Tena's fires.

Epona wondered what was bothering him, but she did not ask. She thought she would never understand him. He was like the climate of the plains, sunny and good-humored one moment, dark and foreboding the next. Epona, shaped by the Blue Mountains, was used to ongoing conversation like the wind in the pine trees, or tranquil periods of contemplation fostered by the lingering twilight of sunseason. The Scythian's moods did not match hers.

That night they camped on the banks of the Duna and Epona fell asleep listening to the river singing to itself, wishing that she, like Uiska, understood the language of the waters. Kazhak stood the first watch and then slept soundly beside her without touching her.

In the dawn light of nextday she could see that the land east of the river was an inviting plain, thickly covered with low bushes that turned it a rich shade of lavender. Nematona would have been very excited by the discovery.

Occasionally they saw people in the distance as they rode, large settlements or long, well-guarded wagon trains carrying merchants to the prosperous southlands. Kazhak went out of his way to avoid such concentrations of people. It appeared the horsemen were quick to slaughter helpless villagers bringing in their first fruits, but were less eager to confront those who had them outnumbered and possessed adequate weaponry.

Epona felt the sting of contempt. A member of the people,

outnumbered or not, would have gone up to the strangers he encountered, holding out an empty knife hand and demonstrating fearlessness. What could harm one of the people anyway? The sky could fall and crush the body, the earth could swallow it, but for an immortal spirit there was really nothing to fear.

A spirit . . . a mental image of Kernunnos flashed before her eyes, and for one heartbeat she had the awful sense of being invaded. He was more than a thought, he was a tangible presence inside her mind during that brief space of time, traveling with her, threatening her . . . she had not escaped him. He was here, somehow. She could feel it. Thinking about him had opened a gate and he had come through; he knew where she was now.

The horses began to grow nervous for no discernible reason. The gray stallion tossed his head again and again, snatching at the bit, and damp patches of sweat appeared on his neck. The others began to shy at nothing, snorting.

Kazhak glanced over his shoulder toward the northwest. His men noticed this and looked back as well; so did Epona. High white clouds with tattered edges were moving swiftly across the sky as if to avoid a darker cloud pursuing them, a cloud of mist and amorphous shape. As Epona watched, the sky took on a green color, dark, menacing, and the rising wind began to hurl leaves and even fragments of soil through the air.

Kazhak said something urgent to his men. They jumped from their horses and began leading the animals into a narrow ravine running back from the river. The sides would provide some protection from the wind and there were no large trees to fall and crush them.

The Scythians took care of their animals first, hobbling them securely in the best shelter they could find. "Is said wind here sometimes blow down ox," Kazhak explained to Epona. "Big storms here, much power, stronger than man. What your horn-headed priest call sacred, is it so? Stronger than man?"

Epona was helping him unpack the nervous stallion. "Storms are the moods of the earth mother," she answered. "They are not to be feared; there are those of my people who know how to control and make use of them."

Kazhak's brows lifted. "Is joke?"

"I speak the truth."

"You can do this thing?" For the first time she heard respect in his voice. She was tempted to tell him she could, indeed, influence the weather. She was born *drui*, was she not? Or so they said?

"No," she answered. "I can't control the weather. Only the *druii* do that, and even they cannot make the weather do whatever they want. They can change it a little, sometimes."

The bards sang of an era many generations ago when the *druii* understood how to use the power of the great stones and had much more influence over many things, including weather, but there was no time to tell this to Kazhak. The storm was upon them now and they were very busy.

"Kazhak not change weather," he told Epona as he pulled a bundle from one of the packs, "but Kazhak can stop rain!" He held up an oiled hide that had been stretched and pounded so thin it folded like fabric. With this and broken branches lying on the ground he quickly constructed a crude tent and urged Epona to go inside. Around them the other Scythians were constructing similar shelters for themselves.

"You go in," Kazhak told the girl. "Dry in there."

She crawled in on her hands and knees and he pushed in after her. Their two bodies crowded the little tent, but he was right; after a struggle to arrange the bearskin cloak to augment the hide covering, the improvised shelter did keep off the rain. Large drops drummed unsuccessfully on the tent above them, seeking admittance.

Kazhak heaved an expansive sigh. "Is good, is it so?"

Their bodies were jammed together in the cramped space. His body heat had already driven out the damp chill. Lying cuddled against him was like lying next to a banked fire.

Epona's wet clothes clung to her skin; their dampness went through to her bones. She pressed more tightly against the Scythian. The rain fell harder. The wind howled, but Kazhak's clever arrangement of branches held the tent firm.

Epona was acutely aware of the man; he seemed now to fill her world to its edges. She did not know how she felt about him. He had, indeed, spared her the life of a *drui*, but what sort of life would she have instead?

Kazhak was like no one she knew. Underneath his superficially jovial attitude, he was capable of a brooding melancholy and a swift, savage temper. She had seen him sit without moving on his horse for half a day at a time, his face closed and cold, his dark eyes lurking deep in their sockets like cunning predators. He could shut his spirit away and keep it selfishly hidden, giving nothing, so that even as she rode behind him with her hands on his body he felt wooden to the touch.

But now, in the little tent, he was neither wooden nor remote. He was big — bigger than she had realized — and warm; flesh and blood. He asked her, "You warm now?" in a tone of genuine concern.

"Yes, your spirit is generous."

He did not understand her thanks. "Spirit? Is no spirit. Is body. Your body warm, Kazhak's body warm. Man needs brother to make warm when rain is cold."

Brother? she thought, surprised.

"I am not your brother," she said.

Kazhak replied, in a voice so low she could hardly hear it above the storm, though his mouth was close to her ear, "You look in Kazhak's eyes, Kazhak look in your eyes. Feel something. Only brothers share eye-bond. Brothers. Friends. Is what you call sacred." He shifted his weight uneasily. "You . . . Kazhak no understand," he said, and she could hear the bewilderment in his voice.

Epona felt sorry for this plainly baffled man who seemed so upset by the very normal occurrence of having his spirit make contact with another spirit. "Among my people," she told him, "men and women often meet eyes and feel something."

"But woman cannot be brother," he said, stubbornly repeating the one thing of which he was certain.

"I am a woman in thislife," she answered, "but I can also be your friend if you will let me. I left all my friends in the Blue Mountains."

Kazhak wanted to get back to areas he understood. Let this person be a woman only; the emotional requirements of women were simple, almost beneath consideration. "You not need friends," he told her abruptly, bringing the conversation to a close. "You will have other women if you want talk."

Without further discussion he rolled over on top of her.

Chapter 16

EPONA HAD THOUGHT SHE KNEW what to expect. All her
life she had seen people coupling, animals coupling. It was a
simple act with variations of position and duration but no more
complicated than eating or drinking.

Or so she believed.

Kazhak was heavy and insistent, but he was not rough. He did
not attempt to cause pain. His hands moved over her body with
the confidence of a man used to women, and at the same time he
employed a certain spirit of exploration, the excitement of an adventurer into unfamiliar territory. This was a woman of the Kelti,
long legged, milky skinned, with firm muscles where women of
his own race were soft as overripe fruit. When he put his hand
between her legs to spread them apart he felt the strong thighs
and paused, enjoying their strangeness.

His fingers were rough and calloused, but Epona discovered it
was exciting to feel them moving so delicately, so close to her
inner self. Kazhak was gentler than the priest had been at her
woman-making. He handled her as a stockman handles a calf still
wobbly and fragile with newness.

His body pinned hers to the earth, but he was not forcibly
holding her down, merely cushioning himself on her softness. His
breathing grew heavier. The limited space within the tent grew
hotter.

Epona had never realized the pressure of another human body on her own could feel so good. She wanted to get even closer to him but there was no way to get closer, their bodies were already touching throughout their length.

No, there was one way to be closer. And Kazhak was ready.

He entered her suddenly, a deft plunge that startled her because his penis was so much larger than she had anticipated. There was a moment of discomfort as her body adjusted itself to the unfamiliar sensation, but as the *gutuiters* had promised, there was no pain. Instead there was an aching that became increasingly pleasurable, an ache that mounted in intensity as Kazhak's hips moved against hers, an ache like a hungry belly demanding to be fed and tantalized by the approaching feast.

She began to move with him.

Bedsports.

Kazhak, accustomed to the passive response of his women on the Sea of Grass, almost stopped moving. "You all right?" he whispered, fearing she might be having some sort of seizure.

"Yes," she answered, thrusting harder against him. *Do not stop now*, she begged him in her mind. *Not now!*

He did not stop. Together they moved closer and closer to . . .

And there it was. She felt it convulse him and she could almost share the sensation sweeping through his body, flooding residually into hers with warmth and pleasure. Aaahhh . . .

The second time would be better. That was the wisdom the matrons shared around the lodgefires. The first time might be awkward, but the second time would definitely be better.

Rigantona had been right; there was no way of understanding without personal experience.

Epona smiled to herself in the darkness, thinking forward to the second time.

The storm blew over them and was gone. Kazhak squirmed out of the shelter, adjusting his clothing as he went. Epona lay in a tumble of incompletion, her body longing for his return, but then she heard his sharp command and a moment later he began dismantling the tent.

"Storm gone, we ride," he said brusquely. Whatever had happened between them was over as far as the Scythian was concerned. Motion was the imperative; they must continue eastward.

Motion was also the way to handle the troubling feelings Kazhak had not experienced before. This woman, this Kelti, was not like women he knew; she was trouble, as he had halfway suspected from the beginning. He had only intended to take a quick pleasure from her while they outwaited the storm, but the unexpected tenderness that welled up in him left him confused and annoyed with himself. Feelings like that could make a man weak. It really might be wise to sell her as a slave, if they met traders along the way who expressed an interest.

That night Epona looked up to find Kazhak staring at her across the campfire. He said nothing to her, nor did he drop his eyes. They were filled with the light of the fire.

He did not stand first watch that night. Aksinya paced the perimeter of the encampment, his hand close to his sword hilt when the distant howling of wolves drifted to him on the wind, and Kazhak lay with Epona, their heads pillowed together on the neck of the gray stallion.

They lay together but nothing more happened. She enjoyed his warmth and the strength of his arms around her, but it was his body inside hers she craved, and he seemed to be thinking of something else. Disappointed, she squirmed against him, and he responded by whispering in her ear, "You see him?"

"Who?" She glanced around, seeing only the bulk of the gray horse and the tiny red eyes of the dying fire beyond which Basl and Dasadas lay sleeping with their mounts.

"Someone watches us," Kazhak answered in a hushed voice.

"I don't see anybody."

"Is there. Kazhak feel. Skin on neck tell Kazhak. Touch, here." He took her hand and held her fingers against the back of his neck, under the hair. She could feel the rising hackles of the skin.

"Someone watches," the Scythian repeated.

His tone made Epona apprehensive. Aksinya paced by them, looking out into the night, and Kazhak said something to him and got up. Both men took the watch together, and when they tired Basl and Dasadas were awakened to take their places.

But they saw no one; heard nothing but a wolf howling, far off.

In the morning they rode again across the broad plain.

The mountains were behind them now, though in response to a question of Epona's Kazhak explained they would eventually have to cross another mountain range, the last that separated them from the Sea of Grass. They had turned away from the Duna, which flowed due south in this region, and were approaching another river, which Kazhak called the Tisa.

The land was dotted with farmsteads, but the Scythians staged no raids on them. Some of these places looked as if they had suffered too many raids already; others, though prosperous, were too well equipped with men of fighting age to tempt a band of only four warriors. The Scythians rode by peaceably and the inhabitants watched them with wary eyes.

Epona looked with interest at these new folk. They were not wealthy by the standards of the Kelti; they usually wore undyed wool and seemed to have little jewelry. The men did sport brightly colored sashes, and many of the women wore shawls of the same material pulled over their heads.

They were a well-nourished people; the land around them, the good farmland the Scythians held in contempt, was generous. In addition to their varied crops, Epona noticed that they built wooden hurdles to pen their sheep; small sheep, lacking the deep wool of mountain stock. They had cattle as well, leggier than Kelti oxen, and shaggy dark dogs that ran out to bark furious challenges at the Scythian horses. Epona saw one woman tending a flock of fat and flightless birds who bobbed around her feet, pecking at the grain she threw them. *Such birds would not require a spear to capture them for the pot; such birds would be welcomed in the village of the Kelti*, Epona thought to herself.

Several times she noticed huge haystacks, like thatched lodges, and speculated about the amount of fodder this land produced. It would feed many animals, animals that could be raised close to home instead of hunted. Kernunnos would resist such an idea.

Do not think of Kernunnos, warned the spirit within.

The farmers were sturdy people, deep-chested, with broad foreheads and cheekbones and ruddy cheeks. The color of their hair ranged from Scythian brown to Kelti blond; they could have belonged to either people. Women worked beside their men in fields of beans and barley, calling to one another in cheerful voices. When Epona caught snatches of their words she did not recognize the language.

"What people are these?" she asked Kazhak, but he was in no mood for questions and did not bother to answer her.

Kazhak had hunted since earliest boyhood. He was keenly sensitive to the interplay between predator and prey, and now he felt himself being hunted by something cunning and dangerous. It was an unpleasant sensation. He had not been able to identify the nature or location of the hunger; he only knew, with atavistic certainty, that something was stalking him, moving ever closer.

He had to get back to his familiar territory, his Sea of Grass, before the thing caught up with him.

His tension was contagious. Epona began to feel anxious without knowing why. Perhaps, she thought, it was because she was so far from home, and moving farther away with every footfall of the horse. Better not to think about it, then; better not to make herself miserable summoning up happy recollections of the Blue Mountains, her friends, everything she had known and loved and left so carelessly, as if her headlong flight were a children's pretend-game that could be undone nextday.

It could not be undone nextday. Nextday there would be only the Scythians, the horses, and whatever was waiting for her on the Sea of Grass.

That night the sky was clear and the stars were bright and close. The Scythians rode until darkness forced a halt, then stopped for sleep in the lee of a hillock surmounted by wind-gnarled trees.

Everyone seemed to have trouble sleeping. Epona could hear the men talking among themselves in low voices. The night grew darker, with a purple-black cast and a dusty-sweet fragrance peculiar to the region. Epona had begun to see a certain beauty in the undulating plains, where once she thought only mountains were beautiful. But this was a new aspect of the earth mother, to be cherished and revered, and it was right she should learn to appreciate it, she told herself.

The Scythians did not see the beauty of the night. Kazhak was asking Dasadas, "Have you seen it since we stopped?"

Dasadas nodded his head in the negative gesture. "No. But there is howling, beyond that gully, coming closer."

"Take your bow and kill it, hunt and kill before it kills us," Kazhak advised. "You can see enough, the night is clear and your eyes were trained on the Sea of Grass. Take Basl with you."

He and Aksinya waited. Epona turned from side to side, annoying the gray stallion, and tried to sleep. She wondered what the men were talking about so softly.

Suddenly Kazhak clapped his hands together. "Hear! The arrows of Dasadas are singing!"

They waited again. The other two Scythians returned to the camp with empty hands.

"You saw it?" Kazhak asked eagerly.

"We saw something. It looked like wolf, silver-colored wolf. Biggest wolf ever. We shot arrows at it from very close."

"Then you killed it, is it so?"

They hung their heads, ashamed. "No. We did not kill it. We shot but the wolf did not fall. It ran away. Our arrows seemed to go right into it but it ran away, and the arrows are gone too."

Kazhak could only stare at them. "You lost wolf? And good arrows?"

"It must be badly wounded," Basl offered.

Kazhak thought about this. "If it is wounded, it will not bother us tonight. We rest. Tomorrow we leave here and leave hurt wolf to die."

He spoke with more confidence than he felt. The wolf — or whatever it was — had been following them for days, behaving in a manner unlike any animal he had known, hiding, skulking, but always narrowing the distance between it and them. They had all caught fleeting glimpses, but no one had seen it clearly. They just knew it was there.

And they had not been able to kill it.

He lay down beside Epona and put his arms around her.

"Was there a wild animal near the camp?" she wanted to know. "Did the men kill it?"

"Scyth great hunters, never miss," he replied. Her body comforted his; the way she lay against him made him think her trusting and submissive. He was a man, he could take care of her. He was a Prince of the Horse; he could take care of all of them.

Feeling more sure of himself, he began rubbing his body against hers and caressing her with his hands. This time she welcomed him with enthusiasm, allowing herself to be enveloped by the delicious new feelings throbbing through her awakened body. When he entered her she was moist and ready for him; she was almost demanding, and she took from him hungrily, feeding on the horseman's passion.

The women around the lodgefires had been right. The second time was much better.

Afterward they lay with their bodies fitted snugly together. Her back was to him and his arms clasped her so closely his breath stirred the little curling hairs at the nape of her neck. It was hard to remember how it had felt to be two separate people with space between them.

Epona thought, *This is how it is in the otherworlds where there is no passage of time and no sense of the body. This lovely warm floating, so complete, so satisfied . . .*

The brilliant stars wheeled above them.

In the darkest part of the night Kazhak whispered her name, just once. In her own language, not his, he called her beautiful.

Dawn found them on the move again. Everyone seemed to have rested better and awakened refreshed — perhaps it was because the predator had been chased from camp. They were all in a better mood. Basl actually spoke to the young woman when he set aside her share of the morning's meat, and Epona smiled at him, amused by the quick way he ducked his head to avoid meeting her eyes.

Even the gray stallion seemed happier. He nickered and pawed the ground, curving his neck into a graceful line of controlled energy, urging them to mount and ride. Ride!

A cool wind blew at their backs, pushing them eastward. For the first time, Epona felt no stiffness in her joints, no soreness in her muscles as she straddled the gray. This was good riding country; Kazhak rarely had her walk now, and she was glad of it. Her body felt oiled and new, perfectly blended into that of the animal beneath it. Her reflexes had learned to match themselves to those of the horse and she sat with easy grace.

She no longer bothered to braid her hair; her hair style could have no meaning to the Scythians anyway. Now it floated around her face and the wind blew long strands of it forward over Kazhak's shoulders. He turned and looked at her with a smile in his eyes, and she smiled back.

"Kelti gold," he said.

The horses cantered over springy earth. There was a glory in riding. The human became part of the animal, attached by invisible wires, muscle connected to muscle and bone merged with bone. Epona felt the strength of the stallion become her strength; its speed and grace were hers, too. She sat on the powerfully thrusting haunches with her head thrown back and her eyes closed, not thinking, just feeling, light and free.

Free. This is what it is to be a horseman.

The day assumed the mood of a festival day. Kazhak was willing to talk again, and he told Epona the names of the plants they saw, teaching her the Scythian words for them. He identified the many animals glimpsed at a distance, the foxes and roebucks and eagles, the herds of dangerous wild pigs. He spoke of creatures they would see farther east, of deer with long backswept horns and big cats like the lions on Hellene pottery.

Kazhak enjoyed having someone at his shoulder to whom he could talk when the mood was on him. Epona was interested and quick-witted; the questions she asked made him think new thoughts and look at things in new ways.

He was aware that his men disapproved of her, and this made him perversely kinder to her, almost flaunting the girl in their faces, showing them he was the leader and could do as he pleased.

Epona began to feel a small sense of power herself. This was more than an escape, this was a new beginning for her, the start of a life unlike any woman of the Kelti had known before. And it was her very own, chosen by herself. She determined to drink it to the bottom of the cup.

"Do you suppose I could have a horse of my own?" she asked Kazhak.

The Scythian snorted. "Women do not ride horses."

"But I am riding a horse right now," she pointed out. "And I could handle one by myself, I know it. I think I could even ride this one without you."

Kazhak scowled. "Women do not ride horses!" He considered the subject inarguable.

The horses slowed to a walk and Kazhak commanded Epona to get off and give the gray stallion a rest. He looked down at her tawny head in wonder. Woman, thinking she could manage a horse! What would his men say if they heard such a wild suggestion?

He chuckled to himself, thinking of it.

Epona walked at the stallion's shoulder, stroking his neck from time to time. The horse had fully accepted her as a companion; he rolled his eye in her direction or slanted an ear toward her to pick up the sound of her voice. A bond had been established between them as Epona had once formed a bond with the cartponies of Toutorix. But those had been very different animals, with their slow reflexes and placid geldings' thoughts.

The Scythian stallion was as quick as starfire, his attention flickering here, there, everywhere; his curiosity a match for Epona's; his passion always simmering beneath his silky hide. The horses of the nomads were exquisitely sensitive in comparison with the stock of the Kelti. The gray stallion responded to every mood of his rider, like an extension of the human body. He could prance and rear in a fine demonstration of defiance, then calm at once and thrust his muzzle into Epona's palm, nuzzling for the clover she pulled for him.

The horse was an emissary to her from the Sea of Grass, making Epona feel more alive than she ever had before. Watching him, she thought the Kelti had nothing that could compare with this Scythian treasure.

But when they camped and ate the unseasoned meats and chunks of indigestible bread the Scythians carried, Epona thought with longing of the Blue Mountains. Her tastebuds remembered the wide variety of food she had taken for granted, and the equally wide variety of ways the Kelti had for preparing the food. Not just burned on the outside and raw on the inside, like the game the Scythians sometimes shot. Kelti meat had been roasted, boiled, simmered in broth, buried beneath the glowing coals of a firepit, browned in goat's butter, steamed in wet leaves . . . Mutton and lamb and venison, hare and coney and cheese pie, tender baby goat, roast suckling pig, stone-ground emmer bread and barley-beer, berries and honeycomb, fresh cress and fish from the lake, Kelti beans, boiled melde . . . And the seasonings! The omnipresent salt, but also the herbs of the country and the spices brought by the traders. Garlic and onion, peppercorns, varieties of mint, lees of wine, kinnamon and . . .

When the Scythians reached their home territory, she assured herself, they would eat better, too. It was not possible that their whole tribe subsisted on such miserable fare as the men carried in their saddlebags.

The land sank and became marshy; they saw blue herons and white storks, and the mud nourished tall weeds that Kazhak said, with contempt, were eaten by "those farmer people. Eat grass like horses."

The plants looked green and juicy. Epona rode past them with wistful eyes.

They came to the Tisa, a smaller river than the Duna, low in this season, and forded it without difficulty. They rode and camped and rode again, and Kazhak entered Epona many times. Her pleasure increased with each encounter as her sensuality blossomed. The horse was part of it. His warmth kindled hers as she sat on the broad, muscular rump. She became aware, through the very pores of her skin, of the aura of the male animal — man, horse, man. Kazhak was sometimes a sexual partner, sometimes a preoccupied stranger, but the horse was a constant, glorying in his gender, neck arched with masculine pride, great full testicles glossy with health, hanging like ripe fruit between his thighs.

Riding the stallion she thought of Kazhak. Lying in Kazhak's arms she imagined riding the stallion. It seemed to her that the two of them merged at times into one being, a statement of beauty and power that made fluid the dividing line between animal and human. She surrendered to the pleasure of being female to their male.

She came to accept the tastelessness of the food and the hardness of the ground on which they slept. Such things were merely a part of the life, the sun and the wind and the riding, riding . . .

They came to a deeply rutted road beside a dry streambed and found the path already occupied by trading wagons piled high with goods. It was a small train, and this time Kazhak did not hesitate to ride forward and salute the leader. The first wagon was driven by a long-skulled, fine-featured man with dark hair and the unmistakable look of a Thracian. Once Thracians had sat with Toutorix around the feasting fire in the Blue Mountains; Epona and the other children used to sneak close to the fire, watching them, mimicking the way they walked and the cadences of their speech.

Sell you as slave to the Thracians, Kazhak had threatened.

Chapter 17

THE WAGONEERS wore hooded felt cloaks, pushed back from their shoulders now because of the warmth of the sun. They had only a few wagons, but in true Thracian style they carried as much music with them as they could afford: a lone lyre player who rode with the driver of the third wagon, strumming his instrument and singing the song of the road. He was not an inspired singer, and they had been on the road a very long time. The other men only occasionally sang with him now.

The traders had spears propped beside them in their wagons, but seemed to be without the usual contingent of armed outriders. They were making a desperate push for the nearest trading center, hoping to sell enough goods there to resupply themselves with guards to replace those they had lost on the journey.

Meeting Scythians was a piece of bad fortune, putting them all out of tune. But at least, the leader thought, there were only four men on the horses; perhaps they were no more prepared for battle than the Thracians. Perhaps they were just another band of weary travelers, anxious to get home. He saluted Kazhak as the obvious leader with an elaborate bow and courteous phrases of greeting. He added an effusive compliment about the gray stallion, and Kazhak replied in a cordial manner.

"Do you know that man?" Epona whispered at his shoulder.

"No, but is horse man," Kazhak answered. "All true horse men are brothers."

He began conversing with the Thracian in a rough approximation of the man's own language, though without the musicality of vowels that made Thracian speech so pleasant. Epona had already learned that Kazhak's gift for languages other than his own was rare among his people, who were suspicious of any foreign customs and ways, but it was a convenient asset for an exploratory expedition. Now she listened with interest, trying to follow the conversation as the two men discussed their animals, exchanging further compliments. She was able to understand more than she expected. Kazhak spoke admiringly of the pair of bay mares pulling the first wagon, and the gray stallion added his own softly nickered comment of praise.

The other three Scythians sat alertly on their horses, ready to follow whatever lead Kazhak gave them. The wagon drivers waited with equal tension.

The Thracian introduced himself as Provaton, nephew of a famed horsebreeder on the Struma. That explained his possession of wagon horses almost as large as Scythian saddle animals, rather than asses or the long-horned cattle sometimes trained to the yoke by southerners.

"Very fine horses," Kazhak said again. "You want to trade?"

Epona sat rigid behind him. What did Kazhak have to trade for Thracian horses? He would never give up the iron swords, she was certain.

Provaton wrapped the leather reins around the bar provided for that purpose at the front of his box-shaped, four-wheeled wagon, and gingerly stepped down, with the stiffness of a man who has spent many days jolting along rutted roads. He rubbed the small of his back and stretched himself, then approached Kazhak.

"What have you to trade?" he asked the Scythian. "And how would I haul my wagons home if I bartered away my good horses?" He kept his voice light and pleasant; this encounter must remain a friendly one, or he might never get home at all.

Before Kazhak could answer, one of the other Thracians called out, "What about the woman?"

Epona dug her fingers into Kazhak's belt.

Provaton looked up at her as she sat on the rump of the gray stallion. A *keltoi* girl, by the looks of her; very fair. Young. Such creamy skin and blue eyes. The southern slave markets were al-

215

ways eager for such merchandise, though they rarely got their hands on one of the northern *keltoi,* who were a powerful people and known to prefer death to enslavement.

Provaton folded his arms and squinted up at Kazhak, inviting the Scythian to make the first offer. "What do you suggest?" he said.

"What you got in wagons?" Kazhak countered.

"Amber, furs, some woven wool. We traded copper and anise for it, and I have a good market waiting in Makedon."

Kazhak's brows drew down, hiding the expression in his eyes. "How much amber?"

Provaton was uneasy. You could never predict what a Scythian was going to do, and though a tenuous peace existed between the two peoples at the time, there were always attacks and skirmishes along the borders, and four Scythians might not hesitate to slaughter a merchant train of Thracians for their amber. His wagoneers were too tired and dispirited to fight well.

"Very little amber, very little," he said hastily. "We were late getting north and the other merchants had been there ahead of us; we got the dregs. Even our furs are inferior this year. Mostly ermine, admired in Moesia and Thrace but very common among your people."

"You know how it is on Sea of Grass?" Kazhak asked with sudden warmth.

"What man who values horseflesh does not? I, myself, have been as far as the great horse fair on the plain at Maikop; with my family I have bought many good animals from your people and loaded them with felt and furs to sell at home."

Kazhak leaned forward eagerly at the mention of Maikop. "You know Kolaxais, Prince of Horses?" he asked, as a man does who is starved of news of home. "Kolaxais takes many horses to Maikop."

The Thracian hesitated. "Who has not heard of Kolaxais?" he asked. There was a falter in his pronunciation of the name and the light went out of Kazhak's eyes. "Never heard of Kolaxais," he whispered in an aside to Epona. "Thracian lie." Kazhak grinned suddenly; the brotherhood of horse men was thereby dissolved, as far as he was concerned.

Kazhak gestured toward Aksinya. "That man my brother," he

said, "has iron knives of the Kelti in pack on horse. You never see such good knives. You know good horses, Sea of Grass, so Kazhak offer you special trade. Pack of Aksinya, unopened, for one of Provaton's wagons, unsearched. Blind trade, between friends. No one looks." He grinned. It was a remarkably innocent grin, all teeth and wide eyes.

"I could not do that," Provaton said stiffly. "How could I explain to my principals at home, who financed this train? A loaded wagon with two good horses is worth more than anything you could possibly be carrying in one pack. Unless you have gold as well as iron, that is."

The grin was fixed on Kazhak's face. "Is well known, Scyth always has gold," he said noncommittally.

The Thracian cast a second glance at the bulging pack on the horse behind Aksinya. Aksinya scowled as a man does who fears he is about to be robbed.

It might be better to accept this trade, no matter how unfair, in hopes the Scythians would be satisfied and let us go on, Provaton thought. And if it was really true about the *keltoi* iron . . . and it could be, they had the woman with them . . .

Suddenly the Thracian tensed and whirled around, looking back along his little line of wagons. He had just realized that the other Scythians had moved away and were now bracketing the train between them, as hunting dogs would work a small herd of deer.

Provaton had been having a discouraging summer. He was definitely very far out of tune.

"What are those men doing?" he asked Kazhak sharply.

Kazhak's reply was bland. "Sitting on horses. No harm." He sounded disinterested.

Provaton did some quick mental calculation. It had been a disastrous trip, with many of his men lost to a fever contracted in a swampy valley between the Elbe and the Oder. His merchandise really was inferior, for the reason he had given Kazhak, but his backers would accept no excuses. If he had some superior iron-work to show them — and there were already rumors about *keltoi* iron —

A gamble on life was better than sure death.

He forced his voice to be hearty, as if there were no threat. "I like your trade," he said to Kazhak. "It amuses me. I might be

217

willing to let you have one wagon . . . that one, with the brown gelding and the chestnut mare . . . in return for your pack, if it really contains *keltoi* iron."

"Shortswords Kelti call daggers," Kazhak informed him. "Best anywhere. My men all wear now."

Epona followed this exchange with relief. She had known a bad moment when the Thracian called attention to her, but now it seemed everything was going to be all right. Kazhak rode his stallion toward the wagon in question and she looked at the two horses, waiting in their traces.

Before the spirit within could warn her to keep silent, she said, "Not that wagon, Kazhak."

Startled, the Thracian leader looked at her a second time, with the appraising eyes of a merchantman. *Such a woman would bring a high price in the great slave market at Thasos, where the Ionian colonials made fabulous offers for unusual females.*

Kazhak turned in his saddle. "Why not this wagon?" he asked her.

"One of the horses is ill," she told him.

Kazhak's dark brows crawled up his forehead like caterpillars. "How you know?"

"I am Kelt," she replied, the only experience she could give. How could she make someone not of the people understand the aura of pain that radiated from the chestnut mare?

"My horses are in perfect health!" Provaton protested.

"Show us," Kazhak ordered.

While they all watched, Epona slid down from the gray stallion and walked to the team in question. The chestnut mare watched her approach, its eyes red rimmed and eloquent with anguish. It suffered silently as horses must, but the pain poured from it in waves, lapping around Epona. She had to brace herself against it; she had to force herself to touch the suffering animal.

She bent and pressed her ear to the mare's belly. She heard none of the customary rumblings and gurglings of a healthy horse's intestines. When she closed her eyes she imagined something burning inside, like fire, eating the mare alive.

She straightened up and turned to Kazhak. "This horse is poisoned," she told him. "She has eaten some weed along the way and it has given her blocked bowels and a terrible pain in her belly. She will not live long."

The driver of the Thracian wagon had not understood many of her words but he understood the familiar gesture of a head pressed against the belly of a horse suffering from colic. He knew his mare, the greedy mare who had snatched feed from the roadside all the way from Moesia to the Baltik and back again.

Now Provaton put his hand on the mare's neck and felt it just beginning to dampen with sweat, the slick, unhealthy sweat of an animal in pain.

How could the girl have known, sitting many paces away on another horse?

The driver got down from his wagon and came to stand beside Epona. His eyes were dark with worry.

The mare's head began to droop lower. As they watched, bloody strings of mucus started running from her nostrils and her eyes half closed. Then suddenly they flared open as a spasm shook her and she tossed her head up wildly, pawing the earth.

The pain was unbearable.

"Take her out of the traces," Epona said.

The Thracian men stared at her. Who was this woman to be giving orders? She had little command of their language but her gestures were expressive; she meant them to be obeyed, just as if she had some degree of authority.

Kazhak narrowed his eyes and glared at Epona, wondering what sort of Kelti trickery this might be. His men watched with cynical amusement. Kazhak had taken this on himself, this peculiar foreign woman. Let him deal with her.

Ignoring them all, Epona began fumbling with the traces and after a moment's hesitation the wagon driver helped her. He jumped back, however, when the mare lashed out in her agony, her hoof narrowly missing his head.

Once free of the wagon the mare reared and pawed at the sky, pulling Epona off the ground as the girl clung to her bridle. The men tried to help then but Epona waved them back, and for some reason none of them could understand, they obeyed her. They stood in a circle, beyond the reach of the desperate, convulsing mare, and left the young woman alone with the horse.

The pain was a living thing, a hand that grabbed the intestines and squeezed. The mare and Epona suffered it together, fighting with crazed fear, but fear was not sufficient. Epona tried to block off that part of her mind so she could think; concentrate. She held

219

on grimly as the mare whirled in a circle, dragging her. She reached out with her inner being, grasping for some touch of the great fire of life, summoning its strength and support.

A moment of peace came to both of them. The mare stopped her frantic struggling and stood with braced legs, fighting for breath. Epona relinquished her hold on the bridle and flattened her body against the body of the mare, her breasts against the heaving sides, vulnerable to any move the horse might make in its dying agony. Behind her closed eyes she spoke to the spirits she knew and the unfamiliar ones that surrounded them in this place. She had not been taught the signs and invocations; she could only fashion them from her own intuition and pray that was sufficient.

The pain had come quickly; it would kill quickly. The mare was finding it agonizing to breathe, which added to her panic. Once her knees buckled and her forequarters sank to the ground, and Epona went down with her, holding on tightly, while the mare's driver moaned and wrung his hands. A horse down was a horse dead.

The mare's eyes were glazing, but somehow she got to her feet again, Epona clinging to her like a burr. The girl's entire being was absorbed by the pain now, but still she prayed to the spirit of life. There was nothing but the pain and the prayer.

The mare convulsed and Kazhak shouted a warning. The girl would be trampled. The mare was so wild none of his men were willing to get close to her and pull Epona free; they could only watch helplessly as she stayed with the plunging, bellowing horse, concentrating with singleminded ferocity on the pain, pulling it, drawing it out, now . . . it will ease . . . now!

They saw her face go white beneath the golden freckles. The mare's eyes rolled in her head in the death agony, and she screamed like a human being. Her mate, still in the traces, whin-nied in sympathy.

The chestnut mare stood on spraddled legs, head hanging, but she did not go down. Even as they watched, unbelieving, the glaze of death passed from her eyes. Her breathing steadied. The flow of bloody mucus from her nostrils slowed, then stopped. She raised her head and pricked her ears with interest when her teammate whinnied a second time.

Epona staggered away and flung herself down on the grass, panting.

The men crowded around her, demanding to know what she had done and how she had done it, but there was respect tinged with awe in their voices. It would have been a heady moment for Epona if she had not felt so sick and exhausted. Her mouth tasted of bile and her insides were sore. She lay propped on one elbow, waiting for the earth to stop spinning around her.

A little distance away the wagon driver was giving his recovered mare a thorough examination, shaking his head in amazement. The mare had defecated and was trying to graze.

Provaton addressed Kazhak. "What will you take for the woman?" he asked bluntly. "One wagon, two? More?"

Kazhak surveyed the wagon train. He did not have enough men to drive it home, and on closer inspection it had the shabby look of something not worth the effort.

But the woman was different.

"She is not for sale," he said.

Epona did not know whether she should feel relieved or dejected. The Thracians were an artistic, creative people on the eastern edge of the increasingly brilliant world of the Hellenes. Life among them might be considered preferable to life on the Sea of Grass, among the nomads.

But she had ridden the horse; she had felt the wind on her teeth and looked ahead to unlimited horizons, knowing that beneath her was the strength to take her there.

She tried to catch Kazhak's eye. She smiled at him, willing him to remember their bodies together.

"I will give you the best possible price," Provaton insisted, trying to keep from begging, which always ruined a deal. But the keltoi woman made his mouth water. He would not sell her to the Ionian colonials; he would take her around to the prosperous horsebreeders in the valley of the Maritsa and let her heal their valuable animals, then sit back and watch as they filled his purse with gold. He would be independently wealthy; there would be no more long months of swallowing dust along the trade routes, fighting to stay alive and make a slim profit. He would be a great man at last, with his own villa and stables. He would step in rhythm for the rest of his days.

"Woman is not for sale," Kazhak reiterated, seeing the lust in the Thracian's eyes. Having acquired Epona almost inadvertently, there were times during the trip when he would have gladly traded her, but not now. Now he knew what he had, even if he did not understand it.

He would be bringing great treasure to the Sea of Grass.

Interest in lesser trades was forgotten. There was a little desultory conversation about the wagon and the pack of iron daggers, but neither side pushed very hard. There was only one prize worth having, it seemed, and the Thracians lacked the strength to take it by force.

Once they reached their homelands, however, they would be quick to tell of the incident, of the great horse-healer of the *keltoi*. It was too good a story to keep. *Perhaps*, thought Provaton, *funds could be raised for an expedition into the Scythian territories to try to find and capture her.*

Or perhaps there were others like her among the *keltoi*. It would be wise to take his wagons into the high mountains next year and do a little business there, see what was available. If he could keep his skin whole and his head on his shoulders until next year.

"You saved my horse," he told Kazhak, "and it would be a great favor to me if you would let me give you a gift in return. You and your men can . . . ah . . . each choose something from the wagons. Whatever you like."

"One thing each?" Kazhak asked, narrowing his eyes. "That is all horse worth to you?"

"I have to make a living," Provaton protested. "I have a wife and six children, and I am a younger son, I rent my house . . ."

Kazhak was bored with this man. "Take," he said to the other Scythians, gesturing toward the wagons. "Take one good thing each, if there is any good thing, and we go. And something for you," he added to Epona, urging her forward to select a bauble.

They left Provaton standing in the road beside his wagons, the dust of their passage settling onto his shoulders, his eyes following Epona's golden head until she and the horsemen were mere specks in the distance.

"Remember that woman," he said to his men. "Remember everything about her."

222

Chapter 18

EVERYTHING WAS CHANGED. Kazhak's men, who had treated Epona with indifference if they acknowledged her presence at all, now looked at her as they would have looked at a two-headed colt born to one of the herd mares, with awe and pride. Something inexplicable had happened at the instigation of the woman: A horse all could see was dying, doomed, had been restored to life. It was not possible, but they had seen it. She had risked her own life to fight for the existence of the crazed mare, and she had won.

None of the men who had seen that would ever look at her in the same way again.

Kazhak was newly careful with her, and no longer made her walk at intervals to rest the stallion. Instead he had one of the other men walk and put Epona on that man's horse, leading it himself. He gave her first choice of the food at night and first drink of water, immediately after the horses.

None of the other men objected.

Kazhak lay beside her at night, looking up at the stars, and thought about the Kelti woman as he had never thought of any other woman, and when he entered her body it was with a tenderness bordering on reverence.

They continued eastward, until the sun rose to greet them above a new range of mountains.

"Carpātos," Kazhak identified them, squinting into the morning light.

The plains lifted toward the mountains in salute to the greater force.

"Not as tall as your mountains," Kazhak commented to Epona. "But very steep. Very dark."

Dark? What could he mean by that? And why was he taking this route? "I thought you didn't like to take horses into mountains," she reminded him. "You said their feet were badly broken by the stones when you came to us."

Kazhak grunted an assent. "Stones break feet, yes. And we could follow Duna south into land of Moesia, then north, then east, crooked way to Black Sea, but there is much swampland that way. Fevers, sickness, for man and horse. So we go shorter way through mountains again, and if horses' feet break you fix, is it so?"

A horse dying of a poison weed was one thing; broken feet, another. To solve the problem of the latter, Goibban had only recently begun making and nailing iron shoes onto the feet of the cartponies, but such skills were beyond Epona's ability. The power had come to her when she summoned it, but she knew deep inside that power had been for a specific purpose, and within the limitations of her own gift. She could not fix a split hoof in the same way.

But it might be wise not to say that to Kazhak. She enjoyed hearing the respect in his voice; she enjoyed being given the more choice morsels of food, instead of having to wait for the leavings.

The plains gave way to woodlands, a thick green fleece climbing the slopes. The Scythians found a stream to follow and all dismounted, leading their horses as the incline grew steeper. Giant crowding conifers created a dense shade. *Perhaps this is what Kazhak meant by dark mountains,* Epona thought.

The first night they camped, though still in the foothills, Epona could already smell the thinner air and feel the difference in altitude in her chest and forehead.

Mountains. This is home for me, she thought. *This feels right.*

Mountains were not home to the Scythians. As they progressed deeper into the Carpātos, following streams and game trails and the occasional paths of trappers or woodcutters, they grew progressively more edgy. All the men darted sidelong glances into the woods, and stopped from time to time to listen, with inheld breath and tense faces.

Autumn had already come to these mountains, and winter was

not far behind, with gray skies and somber colors. A pervasive chill was in the air as Epona and the four Scythians climbed through forests of conifer and oak twisted into grotesque shapes by wind and ice. Great outcroppings of stone broke, with savage thrusts, through the thin soil. Rugged crags brooded above deep valleys blanketed with silence.

Although Epona's heart had warmed to the sight of mountains again, it chilled in her breast in the Carpātos.

Something is wrong, Epona thought. She said nothing to Kazhak, however; the Scythian leader seemed sunk in one of his blackest moods and no one spoke to him more than necessary, fearing a slashing reply or a fist in the mouth. He did not hesitate to hit his men when they angered him.

The Scythians stopped to make camp earlier in the day than they had on the flowered plains, and they built a fire every night, cherishing its bright flame. By unspoken agreement they traveled along the line of settlements strung through the forest, heartened by the sight of human habitation.

Forbidding as these mountains seemed, they were home to a hardy people who lived by trapping and mining. Like the Kelti, they were fiercely independent folk, hard workers who pitted their strength and endurance against the challenge of the earth mother. At night they sat around their own lodgefires and told tales not dissimilar to those of Epona's people.

Some of them saw the Scythians pass by. They did not come out in greeting, offering hospitality as the Kelti would have done. They merely stood beside their snug stone-and-timber huts and watched as the horsemen moved uneasily through their territory.

Even here, in this mountain wilderness, tales were told of the Scythians, and the inhabitants of the Carpātos had no desire to challenge the warriors from the east. Leave them alone and let them pass by.

But the mountain dwellers watched, and saw. And sent runners to the next settlement to spread a warning.

As the Scythians followed a twisting route deeper into the mountains the stories that accompanied them grew more lurid, though they did not know it. All they knew was the uncomfortable feeling at the back of the neck, the raising of hackles that had begun shortly after they left the plains. The horses felt it, too, and were skittish and reluctant to graze when they were unsaddled in the evening. They would only snatch a few bites of the sparse grass that had survived the early frosts, then lift their heads and stand listening, ears flickering back and forth nervously.

They were being followed again.

Kazhak sat by the campfire at night and examined the heads of his arrows, running his thumb along the killing surface again and again, trying to take comfort from the sweetly vicious shape.

But perhaps the thing that followed them was not vulnerable to the triple-edged arrows of the Scythians. Basl and Dasadas said it was not. They claimed they were not afraid of it, but they had acquired much respect for the creature.

None of the Scythians admitted to fear. It was the mountains that made them tense and jumpy; the darkly glowering Carpātos, long the source of wild tales.

Kazhak slept with one eye open, his weapons within easy reach, and listened to the night sounds, the soughing of wind in the pine trees, the little droppings and rustlings and patterings of nocturnal activity. He noted particularly when those sounds ceased and an unnatural quiet descended on the glade where they had made their latest camp. After many long, hard days in difficult terrain, trying to follow the rivers and gorges and avoid the higher peaks, they had at last reached the eastern slope of the Carpātos, and Kazhak had expected to feel in a better mood with the final barrier behind them.

But he was not in a good mood. He was more anxious than ever, and the silence was nerve-wracking. He opened his eyes and looked around.

He saw Basl and Aksinya on watch, just beyond the campfire, and in the other direction he saw something move among the trees.

Kazhak sat up.

Epona was instantly awake, her hand on the hilt of her knife. She heard the silence, too. *Be strong*, she prayed without voice to the spirit of the iron in the knife; Goibban's iron. *If I have enemies, fight them courageously.*

But there were no enemies to be seen. The thing that had flickered among the trees had disappeared.

"Was a man," Kazhak told her, but without conviction.

She removed her hand from the knife hilt.

The morning dawned without sunlight. A pale gray mist enshrouded the landscape and the party of horsemen moved through it like a troop of ghosts, at times scarcely visible to one another. They were mounted again, Epona behind Kazhak. The horses shied at everything that moved; even a branch stirred by the wind frightened them. Epona bent down and stroked the gray stallion's flanks, soothing him, so he behaved better than the others, but his eyes rolled in his head and he snatched at the bit, wanting to run.

They came to a hut built of stones and clay and roofed with untrimmed logs. The small structure stood at the edge of the trail they were following, and beyond it the slope dropped sharply toward a tumbling stream. An old man bundled in furs was squatting in front of the hut, chewing a strip of leather to soften it for making thongs. He stood up as the horses approached.

Epona had grown accustomed to the way people stared at the Scythians, with hostility or fear or naked hatred, but she had never seen anyone so defeated by terror. The old man turned corpse-white and his hands trembled like poplar leaves. He stumbled backward, then bolted into the hut.

He had not been looking at the riders. He had been looking at something on the trail immediately behind them.

Kazhak whirled around in his saddle.

An enormous silvery wolf stood at the edge of dense forest, watching them. Then it was gone; it was simply not there anymore. There were the sounds of a large body crashing through the undergrowth, a heavy stand of mountain laurel: the swishing of branches and snapping of twigs, the thud of feet hitting the earth in a rhythm unknown to any running wolf. One-two, one-two, one-two. Human feet, running.

The old man peered from his hut, his old wife and a grown son crowding close to his shoulders, watching also, their frightened faces pale ovals with staring eyes.

"Was a wolf!" Dasadas cried, fighting to control his plunging, rearing horse.

"Was a man!" Kazhak yelled at him.

"Was both," Aksinya said in a voice barely above a whisper.

They fled down the mountainside toward the cold stream below, careless, for once, of the horses' safety. In their own terror the animals could have stumbled and fallen but they did not. Only when they reached the water did they check their wild gallop and look back, but there was nothing menacing to be seen behind them. The trail was empty except for the mist that swirled and lifted and closed down again, revealing only what it chose to reveal.

Another day's travel, another night's camp, and they would be in the eastern foothills, with the dark Carpātos behind them.

Kazhak was tempted to ride all night, but when Basl made the suggestion first he hit him with a careless backhand across the mouth.

"Kazhak best son of Kolaxais, Prince of Horses," he said. "Not run from anything. Not ride horses at night in rough country. So is man, or wolf. So? What harm? Man cannot hurt us. Wolf cannot hurt us. Let it follow, Kazhak not care."

Epona recognized bravado when she saw it, and was secretly proud of the Scythian. As they rode he began talking to her again, letting his words rebuild his shaken inner confidence.

"On Sea of Grass man can look half day in any direction," he told her. "No surprises. Mountain wolf not follow us there; mountain wolf helpless on Sea of Grass."

Listening to himself made him feel better. "Scythians chase this wolf," he expounded, picturing the hunt, himself riding with a large band of his brothers, many bows and arrows. They would gallop down on this creature and take its head; they would skin it and he would fasten the hide to his tent, where the women would look at it and whisper admiringly among themselves.

He drove his little band eastward at a hard pace.

Meanwhile, the old man in the stone hut by the trail was repeating to a gathering of his kinfolk the description of what he had seen at the edge of the forest. Word passed through the mountains like the piping of the birds and others came to hear, or to repeat similar tales they had already heard as the Scythians rode through their territory.

They told one another, in hushed voices, about the man who changed into a wolf, or the wolf that ran on man's feet after the horsemen, sometimes glimpsed, always terrifying, a creature unlike any seen in the Carpātos before.

When they heard wolves howling in the forest they put new bars on their doors, high up, at the level where a man might try to break the door down.

The Scythians made their last camp in the mountains. Kazhak

prudently chose a site in the lee of a tumble of boulders, with only one possible approach. They camped well before dark, and all dragged deadwood to the site to build a huge fire.

Epona sat crosslegged on the earth, watching the flames and thinking of Tena, She Who Summons Fire. Was the fire animated by the same spirit when the Scythians built it? If she wanted to pray to a Scythian fire, would she need to address it in the language of the firemaker?

She realized how incomplete her knowledge was. There were so many things, now perceived to be important, she should have asked the *druii* when she had the opportunity.

The *druii*. She should not have been thinking of the *druii*, she reminded herself sharply. Those thoughts could send a signal like a bonfire built on the high ground to tell of the death of a chieftain or summon kin-tribes to war. There were those who could follow that signal. She must not . . .

She could not help it. She could feel the shapechanger; he lurked at the edges of her mind as the impossibly large silver wolf had skulked at the edge of the trees, watching with yellow eyes.

She had not escaped him.

They might yet escape; Kazhak seemed to think they could.

Kazhak did not understand the nature of the creature that followed them. And she would not tell him. He might decide to send her back to be rid of it, to deny her the freedom to choose her own life, to choose the galloping horse and the wind in her hair.

Let others sacrifice themselves for the tribe, she thought. *I have put all that behind me. I am going to the Sea of Grass, and you will have no power there, Kernunnos. It is too far to reach, even for you.*

It must be.

The campfire sputtered as it licked the pine knots and showers of sparks flew into the air, looking for their distant brothers, the stars. But the stars were hidden behind heavy clouds. The sky overhead was black and empty, as empty as the night pressing in on the campsite.

Not totally empty, however. Somewhere a wolf howled, and the gray stallion snorted.

Epona was reluctant to fall asleep, to let herself sink, vulnerable, into the dreamworlds, where Kernunnos could so easily reach

229

her. If he were to make one final effort to force her to return to the valley of the Kelti and the priesthood, she felt certain he would make it here, in the mountains, in a landscape familiar to both of them.

The night wore on, as slowly as a night spent in pain.

Five people, none of them sleeping, waited for it to die.

The trees stood very still, keeping watch.

From the heart of the night came a formless shape, gliding over the rough terrain. It flowed like water down sheer precipices; it whispered through the trees like leaves rustling; it was part of the earth, and the dark, and the pattern. It came to reclaim its own.

Before any of the others were aware of it, Epona knew he was watching them again, yellow eyes beyond the safe circle of the campfire.

No! she thought, hurling the message at him silently. *I do not belong to the tribe anymore. These are my people now.*

The fire went out; suddenly, as if a waterskin had been dumped on it. Dasadas sprang to his feet with an oath and notched an arrow to his bowstring, but there was no target.

The darkness moved closer.

Aksinya fumbled in his pack for more flints, but his fingers were numb and he was too clumsy to strike a fire.

The wolf padded around the perimeter of the camp. They could all hear it. It panted hoarsely, loud in the eerie quiet that had fallen. It stepped deliberately on twigs that snapped beneath its weight. It was a very big wolf. It wanted them to know it was there.

The spirit within spoke to Epona. *You are of the Kelti*, it reminded her. *This is not your place. Nor do you belong on the Sea of Grass with these nomads. You are of the same blood as that wolf, and your bones know the songs of his people. He summons you. He summons you home.*

My home is where I make it, she answered inside herself. *I will choose; I am a free person.*

The Kelti are forever free, the spirit within responded. *They are as free as the wind and the water, the trees and the fire. But they are also part of you. You can never escape your own blood.*

The wolf moved closer, its pale coat visible in the darkness, its eyes glowing with their own light. It sat down within six paces of Epona.

Kazhak ran at it, swearing.

It was gone.

Epona clenched her fists and said nothing.

"You see that?" Kazhak shouted, all composure lost. "You all see? Kazhak kill wolf now, stop this. No more. Never no more, that wolf!"

Teeth bared and shortsword in hand he plunged off in the direction he thought the wolf had taken.

"No!" Epona cried, stretching out her hand to him, but he was already beyond her reach. The wolf had insulted him. It had frightened him more badly than he would admit even to himself, then it had walked brazenly into his camp and sat down like a tame hound. He would put a stop to its taunting for all time. Whatever it was, he did not believe it could not be killed.

As he had thought he could kill the stag on the edge of the cliff.

"Stop him!" Epona called to the others. Who could say what might happen to the Scythian in the darkness . . . with the giant wolf?

Basl ran without hesitation to the aid of his leader, although Dasadas shouted a warning and Aksinya urged him to wait. When he was gone, the other two men came and stood beside Epona protectively.

Kazhak scrambled over the rocky ground, breasting his way through a stand of young conifers barely shoulder high, intent on following the fading sounds of the wolf's passage. It had come this way; it was not far ahead of him. He could not shoot it in the dark, but if he could close with it he would hack it to death with sword and knife.

He slowed to a halt, disoriented. The forest around him told no secrets; he heard no footfalls, no branches swishing back into place. The thing had eluded him. Perhaps it had already taken refuge in some rocky lair to wait until daylight and track them again for what reason no man knew.

The animal — it *had* to be an animal — must have the foaming-mouth disease; that was the only explanation for its behavior. Yet he had never heard of an animal acting as this one did.

He heard something behind him and then Basl's welcome voice called out. Kazhak answered. His fury had ebbed away and he was glad of the company of the other man in this choking darkness. He was unsure which way the camp lay; there was no fire-light to guide him.

"Basl, over here!" Kazhak called, starting forward to meet his comrade. But in that moment he heard a sound like the falling of a mighty tree, a tearing and crashing that reverberated through-out the forest, followed by a human yell. Basl's voice. Could a tree fall in a windless forest?

Kazhak floundered toward him, fighting off the branches that cut at his face. He called Basl's name but there was no answer.

There was another sound: the rush of a body through under-growth, very close by. And then one sudden, terrible cry. "It is the wolf! Basl has . . . Aaaiii . . . !"

The cry became a shriek and then a bubbling moan, more chill-ing than any scream. Kazhak had heard that sound before, when a badly aimed blow failed to decapitate a man and left him with a hacked neck, strangling in his own blood.

"Basl!" he cried in anguish, but there was no answer.

The trees and bushes seemed to conspire against him, holding him back as he plunged through them. Under his breath he cursed the mountains and the starless night and the crazy silvery ani-mal . . .

He almost fell over Basl's body. The other Scythian lay doubled up on the ground, making ugly, inhuman sounds. Kazhak scooped him up in his arms and began using his elbows and shoulders to force his way free of the lush growth that entangled them both.

No stars were visible, no guides could lead them back to camp. The wolf might be anywhere in the forest, watching them with the cold amusement of the superior creature. If Kazhak called to his companions it might follow his voice and attack again.

But he had no choice. Basl was dying, or already dead, and he himself was lost. He threw back his head and yelled, the full-throated roar of a nomadic warrior. Perhaps the sound might in-timidate the wolf, though that was a slim hope.

Aksinya answered, unexpectedly close by, and soon Kazhak was stumbling toward the dim but familiar outlines of the horses and his own gray stallion was nickering a greeting.

He laid Basl on the earth and tried to determine the extent of his wounds. Now Aksinya had no trouble starting a fire, and by its light they could see the ragged black hole torn in Basl's throat. It was astonishing he had lived so long with the blood pouring out of his body in great gushes, but even as they watched he went limp and the spirit left him. Epona moved back, to give it room to depart unhindered.

Kazhak moaned with grief. "Brother!" he cried again and again. He collapsed on Basl's body and buried his face against the blood-soaked chest. His shoulders heaved with sobs.

Epona was surprised at these warriors, crying over another warrior's death.

Dasadas was weeping even more loudly than Kazhak, but in spite of his tears he noticed that Basl's dead hand clutched a scrap of something. He pried the fingers open and held the object up to the firelight, so all could see it.

In his death struggle, Basl had cut and hacked at the wolf's head with his new Kelti knife, and had succeeded in tearing away a large flap of flesh and one complete ear.

The mutilated animal must be in agony by now, and losing quantities of blood.

Dasadas lifted the trophy high and shook it in triumph. "Wolf not bother us more!" he cried.

The remaining men crowded around him to examine the torn flesh, and assure one another that they were now free of the creature. They could sleep without fear.

But when Kazhak at last laid his head beside Epona's on the neck of the gray stallion, he muttered, for her ears alone, "Kazhak not so sure wolf is dead. Was bad wound, but Kazhak has seen animals live with worse wounds.

"If it was an animal."

Chapter 19

KAZHAK WANTED TO TRAVEL as quickly as possible. He gave Epona Basl's horse to ride; they would not waste time with a lot of walking. The horse was a brown gelding, almost black in the sunlight except for the lighter-colored hairs on its muzzle and around its eyes. Like the other Scythian horses, its tail and mane had been cut short to avoid spoiling a shot from the bow, but its hair had grown faster than theirs and the mane was already falling over to one side again.

The other men did not offer any objection to Epona's having the horse. Once they would have expressed outrage, but much had happened, and they were changed men. They had originally left the Sea of Grass as part of a large party of tribesmen, thinking of themselves as brothers, avid for new lands and ready, they thought, for anything. They were returning depleted in number and diminished in spirit. Their fire was quenched, temporarily.

The brown gelding was neither as powerful nor as smooth gaited as Kazhak's stallion, but he was a surefooted animal with a good disposition. His only reaction to his new rider was a fretful tossing of his head until Epona got used to managing the reins and the bit. The girl was delighted to realize how easy it was to communicate with the horse, just by the lightest touch on the reins. She taught her hands to be gentle, mastering the rider's art of give and take. Soon she had learned that she could whisper to the horse through her fingers and his mouth. By the end of the first day they were friends.

She rode.

With the horse beneath her, the glory of command surrendered to her hands and her will, the horizon spread beckoning before her . . . she rode.

Every step took them closer to the birthplace of the sun, the Black Sea region, the land of the nomads. On a morning of blue sky and high clouds they left a final strip of woodland and rode down a gentle slope to a shallow stream. Beyond the stream they climbed a steep incline, the horses plunging upward. Then they were at the top and the forests were all behind them. They trotted through a last sparse stand of birches and rode out, blinking against a sudden flood of yellow light, onto the Sea of Grass.

The prairie stretched into forever, dwarfing the flowered plain that had so impressed Epona on the other side of the Carpātos. This tableland had no limits as she knew limits. A human being, riding down from the mountains, out of the embrace of the forests, would feel himself shrinking with every step he took onto the grasslands.

Light was everywhere, a constant like the wind. No longer just above, it went around and through; it dominated. Nothing blocked it. They rode in light as if in the belly of a god.

The land undulated gently; it was a calm sea. When the wind caught the grasses they rippled into waves, reflecting light from their surfaces in constantly changing patterns that gave an impression of watery motion.

At first the unrelieved prairie was a novelty and Epona rode with slack rein, drinking in the landscape with her eyes. Waving stalks still bearing heavy seedheads rose as high as the horses' shoulders, and the animals snatched bites of grass as they traveled, never having to lower their heads to eat. The frost that chilled the mountains had not yet reached the plains.

The relentless sun of summer had scorched the vegetation, so Epona initially thought it was all one color, but when she looked closer she realized the color was not uniform and the various blades of grass were not identical. Some still showed traces of the silvery-green they had worn in spring; others were streaked with russet; still others had broad, dull leaves the horses nosed aside and did not eat. Each stalk of grass was as individual as a person, its nature shaped by the spirit within. In some places were patches where grass had failed to grow and Epona caught glimpses of the

235

bare earth, dark brown like horse dung, starred with blue and yellow blossoms of some bold, late-blooming flower. She leaned from the saddle to get a better look at the plants, but they were only a blur beneath the feet of the trotting horses.

"Can we go more slowly here?" she called to Kazhak.

"Slow for why?"

"I want to look at the grass." Her answer sounded foolish in her own ears, and Kazhak laughed.

"Look!" he cried, dropping the reins on the stallion's neck and flinging his arms wide, as if to embrace the land from horizon to horizon. "Look at grass. Everywhere!"

When her eye tired of the rippling sea of plant life, Epona tilted her head back and looked at the sky, the immense sky that was so much larger than she had realized. It curved over the land like a bowl. Once she had thought the sky was immutably limited by mountains and framed by the vertical slashes of pine trees, but now she saw she had been wrong. The sky could not be so captured.

The Sea of Grass showed her the reality of Sky.

Clouds billowed up into forms she had never seen in the mountains. They became mountains themselves, towering thunderheads that rose above the steppes and carried the day on their shoulders. Theirs was the dazzling white of sunlit snow. She watched them until spots danced in her eyes, trusting the brown horse to follow his companions without her guiding hand on the reins. She was almost blinded by the glare of cloud and sky. She closed her eyes. They felt hot inside her lids and there was no soothing darkness, just a blue burning.

When she opened her eyes again the sky was still there but a strong wind was chasing the thunderheads before it, over the horizon and beyond.

Her mind could not stretch to Beyond.

The sky was too big. It began to oppress her. It crouched above her throughout the day, pushing her down, making her small. Without the cloud pillars to hold it up it might crush her. She wanted to cower beneath it and offer sacrifice, begging for mercy. Yet it went on and on, and they rode on and on beneath it, and nothing changed.

How could men live under such a sky?

She reined the brown gelding close to Kazhak's horse and tried to talk about her feelings. The Scythian listened politely, but he did not understand. The woman seemed to think there was something wrong with the land, whereas he knew that things had just become right again.

He tried to reassure her. "Here on grassland men look big," he told her, speaking from his own feelings. "Men stand tall on Sea of Grass, cast long shadows, is it so? In forest, trees are bigger. In mountains, mountains are bigger. Here, nothing stands taller than Kazhak on horse. Is good place. Is best place."

That might be true for him, but Epona felt diminished by the landscape. How could there be one truth for him and another for her? She turned that question over and over in her curious mind, trying to make both pieces fit together into one whole.

For a while they had seen distant fingerings of woodland stretching out onto the prairie, but soon those too were left behind and the only trees they saw were those marking streams and rivers; waterways that became less frequent as they moved on across the prairie. Epona began looking for those few trees as for familiar faces, hungering for a sight of branch and leaf.

As she had done with water, Epona had always taken trees for granted. The forests were an integral part of Kelti life, satisfying both their physical and spiritual needs. Epona's people lived in lodges built of timber and prayed to the spirits of the trees that supplied the logs. They burned wood for heat and cooking, reduced more wood to charcoal to feed the insatiable appetites of forge and smelter, ate from wooden bowls, used wooden tools and utensils, and shared intimately in the life of the trees; the breathing, sentient beings who occupied space with them on the earth mother.

The Kelti took fruits from the trees and leaves and roots for medicinal purposes; they used bark for dyes and were famed throughout the trade routes for their resins. From studying a given tree, a *drui* could predict the cycles of drought, that his people might prepare for them. A sentry could use that same tree as a lookout post, and when that tree's spirit had moved on to its next-life the trunk might become a rooftree in a lodge, a carved chest for a new wife, or beams or doors or embracing walls.

The tree was not just part of life, it embodied life. Epona had never realized the sight of trees was essential to her inner self until she rode onto the Sea of Grass, and looked at endless, treeless prairie.

Night did not come suddenly on the steppe. Epona only gradually became aware of a change in the light, and the great distance the sun had traveled while they themselves were going the other way. Light that had been yellow in the morning became white, then amber, and at last lay in flat, violet-colored planes across the land as the sun died in the west.

The young woman pulled her cloak more tightly about her. She was not eager to spend a night, naked and vulnerable as she felt, beneath that gaping maw of sky. She hoped they would at least seek a stream bank for their encampment, so she might look at trees before she fell asleep.

The Scythians did not feel the absence of trees. They camped beneath the open sky, simply stopping when it was too dark to see well. They passed the waterskins and made their few preparations for the night as serenely as if there were log walls around them. Beside Epona, Kazhak went to sleep on his back, face turned upward.

Epona could not sleep. She curled herself into the smallest possible ball and closed her eyes tightly, but that only served to make the unfamiliar night sounds of the grasslands more audible. The wind, which had blown all day, now moaned like a tormented spirit. It spoke the language of an unknown place; it was not the familiar wind of the mountains.

Stranger, it said to her. *Foreigner. You do not belong here.*

Epona could not bear to lie with her eyes closed while that great voice swept over her. She rolled over on her back and opened her eyes, looking up.

And the stars looked down at her.

The *stars!*

The earth seemed to heave beneath her. She scrabbled frantically, her fingers clawing the grass and soil on which she lay, clutching for a hold that would keep her from tumbling down . . . up? . . . into the myriad stars. Stars beyond the ability of man to count or mind to understand, stars that robbed her of her equilibrium and left her dazed, staring into the depths of boundless sky.

Epona had been raised with the nearby, familiar spirits of animal and plant, water and fire and stone. She had been taught to understand the aspects of the earth mother upon whom her people had depended for game and timber, copper and salt. She had been taught to revere the sun and moon as distant, less-immediate powers with a strong influence on the earth mother and thereby on her, but at one remove.

She had hardly ever bothered to think about the stars. They were tiny lights in a sky narrowed and framed by mountain peaks; they were eyes that watched but had little meaning.

Now, lying on her back and staring at the immense night sky arching over the broad steppe Epona felt the magnitude of stars for the first time, and was forced to acknowledge them. The bards told of a time in the far past when the people had been more involved with the great lights in the sky than people in thistime, dealing with them in complex ways that no one now remembered or would understand. But that was in the dawn of the race, and much had changed. Snow and ice grind boulders into sand. Now the stars were an alien multitude, watching the earth with glittering indifference, and Epona felt pitifully small in their presence.

I have shrunk away to nothing, she told herself. *I am less than a blade of grass among too many blades of grass, underneath too many stars.*

I was born Kelti, but I am afraid, even so.

I was arrogant; I thought I had importance. Now I have disappeared and no one will ever know or care.

She lay pinned to the earth, the boundaries of her small world blown away.

When she awoke it was to birdsong. She opened her eyes and saw a little bird, even tinier than she had felt the night before, sitting on a blade of grass not far from her head and singing to her without fear. Its size did not matter; its spirit was sufficient.

She smiled at the bird and began to feel better.

Birds on the Sea of Grass sang songs different from those of mountain birds, and it seemed to Epona they sang louder. They began their sunrise prayer with a burst of exultation that came from the very air above, rather than from trees or woodland cover.

As they sang, they were accompanied by a lovely sound Epona eventually identified as the omnipresent wind, harping the grasses.

It was as if the earth mother had known her distress, and sent comfort to Epona on the wings and in the songs of birds.

She raised her head and saw Kazhak awake, looking at her. "It is . . . lovely here, I think," she commented, and his eyes told her he was pleased.

Kazhak arose feeling expansive. He talked, he joked, he tried to cajole Dasadas and Aksinya out of more somber moods. True, Basl was dead, but the pale wolf no longer followed them. Nothing could track them while suffering from such a wound.

"We have lost many brothers," he said, "but death happens. While we live, let us live."

They broke their fast with meat and sips of water and galloped eastward, Kazhak leading, his heels drumming the sides of the gray stallion.

They could not keep up such a pace all day, however, and eventually slowed to a walk to let the horses blow. Kazhak turned to Epona. "Why you smile?"

"I was listening to the birds sing. I think I never appreciated birdsong before."

"You know any songs? Can you sing about the horse, the wind, the feathergrass, maybe?"

"My people don't have songs about those things," she told him.

"What else is to sing about?"

"We sing the songs of the spirits and the history of the people. We sing to remember all that has gone before."

Kazhak frowned. "Is bad custom. Better to forget the past. Day go, night come, new day next. Ride ahead, no look back."

"But the past isn't gone," she argued. "It still influences everything we do and are." She thought it better not to explain that the past was one of the otherworlds, and the *druii* had access to the otherworlds.

Perhaps Kazhak's way was better, after all — ride on and do not look back. Do not turn your head and see the dead farmers in their field, or your abandoned home and friends, or the sha . . .

"Why don't you sing?" she asked Kazhak hurriedly, interrupting her own thoughts.

He chuckled. "Kazhak sing, horses run away."

"Then what about Dasadas and Aksinya?"

"They sing some; they dance better. Ride best. Riding is always best. Only Thracians want music all the time."

Yet he had asked her to sing. He must enjoy music, too.

They rode side by side, their horses' heads nodding in unison. Aksinya and Dasadas followed several paces behind. At Epona's urging, Kazhak began to tell her of the customs of his own people, and their conversation was carried on the wind to the two who followed.

Aksinya paid no attention, but Dasadas listened closely, his ears attuned to the sound of Epona's voice. He was the youngest of the band of Scythians, not many years past childhood but powerfully built, with clearcut features that might have been formed by a craftsman's chisel, and a heavy mane of light-brown hair. Since the incident of the Thracian horse, Dasadas had watched Epona as keenly as Aksinya watched for game to shoot. When Epona gestured, Dasadas noticed. When she spoke, he listened.

Now he watched the back of her head with somber passion, his pale eyes glowing in their deep sockets.

Once, Dasadas had agreed with his friends who thought the Kelti woman was an unnecessary encumbrance and resented Kazhak for bringing her. Then he had watched in disbelief as the girl pressed her body against that of the crazed, dying horse, ignoring the thrashing legs and deadly, striking hooves. Epona had somehow reversed the effects of the poison weed by her physical presence and her will. It was more than magic; to Dasadas it seemed to be the visitation of a god.

He was shaken and dazzled. He no longer saw Epona as a mere woman. She was a supernatural being to him now, the possessor of unknown powers. He thought her both terrible and beautiful. His eyes followed her constantly; he could think of nothing else.

Epona, Epona. Epona sitting on a horse as no woman had done before, head thrown back, yellow hair blowing free, warm voice laughing. Epona, silent and withdrawn, brooding over mysteries. Epona, as elusive as the wind in the Sea of Grass.

Epona, Epona.

"Is bad we had to bury Basl like seed, just stuck in hole in ground," Kazhak was saying. "He will not grow; he will not make nice plant horses can eat." His eyes twinkled. Even in his friend's death, Kazhak could find something to joke about if he was in the right mood. He had done his mourning the night of Basl's death, when he and the others had stabbed their own ear lobes with their knives and shrieked the dead man's name aloud, tearing their hair and their clothes, wild in their grief.

But that was over now; they had ridden away.

"If Basl died on Sea of Grass, among people of the horse," Kazhak told Epona, "would have been big funeral. While some build death house, we feast and mourn forty days to show proper respect for a brother, a comrade. Then we bury Basl in wooden house."

"Forty days!" Epona's mind presented her with a picture of how Basl's body would have looked after forty days, unburied.

Kazhak grinned. "Body keep. Open belly, clean out inside, fill with cypress, parsley seed, frankincense. Sew up skin, seal with wax. Family of Basl put body on wagon and take to visit every tribe in area, say farewell. Men from one tribe accompany body to next tribe, on and on. Forty days. Then back to death house and burial. Everyone gets to see Basl before he is gone. Nice custom, is it so?"

Epona could not think of an appropriate comment. "Are there many tribes of your race?" she asked instead.

Kazhak shook his head in assent. "Many tribes, each different, but all men of the horse. Live from shore of the sea all the way north to the forest land. Kazhak's line is of royal blood from homeland on river Tanais, what blackcloaks call the Don."

"Who are the blackcloaks?"

"Savages, live north of grassland. Not horse people." His voice was contemptuous. "Many savages live on edges of Sea of Grass; smart ones stay out of our way. Man can ride fourteen days, east or west, see only Scythians."

"What are some of those others like, those savages?" Epona wanted to know. It amused her to hear Kazhak so patronizingly refer to others as savage.

"Is race of baldheads," he told her. "Dirt diggers, farmers. Is race who live by wrecking ships on seacoast, people called Tauri; never laugh, those Tauri. Vultures." The shipwreckers were distasteful to him; he spat their name from his mouth.

"Is another race called Budini," he continued. "Good fighters, strong, fire-haired, blue eyes, get angry very easy."

Epona thought of her own people, so many among them with blue eyes and red hair, and wondered if the bellicose Budini were a kin-tribe she had never heard of before.

"Who else?" she asked Kazhak.

"Agathyrsi," he said, curling his lip with scorn. "All men sleep with all women, no man has woman of his own. You see? Savages.

"And is also Androphagi, very interesting. Man eaters."

Epona looked at him with disbelief, thinking she had misunderstood his words. "What do you mean?"

"Cannibals," he replied. "Is hard to believe, is it so? But is true. When man of Androphagi die, his family mix his flesh with mutton and all eat. Worse than all others, those people. Even treat women like men, equal."

His voice dismissed the cannibals, condemned not only for their feeding habits but also for the unforgivable custom of accepting women as equal to men. As the Kelti did.

Epona's good mood melted away. Kazhak did not notice. Once again he was launched on a pleasurable monologue, larding his dissertation on the savages with amusing asides and anecdotes, the sort of stories that had made Epona laugh earlier. He was so entranced by the sound of his own voice he did not hear her silence now.

Dasadas, however, was aware of the way her shoulders slumped; he saw her turn her face from Kazhak and go into a place of her own, inside herself.

The reins went slack on the brown gelding's neck and Epona let him pick his own path, knowing he would wander a little distance away from the gray stallion. Geldings preferred to keep distance between themselves and the unaltered male. Before Kazhak noticed the widening space between them, however, Aksinya called his attention to a deer hiding in the tall grass within easy reach of their arrows.

Kazhak slapped his thigh, delighted with the discovery. Even as he took his bow and arrows from their case, the *gorytus* always worn at his left side, the deer realized its danger and took flight, and Kazhak and Aksinya pounded after it joyously, all else momentarily forgotten.

Epona did not care to watch them pursue and kill the deer. Suddenly she felt a deep desire to be alone; alone with just the horse and the prairie and her own thoughts. Kazhak was not watching, he did not care what she did so long as she did not interfere with the hunt.

Something wild and reckless seized her. She glanced once at the fleeing deer, which was running southward in great bounds, then turned the brown gelding's head toward the north and clamped her legs against its sides. "Go," she ordered, fiercely.

The gelding leaped forward in a headlong gallop.

Epona was not running away; she was not thinking of escape. She just wanted to run, to feel the strength of the horse beneath her and answer the call of the far horizon. To go and go, without limits. To run, as free as the deer, as free as the birds, faster than human could ever run, to gallop and gallop, obsessed with speed and freedom.

The gelding enjoyed the sudden burst of speed as much as his rider did. After the first few bolting strides he settled into a ground-eating gallop. The light weight of the girl on his back was as nothing to him. She had given him his head and now she leaned forward to urge him to go faster. He surrendered gladly to the same impulse that had seized Epona. They raced as one being across the prairie, glorying in their flight.

Out of the corner of his eye, Kazhak saw them go, but it did not interfere with his pursuit of the deer, who had proved to be wily and fast. As a young rider he, too, had been unable to resist racing his horse. He knew Epona would run only so far before the frenzy subsided and she returned to him, walking her lathered horse. She had nowhere else to go.

It was more important to get the deer than to worry unnecessarily about the woman.

Dasadas had also taken up the pursuit, but it was not the deer he chased. He had watched Epona rein her horse aside and kick it violently; he had seen how easily she rode the speeding animal, as if she rode an arrow released from a bow. She rode like a man; no, better than a man, she rode as befitted a goddess.

Dasadas turned his own horse's head toward the north and set off after her.

The brown gelding's running rhythm was music to the woman who rode him. It reverberated through her body, as strong as the priest drum: da da *dum*, da da *dum*, da da *dum*. It was intoxicating, urging her to go ever faster. There seemed no limit to her newfound lust for speed. She lashed the gelding's shoulders with the reins, shouting at him to go faster, leaning low on his neck, and he responded with an additional burst of energy.

But he could not sustain it. Gradually the momentum faded, and she knew it was over. The brown horse dropped back to an easy canter and Epona regretfully prepared to rein him in a wide circle and return to the others.

Then she heard the tattoo of hooves behind her and looked over her shoulder. Dasadas, his face as dark as fury, was riding down on her, whipping his horse. She felt a flash of fear. Kazhak must have misinterpreted her action and sent this man to capture her before she could escape.

She would return willingly, she had never intended otherwise, but she would not let Dasadas drag her back like a runaway slave. She leaned over her horse's mane and called on the brown gelding for new strength with which to outrun their pursuer.

Dasadas saw what she did. She was trying to flee him as the deer fled Kazhak. But Kazhak would get the deer, and he would get the woman. He would have her; he would have her *now;* he would possess this being who filled his thoughts and made his brain whirl with foolish dreams. He, Dasadas, deserved her. Kazhak, who was negligent and had bad judgment, did not.

He put to use the skills developed through years spent in the saddle, matching every rhythm of his body to that of his mount, and began to close the gap.

Epona glanced back and saw Dasadas gaining on her. She lashed the brown gelding with the reins but he had nothing more to give. His rider watched, despairing, as the young Scythian drew abreast of her and guided his horse close to hers. He reached across the space between them and caught hold of her reins, jerking the brown gelding's head against his knee.

Epona fought him; she struck at his face with her fists and called him by the names Kelti women reserved for men they despised, but he hung on grimly, forcing her horse to a halt.

The spirit within her made a small mourning for the beauty of the ride, so cruelly cut short.

Dasadas seized Epona and pulled her off the horse. She fell to the ground between his mount and hers and he fell on top of her, already tearing at her with iron fingers.

The horses shied away.

Chapter 20

S HE TRIED TO FIGHT HIM OFF, but the fall had knocked the wind out of her and she had trouble summoning the necessary strength. Dasadas was very muscular and very determined.

Her body and spirit had accepted Kazhak; she had no desire for Dasadas and no intention of submitting to him. She writhed beneath him, trying to get her knee up into his belly. Then she heard the words he was mumbling.

"Tell, tell, tell," he panted.

"What are you saying?" She brought one arm up at an angle between them, bracing herself so that her elbow kept his chest from hers, but he shoved her arm aside and threw his whole weight on her, pressing her into the earth.

"Tell!" he commanded.

His face was directly over hers, staring down with wild eyes. His features were more finely proportioned than Kazhak's, his brown beard was softer, his lips were fuller, but there was something hopelessly hungry in those eyes that alarmed her. She made her body as rigid as possible to show him she was unwilling to accede to his demands, whatever they might be.

Dasadas made a mighty effort to summon the few words of the Kelti language he could remember, so the woman would understand what he wanted. She had to understand, and give it to him; it was more important than her body, which he could so easily take.

He wanted to be given access to her magic.

His defeat at the hands of Goibban the smith had humiliated Dasadas, and he had been further embarrassed by his own fear of the strange giant wolf that followed them and killed Basl. It was as if his manhood had been under attack since his first meeting with the Kelti, and he was anxious to make up for his loss of prestige in his own eyes by acquiring a special attribute, something that would elevate him to a new plane of self-respect. He would possess the magic woman and her secret. He would have something very special. She must tell him how she had done it.

"Horse," he said, spraying her with spittle in his eagerness to get the words out and be understood. "Horse dead." He could not think of the word for sick. "You. Fix." He glared at her. She must know his thoughts; she was magic.

Epona was baffled. Had one of the horses died, and did he think she could bring it back from the otherworld? She struggled to raise her head and caught a quick glimpse of his mount and hers, grazing together a few paces away, alive and well. What did he mean, then?

He saw the confusion in her eyes and it enraged him. How could she give it to him if she did not understand? Could he acquire the magic merely by possessing her body? But no — if that were possible, Kazhak would already have done so, and being Kazhak he would have bragged about it.

Dasadas had brought down a tremendous trophy from the chase but did not know how to take advantage of his prize. There was both fury and frustration in the face looming over Epona's. Muttering inaudibly, he began tearing at her clothes, determined to have at least that much of her.

Epona was better equipped to deal with a simple physical assault than with an incomprehensible demand. Throughout her childhood, she, like all the girls of the Kelti, had practiced the skills of battle with the boys, against the day they might have to fight beside their husbands. It was an accepted part of education, and if she did not love it as Mahka did, she had at least been very good at it. And now she had recovered her wind.

Dasadas was surprised at the way she fought him. She was stronger than she looked, the slender Kelti woman, and she wrestled with him as a man would have, understanding the advantages of momentum and timing. Her determination was the equal of

247

his; she would not surrender. Dasadas enjoyed that. He felt the quick nervous energy flooding her body, like an unbroken colt's on a spring morning, so full of itself that it would buck wildly rather than submit to a rider. He clamped her with his knees and gritted his teeth, preparing to ride her anyway. His face reflected his arrogant certainty.

Epona pretended to relax, just long enough for him to start fumbling with his clothes, thinking that she had given in. Then she lunged upward suddenly, gouging at his eyes with her thumbs.

She caught him off balance and broke his leg grip. One hand still clamped her shoulder but he had to take that away to defend his face, and all the time she was shrieking at him with the war cry of the Kelti. She was no longer beneath him; she seemed to be swarming all over him, jabbing at him, punching him with a deadly knowledge of his most vulnerable areas. Before the startled Scythian could recover himself she twisted like an eel and rolled clear of him, then was on her feet and running to her horse.

A leap and a swing of her leg and Epona was safely atop the brown gelding, jerking his head up, pulling him away from the grass. She glanced back and saw Dasadas gaping at her with astonishment. He held out his hand as if it could still close on her, but she kicked the horse and rode back to Kazhak.

Dasadas stared after her. He felt as if he were wracked by a fever. The energy the Kelti woman had summoned to fight him had excited him more than any experience he had ever had with a woman. He could still feel the touch of her body along the length of his; his flesh ached with the memory.

He got slowly to his feet. He wanted her more than ever. His body was throbbing with the lust he had thought to relieve between her thighs. And also, more than ever, he was awed by her, and afraid of her; afraid of something so far outside his experience. Epona, Epona.

Gradually becoming aware of the bruised areas where she had pummeled his body, he went to retrieve his horse.

Kazhak, busy skinning the deer, looked up to see Epona riding toward him at a sedate walk. Her horse had sweated but the lather was dry, causing the shaggy, incoming winter hair on his neck to lie in a pattern of waves. The face of the girl was cool, detached. She barely gave Kazhak a nod of greeting before turning away to care for her horse.

Kazhak had been returning with the slain deer when his sharp eyes saw Dasadas and Epona in the distance. He had watched, immobile, as Dasadas caught the girl and pulled her from her horse. He had thrown down the deer and grabbed his sword, even as Aksinya laid a restraining hand on his arm, but then they had both seen, in the far distance, the small figure of the Kelti woman elude the man and head back toward them.

By mutual wordless consent they had returned to the job at hand, preparing the welcome fresh meat to be added to their provisions for the remainder of the journey.

Kazhak watched from underneath his heavy eyebrows as Dasadas returned alone, looking like a thundercloud. There was a bruise starting to grow purple just underneath his eye and he had a split lip.

Kazhak smiled to himself and said nothing, but that night he offered Epona the deer's liver as well as the choice part of the haunch. Dasadas received his meat last, a stringy portion that once would have gone to the woman.

When he glowered at Kazhak he met a frosty stare in return. "No more," Kazhak said, and Dasadas knew what he meant. "She will go into tent of Kazhak. Remember that."

"Her horse ran away, had to be caught," Dasadas said.

Kazhak was not fooled. "Her horse did not run away. She rides better than you."

Dasadas was treading on dangerous ground now, and he knew it. But he could not help himself. Even with Kazhak facing him, glowering at him, he could not keep his eyes from cutting swiftly sideways to steal another look at Epona. Kazhak saw that glance. "She will live in Kazhak's tent," he said again, and he doubled one fist and pounded it onto the open palm of the other to drive those words home. Dasadas hardly even heard them. His ears were still filled with the sound of Epona's voice.

When Kazhak and Epona stretched themselves on the ground for sleeping, Kazhak took her fiercely, again and again, so that no one could misunderstand. Even as she lay beneath him, galloping with his body to the rhythms of pleasure, Epona was aware that

249

Dasadas was watching them from beyond the campfire, and she pitied him. Then the rhythm speeded up, and she forgot Dasadas altogether.

But in the cool gray light of dawn she reflected that bedsports were not as simple as they seemed. Other things were involved, aside from flesh and blood.

The next day they entered a region familiar to the Scythians, though Epona saw no difference between it and other parts of the steppeland. But Kazhak spoke more often now of his tribe, the herds, this and that familiar landmark; and even dour Aksinya seemed more cheerful than he had since the journey eastward began.

The sun was high overhead when they came to the first huddle of wagons and tents at the edge of a mixed herd of horses and cattle, and a small flock of sheep.

Some wagons were mere ox-drawn carts, but several were large enough to support domed tents set up on their beds. These tents, and others set up independently on their own frames upon the earth, were made of overlapped layers of heavy felt, lashed together onto collapsible supports of birch and willow. Epona would later learn that the felt was made by wetting and pounding together wool and animal hair until the fibers interlocked, then waterproofing the material further with grease. The result looked flimsy to the eyes of a Kelt accustomed to timber lodges, but it was sufficient, even for the savage climate of the steppe. The women could set up or dismantle such tents in less than half a day, while their men attended to the herd, and in the larger wagons a family could live with a degree of comfort within snug felt walls.

Epona noticed that the biggest wagon was equipped with a horse hitch and a team; not the leggy saddle horses the Scythians rode, but big, sturdy animals of more common breeding, large-headed like the Thracian horses, and obviously capable of more speed and maneuverability than any Kelti cartpony possessed.

Kazhak rode toward the most ostentatious tent to offer greetings to the leader of the band of nomads. Epona and the men followed at a distance, allowing Kazhak to take the brunt of whatever favor, or disfavor, would be shown. That was always the leader's lot.

Kazhak was certain of a friendly welcome here, however, and he advanced with a grin already spread across his face like the rising sun. Epona followed him closely, turning from side to side to look at the domestic arrangements of the nomads, unlike anything she had seen before.

Whole families seemed to live in, and under, the wagons, and the faces of children peeped shyly out through gaps in the covering. Older children, windburned boys with unkempt hair and darting eyes, abandoned their task of tending the goats and came forward to watch the newcomers ride into camp. The faces of these youngsters showed neither fear nor curiosity, but the inbred mistrust of strangers that they had imbibed with their mother's milk.

There were no girl children visible in the camp, and no women to be seen.

As Kazhak approached the largest tent its owner rode toward him on a thick-necked chestnut horse. The two men roared a greeting at each other, jumped down from their mounts simultaneously, and strode into the tent together, arms around each other.

Epona had only a brief glimpse of the Scythian chief, and found it difficult to guess his age. Sun and wind and bitter winters tanned the hides of the nomads uniformly, so there was little difference between the young and the old. Even the ubiquitous wrinkles around the eyes were a result of squinting across grasslands, and as common among boys as men. This man's worn crimson trousers were the color of drying blood, and instead of a felt cap he kept his hair out of his face with a browband of beaten gold worth a cartload of salt.

Other men were coming into the camp, shouting recognition of Dasadas and Aksinya, and soon the Scythians were surrounded by friends. But no one came near Epona. She sat alone on her horse, wrapped in her bearskin cloak and her dignity, and felt their eyes crawl over her like insects. No one spoke to her. No one spoke of her. They stared at her and waited.

Kazhak emerged from the tent, his friend the chief close behind him. Kazhak repeated the man's name loudly and with affection, "Potor, Potor!" and they clapped each other on the back. Potor had meant to extend an invitation to Kazhak's companions to join them in the tent, but then he got a good look at the lone figure sitting on the dark brown gelding.

251

It was a woman. With yellow hair, and uncovered face!

He muttered an epithet and made a sign to protect himself from evil.

"Is Kelti woman," Kazhak hastened to explain. "Kazhak bring from the land of the salt miners, many days' ride. Very valuable, this woman. Worth more than gold."

Potor took a step backward, away from his friend. "Kazhak has gone mad," he said with pity.

"No, no, is strange story, but when you hear, you will understand. We sit and eat, drink, is it so?"

Potor was unsure. "Woman . . . *riding* a horse?" He still could not believe his eyes.

"She earned it," Kazhak replied.

"You tell Potor," the chief decided. "Now." He went back into the tent, and Kazhak, beckoning to his men to join him, followed.

The tent flap fell closed behind them.

Epona felt eyes staring at her from every wagon, but when she looked, they were not there. The Scythian men had drifted away from the area where she waited, looking over their shoulders at her suspiciously before going about their business. Even the children had melted away, and she was alone with the horses. Yet she knew she was not alone; those hundreds of eyes were watching, watching.

The women must all be in the tents and wagons, kept out of sight. What sort of people did not allow their women to welcome travelers?

What sort of women would willingly stay hidden away from the light and air, imprisoned in cells of felt and leather?

To give herself something to do, Epona dismounted and began tending to the horses. She removed their saddles and rubbed their backs with grass; she offered them a small drink of water each, from the waterskin. She noticed that no one came forward to give her any assistance.

Food smells issued from the tents, and her stomach rumbled.

The men of the tribe stayed at least a dozen gallop strides away as they talked in small clusters or cared for their own horses. True Scythians, they did not dismount unless absolutely necessary. One of them yelled something, and Epona saw a figure swathed in blankets emerge from one of the smaller wagons and carry a bowl to the man, who emptied it while he sat on his horse, drinking in noisy gulps. The person who had served him scurried back to the wagon, face covered so Epona could not see a glimmer of flesh.

But she walked as women walk.

Slaves, Epona thought grimly.

Not me.

There was the sound of masculine laughter in Potor's tent, and someone was playing a flute.

It was hard to believe the camp was normally so quiet. Epona watched as the men rode back to their herds, and she expected to see the women come out of the wagons, but they did not. The felt hanging on the sides of the wagons twitched as if someone moved it from within, and occasionally she heard a whisper or a smothered exclamation. But no one came to bid her welcome.

The gray stallion put his muzzle in the palm of her hand and breathed a soft sigh. She leaned her forehead against his neck and stood close to him, smelling the familiar horse smells, comforted. She was not alone. She had a friend.

Another well-bundled figure emerged from one of the tents and came toward her, carrying a bronze bowl of fine Thracian workmanship, reeking with fermented mares' milk. The servitor set the bowl at Epona's feet and hurried away without speaking.

The mess in the bowl turned the Kelti girl's stomach. She would rather eat the unseasoned meat and leathery bread in the saddlebags. She emptied the bowl onto the trampled earth, where it lay like a puddle of vomit, and hunted in Kazhak's pack for something better. She found the small pouch of white leather he kept here; she had seen him take an herb from it occasionally and chew with obvious pleasure. The Scythians claimed the herb enabled a man — or a horse — to go as much as twelve days without water. Now she decided to try the stuff for herself, as compensation for being abandoned.

The first bite was dry and bitter, but as her saliva mixed with it she was aware of a minty taste that improved each time she chewed. It might not abolish hunger and thirst, but it did make her feel pleasantly relaxed. She no longer minded the passage of the sun overhead or her long wait in the dust with the horses.

The afternoon wore on and she grew sleepy. She ordered the brown gelding to lie down and stretched out next to him, her head pillowed on his neck, her ankles crossed like a man's. One might as well be comfortable.

Knowing that the watchers in the wagons were staring at her amused her. *I am a free person*, she wanted to say to them. *I can do what I like*.

She smiled to herself and fell asleep in the sun.

Kazhak awoke her by kicking the sole of her foot. The expression on his face was one of outrage at her unconventional attitude; yet his eyes were twinkling and she knew he was not really angry, but secretly amused by her.

She had been an astonishing sight, a woman stretched out like a man, sleeping on her horse's neck in broad daylight. The shock and scandal would fuel tongues in this tribe for many days. Kazhak could hear the women, the ordinary women, other men's women, jibber-jabbering.

"We not stay here tonight," he told Epona. "Get up; we ride on."

He did not order her to saddle all the horses, as the watching Scythians expected. Each of the four prepared his — or her — own animal and they mounted together, like comrades, and rode away.

The next day they saw more groups of the horse people: single families driving small herds and occasional larger groups, where several families had come together for trade or to share wagon repairs. Kazhak was hailed as he rode by, for many recognized him, but he did not stop to visit. He had been frustrated enough by his conversation with Potor; he did not want to explain Epona again until he reached his own tribe.

He was now very concerned about his ability to convince Kolaxais and the shamans of Epona's value. And they must believe; he had brought back so little, after leaving with such great expectations. A few splendid Kelti blades, and the girl — that was all he could show to justify his long absence and his tragic expenditure of men and horses.

When he had tried to describe Kelti magic to Potor, to give him an idea of Epona's value, the other Scythian had been dubious. "Thracian horse was not dying," he said. "You were fooled,

Kazhak. You let woman impress you; is sign of great weakness in man. Potor is surprised at you."

"Kazhak knows what he saw. Horse was dead while still standing, Potor. Nothing could have saved it. Kazhak has seen other things, too, things with no explanation but very strong magic."

"Potor has seen this Kelti woman do nothing," his friend replied. "May be as you say, Kazhak, but may be not. Have her show us. Bring her now, have her do magic, some hard thing, and Potor will listen to your words with pricked ears."

But Kazhak did not want to waste Epona on convincing Potor and his men. She must be saved, hoarded like the precious gold he no longer carried; saved to dazzle the shamans and give them new respect for Kazhak.

He assumed a haughty expression to show Potor that such a request was beneath consideration.

"Kelti woman does not do tricks like trained monkey taken from eastern traders," he said with immense dignity. "Her magic is of very high kind. For special use only, Potor. Such magic is to be saved like small drop of water on empty prairie in summertime."

Potor dug into his mouth with one grimy forefinger, hunting for a meat fiber caught between his back teeth. "It is said that there are people in the west who are very skilled with magic," he commented, talking almost inaudibly around his probing finger. He found the meat and fished it out, than ate it again with great satisfaction. "But you cannot bring their magic to your tribe, Kazhak. Is foolish thing to attempt; is dangerous, all magic is dangerous. Even shamans fear the results of their own actions. If woman has such power as you say, you have done stupid thing and you will regret it."

Kazhak set his jaw and folded his arms across his chest. "Kazhak will not regret anything," he said through tight lips, determined to make his words the truth.

As they proceeded eastward, Epona occupied herself with imagining the reception she would receive from Kazhak's tribe. Obviously, she could not expect to be welcomed as she would have been welcomed into one of the kin-tribes of her own people.

My former people, she corrected herself.

She would have to make her own place in this new life, and that might prove harder than she had anticipated. But leaving the Blue Mountains had been hard; turning her back on all she had known and loved had been hard, but she had done it. She could do this, too.

She actually began to look forward to the challenge. She would not cower timidly in a wagon like the Scythian women, nor come trotting, tame as a trained hound, when some man signaled her. She was born of the Kelti.

Spirits of my people, be with me, she prayed.

You rejected them, replied the spirit within.

They saw more bands of nomads, sprawling family encampments and groups of men riding together. The Sea of Grass was more populated than Epona had realized. "There are many horse people," she remarked to Kazhak.

"As many as blades of grass."

"Do the Scythians have a long history?"

"We oldest people on earth," he replied with unassailable certainty.

Epona's temper flared. "How can you say that? You have no history singers. The bards of the Kelti, who are sworn to truth, tell us ours is an ancient race, going back to the first dawn. And you yourself said there had been towns and copper mines in the valley of the Duna for more generations than anyone could count. But if you have no *druii* to teach your children, how can you be so certain of your own past?"

"Scythians oldest people on earth," Kazhak repeated stubbornly. "First people. Best people. Is no argument, is known fact."

"Not to me!" she answered hotly.

When they had spent fourteen nights on the Sea of Grass, Kazhak announced, "Soon we see herds of Kolaxais, is it so? Maybe today." He pushed his horse at an unrelenting pace from the moment they mounted, shortly after dawn, and did not allow his party to walk or draw rein until they caught the sight of the first band of grazing horses Kazhak recognized as his tribe's.

Epona gazed, awed, at the vast number of animals spread across the prairie like a rug of many hues: red and brown and dun-yellow, gray and black and white. Early gelding had given those chosen for riding longer leg bones and necks than most of the breeding animals, but all were beautiful to Epona: finer than any

256

horses she had ever seen. The spirit within rose into her eyes and worshiped the creatures as they grazed.

Kazhak's tribe was the largest they had yet encountered. In this season, when families were gathering to share a communal preparation for winter, Kazhak's people filled more than a hundred tents and wagons, spread over the grassland like a portable city.

As they approached, many of the herdsmen recognized Kazhak and galloped toward him, shouting a welcome. He laughed aloud and drew his knees up against the gray stallion's withers. When he was surrounded by kinsmen he leaped to his feet on the horse's back, as lithe as a cat, and shouted the cry of the horse people, moving his feet in a neat swift pattern atop his saddle.

There were calls of recognition for Dasadas and Aksinya, but there were also many questions, hesitant at first but then coming thick and fast. Where was Ishkapai? Bartatua? Madyes? Was Donya riding behind, soon to join them? What news of Akov and Telek and young Vasilas?

A hush settled over the men crowding around the new arrivals. Eyes turned toward Epona, who had been sitting quietly, a little apart, muffled in her bearskin cloak against the bone-chilling cold now sweeping the steppes. Her bright hair was covered by a warm felt hood she had taken from Basl's pack, making her femininity difficult to detect, but the sharp-eyed Scythians had begun to notice that she was not just another horse man.

"That is one of the geldings of Basl," said an accusing voice, "but Basl does not ride him. Where is Basl, and what is that on his horse?"

A subdued Kazhak slid down to straddle his mount again, the exuberance dying away in him.

"Where is Donya my brother?" someone else demanded to know.

Kazhak saw hostility in the familiar faces surrounding him. "Going west," he began to explain, "we met big tribe of Cimmerians, many warriors, many weapons. Kazhak's men fought well, but many brothers died. Only best fighters survived: Kazhak, Dasadas, Aksinya still live." He grinned, asking them to rejoice in his survival, at least.

"Kazhak lived while brothers died?"

"All were wounded," Kazhak hurried to assure them. "Weak, bleeding, we rode west into mountains where Cimmerians would not follow us. Heard stories there about Kelti smith farther on who forges best swords ever made. So we made hard journey to village of the Kelti, saw the swords, brought them back for great Kolaxais. Brought back other treasure, too, better even than swords, is it so?"

"What is better than swords?" cried a challenging voice.

But Kazhak had said enough; more than he wished. The rest must be told to Kolaxais first. "Where is the Prince of the Horse?" he wanted to know.

"In his tent," came the answer. "With his shamans."

Epona had been watching Kazhak's face. She saw that he was displeased with that answer.

Turning toward her and the others, he said, "We go to Kolaxais now." He deliberately met eyes with Epona. "All go to Kolaxais," he added.

They dismounted, and the crowd of men — not one woman, Epona noted, not one — fell away to let them pass. Young boys materialized from the edge of the throng and caught the horses, leading them off to be unsaddled and watered. Epona was reluctant to follow Kazhak until she was sure the horses would be cared for, but then she realized how absurd that was. These were the people of the horse. As she had learned on the journey, the horse came first.

Kazhak led the way to a tent that could belong only to the chief of so numerous a tribe. It was as large as any two other tents, and a pole stuck into the ground in front of it was decorated with a cluster of human heads, most reduced by time and weather to bare skulls.

They showed their teeth to Epona.

You are empty, she told them silently. *The spirit is gone; you cannot harm me.* She held her head high and walked past.

Epona ducked her head to follow the men through the tent flap. It took a few moments for her eyes to accustom themselves to the gloom within, but then what she saw reminded her very forcibly that she was now in another world, with an alien culture. Her ears and her nose reaffirmed the fact.

The interior of the tent was lined with rugs that appeared to be made of woven wool, though the Scythians did not wear woven wool on their bodies; only felt and leather. Piles of rugs and hides served for furniture, with the exception of small carved chests and a curious stoollike device that emitted the odor of some burning weed.

The tent was cluttered with objects, so that one had to pick one's way between wooden and pottery bowls, stone lamps, leather purses and cases, sacks of fur, flasks, jugs, wooden serving dishes on little feet, copper censers, drums, and stringed musical instruments. The tent of Kolaxais might have been a packrat's nest, though opulent with vivid color and thick with the smells of its inhabitants.

The Scythians, Epona thought to herself, *have no sense of proportion, of symmetry*. Nothing was arranged for artistic effect, as in the lodges of the Kelti; nothing was arranged at all. Like their language, their lifestyle seemed discordant to her. Even the brilliant colors with which they dyed their felts clashed with one another.

Everything was permeated with the scent of wood burned with weeds, and the overriding, nauseous odor of fermented mares' milk and rancid butter.

On the pile of rugs that served him as bed and seat was a man so old he might have been a preserved corpse. Only the black eyes glaring from the recesses of his eye sockets burned with the great fire of life. His face was a mass of wrinkles, seam folded upon seam, all individuality altered by the crumpled skin. Thin strands of white hair escaped the felt hood pulled down over his ears, and the hands resting on his folded knees looked like the claws of a bird.

Epona heard Kazhak take a swift indraft of breath, as if surprised by the appearance of the ancient sitting crosslegged on the rugs. "Prince of Horses," he murmured respectfully, bowing down. The other Scythians bowed as well, but Epona did not.

She realized she was looking at Kolaxais, the great prince of that tribe of Scythians which considered itself royal, destined to rule over all other nomads. She had seen his horses spread out across the Sea of Grass. She could now see the dazzling amount of gold on his person, the fine gold plates worked into a kind of tunic, the massive neckring and other jewels he wore. But she was not impressed, as Rigantona would have been impressed. Kolaxais possessed the things that could be counted and carried, but he was old and wizened and she did not sense an aura of real power, not anymore. A diminished man sat before her, looking out at the world with frightened eyes. Yet strong men like Kazhak bowed down to him. No Kelt would.

Kolaxais was not alone in his tent. Crowding its inward sloping, circular walls were numerous other men, less richly attired, but each with his personal treasure of gold or amber prominently displayed, though the clothes on his body were worn and stained from long seasons in the saddle.

Closest to Kolaxais were two very strange figures. They were men, but they were not dressed as men dress. They wore long skirts of red felt, covered by fur tunics, and on their heads were small, round felt caps, from which hung what appeared to be the entire tails of white horses. More of these long hair pendants were attached to the tunics and to the skirts, so the wearers looked more like white haystacks than human beings.

Their faces were painted with fierce designs, giving an impression of extremely slanted eyes and hollow cheeks. Long fangs were drawn at the sides of the mouth, outlined in red ocher. Snarl lines of charcoal streaked the skin.

Each man held a drum that he pounded monotonously, with no rhythm that Epona recognized. The other men, talking among themselves, shouted over the drums as if they were accustomed to doing so.

Kazhak rose from his bow and addressed Kolaxais. "Kazhak sees you still keep the shamans close," he said, gesturing toward the men in the horsehair tassels. He did not sound pleased. As if his words were a signal the two shamans began beating their drums louder, glaring at him as they did so and mumbling incantations.

Kolaxais did not signal them to be silent. Instead, he raised an old man's whispery voice in a valiant effort to be heard through the din, and said to Kazhak, "Shamans keep Kolaxais alive."

Kazhak grunted. "Shamans keep Kolaxais off his horses, closed in his tent. Prince should be under open sky, where men belong."

Kolaxais cut his eyes toward the chanting shamans. "Demons are in the open air," he said tremulously. "Only shamans can protect me from them. Demons made me sick; shamans keep them from killing me altogether."

"Kolaxais was not sick; was just slight failing that comes with age." Kazhak snorted, then continued, "But shamans took advantage, did things to make you feel worse."

"We had this argument before," Kolaxais replied. "You were wrong then; you are wrong now. You yelled with anger, rode away, did not stay with Kolaxais. But shamans stayed. Shamans have been my only friends and allies."

"They feed on you as jackals feed on carrion!" Kazhak cried, unable to control himself any longer. The watching tribesmen muttered and swayed toward him. Dasadas and Aksinya moved closer to his back, fingering their swords, then seemed to soften like wax and edge away, unwilling to risk the anger of their people.

Epona put one hand on the hilt of her knife and took a long step forward, until her shoulder pressed against the shoulder of Kazhak. She gazed at Kolaxais and his shamans with an impassive warrior's face.

Wrinkles hid any astonishment Kolaxais might have felt, as paint disguised the expressions of the shamans, but one of the priests missed a beat of his drum.

Epona had removed her hood and her hair was ruddy gold in the light of the stone lamps used for illumination. There was no mistaking her gender, nor her absolute readiness to fight beside Kazhak if necessary.

The massed Scythians broke into a gabble of conversation and some of them reached for their own weapons, the bronze daggers thrust through their belts and the swords — bronze and a light-colored, obviously inferior iron — they had dropped at the entrance to the tent.

The shamans glared and the beat of the drums increased in tempo, urging action, urging punishment for Kazhak, who dared to make such an accusation.

Epona bared her teeth at them and lifted her knife, ready for battle.

Chapter 21

E PONA AND HER BEHAVIOR were so surprising to Kolaxais that he briefly forgot the shamans hovering over him. The atmosphere in the tent crackled with menace; yet here was this yellow-haired woman, with a knife in her hand and the unmistakable gleam of battle in her eye, ready to fight beside Kazhak against hopeless odds. In the long experience of Kolaxais, such a situation in a Scythian tent was without precedent.

He made a chopping motion with his hand, demanding silence, with all the vigor Kazhak remembered from earlier days. "Who is this woman?" Kolaxais wanted to know. The unusual strength of his voice did not go unnoticed by the shamans, who reluctantly silenced their drums, nor by the other Scythians, who waited with drawn weapons to see what would happen next.

In accordance with the battle style she had learned as a child, Epona tossed the knife from one hand to the other, demonstrating her dexterity to intimidate her opponents.

The eyes of the Scythians followed the flashing iron with disbelief.

Kazhak raised his voice. "This is Kelti woman," he said. "This is woman of exceptional power."

"*Woman* of power?" Kolaxais' eyes squinted out of their network of wrinkles; then he hawked and spat, to show his contempt. The shamans sneered openly. "How can a woman have any power?" Kolaxais asked.

"This Kelti woman can do magic," Kazhak said carefully, weighing each word before it escaped his mouth and watching Kolaxais for any change of expression. "More magic than you have seen before. She can make a dead horse alive. She can change the weather. Kazhak has brought you this great treasure."

Epona darted an angry glance at him but he was unaware of it. He was boasting more blatantly than a Kelt, claiming abilities she did not possess and could never hope to demonstrate. Who could make the dead alive again after their transition? If these Scythians were angry now, they would be furious when they discovered the truth.

Kazhak had put her in a bad situation; this was certainly an inauspicious beginning for a new life with a new tribe.

The shamans were staring at her. One of them held up a long finger with a very dirty fingernail and pointed it at her. "Women have no power," he said. "This is a trick, Kolaxais. Kazhak is not to be trusted or believed."

Dasadas spoke up, his voice low at first, almost as if he were afraid of being heard, but getting stronger after Epona turned around and looked at him. "Kazhak speaks the truth," he said. "Dasadas has seen this woman do great magic. She saved a poisoned horse, a horse that would be rotting on the plains right now if she had not turned death aside. Dasadas knows horses; Dasadas has seen horses die. Dasadas tells Kolaxais: This woman can save horses that should be dead."

One of the shamans bent over to buzz-buzz in Kolaxais' ear. As the prince listened he seemed to shrink inside his clothes, his brief flash of vitality withering away. He shook his head in assent to the shaman's words.

"You make reckless claims for this woman," he said to Kazhak. Then he hesitated, and once more the shaman whispered to him. The old man began speaking as if his words were an echo of the words hissed in his ear. "Tsaygas says no woman can do magic. Is known fact, no argument. Tsaygas says he will test this woman and show how she has fooled you. Kazhak . . . Kolaxais is ashamed for you."

"No one needs to be ashamed for Kazhak. This woman can do magic. In the western mountains her kind are shamans; we have seen them do more magic than we have ever seen done here." His voice rang with defiance.

263

Epona saw how Kolaxais' hands trembled on his knees; she heard the man's breath rattling in his chest. He was not only old, he was ill, and very frightened. Kazhak's words were frightening him.

"Do not make shamans angry," he said in a whispery voice.

"If shamans are angry, Kazhak has as much power on his side in the strength of this magic person," the Scythian replied, gesturing toward Epona.

"We will test her," one of the shamans said. "We will see. We think you are . . . mistaken, Kazhak, and she has no power, but if she does have the *taltos*, we will see if it is black or white. If white, you are . . . fortunate to have her on your side. If black . . ." The man shrugged, rolling his eyes. "But of course, she cannot do magic," he reiterated. He bared his teeth unpleasantly.

It was the turn of the second shaman to lean over Kolaxais, murmuring instructions, and the prince dutifully repeated, "Is no need for arguments between us, Kazhak, until your claim is tested. But surely you have brought back great treasure for your *han*, after such a long journey. Is there much . . ." His voice faded away and his rheumy eyes drifted shut. The shaman nudged him and he spoke too loudly, as one awakened from a sudden doze. "Did you bring much gold for us? Good heads? Bring in your real treasure, Kazhak; let us see what new glory you bring to your father's tent."

The time of physical danger seemed to have passed. Epona could feel the men in the tent relaxing a little, and she saw Kazhak shift position, holding both his weaponless hands so they were plainly visible. Following his lead, she was the last to put her knife away.

Kazhak had never looked directly at her during this crisis, but he had watched her on the periphery of his vision. He had seen the knife in her hand; in his service. He had thought he was past being astonished by the Kelti, but there seemed no limit to their ability to do the unexpected. None of the women waiting in the wagons he owned would have fought for him. None of them would have dared any of the things Epona dared.

It was hard to believe he had ever possessed such a woman, though when she stood beside him, knife in her hand, he felt more desire for her than he had ever experienced.

But this was not the time to think of a female body. This was

264

the time to tell the story of his expedition, to speak of his lost brothers, to talk of the horses they had not brought back with them and of the swords they had.

The other Scythians listened without comment until Kazhak recounted his defeat at the hands of the numerically superior Cimmerians, describing the way the enemy had destroyed good horses to get at their riders, stringing ropes through grass to cause the Scythian mounts to stumble and then hacking them to death on the ground.

"Savages!" one of the listeners cried, and the others joined noisily in his condemnation of wanton horsekillers.

"You left with many horses. You returned with few. You have diminished the holdings of your prince, the great *han* Kolaxais," one of the shamans accused Kazhak.

Kolaxais roused himself enough to ask, "Did you bring much gold? Shamans need gold to fight demons . . ." His voice faded.

"Kazhak brought back real weapons to fight real men," the Scyth replied, signaling Aksinya to bring in the Kelti swords.

Epona had seen the horsemen pretend indifference to the weapons while in her village, but now they all hefted them admiringly, praising their perfect balance and sharp edge, running their hands lustfully over the decorated hilts.

One man held up a rug of woven wool and slashed at it with a sword. The rug divided into two sections.

There was a gasp of admiration.

Another Scyth offered a wooden shield, hide covered, and the sword bit through both shield and covering, narrowly missing amputating the arm of the man who held it.

"Is better than iron of Assyrians," someone said aloud, and there was general agreement.

"Never break," Kazhak boasted. "And Kelti make many more things with iron; everything others make of bronze. Great metalworkers in western mountains."

Kolaxais waved a skeletal hand. "Scythian gold can hire great metalworkers to copy these swords. Other people have good smiths; we can force them to provide all iron swords we need. Someday we use swords just like these to hack down Cimmerian horsekillers." A spark of his old spirit gleamed briefly in his eyes, and his tribesmen cheered and beat on each other's shoulders with their fists.

Epona smiled inwardly. *No, Kolaxais,* she thought. *You will never find metalworkers to unravel the secrets Goibban alone possesses. I spent my childhood watching him work, and I know. The technique for developing the exact heat, the way to control the carbon in the metal, the patient folding. The knowledge of these things is a gift from the spirits and not to be bought with stolen gold.*

Then she reminded herself that these people were now her kin. She should want the best for them; she should desire their accomplishments to be the equal of any other people's.

But the spirit within did not urge her to tell what she knew of Goibban's techniques for working iron. She pressed her lips together and said nothing.

It was obvious that Kolaxais and the other Scythians were not totally pleased with the results of the expedition Kazhak had led, and the final appraisal of Kazhak's success or failure might well depend upon how much Epona proved to be worth to the nomads. Watching the shamans, Epona was aware they were already disposed against her, as they would be disposed against anything of Kazhak's. They had sucked the spirit out of the old man and controlled his husk, and they would resent anyone and anything that got in their way. As long as Kolaxais was so totally in their power, they ruled his people.

The power of the priests. Yet Kernunnos, with all his power, had never actually attempted to rule the tribe or dictate tribal policy; his gifts were for the benefit of the tribe, not its subjugation. No Kelti would allow anyone, even a priest, such ascendancy.

How strange it is, Epona thought suddenly, *to be thinking kindly of Kernunnos! It must be the influence of this place, so different from anything I have known, and these people.*

My people now. My people.

Kolaxais seemed very tired. He slumped even lower on his pile of rugs and the shamans fussed over him, muttering and making signs. The interview was at an end. In their own time, the shamans would examine the Kelti woman and make a determination as to her gifts and her value, but until then she and Kazhak were dismissed.

Kazhak was confronted with yet another problem. He had thought originally to put Epona into one of his tents with his other

266

women; one more pair of hands to carry dried dung-cakes to the hearth for cooking; one more strong back to bear burdens. But somewhere along the way he had realized this was impossible. He could not put the Kelti woman in with his wives.

He went with some reluctance to the tent now occupied by Talia, his senior wife, and Gala, his second choice, and demanded that it be relinquished to the new woman. The tent must be Epona's, and hers alone. He was quite aware of the resentment this might cause, but it did not matter. Women were always busy hating somebody. Besides, he was confident Epona could take care of herself.

He took her to her new home and demonstrated it with pride. "Is good tent, almost as big as Kazhak's own. Women will take it down, set it up when necessary. You will live here very good all winter, is it so?" He smiled engagingly, willing her to be pleased.

Epona looked around. The small space was, if anything, more packed and cluttered than the tent of Kolaxais. It did not seem possible there might be room for one human being, yet she had seen two women and a scramble of children emerge from this tent and disappear into another one.

"I would rather sleep under the stars, with my head on the neck of my horse," she told Kazhak.

His eyebrows did their familiar upward wriggle. "Man sleep with horse, woman sleep in tent," he said. He saw her face setting itself in stubborn lines. "Is warm in tent," he added as an incentive.

"I don't mind the cold; I am used to it."

"Cold of mountains is not like cold on Sea of Grass."

Her eyes glinted. "Are you ordering me to sleep in the tent?"

Kazhak hesitated, examining his knowledge of the character of this woman. It might be best not to order her to do anything. He widened his smile. "No no, is not order. Would please Kazhak, make Kazhak very proud, but is not order."

Epona relaxed a little. "Very well, then, I will sleep in your tent. But you have to take some of these things out of it; I don't want all these boxes and bags and . . ." She waved her hand helplessly, at a loss for words to describe the jumble of mixed Scythian loot and household articles.

Kazhak could not be seen helping a woman unload a tent; he

had enough problems already. He went to one of his other women, the youngest and most obedient, and ordered her to assist the Kelti woman. It was a blatant break with tradition, asking a woman who was senior to another to serve her, but it was the least undesirable option. Ro-An would make no trouble.

Epona was on her knees in the tent, holding up a small stone lamp and trying to sort through a pile of dirty furs, when she heard a timid voice at her shoulder. Glancing around, she got her first look at a Scythian woman's uncovered face.

Like many of her people, this one was dark of eye and possessed high cheekbones and a strongly chiseled nose. Her mouth was small and soft, however, and her chin melted back into the folds of her clothing. She gave the impression of a fawn glimpsed at the edge of a clearing.

"Ro-An," she said hesitantly, touching her breast.

"Epona," the Kelt responded, smiling to show friendship.

Ro-An did not smile. Her dark eyes grew larger, then she lowered her lids in subjugation and held out both her hands, to show they were in Epona's service.

Epona had sometimes thought of herself as shy, but she was a roaring lion compared to this timid creature. It might be kinder not to speak to her at all, just to load her with disposables and send her scurrying away. Still, she might prove to be an ally, and Epona was starved for the sound of a female voice.

Instead of immediately putting Ro-An to work, she tried to start a conversation. "Are you one of Kazhak's women?" she wanted to know. "You. Kazhak's woman. Yes?"

Ro-An made a tiny sound that could have been a giggle and pulled a fold of her clothing over the lower part of her face.

"Does Kazhak have many wives?" Epona questioned, struggling with her limited knowledge of the Scythian language — a knowledge she had enlarged with each day that passed since leaving the Blue Mountains.

Ro-An giggled again and ducked her head. Epona began to lose patience.

"I . . . Epona . . . will not hurt Ro-An," she said slowly and distinctly.

Ro-An appeared to relax a little. She shook her head in assent and looked up. Epona discovered that women did not share the male taboo about the meeting of eyes; Ro-An looked at her shyly but without hesitation. "Is good of Epona," she said. Her voice was very soft.

"Was this your tent, Ro-An?"

"No, is tent of Kazhak. Kazhak's tent for his women."

"All his women lived here? With Kazhak?"

Ro-An giggled. "No no. Kazhak has big tent for himself, like all men. Women set up, take down, but do not share. Little tents are for women in winter camp. In summer we do not bother to set up, usually sleep in wagons. Some men, not in favor of *han*, have no tents at all. Must live, and their women must live, in wagons all time. Ro-An slept under wagon as a child," she added. "Better now. Kazhak has several tents. One for him, one for . . . you, now. Two more for women. He is favorite son of Kolaxais; Kolaxais allows him much."

Epona, busy trying to arrange her living space, turned over a bag of meal and caught the distinct smell of something rotting underneath, unmasked by kinnamon or any wholesome scent. "Ugh!"

Ro-An leaned forward to see, and Epona got a good whiff of the girl's own body odor, which was goatish.

Now was as good a time as any to ask the question that had been on her mind since leaving the Blue Mountains, the question that had occurred to her again and again when she thought of her approaching existence with the horse people. Now her need was imperative.

"Ro-An, how do women . . . clean themselves here?" She knew it was no good to ask for a cauldron of heated water for washing, though that image had tantalized her mind many times throughout the journey. One good, hot bath . . . the small courtesy the Kelti traditionally offered to any newly arrived traveler. But not here, on the Sea of Grass. Here there were obviously other ways, though she doubted they could be as pleasant.

"Epona wants to clean?" Ro-An asked with surprise.

"Very much," Epona assured her. "Epona is not happy with the feeling of her skin."

A brief friendliness and understanding looked out of Ro-An's eyes. A warm spirit was there, if artfully hidden. Epona longed to reach out to it as she reached out to the spirits of the horses.

"Ro-An help you clean," the Scythian woman said. Pulling a fold of fabric across her face, she left the tent.

Epona waited, alone. She could hear the voices of men outside, shouting to one another and the animals. She heard horses whinny; goats bleat; the ubiquitous wind blowing. Life went on outside the tent, but within it she was the only representative of life, and all alone. Perhaps all the spirits she knew had been left far behind.

Never, said the voice within. *We go with you.*

Ro-An returned with an assortment of bowls and jars. She was apologetic. "Epona should have two women help her clean, not just Ro-An," she said, eyes downcast. "But other woman would not come."

Two shamans; two women to perform a ritual. Was this customary with the nomads? Did they not realize two was an asymmetrical number, having no center? Once again the alien quality of her new life was made clear to Epona.

Ro-An brought an additional bronze brazier, smoldering with something that smelled like horse dung, but it was powerless to lift the gloom within the tent. "We could go outside where there is good light," Epona suggested, but Ro-An recoiled with shock.

"Men would see!"

"What is wrong with that? I am not deformed."

"Your body belongs to Kazhak; no one else must see."

"My body belongs to myself," Epona corrected her. "I am born of the Kelti."

"What is this thing, this Kelti?"

"The tribe of my birth," Epona answered, but that did not seem to be sufficient explanation. "It is more than a tribe, it is what we are. To be Kelt is to be free. I came to Kazhak as a free woman of the Kelti, of my own choice."

Ro-An's dark eyes were blank with lack of understanding. "What means this *free?*" she asked.

Across the barrier of language, there was no way to reach with an explanation.

Ro-an busied herself with her jars and bowls. As Epona watched, the other woman used a stone bulb to pound a combination of cypress, cedar, and frankincense into a fragrant paste. Epona could not determine what this had to do with washing. On the long journey she had sneaked opportunities to bathe herself whenever she could, by going on foot through the rivers and streams they crossed, letting the cold water wash her body. But it was not the same; not what she remembered and desired. Watching Ro-An with her paste, she felt she would die if she could not get really clean, and how could that be done with a compound of beaten wood?

Ro-An signaled that she was to remove her clothes. As Epona uncovered her body, the other woman looked away. "Is body of Kazhak; is not mine to see," she explained timidly. Epona's words had meant nothing to her.

With averted head but skilled and experienced fingers she plastered the thick white paste onto Epona's flesh, covering her face and body thoroughly. Epona felt a tingling sensation. The paste began to harden like drying mud. It was soon difficult to speak, and she realized that she was in a vulnerable situation. With anyone more aggressive than the timorous Ro-An she might have anticipated some sort of attack.

The two women waited. Epona would have liked to talk more with the Scythian, but the paste cracked unpleasantly on her face when she tried to move her lips, and Ro-An volunteered nothing.

At last the Scythian woman grunted to herself and began to pull the plaster away from Epona's skin. The young woman's body hair came with it, making her wince at first, but then she bit her lip and bore the ordeal with fortitude. Only the first moment of discomfort had startled her sufficiently to make her forget her heritage.

It took a long time to get all the paste off her body, but when it was done, Ro-An gave her a folded pad of goats' hair and instructed her to rub herself all over with it to remove the last traces. That done, Epona looked down at her bare skin with astonishment. It glowed rosily in the light of the lamps. It was clean and glossy as polished stone, with a sweet fragrance as good as any bath in perfumed oil might have imparted.

"Do the men do this also?" she could not help asking.

Ro-An giggled and put both hands over her mouth, but her eyes sparkled merrily. "No, is not so good for men. But do not tell. Men make little felt tent, put dish inside full of red-hot stones. Throw hemp seed on stones. Makes vapor; men get very happy, shout for joy. But skin does not feel like this."

Epona had to agree that her skin felt marvelous. Nevertheless, she was curious about the bath of hemp-seed vapor the men took; it sounded almost like a *druii* ritual to her.

When Epona's cleansing was completed and she had dressed herself again, Ro-An left the tent, her arms laden with things Epona wished to discard. She glanced back once and managed a shy smile before disappearing from Epona's view.

The young woman was alone again. She thought of leaving the tent and exploring the camp, but she could not make herself do it. The pleasant interlude with Ro-An had made her more aware than ever of her isolation among these people, the great differences between them and her own kind that would serve as barriers. She did not have the energy, just then, to attempt to scale those barriers.

It would have been much easier for me to stay and go into the magic house, she thought ruefully. *The otherworlds were not so unfamiliar as this place.*

Night was descending on the steppe. By pushing aside a flap, Epona could watch as the Scythians prepared for the dying of the sun. The tents and wagons were arranged in a large irregular circle, and within this area certain animals were held for the night and cooking fires were also built. Women were in evidence now, scurrying back and forth, faces covered, as they prepared the main meal of the nomadic day.

Was Epona expected to join them, to take part in making the food? Whom should she ask?

She waited, uncertain, and at last she began to wonder if she would even be fed at all. She saw food carried into the big tents where the nobles of the tribe gathered, and then distributed among the herders who crouched in circles close to their animals. What scraps remained the women carried away to the wagons, for themselves and the children.

Epona's stomach began to growl, making demands. It would soon turn into a tyrant. *Better take care of it now,* she thought, and started to leave the tent just as she saw Kazhak coming toward her at last.

"Where you go?" he demanded to know.

"I'm hungry."

"Hungry." He said the word as if it had no meaning for him. He had never thought ahead to feeding Epona in the Scythian camp; he had never thought about feeding women in camp at all. That was the sort of thing women took care of; yet obviously no one had done anything about the Kelti woman.

It was a deliberate insult. He glowered, and his voice dropped to a growl. "Wait here," he told her. "There will be food." He marched away like a warrior going out to do battle. Epona watched him, bemused.

Soon he was back, with a dripping piece of meat and a bowl of fermented milk, as well as a pouch containing some unidentifiable and inedible sweet. He returned to the tent with her and sat watching as she ate. "Is very good, is it so?" he asked several times.

Epona, with her mouth full, was spared the necessity of lying.

When her hunger died down and she began chewing more slowly Kazhak started to talk to her, leaning forward earnestly, his elbows on his knees, his eyes watching her face.

"In tent of Kolaxais you would have fought for Kazhak, is so?"

"Is so," she agreed.

"For why? Kazhak and you, both would have been killed."

"What about it?" She wiped her fingers on her sleeve and dipped them into the sticky sweetmeat he had brought, then licked one finger tip tentatively. *Ugh.* The concoction seemed to be composed of smashed insects roasted with honey.

"We be dead, that is what," Kazhak answered. "And you were willing? You would do that for Kazhak?"

She could not understand his surprise. "Of course. I am your wife, you are my husband. A woman's duty is to fight for her man if he needs her to protect his life, just as she protects that life by feeding his belly and warming his back with clothes."

"Kazhak does not know this custom. A wife or favorite woman can be strangled to go into log house with dead man, that makes sense, is good custom. But a woman, fighting with weapons? Is like savages. Who tells you to do that?"

"No one has to tell me to do anything," she said haughtily.

"Kazhak will tell you to do things, and you must, because you are Kazhak's woman."

Her mood changed. "What if I do not do what you order me to do? Will you strike me?" Suddenly her hand was on the hilt of her knife. Kazhak watched her with disbelief.

"Woman would never!" the Scythian exclaimed.

"This woman would," she assured him. "Do not try to make me into what your other women are, Kazhak. I was born Kelt. I am my own person."

273

Her words rang in Kazhak's head like bells. *I am my own person*, she had said. A person who belonged to himself — or herself — and was not a minion of Kolaxais, or a slave to be bought and sold. Could such things be?

The woman excited him. She had had the paste cleansing, he could smell it on her skin and see it in the shine of her cheeks. Her yellow hair — reddish yellow, in this light — lay in waves across her shoulders and down her back. Her face was strong and defiant, and yet he remembered her lying soft beneath him, her body boneless and agile.

He remembered her standing at his shoulder, brandishing the knife in his defense.

"Epona," he said.

He reached out for her because he could not help himself. She was magic; she might have greater power than he could guess; she might wither him away like dead grass, or cause him to be attacked by an evil spirit, or suck the life out of him as the priests sucked it from Kolaxais. It did not matter.

She had said she was his woman. The part of him that was wary of her was not as strong as the part of him that desired her.

"Epona," he said again, letting his voice be soft, holding out his hand.

It had been a long day, and a trying one. Epona's eyes felt gritty with the need for sleep, and there was no hunger in her body for the body of the man. But everything around her was strange, and disturbing; the society with which she would be forcibly joined had already begun rejecting her and she knew it. The coming days would be hard ones, and it was possible she would never learn to feel that this place was home, or these people hers. Only two things here were known and familiar: the horses, and the man.

She did not want to sleep amid the musty rugs and the filthy furs of the Scythian tent, but she thought she could sleep in Kazhak's arms, at least. That would have to be her home, for now.

She smiled at him and took his hand, pressing it against her breasts.

Chapter 22

IN THE MORNING, Epona's life as one of the Scythian tribe must really begin. She awoke alone in the tent, Kazhak having left sometime during the darkness. She would learn that to be a Scythian custom; men who stayed in women's company all night were suspect. A man who had been away, among savages, might have acquired some alien customs, such as sleeping weak as an infant in a woman's bed. All such foreign ideas were despised. Only the gold and the skills of non-Scythians were welcome on the Sea of Grass. Those, and the bodies of their stolen women, who would vanish into the tents and behind the veils, never to be seen again.

Epona had no intention of being such a woman.

Face bare, head uncovered, she emerged from the tent and looked around the encampment. Other women were abroad this morning, tending small cooking fires or caring for the goats that ambled among the wagons. They glanced up as Epona appeared and quickly checked to be sure the lower part of their faces was covered. They watched her through guarded eyes, the spirit locked behind them.

The Scythian women wore felt tunics like the men's, though longer, with a bib over the chest and cumbersome felt leggings. Their clothing was plain by comparison with their men's, though each woman had an ornamented belt trimmed in bronze, and Epona caught glimpses of the flash of gold jewelry as they moved about. She was discouraged to realize they all looked alike to her. How could she ever tell which one was Ro-An, the only person she could hope to claim as a sort of friend?

The women watched her, but no one invited her to approach a cooking fire.

Ignoring her gnawing morning hunger, she lounged across the campground as if she were merely out for a stroll in her own home place; her head was high and proud, her expression was assured to the point of indifference. *Let no one know how you feel inside,* she told herself. Her eyes, meanwhile, devoured every detail of her new environment. She saw women she determined must be senior wives, because they were more colorfully dressed and seemed to do nothing but boss the younger women. These principal wives tended to sit in little groups around cooking fires or in front of their tents, talking and chewing on strips of crisp fat. As she walked by one such group, Epona noted that these women of superior status wore boots of spotted fur, elaborately embroidered and trimmed on the sole with beading, making walking impractical. They sat with their feet turned to display the decorated soles to one another, comfortably idle while the newer wives did the labor of the camp.

On their heads were various headdresses: caps and scarves with detachable veils to cover the lower part of the face. When they unfastened these veils to talk to one another — a symbolic relinquishment of privacy — Epona saw that many of them had blackened and broken or missing teeth.

She felt contempt for the useless women in beaded shoes, the women who had no work to do.

But what kind of work will I do here? she wondered. *How will I fit into this tribe?*

The men had been up since the first light streaked the eastern horizon, and most of them were already gone from the camp, out with the grazing herds of horses or off hunting. The women had taken over the community they deserted, maintaining it on the sufferance of the males until the true owners returned.

Smoke emerged from the smoke holes of the large tents, and Epona wondered if Kazhak might be inside one of those tents with his kinsmen; with Kolaxais, perhaps. She saw that the gray stallion waited, in hobbles, close to her own brown gelding, and she went to release them both and watch them as they grazed so they would not mingle with someone else's herd. The stallion was sniffing the wind for mares in season, though no mare would welcome him in the winter. But hope never left his heart; he was a stallion.

Someone came out of one of the royal tents and walked toward Epona, but it was not Kazhak. Dasadas approached her with his eyes fixed on the space immediately above her head and the faintest trace of a smile on his face, obviously intending to be pleasant.

"Epona has had food?" he inquired.

"Did Kazhak send you to ask about me?"

He hesitated. "No, Kazhak is busy, but Dasadas is not too busy to think of Epona. Are you hungry?"

Epona answered him in his own language, as she had spoken to Ro-An. "Epona is hungry. No one has offered to share food with me."

"They do not know what to think of you," Dasadas told her. "You are not like other captured women; it is already known that shamans want others to ignore you. But come, Dasadas will give you food."

He put a gentle hand on her arm to guide her, a gesture far removed from his violent attempt to possess her body a few days before. Now he seemed anxious to please, a friend in a strange environment, and his offer of food made Epona's stomach growl. She accompanied him eagerly toward a cluster of women surrounding a cooking fire, but their progress was halted by Kazhak's angry voice, ringing across the encampment.

"The hand of Dasadas is on Kazhak's woman!" the Scythian bellowed. "If Kazhak cuts off that hand, no one protests!"

Dasadas abandoned his hold on her arm as abruptly as if Epona's flesh burned him. "She was hungry . . ." he tried to explain, but Kazhak trotted toward them wearing such a fierce expression that he gave up hope of explaining and backed away, keeping his eyes down.

Epona was angry. If Kazhak had not thought to see that she was fed, what was wrong with Dasadas showing her that courtesy? She started to say as much to Kazhak but he brushed her words aside and hustled her back to the privacy of the tent, where her words, and his, would not be overheard.

"No man can put his hand on you now you live in Kazhak's tent," he admonished her. "You should have screamed."

"That is foolishness. He wasn't hurting me; he was only going to get me something to eat. I was very hungry."

"No matter if you are starving; if you die. You must not let other man touch you. Is word of Kolaxais."

"Why should Dasadas be punished for a generous gesture just because of the word of a sick old man? Kolaxais cannot enforce such rules. I was in his tent, remember? The only strength I felt there was not his, but the strength of the shamans."

Kazhak bowed his head in sadness. "Is so, what you say," he told her in a subdued voice. "When Kazhak was young, Kolaxais was very strong, a mighty *han*, made many good rules for the welfare of the tribe. Rules like one which forbids man to lay hands on woman who lives in another man's tent. But now Kolaxais is sick and weak; the rules he makes now are shamans' rules. There is saying on Sea of Grass: 'If horses get sick, dogs get fat. If man gets sick, shamans get fat.' Is so. Shamans get fat and Kolaxais fades away. The heart is dying in our tribe. Shamans make all rules now. There has been no magic to fight them."

"Is that the only reason you brought me here?" Epona asked, horrified at the implications. "You think I can fight the shamans for you?"

"Is not only reason," Kazhak answered, truthfully. "But your people, *you*, can do very strong magic. Kazhak has seen."

Once more her talents were being demanded for the tribe, and not even the Kelti, this time, but these nomads on their windswept alien plain. She had fled to avoid devoting her life to the spirits. It did not seem fair that Kazhak ask that of her now. If she gave him what he wanted — and she did not believe she could, she was not equipped to duel with shamans! — there would be no end to it. On and on, for all of this life, she would crouch over fires and mutter incantations and exhaust her spirit in the service of others, with no life of her own.

"You have made a mistake, Kazhak," she told him. "If you mean to pit my powers against the shamans you will be disappointed, for I can do nothing."

"You cured horse. Dasadas said right; horse would have been dead."

"Perhaps, but that is the only gift I have, and I did not even know I had that one until the spirit within the horse cried out to me. I am *drui*, but I am not trained, I have not learned the . . ."

"Tell Kazhak again, what is *drui?*" he interrupted.

"People who you would say work magic, but I think it is not the kind of magic your shamans practice. The *druii* have learned to understand how things are kept in balance in thisworld through our dealings with the otherworlds, and they tell us how to live in harmony with the earth mother so we are benefited and not deprived in thislife. Everything the *druii* do is for a purpose and fits into the pattern." She listened to herself defending the pattern and was keenly aware of the irony.

"And you are *drui,*" Kazhak insisted.

"Yes, I seem to be, but I left the Blue Mountains before I could be trained."

"You ran away," he reminded her with dawning understanding. "You did not want training."

"That is true," she admitted. "I have no desire to work magic."

"You would fight, die for Kazhak, but not work magic for Kazhak?" He sounded puzzled. He could find no way to coerce the woman into agreeing to the plan that had revealed itself so dazzlingly to him the day she cured the Thracian horse. He had seen it with all the clarity of a dream just before dawn: Epona doing magic that would put the shamans to shame, and Kolaxais coming out of his stupor, thanking Kazhak for bringing this magic person to the tribe, becoming once more the strong leader he had been in his prime.

And there would have been rewards for Kazhak, someday. The other sons of Kolaxais would have torn their hair and gnashed their teeth, but the wagons and women and horses of the great prince would have eventually belonged to his favorite son, Kazhak, who rode west.

Why would Epona not cooperate? How could he force a magic person to do magic?

"The shamans plan to question you," he told her. "They ask many questions of Kazhak: What can you do, what do you know? You must show them something to convince them Kazhak told truth, brought back treasure in you. Otherwise, Kazhak is disgraced."

"You brought back the swords," Epona reminded him.

"Wonderful swords," he agreed, "but not enough to replace what Kazhak lost — horses, brothers. Trip was not successful enough, then Kazhak made matters worse by angering shamans.

They may decide to punish Kazhak; may issue order through mouth of Kolaxais."

"What kind of punishment?"

Kazhak's voice sunk low in his chest, a deep rumbling like that of a bear rubbing itself against a pine tree, grumbling. "For a prince's son? Kazhak would be buried in earth up to his neck, other horse men would ride toward him, galloping. Lean down out of saddle, swing leather thongs. Tear off Kazhak's head." He gazed morosely into the shadows.

Epona swallowed, hard. The spirits seemed to be maneuvering her into a trap from which there was no escape. Yet she knew of nothing within her abilities that would impress the shamans sufficiently to prove the truth behind Kazhak's claims. She could not materialize a dying horse out of the air and then save it on order. This man — this gruff, maddening, sometimes tender man, her husband, her responsibility — might die because of her failure. "When will the shamans question me?" she asked.

"Who can say? Shamans always want to smoke hemp, roll bones, dance. Everything they do requires much muttering, waving of hands, long time before anything happens. Probably long time before they send for you."

Kazhak's words and tone told her he did not believe all of the shamans' ritual was necessary; at some point he had begun to suspect it was mainly for show, to impress and intimidate. Epona, familiar with *druii* magic where everything was done for a purpose, tended to agree with him. In the tent of Kolaxais she had not felt that the shamans were accomplishing anything other than continually emphasizing their presence.

But then, she was untrained; what did she truly know of magic? What questions might they ask her, and how could she answer?

Be quiet and listen, commanded the spirit within. *I will tell you how to live thislife*.

Kazhak saw a slight smile tug at the corners of her mouth and felt reassured. He had done a wise thing in bringing her here; she would not let him down.

"My brothers hunt often; Kazhak will see that you have much food, best food, not get hungry again, is it so?" he promised. "Kazhak's wives cook every day for you, from now on."

"Why can't I cook for myself? And why can't I stay in your tent, if you have a larger one than this?"

Kazhak's pleasant expression faded. Epona might help him, but it was obvious she would also continue to complicate things.

"No woman stays in man's personal tent," he said brusquely. "Is never done. Besides, even Kazhak does not always sleep there. Kazhak thinks man should sleep in open, under stars, unless weather is too cold, too much wind and ice. Sleeping inside felt walls makes man weak; it has weakened Kolaxais. Kazhak puts his women in nice tents, very good, then Kazhak sleeps with horse. Or in tent by himself if weather is bad. Is best way, is it so?"

"That is a very bad way to live, with men and women kept apart," Epona protested.

"No no, is right. Men and women cannot live together without trouble."

"In the Blue Mountains . . ." she began.

"This is Sea of Grass," he interrupted, and she bit off her words and regarded him silently, but without capitulation. "As for cooking," Kazhak continued, "you are person of power, should not be seen cooking. Shamans have no respect for ordinary woman, must see from start that you are not ordinary." He flashed his sudden grin. "Is true, Epona. You are not like other women."

"If I am not to be treated like other women then why can't I live in your tent?"

"Aaannh!" Kazhak threw up his hands. This was why men and women must live apart: to avoid such questions, such arguments. How could he take this female into his tent, his private place, for himself to rest in and entertain his brothers, and open himself up to her way of thinking and her questions?

"Because is not possible!" he thundered, turning on his heel and striding from the tent, anxious to get outside, to his horse. Epona watched through the entrance flap as he saddled the gray stallion and vaulted gracefully onto its back. He was Kazhak; he preferred being on top a fine, fast horse to being anyplace else. Secure in his saddle at last, he rode around the camp, issuing orders at the wagons of his women, and soon Ro-An hurried toward Kazhak's tent to collect the leavings of his dawn meal and bring them to Epona.

At her insistence, Ro-An stayed to keep her company while she ate, and Epona questioned her about Kazhak's other women, and his children. Ro-An's answers were punctuated with giggles, and sometimes the two women could not understand one another at all, when some word eluded them or some concept familiar to one was beyond the grasp of the other. But Epona listened, and learned.

She learned that the children had no training, and ran wild like animals, free to imitate their elders or not as they saw fit. They were given whatever they wanted and otherwise ignored, once they were old enough to leave their mothers' tents. No bard taught them history, no skilled young woman with fast reflexes taught them to use knife and javelin. Kazhak's four women had nine children among them — nine, a good symmetrical number — and five more had died. Ro-An as yet had not conceived, and now that Epona had joined the Scythians, she did not expect to bear a child for quite some time.

"Kazhak will use you most," she told Epona. "He is like that, very odd. When he gets new woman he goes to her only for long time, does not share himself like some other men."

"Have you had other men?"

Ro-An emitted a little shriek of horror. "No! Would be strangled and body thrown out for vultures, not even buried. Woman must look at no man but husband, ever."

"Yet the men have more than one woman," Epona pointed out.

"They are men." Ro-An seemed to think this was a sufficient reason, but Epona did not. She saw it as yet another example of the asymmetric quality of nomadic life.

When Ro-An left her to go about her own duties, Epona tried to find some way to fill the day that yawned as wide and empty as the Sea of Grass. At last she saddled the brown gelding and rode out alone, aware of eyes watching her from behind tent flaps. She took Basl's *gorytus* containing his bow and arrows and amused herself for a long time by experimenting with the weapon, shooting at clumps of grass, dismounting to reclaim her arrows and try another shot. She quickly discovered that the curved bow required a skill she did not possess.

But it was something to do. In the days to come it became almost her only occupation, for want of any other.

Ro-An brought her food and tended to her domestic needs. Kazhak came to her at night, but after lying with her he invariably left the tent and slept alone nearby, under the stars, until bad weather drove him inside his own shelter. Though she expected it every day, the shamans did not send for her. They left her alone to worry and wait.

Epona tried to establish communication with some of the other women, because she was starved for conversation. She soon realized they resented her, not because she was a foreign woman, as the men often brought back foreign women, but because she was a woman so outside their own experience. And also because she had unwittingly dispossessed Kazhak's senior wife, Talia, a plump, graceful person who must have been beautiful in the brief youth of the steppes.

Feeling the currents that swirled around her, Epona questioned Ro-An about making friends with the other women. She longed for the friendships she had left in the Blue Mountains. But Ro-An did not seem to understand what she was talking about.

"Women cannot be friends with other women," the Scythian said. "Each one wants to be husband's favorite, competes with the others, plots to win favor for her sons, tries to make other women look bad. If a woman is not a senior wife, or a favorite, she is nothing. Woman cannot afford to make friends who will learn her secrets, her weaknesses, use them against her."

So it was that Epona learned that life in the Scythian tents was a sort of warfare by itself, with intrigue and skirmishes, uncelebrated victories and unadmitted defeats. Rigantona and Sirona might have understood and even enjoyed it. Epona did not.

She tried stubbornly to befriend the other women, starting with Kazhak's senior wife. From her own small collection of belongings she took the copper bracelet that had marked her entrance to womanhood and sent it to Talia. For several days there was no response, then one morning Ro-An came to her carrying a fur cap with ear flaps, the gift of Talia.

She was occasionally invited to the cooking fires after that, though no one actually allowed her to prepare food, and she was aware of an unremitting reserve on the part of the women around her. However, they did talk to her, and she was able to work at enlarging her vocabulary. Talia's grudging recognition of her did not extend so far as an invitation to join the gossiping senior wives in their beaded boots, but Epona did not mind. She suspected they had little to say that she would care to hear.

She was more interested in learning about the everyday lives of her new people, and in hearing the whispered stories about the savages who lived at the fringes of their world.

Her grasp of the language improved daily. She knew *arima* to mean one; *spou*, eye; *pata*, to kill; and so she easily understood when one of the women spoke of her forefathers having killed many men of the one-eyed race, the Arimaspi. From *oior*, meaning man, and *pata*, she recognized the Scythian name for a race of Mankillers, a race purportedly of women, incredible though that sounded, female warriors who lived somewhere at the fringes of the Sea of Grass and captured men for procreation and slavery.

Some of the Scythian wives admitted to having suspected Epona to be one of these Mankillers, at first. She laughed with delight and assured them that she was not.

The Scythian word for the shortsword was *akinakes*, spoken with affection, and the bronze battle axe, one of the earliest weapons of the horse people, was known as the *balta*. Man. Death. Weapon. These were primary words in the Scythian language.

Epona listened and learned. Much of what she encountered was difficult to understand and harder still to accept, but she tried. These were her people, now; she must find a way to fit in.

You cannot fit into a way of life you will never accept, commented the voice within.

And there was much she could not yet accept.

The man of each family advertised his prowess in battle by arranging his trophy heads on poles around his tent, or hanging their scalps on his horse's bridle. Epona watched one day as a young Scythian calmly peeled the flesh from a human head he had brought into the encampment, using a rib bone as a scraper, then rubbed the scalp back and forth between his hands until it was as clean and hairless as a piece of bleached linen. When he was satisfied with its condition, he tucked the scalp into his belt for utility use, like a napkin.

Men of a neighbor tribe rode into camp sporting cloaks of similar material; many human scalps patiently stitched together. The men seemed very proud of these and stroked them as they sat on their horses, conversing.

Frequent driving rains had begun to force men to seek their tents at night, and many, Kazhak among them, invited their favorite horses into the tent with them. But their women were given no similar invitation. Once Epona saw a man lash out with his foot and kick his wife for no reason as the woman staggered past him, laboring under a massive load of felt rugs and wood strips she meant to bind together for his tent. When the woman fell, her burdens scattering widely around her, her husband turned away without offering to help. He had already lost interest in the momentary amusement.

Yet Epona saw much that she admired about the nomads. Their dedication to their livestock was unstinting and their own tenacious hold on survival demanded respect. They had developed ingenious techniques for dealing with their harsh climate: nearly impenetrable layers of clothing, woven windscreens to break the force of the gale, evolved abilities to go for long periods with little sustenance.

The women created a feast for the eyes from simple scraps of felt and threads of eastern silk, embroidering a fanciful variety of real and imaginary animals with which to color the dull monotony of their lives. The curving dynamic lines of the style appealed to the Kelt in Epona; the representations of animals, so different from the abstractions favored by her own people, touched the spirit within.

Scythian music, unlike any she had heard, lanced through the body and gripped the inner being. It sang with joy and sobbed with sorrow, and when the men danced to it, as they often did, their dance was energetic enough to race the spectators' hearts.

This was a people equally capable of warmth and of cruelty and scarcely differentiating between the two. The men alternated between displays of warriorlike aggressiveness and intense brotherly affection for one another. The women appeared, superficially, to be much more placid; yet from the beginning Epona suspected this was a mold they had been forced into long ago by the circumstances of their lives — a mold that did not reflect the true shape of the spirit within.

This was a proud people, meeting the challenges of life bravely, loving beauty . . . and not so different from the Kelti, Epona decided, as she got to know them. Language and customs separated them, and their natures had been twisted into different shapes by the lands that bred them, but the spirits within were akin.

The last thunderstorms of the year marked the peak of autumn on the steppe with a savage attack of hail and starfire; days following days beneath rolling black clouds and wild weather. When the season passed, the air seemed unnaturally still, as if the earth mother held her breath in anticipation of something worse.

There were no *druii* on the Sea of Grass to keep count of the nights for Epona, or remind her of the dying of the year. Even if she had not seen the light change or felt the cold gathering, she would have known. Her bones, and something older than her bones, kept track of Kelti time.

The feast of Samhain was almost upon them. The Scythians were unfamiliar with the great festivals with which Epona's people marked the change of seasons, and the nomads did not observe the onset of winter as the beginning of a new year. They also seemed unaware that on the pivotal night of Samhain eve the barriers between thisworld and the otherworlds were at their lowest. Spirits could walk freely through the land of the living at the end of each cycle of seasons.

When Epona casually mentioned Samhain Ro-An listened at first, but after a few moments she reacted with such alarm that Epona quickly changed the subject, out of pity. The Scythians had been taught that all spirits were malevolent; the idea of an easy passage between the spirit lands and the world of the living was unbearable to them. Epona talked brightly of other things, of food and clothes and the gossip of the wagons, and Ro-An seemed to relax and forget.

But Epona's blood did not forget. Soon it would be Samhain, and the rituals must be observed.

The first step, at sundown on the eve of Samhain, should be the extinguishing of old fires and the kindling of new. But Epona had no old lodgefire to extinguish, and no *gutuiter* to light a new one. The *druii* taught that an old fire must be given an honorable death by water and earth and water again, according to exactly prescribed ritual, the essential spirits mingling, each action thorough and precise.

Epona had observed that the Scythians had no comprehension of such a balancing of the elements. When they wanted to put out a fire on one of their open cooking hearths they carelessly kicked it to death, or dumped offal on it. Then, when great prairie fires swept across the Sea of Grass, killing game and trapped livestock and reducing precious grazing land to scorched earth, they did not know why.

Wood was scarce on the steppe. There was very little for wagons and tent frames, and fires were customarily fueled with animal dung or fat-filled bones. Yet the Scythians did nothing to propitiate the spirits of the trees. If they came across a rare seedling, fighting for its precarious existence, they might deliberately stamp on it for the pleasure of seeing something die. A member of the Kelti would have built a little stone wall around it as a protection for its infancy, and offered a prayer to the earth mother to keep it safe, and to the spirit of the rain to nourish it.

The Scythians did not concern themselves with the shortage of timber on the arid plains. When all the resources of one area were exhausted, they merely packed their tents onto their wagons and moved on.

Take and go.

Using a few live coals she had begged from one of the Scythian cooking fires, Epona had built a small blaze in a stone-lined firepit she constructed for herself just outside the entrance to her tent. She did not want this particular fire hidden within felt walls, though the smoke-flap would have allowed enough ventilation to keep it alive. This fire should be free, in the open air; in that way it somehow felt closer to the spirits of her people.

For several days she collected water for the ritual extinguishing, a little at a time. The Scythians, who rationed and measured every drop on the arid plains, would be furious if she wasted good drinking water on a fire, so she hid her ration in her mouth and when no one was looking she spat it into a jar. Soon she was tormented by thirst, but she chewed on some of Kazhak's survival weed and saved the water. There must be enough for the ritual, whatever the cost to herself.

So said the spirit within, and now she listened.

She brought fistfuls of earth and stored it under the rugs that made her bed, grieving in her heart for the familiar soil of the earth mother as she had known it in the Blue Mountains. This dirt was alien; taste, touch, smell were all unfamiliar, but it was the best she had.

Samhain eve was marked by a sunset of blood red and burnished gold, and a respite from the shrieking of a daylong wind. Ragged banners of cloud rippled across the sky, waving farewell to the light.

Alone by her firepit, with no help from anyone, Epona strove to keep the ancient harmonies alive.

She watched in a fever of excitement as the sun sank below the rim of the grassland. As the sun died the fire must also die, and be born again under the benevolent gaze of the North Star. She had just completed the ritual extinguishing when she heard Kazhak's voice and saw him coming toward her with a familiar glint in his eye and a broad smile, obviously intending to enjoy a pleasant evening.

But the ritual could not be abandoned.

Bracing herself, she began trying to explain it to Kazhak and make him understand the necessity for allowing her to follow through to the end of the ceremony. At first he seemed puzzled and almost angry, believing this to be some sort of rejection. Then his interest was piqued and he started asking questions. Her replies amused him at first, until they made him uneasy.

"This Samhain magic, it lets in spirits? Evil spirits will come into the tents of Kazhak?"

"Not evil spirits, just beings who have another life than ours. But they are necessary to us; it is important that we show them the proper hospitality. At the death of the old cycle of seasons they are free to come and go as they please."

"Not on the Sea of Grass!" Kazhak interjected.

"Everywhere. We have no power over such things. But if we show proper reverence and maintain the harmonies, we are quite safe."

"Kazhak knew you had strong magic," the Scythian said.

"It is more than magic," Epona replied. "Our rituals are things we . . . *feel*, and we perform them to create symmetry. It is how we follow the pattern."

"What is this pattern?"

How could she explain what she did not totally understand herself? What mutual language could she and Kazhak discover that might make clear to the Scythian those things the Kelt knew only through the voice of the spirit within and the singing in her blood?

The first star was blazing in the sky, though threatened by a bank of purple cloud. Seeing it, Epona reached for the flints. *Tena*

288

would not have needed firestones, she thought, striking them together to summon the new spark.

When she was certain the infant fire would live, given strength by her invocations to the spirits of fire and air, she could pick up the thread of her conversation with Kazhak as she prepared for the next part of the ceremony, the feeding of a stone, bone of the earth mother, with sacrificial blood.

Kazhak watched as she turned away from the new fire. His forehead wrinkled with the effort to understand. "Following a pattern," he murmured. "Is that why you always turn this way" — waving his knife hand — "and never that way?" — gesturing to the cup hand.

"That is one example, yes. If you face south, the stronghold of the sun, you will see that the sun always travels across the sky from your cup hand toward your knife hand. By turning our bodies in the same direction, we stay in harmony; we feel better when we are careful to turn toward the knife hand."

Epona was flattered that Kazhak had noticed this small detail of her behavior. But then he said, "All this magic is too complicated, too much to remember. Kazhak likes things simple."

"It is not too much to remember," she argued. "The spirit within, once awakened, helps us."

"What is this spirit within? Is a demon?"

Epona tried, then, to explain about the great fire of life and the spark from it contained in every living thing. She thought she saw a gleam of comprehension, quickly veiled, in his eyes, but she was disappointed in her own inability to find the words that would give him true understanding. She had not yet been trained to teach, nor had she bothered to memorize the explanations she had been given. *I was always asking questions*, she reminded herself, *but I did not really listen to the answers.*

Kazhak watched curiously as she knelt before the symbolic stone she had set up to represent the goddess, the earth mother. He noticed for the first time the deep purple bruise in the bend of her elbow, where she had opened the vein with her knife and collected her own blood as her lips shaped the prayer to her ancestors — the ancestors still carried in that blood. She drizzled the blood over the stone, offering the fluid of life back to the mother, and whispered fragments of prayers recalled from past Samhains.

Do not hurt us, stones. Stay fixed in your places and do not fall down on our heads, or rise in the night to attack us. We give you life freely; you do not need to take it by force.

When the offering was completed she waited with bowed head and closed eyes, but the spirits of the ancestors did not speak to her here. She was too far from home. Whatever walked on Samhain had nothing to say to the Kelti woman who knelt in silent supplication.

At last she drew a deep breath and opened her eyes. Kazhak was looking at her through lowered lids, and the light of her small fire cast golden shadows on his high cheekbones.

She opened her arms to him then. It seemed a good way to complete the celebration of Samhain.

They went together into the tent, and after their lifemaking Kazhak fell into a deep sleep beside her, and did not return to his own tent. The new little fire stayed alive outside in its carefully constructed firebed, crackling merrily to itself. It stood guard over the sleepers in the tent: a new fire, kindled in the harmonies, fresh and strong to turn away malign influences.

In other tents, in wagons, rolled in their blankets, the people of the horse slept also. But not so soundly as Epona and Kazhak.

At the darkest time of night a great stillness seemed to blanket the encampment. The horses and goats raised their heads and listened, moving about, uneasy. The people slept, also uneasy, for the quality of their dreams had changed.

Spirits walked among them.

In the morning, many of the Scythians would awake from broken sleep with red-rimmed eyes, eyes that still held the shadow of fear. If they had spoken to one another of their dreams, they would have discovered that many shared one dream, a dream of a huge pale wolf who padded into the camp on silent feet, yellow eyes glinting.

The wolf had paced between the tents and wagons, sniffing the air. Its tongue lolled from its mouth. It had moved to the hardy men still sleeping under the stars, rolled in their blankets, and peered into the faces of the sleepers. In their dreams they saw him, but they could not move. They could not run. They lay sweating in terror as he blew his stinking hot breath on them and went on, from one to another, searching.

At last, in their dreams, he came to the tent of Kazhak's Kelti woman and stood on his hind legs, pawing at the felt covering on the side.

The little fire near the entrance hissed a warning.

The wolf sat down a few paces back from the tent and lifted his muzzle. On one long, wavering breath he sang the song of the wolves, a scalp-prickling howl of beauty and loneliness.

The dreamers heard the howl. They clenched their fists and shuddered in their sleep.

The cry died away on the rising night wind, and the wolf went with it, suddenly gone. But for the rest of the night no one slept well outside of Epona's tent.

Chapter 23

A FEW DAYS LATER the shamans sent for Epona. They had been in no hurry to question the girl, expecting she would reveal herself as powerless and a fraud by her actions in the encampment. To this end they had had her watched, but no one had been able to make a satisfactory report. The things she did were not comprehensible to the Scythians. She practiced some form of magic with the fire, that much was certain, and she rode out every day on a horse — like a man! — teaching herself to use bow and arrow. Aside from that, she was a mystery.

The shamans smoked hemp and consulted the bones and one another, sensing a threat, jealous of their position, but unwilling to have the tribe or Kolaxais see that they assigned any importance whatsoever to the woman.

Let her wait, cooling her heels like the women in beaded shoes, until they were ready and had nothing better to do but amuse themselves with her.

When at last the messenger came to her tent to tell Epona the shamans would see her the next morning, the young woman felt suddenly, totally, on guard, like a warrior seeing the signal fires and hearing the battle trumpet.

That night she said to Kazhak, "I am to be examined by your priests tomorrow. What would you have me do?"

"Impress them," Kazhak told her.

"What can I do to impress them?"

Kazhak shrugged his shoulders with impatience. This was not familiar ground to him, this business of magic. "You are healer; heal Kolaxais. Take away influence of shamans."

He is like a child, Epona thought. *He thinks it is so simple because he does not understand all that is involved.*

Uiska had once said to her, "Seen from above, the lake is flat like a sheet of metal. You must look beneath the surface to understand the true nature of the lake."

"I am not trained in the healing arts," Epona said aloud, "and even if there were something I could do for Kolaxais, the shamans would never let me get close enough to examine him and determine what is out of harmony in his body."

"Then do something else, but show them you have power, and remind them Kazhak has you. Is important, Epona. Is important."

His urgency communicated itself to the girl. She was his wife; it was her responsibility to help him in thislife, or she would accrue debts that must be paid in the next. "I will do the best I can," she promised, with a confidence she did not feel.

Epona awoke before dawn. Emerging from the tent, she went directly to her firepit and poked among the remnants of lastday's fire for a live coal, safely hidden in the banked ashes. When thisday's fire was burning she felt somewhat comforted, warmed by the greeting of the friendly spirit.

She dressed in what little finery she possessed and set out for the tent of the shamans, but she had gone only a few paces when she stopped in her tracks. A tree branch lay exactly in line with the path she must take, blown there by the wind, perhaps, but there were no trees from horizon to horizon from which it might have come.

The branch was bent halfway along its length like a broken arm, and at its end, one twig pointed a threatening finger toward Epona.

She sucked in her breath and squinted at the omen, feeling the swirl of invisible forces around her. Was this the doing of the shamans, or of other, more powerful but as yet unguessed spirits? She was a stranger in this place; she might already have made enemies she did not know.

She had hoped to have a final word with Kazhak this morning before her ordeal, but she glimpsed him in the distance, riding with the other horsemen in search of game, thoroughly involved in his own business.

What would be done, she must do for herself.

First, however, she needed the small satisfaction of an ally, a word with a friend, a warmth passed between kindred spirits. She turned toward the hobbled saddle horses held within the circle of tents and wagons.

Kazhak's gray stallion was among them. This morning the Scythian had taken a bay gelding he was training, a leggy animal with a vicious streak that would make him a valuable war-horse if they ever encountered the Cimmerians again. The gray, whose training was complete and dependable, was left in the encampment.

The stallion lifted his head and nickered a greeting as Epona approached.

She put her arms around the stallion's neck and pressed her cheek to his skin, furred now with its winter protection. He smelled good. He felt strong and sure. She inhaled deeply, trying to draw some of his assurance into her troubled self.

The gray horse fidgeted, pawing the earth and swinging his hindquarters away from her. When Epona raised her head and looked at him she saw a familiar tension in his body, making the muscles stand out in sharp relief in spite of his heavy coat. His eyes had a certain glint; his ears flicked with a particular nervousness she had seen before. His were the actions of a sensitive horse anticipating a bad storm.

Yet the sky was cloudless, a bleak winter sky from horizon to horizon, containing only diluted light. There was no storm.

The horse said there was.

She pressed her body against his, trying to merge her thoughts with the wisdom of the horse. She dilated her nostrils as much as she could, scenting the wind as he did, searching out the first small hint of rain.

There it was — still too faint to be noticed by anyone else, merely the echo of something very far away. In the encampment of the Scythians only Kazhak's stallion suspected its presence. Only the stallion — and now Epona — were aware that the weather might change.

She ran her hand lovingly down the stallion's neck and whispered her thanks to him.

The shamans were waiting for her in their tent, attired in their ceremonial robes and painted faces. Two well-nourished hard-eyed men who did not let her sit down but had her stand in the center of the tent, penned between them, so she had to face first one way and then the other as they fired their questions at her, dividing the interrogation equally.

She was always careful to turn toward the knife hand.

They asked a few general questions about her tribe, then narrowed their interest down to the priests, demanding to know everything she could tell them of Kelti ritual and magic. They boasted to her of their ability as healers and described various ailments that they could treat, asking how the Kelti healers would have dealt with this or that sickness or injury. They wanted exact details, but when she told them what she knew they scoffed contemptuously.

Tsaygas, the *bo-han*, or chief shaman, said, "Woman is ignorant woman knows nothing Kelti know nothing. Illness is not caused by disharmony. Illness is caused by demon that enters man and tears away his breath or feeds on his body. Only shaman can fight this evil force. Only shamans sing the songs know the dances good shamans good *taltos;* white shamans white *taltos* sing the songs know the dances . . ."

He flung himself into a whirling dance, the white horses' tails swinging around his body, his hands slamming the priest drum hung around his neck on thongs. The other shaman joined him in a deafening monotone, discordant and painful to the ears.

There was no harmony in them. No symmetry, no pattern.

Epona stood without moving until the dance died of its own momentum, and the two men closed in on her once more with questions and denunciations. It was obvious they would not allow an open discussion and then arrive at a balanced judgment, as the tribal council of the Kelti judged. But what could one expect of these nomads who let a sick old man hold the reins of power instead of electing a strong young one? It was not surprising the shamans had usurped the power of the prince.

It was only surprising that Kazhak thought she, Epona, could in some way alter this balance of power. And maybe she could, thanks to the horse.

Tsaygas extended his hand to show her a large, smoothly polished stone. Then he closed his fingers over the stone and began to chant an incantation. A few pebbles trickled through his closed fingers, turning into a cascade that built a little pile of rocks at his feet. Yet when he opened his hand the original stone was still there, uncrushed and intact.

The shaman's eyes glittered in triumph. "Magic of shamans magic of *taltos* magic of shamans," he chanted, nodding his head rhythmically, grinning at her between his painted fangs.

A trick, Epona thought. *The earth mother would not allow such a thing to actually happen, for it serves no purpose. He means to fool me with tricks.*

The *druii* would have looked upon such pretense with contempt, as Epona did now. She would not have to resort to such obvious deception; the horse had shown her a better way.

The questions went on, stabbing at her like knives, and she no longer tried to answer them seriously. She shaped her answers in the Kelti way by talking around them, wandering down attractive paths and side trails. When Tsaygas demanded to know how she could heal a dying horse — what spells she used, what signs she drew on the earth to protect the animal from the invasion of demons — she replied with a rambling story about a cartpony of the Kelti that had been lost in the Blue Mountains.

The shamans did not have the patience to wait for the ultimate end of that story. They could not get straight answers, or what they perceived to be straight answers, from the woman, and that confirmed their suspicions. She knew nothing, she had no skills and certainly no power. She was not worth either fear or respect, and she was no barrier to their plan to discredit Kazhak completely with Kolaxais.

They would tell the old *han* that this favorite among his few living sons had tried to defraud him by presenting a mere woman as a trophy of war, and Kolaxais would order Kazhak to leave the protection of the family and strike out on his own.

In such a situation, his horses, of course, would remain with the herd of Kolaxais. And the control of the tribe would remain with the shamans.

Anticipation made the shamans careless. Unlike the Kelti, they did not pay close attention to small details. They did not notice the way Epona's eyes turned again and again to the tent flap, which she had left slightly folded back upon entering, so she might judge the light of the sky beyond. They did not notice her sniffing the air.

When they decided the interview was concluded, they dismissed Epona. "Go back to tent of Kazhak," Tsaygas ordered her, "and do not make claims. You are woman; you live or die at word from Kazhak, and Kazhak lives or dies at word from Kolaxais. You are less than nothing, Kelti woman."

The shaman spat on her chest and shoved her toward the tent entrance.

When she stepped outside she felt her heart sink. The sky, though pale and lifeless, its blue drained away, did not contain any hint of a coming storm. The air was calm and even held a trace of warmth from the watery sun lying to the south. Had the stallion been mistaken?

She could not let herself believe that, or she would lose the only weapon she carried.

She turned to face the shamans, who were still watching her from the entrance to the tent. "The magic of the Kelti is not like the magic of the shamans," she said, lifting her voice so it would draw the attention of others in the camp. If this worked — and it must work, it *had* to work — she would need witnesses other than the shamans. Magic was sometimes a private thing, but these nomads would not believe any magic unless it was publicly done and they could see it with their own ignorant eyes.

The witnesses would see her fail, too; if she failed.

Be with me now, she said to the spirit within.

She raised her arms and made the first signs. The shamans, suddenly suspicious, watched her closely but made no effort to stop her. Whatever she did could not amount to much.

She closed her eyes and tried to hear the wind of an approaching storm. She made herself see a curtain of rain moving across the land; she willed herself to smell the moisture in the air.

She heard the rustle of people gathering around her, watching this strange thing, but nothing else happened.

I was a fool to try this, she said to herself.

Be still! ordered the spirit within. *You known how; do it.* You ARE DRUI.

Uiska. I thought of Uiska lastday. Voice of the Waters. She whose inner being was mist and fog and snow; drops of rain; pearls of dew. Uiska, who could locate hidden springs. And summon clouds.

As a child, Epona had often seen Uiska standing alone at the

297

edge of the lake, absorbed in meditation. The woman would tilt back her head and gaze at the sky, lips murmuring. She might have been singing. Her hands shaped patterns in the air. She whistled a tune that was not a tune, very high, like the piping of a bird, but piercing enough to carry long distances. It was the loudest sound Uiska ever made. And after that the clouds would come sweeping across the lake and rain would refresh the earth, or snow would blanket the village, insulating against the cold.

To locate a spring, Uiska had walked back and forth with her two hands held out in front of her body. Sometimes she carried a willow wand but it was not really necessary. Her spirit within knew where the water was; its sister spirit. She heard its voice murmuring to her night and day; she dreamed of cascades of pure, rippling, lifegiving water. In the Blue Mountains Uiska's gift was not as urgently needed as that of Kernunnos, or Tena, but all knew that without water existence in thisworld was impossible, and therefore honored the *drui* woman as being a person of great importance.

Uiska, Epona said to herself. *Uiska.*

She shaped her lips to form a whistle, imitating the whistle Voice of the Waters had used. She had never had the temerity to try such a thing before; she was shocked at how unlike her it sounded.

She heard the watching Scythians begin to mutter to each other.

Kazhak himself had told her that once winter set in, there were no more thunderstorms on the Sea of Grass.

But she could not allow herself to doubt. The horse had predicted it for her, and now the spirit within urged her on.

Suddenly she felt it again, the power she had felt when she was with the Thracian mare. Then it had been fleeting, a few moments of strength and exultation that swiftly faded. Now it was stronger, gripping her with the unshakable certainty of the stones, the trees. She *knew.* There were no limits to those who believed. Whatever she chose to do now, in this time and place, she could achieve.

She held her head high and smiled with old wisdom in a young face.

Once more she pictured the storm, the coming storm. And now she really did smell the rain, really felt the tension building that preceded the thunder and the starfire. With the power pouring through her she had a sense of being a vessel only, and she opened to the magic, the strength, welcoming it, letting it work through her.

Once more she pursed her lips and a piercing whistle shot through the camp like a Scythian arrow.

Concentrate on the wind. Take it into your skin and your blood and your bones. Know what the wind feels like: movement; cold. Coming, coming. Draw it into you. Become the wind. The wind. The wind.

In a soft voice, arms still upraised, eyes closed, she began chanting the names of the spirits of the air and the water, chanting in a soft voice not meant for Scythian ears, for these were sacred names.

She pulled herself into herself, dwindling away into a hard, tight core, calling the wind, drawing it, drawing it . . .

The mighty storm came blasting across the Sea of Grass, howling like a creature in agony.

Chapter 24

IT MIGHT HAVE COME ANYWAY; the horse had believed it would. Even Epona could not be certain, afterward. She had felt the power fill her, the quiet, clenched sensation of pulling her energies into a vortex that demanded all her attention, as a mother might concentrate on the life within her womb to the exclusion of everything else, awaiting the moment of birth. The wind had come then, but it might have been coming anyway.

Yet the sky had been cloudless, and the air had been still.

The Scythians were shocked by the sudden fury of the unseasonable thunderstorm. The great booming rolled repeatedly across the sky as a massive curtain of black cloud raced toward the encampment. Starfire crackled and crashed. The wall of wind slammed into the tents, threatening to tear them from their moorings, though Scythian tents were attached to a sturdy wooden framework intended to withstand almost any savagery of weather. Cloaks and rugs and saddlecloths developed wings and flew away, their owners running after them. Man and his animals had beaten the surrounding earth to bare clay and dust, and now the dust rose in clouds, stinging their eyes.

Panic crackled over the backs of the herds like starfire.

The domestic animals, goats and sheep and hobbled saddle horses, were spooked into aimless movement, and little boys ran after them, trying to keep them from breaking out of the camp.

On the grasslands beyond, the immense horse herd began to

move as well, seething like the contents of a boiling pot, on the verge of a stampede as the whiplash of starfire frightened and drove them.

Epona slowly lowered her arms. She was surprised to find that they ached, and her fingers refused to flex.

The rain fell with her falling arms, pouring down in incredible volume, soaking the spirit and quelling rebellion. Drenched, half-drowned, the livestock calmed; the horse herd did not stampede. The Scythians sought cover and waited for the storm to abate.

Epona stood alone in the open, head up, unafraid of the starfire. Had she not nourished the fire and honored its spirit?

The storm passed over and was gone, as quickly as it had come.

The Scythians emerged hesitantly from their tents and wagons and saw the Kelti woman still standing there calmly, undismayed by the elemental display. Tsaygas and his fellow shaman, Mitkezh, who had sought safety within their tent, peered out at Epona through the tent flap but came no farther. They looked at her as weasels watch from their holes, dark eyes cold and hostile, observing a new predator in their territory.

I am very tired, Epona said to herself. *I have to sleep.* Saying nothing to anyone, she made her way back to her tent without paying any attention to the faces that stared at her or the whispers that followed her. Numbly, she stripped off her wet clothes, wrapped herself in her bearskin cloak, and collapsed on her sleeping rugs.

She fell instantly and deeply asleep, and did not waken until Kazhak tugged at her shoulder and called her name.

She sat up, groggy and disoriented. At first she did not know where she was or who the man was, and she tried to push him away, wanting only to sink back into the restful nothingness, but he would not let her.

"Epona. Epona! Sit up. Up! Yes, better, is it so? You must tell Kazhak what happened. The storm . . . everyone is talking, and the shamans are . . . Epona, what did you do?"

She sat with slumped shoulders, shivering. In spite of her heavy cloak she was cold, and still very tired. "I did what I could to impress them," she answered him.

"You told Kazhak you had no power over the weather."

"I did not think I did. I still don't know . . . I tried, that's all."

"It is being said that Epona brought the thunderstorm, and

there should be no thunderstorm on the Sea of Grass in this season."

"What do the shamans say?"

Kazhak chewed on his lip. "The shamans have said nothing. They are in their tent, beating the drums, chanting. Shamans are upset."

"Isn't that what you wanted?"

Instead of answering her with words, awkward words, Kazhak threw his arms around Epona and came very close to cracking most of her bones with a mighty hug.

As if the thunderstorm had permanently altered the climate of the steppe, the atmosphere in the encampment seemed changed from that day on. The Scythians could no longer pretend Epona did not exist. The men still would not meet eyes with her, of course, but she was aware that they watched her with varying degrees of respect and awe, as one who had matched power with the shamans and forced those men to hide in their tent, unable to turn aside the storm she brought down upon them.

The women were shyly proud of her, now. She was of their own sex, a despised female; yet she had somehow transcended her gender and earned respect. Respect!

It was frightening to think that such an honor could come to one of their own kind, but it was tantalizing, too. The other women, even the senior wives in their beaded boots, began to vie for her attention, to invite her to share their cooking fires and their days, to take part in their gossip and enter into the myriad details of the life they had constructed for themselves apart from the men.

Even the shamans must, temporarily, pay her grudging respect, the respect of the professional for a colleague. Until they could truly determine the extent of her powers and the threat she might pose to their own position they walked softly in her vicinity, unwilling to bring something to life for which they were unprepared.

But they hated her now. She knew it. She could feel it in the rising hair on the nape of her neck and the tingling in her thumbs whenever one of the Scythian priests was anywhere near her.

Kazhak was mightily pleased. "Shamans will do nothing more to Kolaxais," he told Epona, "while they fear Epona. Kazhak was afraid they would let the old prince die, then keep him sitting up and speak through his mouth, but now they will not do that."

"Is that the sort of magic your shamans practice?" Epona asked with contempt. "That is an unclean act, an insult to the body that housed a spirit."

"Shamans do many things," Kazhak told her. "Many things Kazhak does not think you would like. It is so, they heal sickness. Sometimes. But Kazhak thinks they sometimes cause it, too, when they can benefit from it."

"That's disgusting."

"Is it not so among your priests?"

"Of course not. They would be punished by the spirits, in this-world or the next, if they tried to use their gifts to increase their personal power."

"Then they are not like our shamans," Kazhak concluded. "Epona is right; your magic is not our magic. There are no *druii* like you on Sea of Grass."

He meant it as a compliment, but she could not honestly allow his statement to stand.

"There might be, somewhere," she said. "The *druii* teach that there are people with the spirit gifts in every land and among all races. Sometimes they do not even know what they are themselves, but in the dreamworld they meet one another and exchange information. In the dreamworld they can see the pattern clearly from both ends, from the long ago time of the first great *druii* kingdoms to the far away time when the earth mother will call on the *druii* to save her from destruction."

Kazhak was astonished. "This is true thing?"

"It is what I was taught."

"And you believe?"

"Of course. I can feel the truth of it. I more than believe."

"Shamans would not believe," Kazhak said with certainty.

"No. But Tsaygas and Mitkezh are not *druii*, I am sure of that."

"What of their magic? Is it real? Is any magic real, or is all tricks? Who can know? Kazhak does not feel it, as you say you do. Kazhak does not know what to believe."

Epona felt sorry for the man. She suspected it had been a long time since he had had much faith in the shamans, and now even that was gone, replaced by a partial belief in her and something she might not even be able to do. But she was more fortunate: She knew her limitations; yet she also knew that the magic was real, and possible.

Only not, perhaps, for her. It was herself she did not fully believe in. She lay in her tent and wondered, *Did I really summon the storm? Did I really save a dying horse?*

Doubt assailed her as her brief moments of magnificence shrank into the past, two isolated spots of light.

Perhaps the shamans were causing the doubt; perhaps they were casting spells to weaken her. She knew this was a possibility and struggled to hold on to her memories: the power singing within her, the sense of being used by something larger and more important than herself. She longed for it again, that soaring sensation of invincibility, of taking nature into her two hands and bending it to her will.

Was that feeling of power — so heady, so tempting — akin to the power the shamans sought? Why should it be right for her and wrong for them? Why had she once resisted it?

She did not like these thoughts; she suspected they would have never come to her in the Blue Mountains.

Winter attacked the Sea of Grass with a vengeance. It was not an alpine winter, with the sky gradually fading into the soft gray of a dove's breast and the silent, sweet falling of snow blanketing the earth mother, keeping her snug for the gestation of new life. Winter on the grasslands was controlled, like every other season, by the tireless spirit of the wind that swept across the prairie, scattering seed and animal and man.

Wind howled and tore. It drove particles of stinging ice into the eyes and through the clothing. It pelted the unprotected with a granular snow like tiny hailstones; it came in the blink of an eye and could catch and kill you within a short walk from your wagon. The wind could whip a smothering whiteness across the land, composed of snow so heavy it was suffocating, making breathing all but impossible, and what breath remained was sucked out of the lungs by the pervasive cold. Terrible cold. Cold that sank through the flesh and gnawed the marrow within the bones.

Kazhak told Epona of the worst blizzard within his memory, a storm during which deer had turned their rumps to the wind until such masses of ice built up on their hindquarters that the living flesh pulled away in long strips. The dazed, suffering animals wandered aimlessly across the prairie when the storm was over, and the Scythians hunted them down without effort.

Driving ice crystals could blind livestock unless sufficient precautions were taken. When the sky turned a particular dead-white color, Epona watched as the herders wrapped the heads of the most valuable horses with cloth to protect them. When the storm had passed, they found the cloth shredded and many horses had bleeding faces.

The Scythians had spent many generations surviving in this brutal climate. Now that she lived among them, their women taught Epona how to dress for warmth, how to cover her face, how to build a tent for her man by constructing a round lattice-work frame of wood, then lashing felt rugs securely to this support with hair ropes capable of resisting the wind.

The wind that was like a member of the tribe, always to be considered on the Sea of Grass.

It was not surprising the nomads looked with awe at a woman who seemed able to summon such a force.

Epona began, for the first time in her life, to resent the weather, although she knew it was only an aspect of the earth mother and not a being bent on thwarting her personally. But it forced her to spend most of her time in the wagon — trapped in the wagon, that was how she thought of it — denied the freedom of the horse's back and the beckoning grassland. In a large, snug lodge, filled with family and the cheer of the fire spirit, the Kelt had spent many long winters without discomfort, but that was far different from the cramped, dark wagon she now occupied.

"Why can't I at least have Ro-An come and share this tent with me?" she asked Kazhak. "Other women share space; none of them have to live alone, as I do."

"Who would live with a magic person?" Kazhak replied. He did not want any of his other women in the tent with Epona; that would lessen her status in the eyes of the shamans, it would make her appear to be no different from the others. "Go, visit with other women," he advised Epona. "But sleep in this place alone except for Kazhak."

"Then, how soon can I ride again? When can I take my horse and . . ."

"It is winter. You cannot ride out alone; storms come too fast, is not safe."

"They tell you I called the storm," she reminded him. "Do you think it would hurt me?"

"Is one thing to call something; is another to control it. Could be, you would be safe, but Kazhak does not want to take chance."

Having seen ice storms, Epona did not think she would be safe, either, but she at least wanted the freedom of choice. If he had told her she might ride when she pleased, she would probably have stayed safely in the encampment until spring. Since he refused to allow her to go out, she could think of little else.

Feeling the rebellion in her, Kazhak took the brown gelding out of the encampment and turned him loose with the main herd.

"He was my horse!" Epona protested.

"Was Basl's horse," Kazhak corrected her, "as long as Basl lived. Basl is dead, horse belongs to Kolaxais again. No woman owns horse. How can woman own property?"

Another argument was simmering, ready to boil over. No matter how much she tried to explain, Kazhak would never understand, and eventually he would lose patience with her and the bonds of their friendship would be severely strained. She did not want to jeopardize that relationship. It was all she had.

Until she had begun spending time in the company of the Scythian women, Epona had never known the meaning of loneliness. Now, surrounded by people with whom she had nothing in common, she learned the painful depths of that emotion. She could talk to the women, learn from them, see the same faces and hear the same voices day after day, and yet they never became friends. Even Ro-An would never be close to her in spirit. If she tried too hard to reach out to them they withdrew behind their veils, reminded of the ancient suspicion of the nomad for the outsider. If Epona displayed any overt signs of friendship to one, she later learned that the woman suffered for it at the hands of the others. Bored wives, their lives consisting of endless drudgery or unrelieved isolation, they could be savage to one another.

"I would like to have some work of my own to do," Epona suggested to Kazhak. "None of the women's chores are allowed me. I know how to set up a tent, but I have no opportunity to do it. I cannot cook, I am given no materials to sew with, what am I supposed to do?"

"You should be glad Kazhak has so many women to tend your needs," he replied. "You live easier than favorite wife of Kolaxais. Everyone notice. Shamans notice, you are very different from other women."

Epona clenched her useless hands into futile fists. "I am tired of being different!" she complained. But he did not listen.

He saw how the shamans avoided walking too close to Epona's tent. He himself was once more welcomed to the tent of the *han*, though not as cordially as in times past. At least he was not reminded of the men and horses he had lost, or the paucity of loot he had brought back for his prince. He heard many compliments given the Kelti swords, and murmured admiration expressed for the Kelti woman. The special woman. As long as Tsaygas and Mitkezh were wary of Epona, Kazhak held a weapon that no one challenged.

It was not his intention to overthrow the practice of shamanism on the Sea of Grass; such a suggestion would have horrified him. Though Kazhak himself had lost faith in the shamans he was still emotionally bound by the traditions of his race; it would never have occurred to him to try to introduce a new religion. If Tsaygas and Mitkezh had not attempted such a blatant usurpation of the authority of Kolaxais, issuing new orders in his name without even consulting the old *han*, demanding the prince's share of warrior loot as a reward for their ceaseless war with demons, Kazhak would never have interfered.

All his life he had enjoyed the unfettered existence of the horse, giving little thought either to magic or to the dynastic power struggles common among the Scyth. As the favorite son of Kolaxais, he took it for granted that he would be the prince's heir, the next *han* of the tribe. Meanwhile, life had been a cup to be drained with gusto. If he had experienced periods of deep melancholy they were only a part of life, as shadows were the children of Tabiti, the sun. Kazhak had lived his life in the sun and expected the concomitant shadows. He was mortal and would die; everything he might care for would die, so he had let himself care deeply for nothing. He had matched the climate cruelty for cruelty, indifference for indifference, taking what he wanted while life lasted and never thinking beyond tomorrow.

Then he had seen Kolaxais grow weak and ill, and the shamans fall on him to pick his bones before he was even dead.

That was the real reason Kazhak had been so anxious to take his band of comrades and ride away from the Sea of Grass: He could not bear to watch what was happening to Kolaxais and, through him, to the tribe. Daily Kazhak had seen the power of the shamans increase; daily the tribe became more and more afraid of the spirit world with which the magic men threatened them, until the people cowered in their tents and wagons, frightened by every small incident that might be interpreted as an unfavorable omen.

Yet Kazhak had never thought to challenge the shamans. Who could challenge shamans?

Until he saw the strength of Kelti magic. Until he knew Epona.

But she was a difficult weapon with sharp edges, and he was not certain how to handle her. Still, because of her, the shamans were treating him with grudging respect and were being careful not to provoke him.

If they ever suspected Epona had no magic powers both her life and Kazhak's would be forfeit, the Scythian realized fully. But she *was* magic. She was that thing called *drui*.

And more than that — she had shared with him the brotherhood of the eyes.

Against his will, Kazhak had come to care for the yellow-haired woman. And perhaps that was the greatest jeopardy of all. Now he must be willing to die for her, as he would have died for a brother; to die for a creature as alien to him as the wind and the fire.

Meanwhile he must keep her safe in spite of herself, and let her unknown powers tug at the shamans, a weapon of intimidation only, a weapon Kazhak did not know how to use.

The winter dragged on and on. The countless horses in the great herd lost flesh until a man could sink his knuckles between their ribs, and many of the older ones died, but no one suggested Epona try to cure them. They died at night, in the cold, and their frozen carcasses were found by the herders in the morning, obviously past even the strongest magic.

There was nothing for Epona to do at all.

She attempted to amuse herself by talking with the Scythian women, questioning them about the ways of the nomads. Talia, Kazhak's senior wife, was at first suspicious of such questions, but Epona soon learned that the older woman felt reassured by the ignorance of others. When Epona deliberately displayed a child-like lack of knowledge about the most rudimentary aspects of life on the steppe, Talia was willing to enlighten her.

The senior wife was even willing to tell Epona what she knew of shamanistic ritual, a subject that interested Epona more than she was willing to show to the other woman. If Kazhak meant to put her on the balance scale against the shamans, she must learn all she could about them for her own defense.

"The *taltos* is the magic spirit," Talia explained to her. "Is inherited. Is either white *taltos*, good, or black *taltos*, bad. No one can say which spirit he will get. Black *taltos* puts curses on people, looks at them with evil eye, does many bad things. Only white *taltos* can fight him, keep off harm."

Though she said nothing, Epona was secretly shocked. How could magic — the understanding and use of the forces of life — be black, be evil? The *druii* taught that it was to be used only for the maintenance and nurturing of life.

Talia continued, "*Taltos* is not welcome gift. Shamans are always tortured by illness before they are willing to accept their shamanism and begin to practice. The body or the mind must be very sick, very weak, before *taltos* can emerge and take over."

"Aside from fighting the black *taltos*, what magic do the white shamans do?" Epona wanted to know.

"They keep away sickness. They predict the future."

"Epona has seen them do a thing with stones," she said, and told Talia about Tsaygas and his little pile of pebbles.

Talia shook her head in agreement. "Shamans do many things that cannot be explained. Much magic," she said, a tinge of awe in her voice. "Beat drums and fall into *taltos* sleep, very special sleep, and in that way shamans can swallow live coals, or run knives through body and never bleed. Much magic."

"But what purpose do such things serve?" Epona inquired.

"Purpose? Is no purpose, is magic."

"The shamans do not explain the reason for the rituals?" Epona felt the gulf widen between herself and the Scythians. Among the

Kelti it was important to educate the people in dealings with the spirit world, so they might understand the forces that guided their lives and behave correctly, with proper respect.

I did not show proper respect, Epona thought suddenly, with a stab of pain.

"Shamans explain nothing," Talia was saying.

"Then what have you observed when you attended the ceremonies and the sacrifices? Surely that has given you some knowledge . . ."

Talia interrupted, "No no! Women never attend magic ceremonies; is only for men."

Epona was horrified. These women were denied the privilege of access to the spirits! Such an interdiction was one of the gravest punishments the Kelti tribal council could call down on a member of the people who committed a serious crime.

"How do you know what the shamans do, if you are never allowed to participate in the rituals?" she asked Talia.

A sly spirit peeked briefly through Talia's dark eyes, then ducked back out of sight again. "Children are curious, is it so? Hide, peek through tent flaps, carry tales." She giggled behind her veil. "Talia was child once. Epona also. You remember how it was."

Epona could not help smiling. "Epona remembers." *But I would not have gone to the magic house and peeked through Kernunnos' door*, she thought to herself.

"I have seen sticks the shamans carry," she told Talia, "sticks of carved wood with a hoof at the bottom, like a horse's foot. Do you know what purpose those serve, at least?"

Talia shook her head. "Oh yes. On shaman-sticks, the priests can fly. It is so," she assured Epona, seeing the disbelief in her eyes. "Everyone knows they use shaman-sticks to fly to the land of the demons where they fight them, keep them away from us. Sticks are horses with special magic."

"What sort of demons?"

"Demons that cause us to sicken, to die. Without white *taltos* to protect us, the spotted guest would come to kill us all." Upon saying these words, Talia made a sign in the air with her hands and drew her veil completely over her head.

"What is the spotted guest?" Epona asked, but the mere mention of it seemed to have reduced the older woman to such a nervous state that all further discussion was impossible.

The spotted guest must be terrible indeed. If the shamans actually did protect the tribe from it, their power was greater than Epona had realized. She must be very careful.

That night when Kazhak came to her tent, Epona asked him about the spotted guest. His reaction was not as extreme as Talia's but he was obviously uncomfortable with the subject. "Is demon, walks on face and body, leaves red footprints. Whole body burns with fire. Men, women, children, all die when spotted guest comes."

Epona was horrified. "Does no one survive?"

"Few. Very few. But always wear spots on face, deep holes to show where demon walked."

"Talia says that the shamans protect you from the spotted guest."

"Tribe has not been attacked by that particular demon for long time," Kazhak replied. "Maybe shamans protect. Maybe demon busy elsewhere. Is known fact, he attacks all peoples."

"Not in the Blue Mountains," Epona said. "There is no spotted guest in the Blue Mountains."

Kazhak's face shone as if a lighted candle had been placed inside his skull. "Is it so? Kelti can protect against spotted guest completely?"

Why did the spirit within not warn me before I spoke? she asked herself ruefully. "I have never seen the sickness you describe," she told Kazhak, "and I know nothing about protections against it."

"But you do not have it. You said. Must be magic your people do, you can do, better than shamans . . ." He was growing more excited with every word, as if he would grab her by the arm and drag her to the tent of the shamans this very moment, claiming this superlative and decisive power for her.

"I cannot cure the spotted guest sickness," she insisted. "If it attacked me I would die just like the rest of you."

Kazhak glowered at her. "Do not say that. Do not ever say what you cannot do. Tell no one what you cannot do. You understand?"

She lowered her eyes before the expression in his. "I understand."

311

Her curiosity unquenched, Epona continued to ask questions about the shamans, but she was careful not to talk too long to any one woman. From Ro-An she learned that when a shaman died, he was not buried in a wooden house but "in the air," his body placed on a platform raised on poles above the earth, so he could continue to fly as he had once flown on his stick horse.

From a squat elderly woman with blackened teeth, Vilma, a discarded wife of Kolaxais, allowed to live on sufferance with the other old women of the tribe, Epona learned that the shamans also took wives. "They only take women from shaman families," Vilma explained, "women who will bear shaman children."

"But those women practice no magic themselves?"

Vilma looked shocked and drew her veil across her ruined teeth. She stared at Epona without answering.

Ari-Ki, the woman of Aksinya, contributed another nugget of knowledge about the personal lives of the shamans. "Among the people of the horse," she told Epona, "if woman does not belong to a man and take his body into hers by her twentieth name-day she will never be able to give birth without difficulty. When woman goes past her twentieth name-day and is not chosen by a man, shamans can have her for slave."

Epona had already learned that bought slaves such as the Hellenes enjoyed were unknown on the Sea of Grass, and that nobles sometimes took people of their own tribe into slavery to serve them — such as Kolaxais' little cupbearer, a hazel-eyed boy with a merry laugh. But she was somehow shocked to hear of shamans enslaving their own race.

I would not have been a slave in the magic house, she thought. *I would have had honor equal to that of the* gutuiters, *or perhaps Kernunnos himself. If. If. My mother traded me, but not into slavery.*

It was apparent the shamans had considerable power, not the least of it being the strength of fear they held over the heads of the nomads. With each passing day, Epona felt more certain that Kazhak's faith in her was misplaced. Her gifts were so small, so undeveloped; her ignorance was so vast. Soon the shamans would see through her as Uiska saw through opaque water, and know she could not threaten them. Then they would feel free to do whatever they liked to old Kolaxais, and to Kazhak, who had tried to defy them with only the poor strength of a foolish Kelti girl.

The shamans would be unforgiving. She would die friendless, in a place not known to the spirits of her people, and there would be no proper transition ritual. Anything might happen to her, afterward.

She lay sleepless at night and sipped the bitter cup of fear. The hairs of the bearskin cloak tickled the side of her face; the never-subsiding odors of felt and leather and rancid fat filled her nostrils. Outside her tent, the tiny fire she kept alive with scavenged charcoal and dried dung stood watch.

The Scythians around her slept, and dreamed, and in their dreams they saw strange sights.

Sometimes they saw a huge silver wolf that came again and again to the encampment, its lips drawn back from its fangs and its eyes glowing with hunger.

Chapter 25

I N ITS OWN TIME, and with reluctance, winter loosened its grip on the Sea of Grass. The days grew longer. The women began talking among themselves of the coming spring, when rain would bestow a fleeting lushness to the arid steppe. Then the community of nomads would pack up its tents and disperse, each family taking an assigned portion of the sheep and goats, cattle and horses, in search of good grazing. They would not be re-united as a tribe until the next winter, when they must come together for the annual great sacrifice, the Taylga, and give an accounting to the *han*. All the livestock belonged to Kolaxais; all young animals born during the spring and summer, all booty taken by parties of warriors, was ultimately his.

Epona had difficulty understanding that everyone and every-thing belonged to one man, and that the others accepted this. Once it was clear to her, she appreciated the depth of Kazhak's resentment of the shamans. But she never thought of herself as belonging to the *han*.

With the change of seasons her way of living would change, and she was eager to learn what to expect once the tribe scattered in search of summer pastures. She tried questioning Ro-An and Talia, but their answers frustrated her. They would tell her the bare facts only, uncolored by opinion or emotion. She could not tell if they preferred the winter camp or the summer wandering;

she could not base her own anticipation upon any feelings they displayed, for they displayed none.

This was still another aspect of Scythian nature that baffled the Kelt. A nomad woman's reaction to things that happened to her personally or within the community was one of studied indifference. Nothing appeared to please or displease her; nothing excited her. If Epona asked one of the other women her feelings about some matter, the reply was always, "It makes no difference." If asked her opinion, a Scythian woman said, "Ro-An (or Ari-Ki, or Gala) does not know." If pressed further she elaborated by adding, "Ro-An does not care."

"Whatever you want," was the nearest expression the women made of a personal preference, so Epona took them at their word and did as she pleased within the narrow limits of their shared society. But the overriding apathy irritated her. The Scythian women suffered life to happen to them; aside from their infighting for a husband's favor, they took no active part in shaping the pattern of their own lives. They were willingly passive, allowing the restriction of their lives without protest. Like water running from the mountains, they took the easiest way.

Epona came to hate that phrase, "Whatever you want." It goaded her as a herder's switch goaded the animals. "What do *you* want?" she demanded to know more than once, but the women merely stared at her with blank eyes.

They are as dull as sheep, she thought. *Duller, for even a sheep will select a choice tuft of grass for itself. These women pretend that nothing in life matters to them. It must be pretense, for who could really be so uncaring? Everything in this life matters.*

Her own caring burned within her like a flame.

Before the nomads dispersed, they celebrated the great festival of the sun, the sacrifice to Tabiti, which they held each year to entreat the sun to return to northern skies.

When Epona was reminded that all women were excluded from the ceremony, she and Kazhak had yet another quarrel.

"Tabiti is a principal god of the Scythians; of Scythian men and of Scythian women," she argued. "So why are women not allowed to take part in the sacrifice?"

"Women are not needed. They have no influence."

"You want my influence to counteract that of the shamans," she

315

reminded Kazhak. "So obviously you think I have some power with the spirits. Yet I will not be allowed to attend the ritual?"

"Is so. You are woman."

"But I am your wife, Kazhak! Does that not give me some status within the tribe, some special rights?"

Kazhak scowled. This matter of words seemed very important to the people of the Kelti; each word had its own subtle meaning, and he realized he had made a mistake in letting Epona use the wrong one for so long. "You are Kazhak's *woman*," he said in a belated attempt to clarify the situation. "Not wife. Only a woman of Scythian blood can be wife to a Scythian."

"But I will bear your children! What about them?"

"Kazhak's children will be Scythian," he assured her. It would be pleasant if this woman did not argue so much, but Kazhak knew Epona well enough by now to realize this was a futile wish. Her cheeks were already flaming with anger.

"You were the first man to enter my body," she said. "By the laws of my people, that makes me your wife, and part of your tribe. So I am Scythian."

"Is not so. Can never be. You were not born to people of the horse so you are outsider. Outsiders are different, can never be Scythian."

"Your word for outsider is the same as your word for enemy!" Epona pointed out.

"Outsider *is* enemy. When outsider meets Scyth, there is war. Has always been. Must always be so."

Epona could not accept the inevitability of that statement. "Why, Kazhak? The Kelti live in peace and do business with many outsiders, those not of our own people. We do not hate them because they are different. Trees and animals are different, too, but we get along with them, so why should we consider men of other races, who are so much more like us than trees and animals, to be our enemies?"

"Outsiders hated us first," Kazhak replied, and there were millennia of bitter warfare in his voice. "Once, grandfathers of our grandfathers lived many days to the east, raised livestock. Then Tabiti grew angry, scorched the land. Grass became sand and blew away. Where to go, what to do? Scythians moved west, seeking new pasture, but people on new land would not let us graze. Animals were starving. We must fight or die, so learned to fight.

To survive better than all others. Soon we held all new land. We had bigger, fatter, healthier herds; our defeated enemies went somewhere else.

"Then more drought, sickness; we move again. New people resist us. We fight, win, drive them away. They become outsiders, hate us, but man must eat, is it so? Children are born, the tribe gets larger, there must be food, space. We must survive. We take what we need, what else can we do? But all others hate us, try to harm us. They are our enemies, not to be trusted. Outsiders."

"Then I am an outsider," she said.

Kazhak would not meet her eyes. "Yes. Is so."

"But your people and mine are not at war."

"Not today. But your people are wealthy, they have many things my people need. Someday, when there is no more good grass here, we will bring herds west, into valley of the Duna and beyond, even to land of your people. We will leave herds in the lowlands and bring armies into the mountains. We will take your gold, your iron, your heads."

"My people are mighty warriors! We will never let you into our mountains!"

"Mighty warriors die. All men die. Like grass, like even strong horses, all men die. We know how to kill," he reminded her.

"You are defying the great fire of life," she argued. "You accept no one else's right to live; you try to extinguish sparks that are part of yourself."

Kazhak nodded stubbornly, refusing to understand. He was like a horse that would not be led, but planted its feet and insisted on its own way or nothing. "We take what we need."

She could have wept with frustration, but she had not allowed herself to weep since she first thought of herself as Scythian. The Kelti wept easily, over the many things that touched the spirit within, but she had observed the nomads to weep only over the death of a brother. To be Scythian, she had learned to dry her well of tears.

But she was not Scythian. She was not even a wife.

You are Kelti, said the spirit within.

Yes! she responded silently, with sudden fierce joy. *I will be of the Kelti forever!*

She turned a cold, set face toward Kazhak. "If you ever attack my people you will regret it," she told him through clenched teeth. "Even the smallest of our girl children is trained in the skills of combat. No one who knows us dares war on us anymore. I promise you, Scythian: If you ever try to drive us from our land the Kelti will drown you in your own blood!" She threw back her head and glared at him, defying him and all his kind, the spirit of her people fully awake within her.

Kazhak's eyes locked with hers. Not as brother to brother, but as warrior to warrior, over swords.

"We will bury you," he said at last.

He had not meant to say those words, not to that woman. But they had shaped themselves inevitably in his mouth. It had always been so; it would always be so. Peace was an illusion, like a trick shamans performed. It was not, could not be, peace that kept the people of the Kelti so prosperous in their steep mountains. No! Epona had said the words herself: They were skilled warriors and none dared stand against them. That was their secret; that, and the magic they could do.

The magic . . . he had not meant to alienate Epona; that was the last thing he wanted. Too late, he tried to make amends, but his words were clumsy and his gestures futile. She wrapped herself in hauteur and turned her back on him, unwilling to talk further.

"Kazhak will bring the brown gelding for you, from the herd," the Scythian promised. "In the morning. Epona can ride. Go anywhere." He smiled hopefully, but she would not answer or even look at him.

Trouble, nothing but trouble; women were always trouble if you let them get close to you . . . how had this one gotten so close to him? Was that Kelti magic, too? Was he bewitched? Should he go to the shamans for a spell to fight off demons?

Kazhak shook his head in baffled rage. That was how the shamans fastened on to a person like leeches in a swamp, never to let go. The cure was as bad as the sickness. Epona was meant to be a weapon against the shamans, not the other way around . . . everything got so confused when the Kelti were involved. But he must not make an enemy of her, that would be a dangerous mistake. She could hurt him . . .

She could shut herself away from him, that spirit within could hide itself and never again smile out of her eyes at him. Then Kazhak would be alone, as truly and deeply alone as he had been before he met Epona. At one time he had not minded; he had not known he was lonely.

But now he knew. Without her, he would be as desolate as winter twilight on the Sea of Grass.

He tried to talk to her, to change the words somehow, but he could not. They were true words and a man could not unmake the truth. Everything he said seemed to make matters worse. At last, defeated, he left the tent.

When he was gone, Epona turned around and looked at the place where he had stood. *The Kelt will outlast the Scyth, Kazhak*, she said to him in her mind. *You will not bury us.*

In the morning she found the brown gelding hobbled beside her tent, a new saddle on his back, brilliant with red horsehair tassels and leather medallions depicting predator animals clawing and devouring their prey.

Epona did not even look around to see if Kazhak was watching. She unhobbled the horse and mounted quickly, hungry for his back and the open plains.

The dying winter had left the steppe a sea of mud. In the distance she saw the herders already busy among the sprawling mass of horses and cattle, sheep and goats, that stretched almost to the horizon. The stock must be divided into smaller, more manageable bands, and before the tribe left the winter gathering place these bands would be assigned to various men and their families.

Each man with wives and wagons was expected to take his share of the animals and care for it throughout the spring and summer, to be returned in improved condition to Kolaxais at the winter ingathering. The herders could trade animals for better animals; they could enlarge their bands through theft and raiding; they could eat the meat of the cattle, drink the milk of the mares, weave the wool of the sheep and goats. But every animal belonged ultimately to the *han* and must be accounted for to him. Every newborn must be marked with the prince's mark and brought back in the autumn for his eyes to see, so he would know the extent of his wealth.

A man who did not bring back more animals than he took was given a reduced allotment the next season, so that poverty grew as his herd shrank. A man with few horses, or no sheep, could not support many wives, could not have many children. Could not be counted as much of a man.

If a group of warriors set out, as Kazhak and his men had done, to scout for new pastures or seize new treasure to enrich the prince and win his favor, they appointed brothers to care for their allotment of livestock while they were gone, and to guard the women in their wagons. Some of the Scythians had been responsible for other men's wagons for years, the owners having gone off to fight as mercenaries for the Assyrians and never returned. Those who stayed behind sent their women to feed the widows, and counted the children among their own children, and they were assigned enough animals by the prince to support all the mouths they had to feed. For them, there could be fat on the belly and meat in the pot.

If a man betrayed his trust with his brother's livestock or women he was outcast, sent from the sight of the prince forever, all that he was allowed being one horse and his *gorytus*. Such men formed small bands of their own, ranging the steppe, living by theft and stealth, dangerous to all whom they met.

"Dasadas will ride with them someday," Kazhak had once confided to Epona. "He watches you, watches you, all the time. Day will come when Kazhak will announce Dasadas is no longer his brother."

Epona had been equally aware of the eyes of Dasadas, following her around the encampment, but she had paid no attention. Kazhak was her man; as long as he satisfied her it would have been dishonorable, by the laws of the Kelti, to look at any other.

But on this muddy morning she was not satisfied with Kazhak. Instead of temporary anger, flaring up like a spark and dying away in his arms, she felt a cold and permanent rage, like a stone in her belly. Kazhak had betrayed her, he had never intended to make her part of his tribe. She was just a useful possession.

And she would not be possessed.

As she rode away from the encampment, letting her body refamiliarize itself with the movements of the horse, the shifts of weight and balance necessary for riding, she caught sight of another lone rider also setting out from the huddle of wagons. She squinted her eyes against the sun.

The solitary rider was Dasadas.

At Epona's signal the brown gelding broke into a trot, lifting his knees high to pull his feet out of the sticky mud. Epona remembered a fold in the land some distance from the encampment, an undulation of the earth containing a long-dry streambed. A few stunted, dead trees were there, and before winter she had ridden to that place to practice with bow and arrow, out of sight of the Scythians who might have laughed at her clumsiness.

Today she yearned to be out of sight of the Scythians again. She headed for the dry streambed, and Dasadas reined his own horse in the same general direction.

She knew it, but she did not care.

I do not belong to you, Kazhak, she said silently, clenching her jaw, pushing the horse to go faster.

The streambed was not dry now; a thin trickle of melted ice lay at its bottom, and one of the trees might not be dead. Two or three tiny green leaves were struggling for life on a topmost branch.

Epona sat on the horse, looking up at that unequal struggle, the weak leaves against the wind and the sun and the barren earth. She got off her horse and knelt at the base of the tree, fumbling with the brooch that held her bearskin cloak. She used the point of the brooch-pin to scratch her wrist, and dripped a few tiny droplets of blood onto the tree roots, whispering an invocation.

"What you do?" a voice challenged.

"Offering a sacrifice so this tree will live," she answered. She did not look over her shoulder, but she was aware that Dasadas had dismounted and was standing behind her. She could smell his body, a different smell from that of Kazhak; more acid, more bitter.

"Can you make tree live?"

"I can help." She completed the sacrifice and stood up, rubbing her arm. "If the spirits wish; if they accept my offering."

"Why you care?" Dasadas stepped in front of her so she had to look at him. He was thinner than she remembered, his flesh burned by the intensity of the spirit within until it had melted from his bones, leaving his face as sculptured as an Ionian figurine.

"I have an obligation to life," she told him, knowing he would not understand.

"Would you . . ." Dasadas hesitated, licking his lips. Beautifully shaped lips, Epona thought to herself, looking at them for the first time. There were those who would have said Dasadas was a beautiful young man.

"Would you . . . teach Dasadas your magic?" the Scythian asked hesitantly.

Epona stared at him. "You have to be born with the gift," she said. "I cannot make you *drui*. If you have a talent, you can be taught how to use it, that is all."

"You will not teach?" He looked like a disappointed child. "Dasadas give you something in return, if you teach. Dasadas best archer of all Royal Scyths. Dasadas show you how make bow, arrows, kill anything. Is trade?"

The *druii* could be born anywhere, among any people; so it was taught. Perhaps this Dasadas did have the gift. If the link had been broken between herself and Kazhak, perhaps this young man who stood before her, trembling with some strange passion, would be a friend to her spirit.

Who cared for the stupid laws of Kolaxais and the shamans?

Epona smiled at Dasadas, a wide, reckless smile, white teeth framed by chapped red lips. "Teach me to use the bow first," she said. "Then we will see about the magic."

Dasadas agreed without hesitation. He would have agreed to anything to be close to the yellow-haired woman, to hear her voice, to feel the excitement that coursed through him only when he was in her presence. The magic. The magic!

They hobbled the horses and sat on the ground together, and Dasadas explained about the bow as he would have explained to a son of his. The only way to become a great archer was to know every aspect of the bow as well as you knew the veins and hairs on the backs of your hands. Dasadas began by telling Epona how the bow was manufactured, that she might know its most intimate secrets. She had learned the Scythian language very well, for an outsider; it was not as difficult to explain to her as he would have thought, and her mind grasped a concept as quickly as a man's.

The Scythian bow, the most accurate weapon of its kind, was a short reflex bow consisting of a wooden heart, very thick and almost entirely rigid on both sides of the handgrip, but thinning away to form a very slender limb like a willow sapling. Sometimes this was composed of several leaves of wood doweled together, but more often it was cut from a single stave. It was always curved, with the back forming a pronounced concavity in the direction of the arrow's flight, and with a symmetry that spoke to the Kelti spirit within Epona. Looking at the bow, she saw beauty.

As Dasadas explained, after the wood was formed, a thick layer of sinew steeped in a urine compound was laid on the back of the bow and pressed into place. This solidified into a rock-hard layer that was both firm and curiously elastic, almost inseparable from the wood. The belly of the bow was similarly fitted with long plates of curved horn, lying to the wood without tension in any part. These processes alone might take a man several winters. The contact surfaces of the horn and wood were patiently rasped in preparation for the boiled fish glue that would hold them together, and the glue was applied in many thin layers. When a man undertook to make a bow for himself, he was dedicating years of his life to the task, allowing the weapon many long months of resting and drying out before the next step was taken.

The final result was an object of deadly beauty and harmony, a perfect instrument as valuable to its owner as his horse or his wagons.

Epona looked with newly appreciative eyes on the bow she had inherited from Basl. It was as if the dead man's spirit lay obediently in her hands, ready to kill at her command.

Next Dasadas set up targets for her and coached her in the technique for drawing the bow and for sighting her quarry. He was patient and skillful, but his hands trembled violently when he had to touch her to adjust her fingers on the string. Epona remembered that under the Scythian rule he could be killed for touching another man's woman, and thought that was why he trembled.

Wherever Dasadas made contact with Epona's bare flesh, his own flesh burned as if he had touched fire. Magic, it was magic. She was sharing the magic with him, he said to himself. This was the way, then; he could not take it by force, but she would give it to him if he humbled himself. No Scythian ever humbled himself for a woman, but to Dasadas the sacrifice did not seem too great in return for the way he felt when he was in her presence.

Epona, Epona. Shoot the arrow, Epona.

She did, and when she hit her mark she laughed with delight.

Dasadas stood as close to her as he dared, aching for more of her, but he was aware it was not her body he wanted. Not exactly. It was something else he longed to capture, that special quality that enchanted him, that light and laughter and energy so different from the nature of any woman he knew. When he thought of the women who were his wives, he hated them. As he hated Kazhak, for possessing Epona.

Tabiti fled across the sky, and at last caution summoned Dasadas from his madness. If Kazhak came looking for the Kelt and found them together he would be merciless to the younger man. Life had never seemed particularly sweet to Dasadas. Life was harsh, and violent, and often exciting, but not sweet. Yet in Epona's presence he had the feeling there were many faces to life that he had not seen, and there might be sweetness, too. Somehow, somewhere, as part of the magic. He wanted to live a long time; he wanted to live long enough to taste the honey and feel the magic coursing through his veins.

He might not live longer than a few heartbeats more if Kazhak found them alone together, so far from the encampment.

"You must go back," he told the woman with sudden urgency. "You ride back to wagons from north. Dasadas will wait until nearly sundown; ride in from south. But you go now, quickly, before Kazhak looks for you."

Epona understood, but she had not yet fulfilled her part of the bargain. She had not begun to discuss the powers of the spirits with Dasadas. He had generously given all their time together to her, teaching her to shoot the bow. When she tried to protest he waved her objections aside, however.

"If we are careful now, there will be another time," he told her. Her face was soft and open to him; he felt he had made great strides today. He was stalking a new kind of game, something as quick to run as an antelope, but capable of the savagery of a lion. The hunt might take a long time, and much careful strategy, but it would be worth it. It would be worth anything.

He told her, "In only few days, mud will begin to dry on Sea of Grass. It will be possible for wagons to move again. Men will go in every direction, seeking fresh pasture. Some, good brothers, will follow Kazhak, but not many. Every man likes to go his own way. Aksinya may go with Kazhak, but Dasadas will not be welcome."

There was truth to his words. Epona shook her head in silent agreement.

"So, is few days," Dasadas continued. "You ride out, Dasadas ride out and meet you. Different places. Be very careful. You will soon shoot arrows as good as . . . as Basl did. You will tell Dasadas about magic, maybe teach him a little, yes?" He smiled disarmingly, crinkling the skin around his eyes into unfamiliar folds.

He was a young man, handsome to Epona, now that she was used to the faces of the Scythians. And when he was near her, he burned with a fire that lit up his eyes and radiated its heat to her. She was both flattered and intrigued. To be wanted so desperately, so obviously, was soothing to her bruised spirit. When she thought about Kazhak she blamed him bitterly for desiring her as nothing more than a trading piece to be used in the elaborate game he was playing with the shamans. Dasadas wanted her for herself. He wanted to be with her. He wanted to listen to what she had to say.

And he wanted her for bedsports, too. She knew that; what woman would not? It was unfortunate that she felt no desire for his body, but perhaps that would happen if they were together more. She had grown accustomed to the pleasures of the body, but she no longer intended to share lifemaking with Kazhak. She would punish him.

Perhaps she would punish him with Dasadas.

She laughed suddenly, tossing her head so the heavy yellow hair with its copper threads swung free across her back. "I will ride out and meet you, Dasadas," she said. "We will shoot arrows together. We will talk about magic. Until the mud dries; until the wagons move."

She sounded so reckless he was frightened for her. No nomad woman, undertaking a forbidden relationship, would have spoken above a whisper. "You will be careful?" he urged.

"Careful?" Epona laughed again. "Hai, Dasadas, I have never been careful!"

Chapter 26

After the long torpor of the winter, when mere survival was difficult enough and no additional effort was possible, the nomads were bursting with the fresh energies of oncoming spring. The tribe of Kolaxais became frantically busy, preparing for its dispersal. Tents had to be struck, the framework carefully repaired and stored in the wagons; the wagons themselves required a final checking and provisioning before the trek began in search of summer pastures; there were good-byes to be said, the men embracing each other warmly, the women sharing a last pot of root tea with their social equals; the livestock had to be rounded up, counted, and allotted.

This last, the most serious task of the spring, kept all able-bodied men busy. No one had time to notice that Epona and Dasadas were absent from the encampment part of each day.

The forbidden meetings gave Epona a heady sense of defiance. It was this that intoxicated her, more than Dasadas' devotion. She rode out each morning with a pounding heart, eyes scanning the horizon, and on one level of her being she almost hoped to see Kazhak riding toward her. She wanted to stand before him and acknowledge that she had betrayed him, as she felt he had betrayed her. She wanted to laugh in his face, to challenge him, to defy all the restrictions and conventions of his people — his people, not hers — and fight to the death, if necessary, for her freedom.

Fight to the death, as she now wished she had fought beside the farmers in their field, when the Scythians galloped down on them.

And yet she was in no hurry for her transition. Even when the pattern went against her, she enjoyed this life too much to be eager to leave it, and she was always curious about what might happen nextday. She did not really want Kazhak to come upon her and Dasadas and strike them down.

She did not really want to see the look in his eyes, if he found her with another man.

She rode out, and she met Dasadas in different places, each of them a long gallop from the encampment, hidden from casual eyes by the roll of the land or a sheltering gully. She became proficient, then deadly, in her use of the bow, learning the skill with a speed that astonished Dasadas and gave him yet another reason to admire her. She kept her share of the bargain as well, explaining to him, slowly and patiently, the teachings of the *druii*. She was careful not to make the mistakes she had made with Kazhak, speaking to him as an equal who should surely grasp what she was talking about. She tried to teach Dasadas as one would teach a small child, with clear, simple examples, things any mind could grasp.

And she was disappointed. Kazhak had rarely listened, professing impatience with all that was magic, but from time to time his mind had reached out to hers and she had been aware that he knew exactly what she meant. This never happened with Dasadas. He furrowed his forehead in his effort to follow her explanations, but it was soon obvious he had no gift. He could not understand what she tried to teach him. He yearned for the knowledge, the magic, but he had no ability to absorb or use it. He never felt it deep inside, where such magic must originate; he kept trying to get her to teach him to do simple tricks, things she felt were more typical of the shamans than the *druii*.

There was no link between them; Epona and Dasadas never locked eyes and let their spirits speak to one another. And it was not a thing you could ask a man to do. The spirit within Epona knew that such a meeting happened of its own accord, or not at all.

Without that link, there was no desire. When Dasadas stood close to her, his eagerness as tangible as flesh and blood, she felt

327

nothing for him, and each time he tried to touch her more intimately than was necessary for teaching the use of bow and arrow she moved away from him.

At last, in frustration, he grew angry with her. "Why you meet Dasadas if not to touch?"

"We made a trade, your knowledge for mine. The Kelti always honor their word."

"Is more than trade, Epona! Is . . . you are so much, so much more than other women, do you understand? You are . . . you are in the dreams of Dasadas, all the time, like the wolf."

Epona stiffened. "What wolf?"

"The giant wolf, the one we killed. He still comes to Dasadas in dreams. Aksinya says he dreams of wolf, too."

Epona felt as if a cold wind had blown across the Sea of Grass, sending a shiver up her back. "Are you and Aksinya the only ones who dream of this wolf?" she wanted to know.

Dasadas looked puzzled "Is strange, we are only ones who saw silver wolf in Carpātos, but Dasadas has heard two brothers, maybe three, mention dreaming of him. Very strange."

I should not be surprised, Epona thought. *I should have known this would happen.*

"Dasadas, I want you to do something for me."

"What?" His voice held the surly undertone of unrelieved lust, his hunger for her souring in his belly.

"Ask other men if they have dreamed of the silver wolf. Ask men who have not heard what happened to us in the Carpātos."

"If Dasadas does that for you, what will you do for Dasadas?" the Scythian asked slyly. "Kelti are such good traders; what will you trade?"

She had begun this game thoughtlessly, like a child, but she was not playing it with a child. His quick breathing and demanding eyes reminded her of that. A time would come when he would reach for her and she could not honorably pull away, having made an unspoken but implicit offer they both understood. Yet her flesh did not desire his, would never desire his. She knew that now. "What do you want?" she asked him.

"To be near you."

"You are near me now."

"All summer. Ask Kazhak to let Dasadas and his wagons come

with you to the summer grazing. If Epona asks, Kazhak will agree."

She was not so certain of her ability to persuade Kazhak, and she was not sure it would be prudent to have Dasadas in close proximity throughout the long summer. What she had begun as a few days' sport, in defiance and out of anger, could become deadly for all involved during the pastoral days and star-filled nights. But if Dasadas told the truth, if the giant wolf was really following them through the dreamworlds, it would be comforting to have him nearby, a proven ally.

"I will ask Kazhak," she promised. "And you will question the other men, see how many have experienced the same dream?"

"Dasadas will do that," the Scythian agreed.

The days were growing longer, the time for preparation shorter. Already the first small groups of herders had set out from the encampment, riding their horses and cracking their whips to establish early dominance over the animals in their care, their women and children following in the wagons. The weakest animals were assigned first; the choice of the herds would be apportioned last, to Kazhak and the other members of Kolaxais' own family . . . and to the kin of the shamans, who had been promised well-bred horses and healthy young livestock.

"In three days, we will leave, too," Kazhak told Epona.

The next morning she hurried to her arranged meeting with Dasadas, but he was a long time in coming. When at last he rode into view his handsome face was troubled. "Almost every man has dreamed of the wolf," he told her without getting off his horse. "Is very bad thing, Epona. Is not discussed, because what man cries aloud over bad dreams? But Dasadas asks; they tell. That wolf, that strange wolf we saw, wolf that killed Basl, has walked through this camp many times. Many times. Is a demon, a terrible thing! We must tell the shamans, they must fight it."

"No!" Epona said quickly, laying her hand on his arm to stop him physically. "Don't tell the shamans, Dasadas."

"For why?"

Why? Because the shamans would want to know where the silver wolf came from, and why it was plaguing the dreamworld of the Scythians. They were not stupid men, Tsaygas and Mitkezh; it would not take them long to find out that the dreams had begun with Epona's arrival. It would not take them long to determine that it was the Kelti woman who had led the silver wolf onto the Sea of Grass.

"There is no need to tell the shamans because I have the magic to protect the people from the wolf," Epona told Dasadas. "When the camp breaks up, your brothers will no longer have bad dreams about that demon."

Dasadas' face flooded with new admiration. He never doubted her ability to do as she said, which both touched Epona and put a new responsibility on her shoulders. "You can take away the wolf? Is wonderful thing, Epona! But . . . why did you not do this when we were riding here, when wolf chased us, when wolf killed Basl? Why did you not use your magic to save Basl?"

"All magic is limited, Dasadas," she explained, hoping this time he would understand. "I can draw the wolf away from your people, but I will not kill it."

"You cannot kill wolf? Demon cannot be destroyed?"

"It can be destroyed," Epona told him truthfully, though she felt a strange reluctance to say those words. "But I am not the one to do it. It is better just to lure him away and let the people forget about him."

"Dasadas believes you," said the Scythian, his eyes shining with something very near worship. "Now, will you do as you said? Will Kazhak make welcome the wagons, the herds of Dasadas for the summer grazing?"

That was a hard promise to fulfill. When she broached the idea to Kazhak, his immediate reaction was one of anger. "Why does Dasadas want to graze his horses with my horses? Let him find his own pastures!"

"You and he have traveled together before," Epona reminded him. "Every summer, your wagons have followed the same ruts as his; you have always been brothers."

"Now he wants to share more than my grass," Kazhak said suspiciously.

Epona told him, then, of the dreams of the huge wolf, but she did not say she had learned of these dreams through conversations with Dasadas. She let Kazhak think it was the talk of the women, gossip heard over mares' milk and root tea.

Kazhak was surprised. "Many people have dreamed this?"

"So I understand. Have you never had such a dream?"

330

He thought for a moment. "When we hurt the wolf, back in the Carpātos, that was the last Kazhak saw of it, awake or asleep. If my brothers dream of the demon wolf, why does it not come to Kazhak?"

Because you have slept within range of my guardian fire, Epona answered him in her head. *The fire I built with my two hands according to the old ways, and gave special charge over my safety. The sacred ritual fire.*

Wise are the ways of the people, who taught you these things, said the spirit within. *You were wrong to turn your back on such wisdom.*

But she had turned her back. She had set her face toward the east, and she must deal with thisday as she found it. She would do what she could to alleviate the nightmares of Kazhak's people. To this end, she told Kazhak what she had told Dasadas, that she would be able to lure the wolf away from the main body of the tribe so that it followed his wagons and left the others in peace. "I think it is better for us to face the wolf, for we have dealt with it before," she said. She did not tell him that there was no choice; she did not tell him what the wolf wanted. "But it would be better still if we had other experienced warriors with us, who know the ways of this thing. Aksinya and Dasadas would be a valuable addition to our family for this grazing season."

Kazhak was not pleased to hear Dasadas' name mentioned, but he agreed with her thinking. "Let it be, then. Those two who have fought that wolf before will come with us. You will make that wolf follow. Take him away from tribe before shamans learn of him; before shamans accuse Kazhak of bringing him here." That was a danger he had already foreseen.

Nevertheless, Kazhak intended to watch Dasadas very closely. The man's arrows and sword would be welcome, but his attentions to Epona would not. Kazhak would spend the grazing season on guard against both specter and man.

The last tents were struck, the last wagons packed, the last families moved away from the site of the winter encampment. Kolaxais' women transferred the old man, tent and all, into a splendid wagon painted in brilliant blues and reds, fine new felts in place, trophy heads flaunted along both sides. In the grazing season even the *han* followed in the nomadic footsteps of his people, taking with him the choicest animals.

331

And the shamans, who never left his side now.

Epona looked forward to the seasonal trek with almost unbearable eagerness. After the stifling boredom of the camp, the wagons, the exclusive company of women, she would be on the move again, with things happening around her, fresh horizons unfolding. She was anxious to test her newly acquired skill with bow and arrow on the open steppes, and to watch the brood mares grow heavy with foal. She could hardly wait to see the colts of the gray stallion take their first wobbly steps on the Sea of Grass.

It did not matter so much if the silver wolf followed her. He could do little to her but watch, as she lived thislife.

Thislife, that would surely be better now, away from the encampment and the crowds of passive women.

She would not be the only woman, of course. Kazhak's other women, as well as the wives of Aksinya and Dasadas, would accompany them, but only Epona would know the freedom of the horse's back and the open sky.

The ground was not yet thoroughly dried out when the wagons began creaking across it, but that did not matter. Excitement infected everyone. Kazhak himself seemed in a better humor; Epona even observed him riding with Dasadas, talking brother to brother, as if he did not suspect the other man had looked at his woman with covetous eyes.

Kazhak rode one of the young horses, and released the gray stallion to run with his herd, following the lead of a wise old mare who had guided herds before the gray stallion took his first faltering steps. Epona longed to be on her brown gelding, riding with the others, but she was needed to drive the wagon carrying her tent and household. She could mount a horse only when the herds were at peace, grazing; as long as the nomads were on the move she must sit in the wagon behind a pair of inferior draft horses, coarse-headed, slow-witted creatures. Sighting between their ears as she would sight along the flight path of an arrow, she could see the riding horses flowing gracefully across the steppe. They filled her vision and her heart.

Now that there were fewer women to do the labor — and no watching shamans to be impressed — Epona was allowed her share of the chores of nomad life. Unless they were lucky enough to find wood, dung must be gathered and stacked to dry, to use as fuel. If there was a water source nearby, it was up to the women to fetch water for drinking and cooking. They also had to milk the mares and goats and take responsibility for the sheep, who behaved according to incomprehensible whims of their own and needed constant supervision. There was grain to be ground and bread to be baked, the leathery bread of the prairies, not the soft chewy bread of the Blue Mountains. Mares' milk, fermenting in a leather bag, must be churned continually, a tiresome and repetitive task some of the women relegated to their older children. Epona, having no child, performed this task herself.

She was aware that there was speculation about her narrow waist and flat belly, but Ro-An told her, "Is hard to have children. Women do not conceive easily among our people. You may wait long time for first baby."

Among the Kelti, she would not have had to wait so long. The *gutuiters* would have prayed the prayers, offered the sacrifices, given her the potions and compounds that encouraged fertility, but there were no *gutuiters* on the empty prairie. Only women more ignorant than she, watching her with bright and jealous eyes.

To conceive, a woman had to lifemake with a man, and for many days Epona had used one pretext after another to keep from sharing bedsports with Kazhak. Her anger still burned strong within her. The Scythians had a strange aversion to a woman's bleedingtime, so she had told him she was bleeding and thus kept him away for a while. A Scythian man would not lifemake with a woman he thought was "unclean," a custom that amused Epona. What could be unclean about blood, the fluid of life itself? Among the Kelti, a woman undergoing her bleedingtime was treated with respect, even brought little presents and honored with special foods, to help call attention to her favorably, so the spirits awaiting housing would take notice of her.

Among the Scythians she hid away in her wagon, letting no one see her face, and when the period was over she had to undergo purification rites. At least, Epona thought, sitting patiently as Ro-An scraped the cleansing paste from her skin, it gave one a good excuse for the nomadic version of a bath.

But Kazhak would not be put off forever. While the herd was on the move he was kept busy, but when at last a good grazing site was located, with water nearby in the form of a shallow river, and the early growth of silver-headed grass promising abundance, he meant to return to Epona's bed. He knew she had long sim-

333

mered with anger, and he wanted that anger to be set aside. He was surprised by his own patience with her.

Every time he looked at her he remembered the way things had been between them — the warmth, the laughter, the talking — and he was anxious to restore that sense of camaraderie.

How strange it was that a man could feel that way about a mere woman! But of course she was not a mere woman.

He had been sleeping close beside her wagon each night, willfully ignoring the tradition that required a man to sleep far away from a bleeding woman. But the night they reached summer pasture he stood watch over the combined herds, and sometime before dawn he slept in his saddle.

And saw, in a dream, a huge silver wolf detach itself from the shadows and pad silently past the herd, its pale coat absorbing rather than reflecting the starlight. He watched, unable to move, as it slunk around the wagons of Aksinya and Dasadas, then stopped a little distance away from Epona's wagon and drew its teeth back from its lips in a silent snarl. It did not advance any closer than the perimeter of the small fire Epona had kindled as soon as they stopped, but its specific interest in her wagon was obvious.

Kazhak fought to arouse himself from his dream. It took an actual physical effort to raise his eyelids, to sit up in the saddle and look around. There was no wolf to be seen, only the herd, the wagons . . . the Sea of Grass, spreading forever under the stars.

In the morning he spoke to Aksinya and Dasadas. They, too, had dreamed of the wolf.

"Epona is right," Kazhak said. "It has followed us; it does not bother the rest of the tribe."

"She has strong magic to draw it away from them," Dasadas commented.

Kazhak pondered before answering. "May be. Or may be it is one of us the wolf follows, brothers, is it so?"

Aksinya and Dasadas exchanged glances.

Kazhak continued slowly, thinking as he spoke. "The wolf followed us . . . long time. Long time before we first saw it, Kazhak knew we were being hunted. Kazhak could feel it. Now Kazhak thinks it has been after us since we left the tribe of Taranis and the Kelti. Why? What does it want?"

"The swords?" Aksinya suggested.

"Kelti can make more swords. Besides, it is a demon; what use has demon for swords? No, Kazhak thinks it comes for another reason. Kazhak thinks it has followed us because we took Epona. The wolf means to punish us for stealing the woman."

"We did not steal her. She asked to come."

Kazhak sighed. "That may not matter to the wolf-demon."

Dasadas looked past Kazhak to the small cluster of wagons at the edge of their combined herds. The animals were avidly cropping the new grass just breaking through the soil; the women were spreading clothing on cord strung between the wagons so that sun and wind might freshen it. Epona was standing off to one side, watching, remembering the water-washed clothes she had worn in the Blue Mountains.

Her slender form drew Dasadas' eyes and held them. With an effort he looked away, before Kazhak saw the direction of his gaze. "You are saying Epona has not used magic to make the wolf follow us, and spare the rest of the tribe?" he asked.

"Kazhak has begun to think the wolf would have followed us anyway. It is us he wants, that wolf. Basl's blood was not enough for him." Kazhak could see it clearly, now, and he was glad Epona had urged him to invite Dasadas to join them. They should make their stand together against this thing, because it would undoubtedly hunt them down separately otherwise. Together, perhaps they did have a chance against it.

Aksinya said, "If wolf wants to punish us for taking Epona, why not just send Kelti woman back where she came from?"

Kazhak whirled to face Aksinya. "No!" he thundered. "Is my woman, that woman! Kazhak does not send her away, Kazhak does not give her away, Kazhak does not share her. You understand? You *both* understand?" He looked directly at Dasadas for a moment. "We keep her. And we will fight wolf if we must. Is agreed?"

They could not meet the savagery in his eyes. Both men looked down at the ground, shaking their heads. "Is agreed," Dasadas said.

Epona, he said in his heart. *Epona. We will have to be very careful, Epona. But at least you are in my eyes every day. Perhaps that will be enough.*

It would not be enough, but he was willing to wait. A hunter

335

sometimes had to be very patient, if he wanted to bring down a great prize.

Life on the steppes in summer was, as Epona had foreseen, very different from life in the winter encampment. The bitterest weather was a time of huddling and surviving, of protecting the flicker of life until spring, but the coming of spring heralded the return of true nomadic life, a sweeping, unfettered existence ideally suited to the vast steppes.

All nomadic life revolved around the livestock. The Scythians did not merely breed and ride their horses; they merged their lives with those of the animals to such an extent that they came very close to being the *kentaurs* of Hellene fable. Living, eating — even sleeping — on their mounts, they followed the horse in his constant search for better grass, and brought with them the cattle and goats and sheep upon whom their own existence also depended. Their women were occupied throughout the warm season with caring for these animals, making felts and curing hides and shearing the sheep of their thick winter wool, but the men gave themselves over, totally, to the horse.

For the Scyth, in the summertime, nothing else mattered. Small groups of herders, such as that of Kazhak, formed little rings on the Sea of Grass, like raindrops forming rings on the surface of a pond. These rings widened and touched the other rings of other herders from other tribes. There was trading and boasting and contesting; horse races to determine the best breeding animals; a constant fever of excitement over breeding or foaling or training young stock. The days were long and filled with horses. The nights were starry, and filled with talk of the horse.

Epona loved it. *This is what I came for*, she thought. *This is what I always wanted.*

Kazhak had been deeply upset by the breach between them, though he had not let her see his unhappiness. Anger, arguments, yes; he could deal with those, knowing she would laugh and forget. But this latest quarrel had gone too deep for laughter and was too strong to be forgotten. Since learning she was not his wife, would never be considered one of the Scythians, Epona had shut herself away from him in every way. He missed her body, but to his own surprise he missed her spirit more.

As he had foreseen, the twilights were very blue and lonely when he did not spend them in Epona's company. His other women — Talia, Gala, Nedja, Ro-An — did not assuage Kazhak's deep sense of loss. It was as if a brother had died.

Something more than a brother. Something dearer, closer even; something he had not known existed until he was torn by its loss.

He tried to win her back.

As a gesture of goodwill he offered to let her ride any of his horses she liked, except for his stallion. Unique among the women of the nomads, Epona was not restricted to the wagons and the chores. Mounted on a good gelding, her bow and arrows in her *gorytus*, she was allowed to ride the perimeter of the herd with the men, keeping the horses within a manageable area, watching for strays, checking for illness or injuries.

The other women might have resented Epona's unparalleled freedom if they had desired any of it for themselves, but they did not. They could not understand how she could enjoy such masculine activities. Ro-An bemoaned the dark tan the Kelti woman's fair skin was acquiring, after a long and painful period of sun- and windburn, and peeling. "Epona will not be beautiful," she complained, urging the other woman to try a bleaching paste she had prepared, a smelly concoction whose preparation Epona had watched with misgivings.

Epona was amused. "Why should you care if Epona is not beautiful? The uglier Epona is, the better for the other women, is it so?"

Ro-An hid her face. "Ro-An cares," she admitted, very low. "Is such white skin, so soft, so nice. You should take good care of it. Ro-An would be sad to see you get ugly." It was the closest admission the other woman could ever make to friendship.

Epona's days were spent beneath open sky, but her nights were not. Rather than effect the more permanent arrangement of setting the tents up on the earth, Kazhak had ordered that all women live within their wagons, while he and the men stood guard nearby, or took turns watching over the herd. Kazhak kept one eye on Epona and one eye on Dasadas; he usually slept beside the front wheel of the Kelti woman's wagon. But he did not try to enter; Epona was adamant about refusing him admittance.

337

When he slept by her wagon, and her fire, he slept deep and without dreams; when he slept with the herd he sometimes saw the huge wolf in his dreams, and once it came so close to him he got a clear look at the terrible mutilation on the side of its head, where the ear had been torn away by the knife Basl brought with him from the village of the Kelti. Massive scar tissue had pulled the wolf's face into a permanent grimace.

The wolf prowled, but it did not attack. It seemed to be watching and waiting, just like the men. It seemed to grow more gaunt as time passed. Kazhak wondered how it fed.

To avoid spending all her evenings alone, Epona sometimes went to one of the other wagons, either one belonging to Kazhak or Aksinya. Epona and the two wives of Dasadas did not care for each other's company. Dasadas' senior wife, Onyot, an angular woman given to angular gestures, had occasionally thrown her slops from the wagon just as Epona was passing by.

It was safe to approach another woman's wagon so long as her man's saddle was not placed in front of the entrance. The first time Epona had seen Kazhak's saddle in front of a wagon other than her own she had felt a sharp pain in her chest, surprising her, but it was not a pain she encountered often. Kazhak's loneliness did not drive him to the wagons of the other women; it drove him instead to the back of the gray stallion, to sit silent for long stretches of time, gazing toward the horizon.

Women's talk, at night, in the wagons, bored Epona, it was so limited in experience or understanding. But it was easier to endure than being alone in her own wagon, looking through the flap at Kazhak's lonely, proud figure in the distance, knowing she would not signal to him, thinking she could never forgive him.

Bit by bit, like patching little scraps of leather together to make a cloak, Epona began introducing topics that interested her into the conversation of the Scythian women. At first she only spoke of medicaments and herbals used by her own people, and then she expanded that subject to include the stains and dyes women of the Kelti used to enhance their beauty. From that point, the talk drifted naturally, easily, to other styles and customs, and soon she found herself teaching an audience that was, if not eager, at least responsive. Some of what she told them they accepted; much of it they questioned, or derided. But at least they listened, and

338

talking about her own people and her Blue Mountains lifted a little of the soreness from Epona's spirit.

She talked, long into the night, of the multiplicity of spirits with whom her people shared the earth mother, and of the beneficence that could be extracted from these spirits with the proper rituals. She regretted that she could not explain all the rituals in detail, for she noticed Gala and Nedja particularly paying close attention and asking questions. Talia remained aloof, resistant to new thoughts, already crusted with the callus of passing time, and Ro-An would never think beyond the wagons and her hoped-for babies.

But some of the other women might. And they might teach their children, as Epona endeavored to teach *them*. The customs of the earth mother might yet come alive in this strange, ignorant place.

One evening, just as Epona was preparing to leave the wagon of Ari-Ki, Aksinya's wife, the women heard a commotion outside. The men were shouting to one another with urgency in their voices, and the quick anger of men faced with a situation they are temporarily unable to handle.

Ignoring formalities, Kazhak thrust his face through the entrance flap of Ari-Ki's wagon. "Epona? You here? Is good; come with Kazhak. Quick!"

His peremptory command left no room for argument. Murmuring a hasty farewell to Ari-Ki, Epona wrapped her cloak around her body to protect her from the lingering chill of spring evenings, and stepped from the wagon.

All three men were waiting for her. "Is the big bay mare," Dasadas explained. "Best mare of all horses in my care; has had a healthy foal every year, no trouble." His words tripped over one another in their eagerness to reach Epona's ears. "She was bred to gray stallion last year; now she tries to give birth to first horse of this new season. But something is wrong, Epona. Mare has been laboring long time, but colt will not come. She grows very weak now. She may die. It would be very bad omen to lose first foal of year. Kolaxais would never entrust another mare so fine to Dasadas."

Epona involuntarily looked westward. The rays of the setting sun reached out toward her: imploring hands, made of golden light.

"You will help," Kazhak said. "Come."

He led the way to the edge of the herd, where the pregnant mare lay on the earth. The other horses had drawn back to give her space, though the gray stallion paced back and forth where he could keep an eye on her, establishing that this was his place and his mare. A mare due to foal often tried to leave the herd and give birth in some hidden spot, but the herders had been careful to avoid having that happen with this mare, whose deliverance of the first healthy, living foal of the season was considered a very necessary example for the other pregnant mares.

The mare made no effort to resist as they knelt beside her and examined her. It was evident from her sunken eyes and heaving flanks that she had been in labor a long time, and now her strength was gone but the foal was still unborn.

The men looked at Epona expectantly. She put her arms around the mare's neck and waited to feel something, but nothing happened. Nothing at all. In constant pain, the mare sweated within the woman's embrace but got no closer to giving birth. Epona closed her eyes and concentrated, reaching out, and still nothing happened.

The mare groaned softly. Dasadas swore under his breath.

Epona looked up at Kazhak. "I don't know what to do to help her," she said.

"Help her like you helped Thracian mare."

"That was different. I can't explain how, but I can feel; it is very different now. What I did then will not work for this horse. I cannot draw the foal out of her body with my body, or my magic."

Her own eyes were filled with pain at having to say those words. In addition to feeling the mare's suffering, she was suffering from her inability to help. It wrung her heart to crouch there in the twilight, feeling two lives slip away.

She tried again, with all the strength she possessed, her lips shaping the prayers, her whole spirit reaching out with desperate urgency.

340

The mare grunted and found a little additional strength, somewhere.

"Aksinya, put cloths over her to keep her warm," Epona ordered, and Aksinya hurried to do her bidding. Meanwhile, Kazhak and Dasadas squatted on their heels behind the mare, holding her tail out of the way and trying to reach the foal.

"Is turned around," Kazhak said at last. "Is very bad; rump is large; is stuck. Horses should not be born this way. It tears the mares; foals often come dead. If we cannot get it free . . ." He grunted and struggled, trying to insert an arm beside the breech-positioned foal in order to turn it. The mare heaved again.

Fight, Epona told her in silence. *Fight for life. I will help you.*

We will help you, said the spirit within.

Time passed. Aksinya brought torches for light, and still the mare clung to life as the foal remained jammed in the birth canal. Both Kazhak and Dasadas were bloody to their elbows, but neither would give up.

"Foal must be dead by now," Dasadas said, but Kazhak merely changed his own position and made another effort, biting his lip as he did so. Suddenly he sat up. "Epona! Your arm is smaller than any man's. You are strong. Come here."

She joined him quickly, and he explained what she must do; how she must reach inside the mare and feel for a little hind leg; how to position and guide the body of the unborn horse so that it could move down the birth canal and be delivered at last.

She had never done it, but Kazhak's strong voice told her he believed she could. He patiently instructed her and she did as he said, groping in darkness, reaching for life.

Dasadas could take no more. He stood up and walked away, his back turned to them, his head sunk low between his shoulders. If his best mare died, as well as the first foal of the year, it would be a sign to all that he and his herd were cursed. The silver wolf, perhaps. Demons. Kazhak would surely drive him away before the contagion could spread to the other pregnant mares.

Epona felt a tiny ankle within her grasp and uttered an exclamation of relief. Kazhak was leaning against her shoulder now, helping her brace herself, talking her through every step as she worked with the unborn horse, shifting it by imperceptible degrees inside its mother. And then both hind legs were free, and

341

extended; a controlled pull and the mare's long labor would be over. If the mare could survive any more.

Kazhak locked his arms around Epona's waist and they pulled together. The mare moaned, and then the foal, wrapped like a present in its glistening sac, slipped into the world as if being born were the easiest of accomplishments.

Epona quickly tore the membrane from around the little creature's muzzle. Whispering a prayer to the spirits of the air, she began forcing her own living breath into the small, unresponsive nostrils. Meanwhile, Kazhak went to the mare's head to ascertain her condition. She was alive, though very weak. He turned back to Epona.

"How is foal?"

Hearing Kazhak's words, Dasadas spun around. "Foal is born?" he asked, hardly daring to hope.

Epona did not have time or breath to answer him. All her energies were going into the small wet creature lying half in her lap. She breathed into its nostrils, she pressed its fragile ribs, trying to feel the beat of a living heart; she prayed for it as she would have prayed for her own infant.

And then it drew a long, quavering breath, and she felt the hot tears of joy running down her own face. "It is alive," she sobbed, looking at Kazhak.

Light came into the Scythian's face. "Alive," he repeated softly. In a moment he was kneeling beside her, helping her finish cleaning the birth sac from the foal — a lovely filly foal — and rub it dry.

Dasadas crowded close to see the newest member of his allotted herd, but they were oblivious to him. Epona and Kazhak looked first at the newborn horse, then at each other, then at the foal again.

Dasadas, feeling shut out, went to his mare, and was at least comforted to see that she, too, was alive, and gradually regaining some strength. As he watched, she raised her head and turned her neck so she could see her newborn. Her nostrils shaped a tender nicker.

"Mare will live," Dasadas said, overjoyed. "And colt, too?"

"Filly," Epona corrected him. "Yes, she will live."

"Was your magic," Dasadas said with certainty. "Very strong; too strong even for the silver wolf. That demon put a bad curse

342

on horse, but you have saved. Epona has saved the horses of Dasadas!" His face was radiant with excitement, but Epona was embarrassed. She had performed no magic; she had not felt the power singing through her. She and Kazhak together, fighting, refusing to give up, had physically delivered the foal and kept the spark alive in it and its mother.

Yet Dasadas would never believe that. His belief in Epona's abilities was stronger than ever; it filled his eyes with a fanatic light. The light made Epona uncomfortable and suddenly she longed to be inside her wagon, hidden away behind the felt and leather.

Dasadas and Aksinya would stay with the mare for the rest of the night, and if the foal did not strengthen quickly they would bring it goats' milk and honey and perform those tasks they had performed before, as servitors to the horse. But Epona was satisfied that all would go well, now; the atmosphere around mare and foal was benign.

She trudged back toward her wagon, so deep in thought she did not hear footsteps behind her until Kazhak's voice said, right at her shoulder, "Kazhak does not want to sleep alone tonight. Is man with bloody hands welcome in wagon of Epona?"

She turned and looked at him. The stars were bright overhead and there was a sliver of a moon providing enough light to reveal his features. Not savage features, but kind, with eyes she knew. The Scythian, who had always subscribed to the philosophy of take and go, would not force himself on her. He was asking, as one free person asks another.

She stood still, not knowing how to answer. And then the words came to her lips unbidden, as if the spirit within had said them of its own accord.

"Blood is life, Kazhak. Life is always welcome in my wagon."

Chapter 27

THE ANGER AND RESENTMENT were still in her, just beneath the surface, festering like a wood tick under the skin. But they were hurting Epona beyond bearing by denying her the pleasure of his embrace and the warmth of his body, plus the bond between them that existed nowhere else. Her skin cried aloud for that warmth; her spirit thirsted for that bond. When Kazhak's voice came rumbling up from deep in his chest, and his eyes sought and held hers as if nothing else on earth was worth looking at, she could not refuse him. The embrace of anger was a poor substitute for Kazhak's arms.

I am not your wife. I have not been made one of your tribe. I have no real place in the world. She said the words in her head, the bitter words, but they did not reach her lips. They were too bitter; they would ruin the taste of this moment, when the magic of new life was strong in both of them and the tender memory of the little filly drew them together in a sort of worship. Worship for the great fire; that was the important thing.

And this was the way to celebrate it.

Epona closed her eyes and willingly lost herself in Kazhak's strong arms.

He felt a residue of stiffness in her spine, but he hugged her until even that melted away. He would not be stopped, not tonight. He had seen the irresistible beauty in her face as she cuddled the newborn horse against her own body.

He unfastened the Kelti brooch holding Epona's bearskin robe, and his fingers were unusually clumsy freeing the pin from the catch. Such complicated fasteners were not used on the Sea of Grass. The style of the pin, unique to the Kelti, had always seemed to Kazhak to be yet another example of the way those people made simple things complex.

Yet there was no denying, the brooches fastened and held cloth better than any other device the Scythian had ever encountered.

The bearskin cloak lay at Epona's feet, and Kazhak gently pressed her down upon it. It was dark in the wagon, but he could see her face so clearly in his mind that he was not aware of the darkness. He moved his hands down her body and every part of that was familiar to him, too, yet always new and exciting. He fitted her hips against his, letting her feel the male hunger awaiting her, and was gratified by the way her breathing quickened and she pressed eagerly against him.

Epona had never assumed the Scythian style of passivity with a man. There would have been no enjoyment for her in such a lack of participation. It was enthusiasm, and the mutual giving and taking of pleasure, that made bedsports so delicious. Once committed, she held nothing back, guiding Kazhak with her hands and her words, touching him . . . here, there, all the sensitive places she had learned . . . until he moaned with pleasure, and reciprocated gladly, taking her with him into that otherworld only the two of them had ever shared.

Later, as they lay together in the darkness, their breathing matched to one rhythm like a good team of wagon horses, Kazhak thought to himself, *This woman is more wife to me than any of those other women in my wagons.*

Yet he could never say such words aloud to Epona. It would be unthinkable.

Many things that had previously seemed unthinkable worked their way to the surface of the Scythian's mind when he was near Epona. He realized she was furious because their relationship had not made her Scyth; yet when he was with her, Kazhak was not aware of himself as a Scythian, either. He and she together were something new, almost like a new tribe. Though they appeared to have little in common, Kazhak could see that their differences were the result of things beyond themselves and outside their control, indifferent forces that did not take individual beings into account. Customs, beliefs, attitudes — these were the external pressures that shaped them, but he and Epona contained something else that refused to be so shaped.

The essence Epona called the spirit within seemed to be the same in both of them. When their eyes met, they understood each other without words. When he was inside her body, it was as if they had only one body between them.

Kazhak lay beside Epona and thought about these things as he had never forced himself to think before. It was difficult to contemplate such abstractions — Kelti thinking — but practice made it easier, and it gave him access to a new freedom inside his own head.

Freedom. That concept meant so much to Epona; yet until she challenged his thinking Kazhak had never considered himself to be lacking in freedom. He rode the horse, which gave him unlimited mobility. He had all the gold he wanted, the gift of Kolaxais — as long as it pleased Kolaxais to let him keep it. But after listening to Epona and remembering the way of life he had observed in her village, he realized his horizons had limits he had never acknowledged.

The horse he rode, the herds he used for food and raw materials; these belonged, in the final accounting, to Kolaxais. Kazhak could live as he pleased — as long as it pleased the *han*. His freedom did not belong to him; it was only allowed him at the prince's pleasure: the prince who was not a chosen representative of his people but who ruled them by divine right as a kinsman of Tabiti, and who could threaten them with ostracism or execution if they displeased him.

And now Kolaxais himself was owned by the shamans, who threatened him — and his tribe — with demons if they refused to submit. To whom did the shamans belong? Were they in turn captives of the same fear they used to intimidate the nomads?

Epona's race did not appear overly fearful of the spirits. They respected them, interacting with them in much the same way one Scythian tribe interacted with another, for mutual benefit. But the Kelti were not enslaved by demons.

They belonged to themselves, the Kelti. Only to themselves,

and to the spark of life each cherished within. That was what Epona said. Kazhak lay sleepless, thinking these troubling thoughts long after Epona's breath had slowed into sleep beside him.

Epona awakened as the stars were dissolving in the first milky light of dawn. To her surprise she found Kazhak still beside her, fast asleep now, one heavy arm thrown across her body.

Trying not to distrub him, she slipped from beneath it and went out into the morning to tend the fire and prepare a small and private sacrifice to the spirits. She was not the Scythian's wife, but she would bear his child if the great fire was willing to send her a spark to nourish within her body.

She crouched alone over the tiny ceremonial blaze, her soft voice chanting the ancient invocations of her people.

Foaling season was soon upon them in earnest, and there were sleepless nights when Epona was summoned again and again to lend her strength, her energy, her . . . magic . . . to the mares bringing new life into the world. Usually the horses gave birth without difficulty, but when they did not, Epona sometimes felt there was difficulty even before one of the men with the herd came for her. She would grow uneasy, even physically uncomfortable, and eventually emerge from her wagon, looking for Kazhak. "Is everything all right?" she would ask, and he would tell her. A dun mare, really too young to be bred, was down and could not get up. A black horse colt had been born to one of Aksinya's mares but had not started breathing. One of the oldest mares had wandered away from the herd and they were certain she was in labor but could not find her . . .

"Can you feel her, Epona? Can you lead us to her?"

She found the mare. She made preparations from weeds and herbs according to half-remembered recipes from her own childhood, and applied them to horses with legs swollen by snakebite or sprained by falling into holes. She sat without sleep for three nights and three days, massaging the twisted body of a young foal that had suffered some injury while running with its mother, throwing all its limbs into disharmony, and in the fourth dawn she watched with a lump in her throat as the little creature struggled to its feet and stood to nurse, and live.

Spring became summer, the brief, lush beauty of the steppe in one of its rare good moods unfolding like a giant flower. Snowmelt gave way to intensely green moss, and that in its turn was replaced by tiny white flowers called sheeplick, then larger blossoms of sunface and skyblue and nightpurple. The last wild hyacinths surrendered to the silver-green plumes of feathergrass, the ocean foam of the Sea of Grass, billowing above an undertow of sage. For a short time, Tabiti was gentle and merciful. The prairie bloomed and life was filled with promise.

Word of Epona's gift spread across the steppe like ripples on a pond, and within one long summer nomads were traveling considerable distances to ask her help; a help Kazhak gladly offered, knowing word would get back to Kolaxais and the shamans. Epona asked one thing in return — to be taught how to break and train the young horses for riding.

Kazhak's immediate reaction was predictable, but she persevered, and at last he grunted an assenting syllable, heavy with reluctance. "Kazhak will show you, a few things only. But if you get hurt, is your own fault, Epona. Kazhak will not take blame."

He took her out onto the summer-brilliant plain, silvery with drying grass, gilded with boundless sunlight. He taught her how to approach the wary young colts selected for breaking, and was pleased to see that she mastered the art quickly. Soon she could put her hand on a horse's neck before any of the men could get near it.

The next step was to learn the use of the rope, a long woven strand to be slipped over a horse's neck and skillfully tossed so that an additional loop encircled his nose, cutting off his wind before he could break away. This was rough work, and men were often dragged or kicked trying to subdue the colts, but Epona never shrank from the task. She was agile and sure of eye; only her light weight kept her from being as effective as the men.

Colts were then snubbed to older, calmer saddle horses, so they might accustom themselves to the sight and proximity of saddle and rider. Kazhak explained the importance of these older horses to Epona by saying, "Is like your *druii*, these old ones. They teach the young, is it so? Show them they have nothing to fear?"

Each step of the training was planned in advance and designed to convince the unbroken animal of man's supremacy, without destroying the horse's own spirit. The Scythians had only contempt for docile animals who never showed fight; they spoke of such horses, no matter what their sex, as "she," a point not lost on Epona. The passivity the nomads demanded from their women they found contemptible in their horses.

A horse who fought, however, who reared and bucked and plunged, was much admired by all men, and the rider who finally won his trust and cooperation gained greatly in stature among the nomads. Aksinya once told Epona that Kazhak's gray stallion had taken a year to break, and had fought every step of the way. For this reason his blood was especially desired on the steppe, and other herders brought their mares to him, offering Kazhak gold in exchange for his services.

"He is the strongest horse," Kazhak boasted. "His heart is as big and as hot as Tabiti!"

When a young horse was used to the touch and presence of men, a saddlecloth was placed on his back for the first time and bound around the belly with a goathair girth. The tightening of the girth usually provoked another fight, and when a saddle was added renewed resistance was expected.

It would have been possible to throw the horse to the ground, strap riding gear on him, let a man seat himself on the animal's back, and then turn them loose to fight it out together; Kazhak told Epona this method of horsebreaking was practiced among some other tribes, but it was not the way of his people. They preferred to go slowly, taking care with each animal so the horse remained willing to learn and could be trusted later.

The first mounting of the saddled gelding or stallion — the Scythians never rode their mares — was an event of prime importance, as it established the permanent relationship between horse and rider. If it went well, a celebration was in order, and the successful trainer of the horse was tossed in the air by his fellows amid much laughter and good-natured roughhousing. But the development of the horse did not end there; it must be continued until the animal was instantly responsive to the signals given him through reins and bridle, through shift of weight and thrust of rider's leg. Once those obediences were acquired a horse who had shown valor in the earlier breaking process was given additional training to make him a combat animal, a full partner in the team, who would maneuver his rider into battle position and even defend a fallen man with teeth and hooves.

The trained war-horse of the Scythians was a terrifying weapon in his own right.

As the summer waned, the men were quick to notice that Epona's light weight and intuitive understanding of the horses gave her an advantage they did not possess. The colts she worked with learned faster and seemed more willing. Now she was dividing her time between the flat, now-dusty plain used for training and the pen where the young horse colts were brought for gelding. During the gelding she stayed close to the animal, whispering to it, applying a paste of her own concoction to its wound to speed the healing process; but anyone looking in her eyes could see that her heart was not in the gelding pen; it was out on the plains with the herd, galloping, mane blowing in the wind.

She had rapidly become indispensable with the horses, and Kazhak again ordered his women to take over her share of female's work. This time Epona did not object. She gladly gave up any pretense of trying to fit into the world of the women. During the long days, under the endless sky, she often forgot that she was a woman. She was just part of the horses, and the steppe. Only in Kazhak's arms at night was she reminded of her sex — or when she saw the eyes of Dasadas following her, following her.

Since returning to her bed, Kazhak had become more tolerant of Dasadas. He even made occasional jokes about the man's obsession with Epona. Out of Dasadas' hearing, he amused Aksinya with an acidic imitation of the younger man. "Epona," he sighed, his eyes bugging, his jaw gaping, his arms hanging loosely at his sides as if his wits had deserted him. He walked in an aimless circle, gazing worshipfully at an imaginary woman.

"Epona," he murmured, and Aksinya laughed.

Epona saw the performance too, and laughed in spite of herself. Yet she knew, with a woman's instinct, that Dasadas was biding his time, waiting for his chance at her. And sooner or later he would force the issue.

Not only Dasadas was waiting. A giant wolf still followed the men through their dreamworlds, and as the season wore on it grew bolder, even appearing to the women in their wagons and causing the children to wake suddenly from sleep with frightened cries. "A man turned into a wolf; he growled at me!" Gala's young son sobbed, burying his face in his mother's lap and shivering with terror.

"Hush, hush, is only a dream," Gala soothed the boy. But her eyes were troubled, for she had had the same dream.

Potor arrived, bringing a string of horses he wished to test by racing with the fastest animals in Kazhak's collection. Though Kazhak boasted to everyone of Epona's skills at healing, now he asked her to refrain from riding and training the young geldings during Potor's visit.

This provoked another argument, of course.

"Other men will have no respect for me," Kazhak sought to explain. "Potor will say Kazhak's woman has turned into a man. Will laugh. Ha, ha," he added morosely, already sorry for himself, feeling the weight of his friend's ridicule.

"*You* know I am not a man. Why should I give up something I enjoy? Just for Potor?"

"Kazhak . . . asks. For Kazhak, Epona."

She hesitated. "Will you let me ride the gray stallion?"

He scowled. "Kelt must always make a trade," he complained, not for the first time.

"You said I could never be Scythian, so of course I am Kelt," she reminded him with malicious pleasure. "Let me ride your horse sometimes, now that breeding season is over. In trade, I will not train any horses until Potor leaves."

His face closed. "Kazhak will tell you what you can or cannot do. You see these trousers? *Man* wears trousers!"

But in the morning she found the gray stallion hobbled close to her wagon, and she put her own saddle on him. Kazhak was already out riding with Potor, showing off a dun gelding Epona had trained herself. When the two men returned, Potor was effusive in his praise of the horse.

"Is wonderful animal, Kazhak; is quick, obedient, very fast. Will you make trade for him, here, now?"

Kazhak considered. "Kazhak plans to take this one with some others to horse fair at Maikop, before season of Taylga. Get good price for horses like this."

Potor agreed. "They are worth much gold. Potor never realized before, but you are one of the best horse trainers, Kazhak. Would you be willing to train some colts for my tribe?"

Kazhak chewed his lip. "Is too busy," he said at last.

That night, as Potor and the men who had accompanied him slept, a sense of brooding malignity stole over the camp. The herd grew restless and Aksinya summoned Dasadas to stand watch over it with him, fearing the possibility of stampede. The nomads tossed and muttered in their sleep. Halfway through the night a sudden, driving rain attacked the Sea of Grass, coming so unexpectedly in the dry season that no preparations had been made for it and Epona's little fire was drowned, hissing, in its stone circle.

When that small fire went out an unnatural darkness settled over the wagons and the herd.

With Potor nearby, Kazhak would not spend the night in Epona's wagon, so the Kelt was sleeping alone when something scratched at the felt hanging over the entrance. Epona was instantly awake, staring into the darkness.

She heard a sound like claws being raked across wood, and then a snuffling, as if an animal's nose was seeking its way through the felt hangings. It might be one of the lean, half-wild dogs who hung around the edge of nomadic life, fighting over scraps, but . . . the smell entered the wagon; bitter, musky, and she knew.

Even in the total darkness she felt his presence as tangibly as if she were looking into his face. "Kernunnos," she said. It was not a question.

He was standing beside her, so close she could hear his breathing: the breathing of a man, not an animal. He must be stooping slightly, for the wagon was built to Scythian proportions and would not accommodate a man of the shapechanger's height.

"Kernunnos," she said again. She wanted to hear his voice confirm what she already knew beyond doubt.

"Yes, Epona." It was a harsh whisper, but it was a voice she recognized.

"Am I dreaming?"

"Does it matter?"

"You have been haunting these people through the dream-worlds, Kernunnos; people who have done you no harm. And you killed Basl. It was you who killed Basl, wasn't it?"

"Does it matter?" he asked again. "Those Scythians are not important to you and me, Epona. The tribe, that is important. And your talents belong to the tribe. You had no right to run away. You must go back."

She felt invaded; her very spirit seemed raped by his intrusion into her wagon. Summoning bravado as a defense, she asked, in an angry voice, "Can you carry me away, priest? Can you pick me up in your arms and take me back to the Blue Mountains with you?"

He answered her with silence, and she knew then that by whatever means the shapechanger had reached her, at least he could not remove her living body from the Sea of Grass. To that degree she was safe from him.

"I will never do what you ask," she told him. "My life is here now, with . . . my husband. You have no right to claim me, for I am no longer a dependent living under my mother's roof. I am a wife; I am free of Rigantona's authority."

She heard a sound like laughter, but she could not be certain it was an audible laugh. It might only have been in her head, as Kernunnos' voice might only have been in her head. It did not have the resonance to be expected from a real man standing beside her in the stuffy wagon. "You are not a wife," the metallic voice, the insect's voice, told her.

How could he know that? She shrank back against the rugs that were her bed, striving to see him in the darkness, but she could only make out an indistinct shape, blacker than black, looming over her.

"You are not a wife," the shapechanger repeated. "Your place is with your tribe. Our strength is not what it was; only four *druii*, a weak number. You are desperately needed to help us hold the pattern.

"Just since you left, much has changed in the village. The new ideas that rode to us with the Scythians have corrupted our young men. They talk constantly of going out of the mountains to find new land. Like you, they foolishly turn their faces away from all we have and hunger for new places and different lives. They talk of loot, of battle and glory, and the village rings with the songs of war. They have turned Goibban's head with praise, so he labors ceaselessly at the forge creating new weapons. He thinks only of the objects he creates and does not consider their ultimate purpose."

She could reach out and touch him if she wanted to, she thought to herself. She could put her hand on his lean thigh and feel the flesh, know if he was real, know the true extent of his power. The power she might also learn to wield, as his apprentice in the magic house. The shapechanger at her shoulder, talking, teaching, over-laying her personality with his, making her into something she never wanted . . .

She knotted her hands into fists and kept them under her blanket, making no effort to touch the priest.

"What has any of this to do with me?" she asked.

"You are strong in the spirit. You are young and very gifted; you could have great influence with the people. They might admire and listen to you; they do not . . . like . . . to listen to me. Under your influence they might be persuaded to give up this madness. You are young, as I said. You do not yet realize how influential you could be, but I will teach you, I will help . . ."

"And Taranis?" Epona interrupted. "How has Taranis reacted to all this?"

"He wants to make a greater name for himself than his predecessor," Kernunnos replied. "He has begun to think he can do that by enlarging the tribal holdings of land. He is ambitious for himself and is not committed to putting the welfare of the tribe above all else. He hears the young men talking about leaving, establishing colonies in other places — by force, by killing, Epona — and he does not object. He sees them grow careless with the rituals; he knows they are no longer listening to the spirit within but thinking only of their own greed and desires, but he does not try to discourage them."

What was it Kazhak had said? "Man must survive. We take what we need, what else can we do?"

"The village of the Kelti is very crowded, Kernunnos," she said to the priest. "There is no room to build more lodges and no land for farming. If the tribe is to continue to grow and prosper, perhaps it does need to seek additional land and learn new skills. All life is change, is it not? That is the teaching of the *druii* themselves."

She felt his anger like hot sun on her face. "You are tainted by contact with these Scythians!" he accused.

"These are not Scythian thoughts, but my own," she told him. "How do I know it is right for the Kelti to cling to the old ways? Perhaps the time has come for us to grow as a people, to break out of the womb of the earth mother and see just how far we can reach. We need not kill to do that. There are empty lands and far

354

horizons waiting for us. I have even dreamed . . ." She stopped abruptly, warned by the spirit within.

Kernunnos was instantly leaning over her, and she could actually feel hot breath on her face. "You have dreamed what? What?"

His force was so potent she could not resist it. "I have seen, in the dreamworlds, lands lying far to the west. To the south. Across seas." Her voice softened and seemed to drift away from her, drifting on sea-fog and dream-memories. "Iberia," she whispered. "Albion." Her voice was very low, and warm, as if with love. "Ierne. The green island at the edge of the world."

"You see!" Kernunnos crowed with triumph. "You see what you have, what you are! You must come back to us, Epona, and let me train you to use your skills for the good of the tribe."

His insistence dragged her back from some far place, recalling her to the here and now, and a sense of danger. "Never!" she cried with a suddenly strong voice. "I want nothing to do with you, priest!"

He heard the revulsion in her tone. "You hate me that much, girl?"

She lay still, searching her memory for her earliest feelings about Kernunnos. "Yes," she said honestly. "From the beginning, the sight of you has been like sand in my eyes. I don't know why."

The priest sighed. "Other lives," he whispered. "Other worlds. We have been enemies before, perhaps. I sense it, but I have been too busy to investigate the fabric of the past as you and I have woven it together. And now, when I need you most, you turn away from me." His voice was fading strangely, as if he were receding farther and farther away. "Our way of life will be destroyed unless we fight for it, Epona. Our people, as we know them, will change until we do not know them at all. You must come back. You must help us . . ."

"Perhaps everything should change," she told him. "Perhaps it is time for something new to be born." Behind her eyelids she had a quick mental image of a horse galloping free toward an unlimited horizon. Free. Unlimited.

The priest gave a cry of despair and fell forward toward her. He was panting like a thirsty animal and his voice had grown very

355

weak. She felt something brush across her throat, something hairy, like a man's beard, and there was the quick, hot touch of his lips against the vein where her life pulsed.

She struck out violently and screamed. Something staggered back, falling against stacked pots and harness, and Epona fumbled at her waist for her knife, only to remember too late that it was night, and her weapon lay with her clothing for the morning.

Something lumbered past her and was gone, leaving her alone in the wagon with a racing heart and a dry mouth. She was wide awake. "Kernunnos?" she asked tentatively, but there was no answer.

"Epona!" Kazhak cried, bursting in upon her. "What is? You scream." He grabbed her in a powerful embrace, shaking her so that her heavy, unbound hair whipped around them both.

"I'm all right except for the mauling you're giving me," she managed to protest. "It was . . ."

"Yes?"

"It was a dream. A bad dream."

He pulled back and tried to see her face in the darkness. "You dream of the wolf, is it so?"

She did not answer him.

In the morning they found one of Potor's men lying a little distance away, crumpled as if he had been dropped there, his throat torn out and only a small pool of congealed blood remaining to show that once he had contained life.

Chapter 28

A T LAST Epona could believe in her own power. Kernunnos would not have come so far, or risked so much, unless she was very valuable indeed. But even the strength of the shape-changer was limited. At such a distance from the magic house where his thislife body must lie sleeping, he could not sustain the image of himself for long without blood sacrifice, life taken to support life. And it was obviously human blood he required. As long as he tried to stay close to Epona, he would continue to exact a toll from the Scythians, taking his sacrifice from the members of her tribe.

Not my tribe. I am of the Kelti.

Even so, for her sake, people of the horse had been slain. The responsibility sat heavily upon her.

Kazhak told Potor only that a large wolf had been haunting the outskirts of the herd for some time, and Potor eagerly demanded to take part in the wolf hunt. The men scoured the area but found nothing, and finally Potor had to take his dead brother home unavenged.

But Kazhak had more to say about the wolf, in private, to Epona. "Demon wolf will kill us all, one by one. Is punishment for stealing you. What magic can you do to stop it?"

She lowered her eyes. "None. I do not know the magic to stop it. Only the fire holds it back, but even fire can be killed." Then she remembered. Basl had not killed the wolf, but at least he had succeeded in injuring it badly. He had cut off its ear with the iron knife acquired from the Kelti smith, after Scythian arrows had proved harmless to the creature.

Perhaps Goibban's iron had a strength to equal Kernunnos' passion.

"Keep your iron weapons close to your hands at all times," Epona advised Kazhak and the others. "It may be they have some special power over the wolf."

"Kazhak knows a better weapon," the Scythian growled. "The speed of the horse, *that* nothing can resist. When we left dark mountains we galloped fast, outran this wolf. We will again. We will leave demon wolf behind us to starve on Sea of Grass."

At his order, the herd was readied, and by early the next day the women in the wagons were whipping the draft horses, thankful that none of them rode in slow ox-carts. They drove at top speed across the prairie, fleeing southward, while the men herded the domestic animals and the horses at an unrelenting pace. They did not stop until the animals were exhausted, but that night no one dreamed of the wolf.

"Is good," Kazhak remarked next dawn. "Always, the horse proves faster than his enemies. Man with horse has everything, Epona. Everything."

Perhaps flight was the answer. As long as they pushed themselves to the limit each day, their pursuer did not seem to be able to catch up with them. But if they stopped for any length of time to allow the herd to rest and graze, someone invariably awoke in the night with pounding heart and staring eyes, to whisper of a giant wolf prowling about the camp.

When their paths crossed those of other herders, it was inevitable that the story of the silvery wolf was passed on, by women gossiping or children playing, or even other men, suddenly glimpsing it near their own wagons. The largest wolf ever seen on the steppe could not pass without comment. It was hunted, but no Scythian arrow could bring it down.

Summer drew to a close, accompanied by the onset of severe thunderstorms and occasional pelting hail. On a dark and sodden day, Kazhak's band passed a singular monument on a slight rise of ground and paused to do it honor. Epona stared in wonder at the Scythian tomb.

It was, as Kazhak had once said, a timbered house, large enough to serve as a lodge for a Kelti family. Beyond its four corners were posts driven into the ground in sets of two pairs each, with a wooden wheel between the posts, and the rotting body of a saddled, bridled horse mounted upon the wheel in a lifelike posture, its legs dangling. Each horse carried a dead rider, a stake driven down from his neck through his spine and attached to the pole holding the horse in place. This grisly guard stood watch over the tomb of some nomad noble, scanning the horizon with emptied eye-sockets.

"Brave young men were strangled to be with their prince," Kazhak commented. "Great honor, is it so?"

When they rode on again in solemn silence, Epona turned for one more look at that decaying company. She saw the precious metals tarnishing on the fading splendor of the horses' trappings; she saw the bows and arrows waiting in each rider's *gorytus* to be fired at some unguessable enemy. She saw the rain beating down on the heads of the dead men and dripping from the hooves of the dead horses as they hung suspended in midair.

The rain ran from the dead to the living, to be absorbed once more into the earth mother and send back new life.

It is always so, said the spirit within.

The animals were growing more and more tired and thin as they were pushed on and on, trying to sustain themselves with an inadequate amount of forage snatched during too-brief pauses. The women in the wagons were peevish with exhaustion; the children were querulous and fretful. A baby wailed endlessly in one of Aksinya's wagons. When Kazhak at last sighted one of the great horse fairs dotting the steppe in this season, everyone drew a breath of relief. Surely they could stop for a while, and rest. The women could sit on something unmoving and exchange gossip with other wives from other tribes of the Scyth; their families could enjoy the security of being surrounded by numerous capable warriors.

A horse fair was the one occasion when many different nomad tribes came together in a loose confederacy, all other interests set aside in favor of exchanging animals and improving their breeding stock. Corrals to hold the mares were built of scarce and precious timber, and surrounded by traders' booths piled high with brilliantly colored rugs, wagon crafts, and horse harness. Wagon camps dotted the landscape. Driving past them, Epona was sur-

359

prised to realize that she had grown accustomed to many things she once thought she could never accept. The heads, for example. Grinning, rotting, stinking. Protecting. A sign of status she had come to respect, her eyes widening in admiration when she saw a particularly fine trophy or a tent decorated with an impressive number of skulls. Without being aware of it, she had absorbed the Scythian concept of the head representing the man, and now she was reassured by the number of bodiless warriors that stood on tireless guard throughout the area of the horse fair.

Business was already very good. Men sat on saddlecloths spread on the ground, ignoring the dust that swirled around them, and bickered good-naturedly or did hard trading, fingers flying and eyes flashing. When one man felt another was taking advantage of him, the standard complaint of the Scythian was howled to the heavens: "This person is of the oldest race on earth! This person is suffering! Why? Who will rid this person of the thief who means to take the teeth from my head?"

Kazhak and the other men set up their own area in a favorable location, and soon they had a crowd around them, admiring their horses — though commenting about the leanness of the animals — and showing even more admiration for the Kelti iron each Scyth wore at his waist, the knife and sword they never put aside.

Out of deference to Kazhak, Epona stayed in her wagon most of the time, though occasionally she could not resist wrapping herself up so that even her golden hair was covered, and wandering among the displays, watching the races and contests, listening to the boasting and complaining. She stood on the edge of a group of bystanders as Dasadas traded four fine mares and an equal number of cattle, as well as his entire allotment of sheep, for a young bay stallion not yet proven at racing or with the mares.

Kazhak grumbled about the trade. "Is a fool's trade, Dasadas. What you need with this horse? You have use of my stallion for your mares, best stallion anywhere."

Dasadas defended himself. "This horse has longer legs, will be bigger, maybe faster, even. And is already trained to saddle. Is riding horse; Dasadas will not have to ride a gelding now."

Kazhak snorted. "Kazhak rides stallion, so Dasadas wants to ride stallion. You cannot always have what Kazhak has, Dasadas." The other man met his eyes and they glared at each other, bristling like male dogs circling one another stiff-legged, ready to fight.

360

Epona stepped between them. "You must be brothers. Brothers stand together," she reminded them. "You have a common enemy."

The moment passed, but they all knew it was not forgotten.

Kazhak was disappointed with the showing his horses made; in past years they had been among the best, but now they were in poor condition and did not command the attention they had in former days. Still, Epona thought, watching them, they were the most magnificent creatures on earth. They did not seem to belong to the same species as the stubby little draft animals — shaggy, primitive ponies, really — used for hauling wagons and carts in the west. She looked at Kazhak sitting on his gray stallion; she watched him and the others racing, contesting, staging mock battles on horseback to demonstrate the training of their animals, and she saw what their enemies must see: The mounted horseman on the splendid steed of the Scythian was a new being, larger than any other, commanding the horizon. Invincible.

They left the site of the horse fair earlier than Kazhak customarily did, and when Aksinya grumbled, Kazhak told him, "We will not stay too long in one place. Is not wise. And we are not doing so good here, is it so? What you get for your best horses, Aksinya?"

The other man spat in the dirt, and Kazhak shook his head in agreement. "So we go on. Next year, may be better. If we are no longer cursed by demon. Since that wolf started following us, many things have gone bad for us."

The more he thought about it, the more certain Kazhak was that the wolf was interfering with every aspect of his life. Epona had not yet conceived, though he was with her often, and that was a bad sign. The other women, too, were causing unfamiliar trouble, complaining and making demands that had Dasadas and Aksinya avoiding their own wagons. Eventually Aksinya mentioned his problem to Kazhak, and Kazhak spoke to Epona.

"You are talking to the women too much about things they cannot understand," he told her. "You upset other women. Is not good, Epona. You tell them they have a right to do this, should be able to do that, but is not true. They are only women; they have no rights. You just make trouble for them."

"I'm not trying to make trouble. I've merely been telling them the custom of the Kelti, the way women are considered partners of their husbands and holders of their own property."

Kazhak's face was troubled. "Men blame me for not controlling your tongue, Epona. Other women are trained good, you are not. Kazhak will lose support of their men. Kazhak needs all brothers now, if we are to win tribe away from bad influence of shamans."

"Is that possible?"

"Kazhak hopes," he replied. "May be is too late already; may be was too late when Kazhak first left Sea of Grass. But we cannot surrender without a fight, so you must not turn men against Kazhak by talking to their women about freedom."

"Does that mean you plan to join the rest of the Royal Tribe at the winter encampment, even though we may still be followed by the wolf?"

"Is so. Is needful that we be present for the Taylga, the Horse Sacrifice. Kazhak missed last year; perhaps that was big mistake. Kazhak should have been present at great ceremony that brings strength to the *han*. For the sake of the tribe."

Those words again. *For the sake of the tribe.* The spirit within told Epona there was no arguing with those words, so she looked down and said nothing. *Yes, Kernunnos,* she thought. *For the sake of the tribe.* But Kazhak knew her too well to mistake acquiescence on one issue for agreement to all his demands.

"Now, Epona, you must give word: You will not talk more to the women about freedom."

"They are just starting to get interested. They ask me questions, Kazhak — as you ask me questions. What am I to say?"

"Say nothing. Talk of freedom only makes trouble."

"Are you trying to order me . . ."

"Am asking, Epona. For Kazhak, who needs your help."

She could not resist that. But neither could she resist one last dig in his ribs with her elbow. "And what about you, Kazhak? Shall I not speak to you of freedom anymore, either?" A smile twitched the corners of her lips and she watched him from under lowered lashes.

"Kazhak is free!" he proclaimed. "Kazhak on his horse is freest man anywhere."

But it was not true, and that was amply demonstrated by the welcome Kazhak received as soon as his band reached the winter encampment. The royal tents, many of them, were already in place, and there was the bustle of activity Epona remembered from the previous season. But there was one major change. The display of trophy heads that identified the tent of Kolaxais was in front of a slightly smaller tent now, and the old *han*'s shelter was occupied by the shamans, who appeared as soon as Kazhak rode up.

Their painted cheeks were fuller. Tsaygas and Mitkezh had eaten well during the grazing season; plenty of fat lamb had gone into their bellies. After a cursory salute, they immediately demanded to know of Kazhak how much his herd had increased, how many foals had been born, what advantageous trades he had made.

"Kazhak reports to Kolaxais," the Scythian told them through tight lips. "These horses belong to the prince; it is for him to know."

"We will tell him," Tsaygas said in a voice greasy with mutton oil. "He trusts us to do the counting, to do the allotting now. He is too old, too tired to be bothered."

The Scythian did not dismount from his gray stallion. "Kazhak must see for himself," he said stubbornly.

Tsaygas' eyes flashed. "Is not possible. *Han* is under protection of good *taltos* white *taltos;* demons might come with you. We have heard, yes, we have heard. Kazhak cannot see Kolaxais."

The gibbering chant of the shamans became a high, keening wail, causing the horses to flatten their ears against their heads and move their feet nervously. Out of the corner of her eye, Epona saw how the Scythians who had come forward to welcome Kazhak swiftly withdrew, finding business with their own herds and wagons, too frightened to stay.

Kazhak saw it, too. Things were worse than he feared. The shamans had Kolaxais sequestered and were refusing admittance to him. He might even be dead, his heir officially unnamed, and the shamans had so extended their grasp that others were reluctant to challenge them. He would need time to learn the extent to which they had consolidated their power; surely not all his brothers had given in to the threats, the demons, the gibbered prophecies, and the terrors summoned from the hemp fumes.

Suddenly he grinned; the expansive Kazhak-grin that could reveal everything or nothing. "Demons come with Kazhak? No! Ka-

363

zhak returns with herd and brothers only. Kazhak brings magic woman, good woman, to heal sick horses."

The voice of Mitkezh was like a northern wind; cold, with a cutting edge. "Is well known on Sea of Grass that a wolf-demon accompanies Kazhak. We now know it was even with you here, last winter. We have made preparations to protect our people. Kolaxais, in his wisdom, has decreed that Kazhak is no longer his son, for Kazhak once swore on his father's hearth that he would bring only honor to his prince and enrich his tribe. Kazhak has broken that oath. Kazhak has brought harm. Shamans know how to punish man who makes false oath."

Kazhak sat on his horse as if stunned. The color had drained from his face. "Kolaxais says . . . Kazhak is no longer his son? That cannot be. Kazhak is good son, Kolaxais has loaned him much gold, many horses, shared his meat . . ."

"Kolaxais does not say your name," Mitkezh told him. "It goes unspoken, like the names of the dead. After the Taylga we will deal with you, white *taltos* good *taltos* will punish the oath-breaker, yes yes . . ." He fell into the chant, lost in it, spinning and weaving so his horse-tail pendants whirled about him.

Tsaygas took up the thread of his speech, with a warning to Kazhak. "For now, pitch your tent, man without a name. Your animals will be counted for adding to the *han*'s herd. After Taylga, we will read entrails of sacrifice; we will determine your punishment.

"We will prepare great ceremony to protect our people from demon you have brought, man without a name. Only shamans can protect. Go now. Go from sight of Tsaygas. You offend our eyes."

The shaman turned and strode back to the great tent that had formerly housed the Prince of the Horse. Epona noticed a small boy she recognized as Kolaxais' own cupbearer holding the entrance flap aside for Tsaygas, and bowing low as he passed.

The expression in Kazhak's face affected Epona as if an arrow had been driven into her own breast. She tried to offer him some useless word of comfort but he brushed her aside. He was too tightly wrapped around his pain to be able to open himself to her.

Searching for some distraction, Epona joined the other women in setting up the tents. For once Kazhak did not object to her participation in the work; he was too preoccupied to notice. The Scythian was moving around the encampment, greeting other men, trying to determine the extent to which the shamans had already turned his brothers against him.

Many men avoided him, but a few greeted Kazhak as they always had and welcomed him into their tents. These few gave him hope. They, too, resented the shamans' blatant seizure of the vast wealth of the *han*.

Vladmir, a stocky Scyth doomed to the life of the tents by a broken hip that had never healed properly, expressed the opinion these men held. "Kolaxais always hard, but fair, Kazhak. When man needed help, Kolaxais would give. Shamans give nothing. Just take, then demand more. They make new rules daily, rules they say are necessary. But people do not understand rules; people break them out of ignorance. Then shamans punish. They take what little we have but still want more."

"They have taken Kolaxais' tent," Kazhak said. His dark eyes seemed to have sunk in his head, just in the short time he had been in the winter encampment.

"Is so," Vladmir affirmed. "Shamans now hold the gold, too."

Kazhak's shock was visible. "The gold of Kolaxais? The wealth of the tribe? But gold is blood of Tabiti; it must stay with the *han*. Is symbol of his chiefdom, of our royal descent. If shamans hold gold, who will let us use it when we need?"

"Shamans have set a guard over the gold," Vladmir said. "The guard is warned: If he falls asleep on duty he will be strangled, then flayed.

"Many men already put to death, Kazhak. Brothers we not see again. Shamans promised some men rewards; some men were greedy. Accepted. Then, as each family came to winter camp, animals were counted by shamans. If herder did not bring back enough animals to satisfy Tsaygas, Mitkezh, these bought men killed their brothers. Dead man's possessions were taken by shamans to placate demons. Or so they say."

"Why did you not resist?" Kazhak wanted to know.

Vladmir held his hands palms up. "Happened little by little. Happened as each man returned, before he could talk to others. Soon fear was in the camp. When new ones came, they felt it. It is like a demon, that fear. It walks between tents, makes people cower inside."

Like a silver wolf, Kazhak thought.

"One man must speak out against shamans, call his brothers in a loud voice to stand with him," Kazhak said.

Vladmir drew back his lips to reveal dark stumps of teeth. He reached for the little brazier burning nearby and threw a handful of hemp seeds onto it, welcoming the smoke that clouded painful thoughts. "You, Kazhak? No. Not enough would listen to you, now. Men are afraid for their lives.

"As shamans control more property, they have more to buy weak men with. Such men forget Kazhak is brother. They listen to words of shamans, then go around camp to talk against Kazhak. Say Kazhak is bad son to the *han;* tell of demon Kazhak brought to Sea of Grass to kill Kolaxais, so Kazhak could take his place."

"You do not believe that!"

"No. But some do."

"Is Kolaxais still alive?" Kazhak had to ask, fearing the answer.

"We think so, but no one has seen. When he dies, it is believed shamans will say he chose new *han,* telling only them. New *han* will not be strong prince; will be someone shamans can control."

"All brothers know Kolaxais said, many times, Kazhak would succeed him as *han.* You have heard, Vladmir."

"When people are afraid, they forget what they heard," Vladmir told him. "They will not argue now. They were used to following orders of Kolaxais; now men say is not much different to follow orders of shamans. Is easier than dying."

"Do they not want to be free?" Kazhak burst out, and Vladmir stared at him.

"Free of what, Kazhak? Man is always ruled by something, yes?"

Kazhak stumbled from his friend's tent, fighting off the fumes of the hemp that could weaken a man and take the bone from his back.

He returned to Epona. "Shamans have been very busy," he told her. She was shocked by his appearance; he had aged seasons in just one day. "They know all about silver wolf now, blame Kazhak. Turn brothers against Kazhak. Even Kolaxais . . ."

"Hai," Epona said softly, opening her arms to him as a mother would invite a weary child.

He swayed toward her, but at the last moment he pulled back.

"No no. Kazhak very strong, no problem," he assured her, forcing his voice to be hearty and confident. "Kazhak will not be driven away again by shamans and demons. Will stay, talk with brothers, win them back. You see. You watch, Epona."

"What happens if the shamans are too strong? Will you just wait for them to kill you?"

Kazhak knotted his fists and pounded them against his thighs. "No! Kazhak is not ready to go into wooden house. Kazhak is a man of the horse; when there is no way at all to win battle, Kazhak rides away. Lives, to fight again. But this battle is not lost. Kazhak will stay; fight."

"Why? Why do you have to stay, when you know they mean to destroy you?"

His voice was husky as he answered, "Among my people, father is sacred, is it so? Papaeus? Kazhak let shamans separate son from father. Was big mistake. Kazhak got mad, took brothers, rode away; did not stay to protect father. Kazhak dishonored father. Kolaxais is right to turn his face from me now. Kazhak can get name back only by fighting for Kolaxais, winning his forgiveness. Winning him away from shamans." His shoulders slumped beneath the weight of the burden they had assumed and he turned away from Epona. He stumbled out into the night, seeking the gray stallion. He would sleep with his horse.

The power of the spirits, Epona thought sadly. *It can be a basket brimming with bread and fruit, or it can be a sword to cut a strong man down.*

She awoke to find that sword hanging over her own head. Two women she had never seen before were in the tent with her, and a man stood at the door. An armed man, with an Assyrian sword in his hand and a bronze Makedonian helmet, complete with noseguard, on his head. He was obviously well prepared for physical conflict, if it came to that.

In one hand he held Epona's own knife, slipped from her belongings while she slept. When she saw Goibban's iron in that hand, a little of the strength went out of her arms.

"Epona of the Kelti," one of the women said, "we are your attendants."

"I need no attendants."

The man spoke. "Shamans say you are magic person, you are to be treated with great respect. Shamans offer you high honor, Kelti woman. Attendants are one mark of that honor."

She was rigid with suspicion. "Where is Kazhak? Does he know of this?"

"Is not Kazhak's business," the Scythian replied.

The women crowded closer to Epona. One held a cup brimming with dark liquid. "Drink," she urged, but Epona pulled away. In one long stride the man stood next to her, his hand behind her skull, holding her head still as the women forced the cup against her lips and pried open her jaw. She fought them, but the three together were stronger than she and some of the liquid got into her mouth and down her throat. She felt the flesh numbing where it touched.

The women stood back and watched her, waiting for the drug to take effect.

Mitkezh entered the tent. A glance at Epona's eyes told him she was fighting the potion, but he was confident of its power. Even a strong shaman could not fight off the effects of Scythian rue. Soon the woman's spirit would have no strength of its own, and she would answer whatever questions he put to her. He would learn as much as she knew of the magic of her people: the powers, the rituals. From such a wealth of information there might be much that could be added to the shamans' own usage.

And when she was wrung dry, as a sacrificial cloth was wrung dry of blood, there were other uses for her. Fitting uses for a woman who had foolishly laid claim to power in her own right, and challenged the strength of the shamans.

They were not afraid of her now. Their own grip on the tribe had tightened to such an extent that they did not need to cower before this person who could summon the wind. What was the wind? Not as frightening as the predators who slunk around the camp; not as terrifying as the giant wolf for which Kazhak was responsible.

But the Taylga would drive all these demons away. The Sacrifice of the White Horse, performed as it would be this time, in

368

this season, with new and special power, would give incomparable strength to those who offered it.

Mitkezh smiled, watching Epona slowly lose the fight and become drowsy. "Send for Tsaygas now," he ordered the guard. "Is time."

She could hear their voices at a great distance. They called her by name; they asked questions. To her vast surprise she heard her own voice answering them like that of a sleepy child. She tried to close her mouth and bite off the words, but the commands of her spirit did not reach the hinges of her jaw.

The questioning went on and on. She was dimly aware that even in her helplessness they treated her with a certain care, a certain respect. A respect they had never accorded a woman before. That much, she had achieved.

At last they went away. Or perhaps they did not; perhaps it was only this world that went away, and Epona felt herself sinking downward with familiar swoop and slide into otherworlds.

Otherworlds, where she might escape.

Otherworlds, where there were names she could call on and help she could seek.

In a swirling gray darkness she called to the spirits of her people. She reached out, summoning, aware of vast distances of time and space, frantically searching for the familiar.

And from far, far away, she at last heard a voice. A harsh metallic voice.

"Epona," Kernunnos said.

She shuddered and surrendered the fight.

When she came to herself she was lying in another tent, and as she climbed upward from the drugged sleep she realized that her hands and feet were bound. One of her female "attendants" stood over her, smiling a false smile. "You are feeling better now, Kelt?" the woman asked.

"Where am I?"

"In safe place. Man without a name is searching for you, but he will not find you here. He will not see you again until the Taylga."

The Taylga. This concerns you, warned the spirit within. Epona wanted to close her eyes and sleep, just sleep . . . but the spirit within would not allow it.

"What happens at the Taylga?" it forced her to ask.

The other woman lowered her eyes. "Women do not attend sacrifice."

"But surely you know . . ." Epona put flattery into her voice, smearing it like honey on bread. "You are obviously a favorite of the shamans."

The woman smirked. "Is so. First slave of Tsaygas. Warm his bed, taste his food for poison."

"Then you must know about the sacrifice. Women always know more than they admit."

The smirk became a smile, as of a shared sisterhood. "Is so. This Taylga will be most special, it is said. Last Taylga was just over when you came here; it was not big success. Sacrifice was not sufficiently fine. But this season we have two splendid horses: black one to placate evil spirits, white one to be sent as messenger to Tabiti, to insure that strength of prince is renewed for coming year."

Kolaxais is alive then, Epona thought with relief. Kazhak would be glad to hear that — if she could get to Kazhak and tell him. "The white horse will be sacrificed to ask strength for Kolaxais?" she inquired, to be sure.

"For ruler of tribe," the woman answered guardedly. "Sacrifice of white horse is always to strengthen bonds between royal Tabiti and prince of Royal Scythians, representative of Papaeus. Tabiti is father in sky; *han* is father of tribe."

Perhaps Kolaxais is already dead. Perhaps a new prince sits in his place, on his rugs, listening to the shrieking of the shamans.

Not Kazhak. It would not be Kazhak.

"Is another purpose for Taylga," the woman said, putting one hand on her belly. "At Taylga, woman is offered to white horse before sacrifice. If horse accepts her, means tribe will be much more fertile in new season. Since Kazhak brought wolf-demon to threaten Kolaxais, not enough babies have been born to our people. This body" — her hand caressed her flat stomach — "should have swelled with child of shaman, but is empty. After Taylga, womb will hold new shaman. Tsaygas has promised."

"What do you mean, a woman is offered to the white horse?"

"Is a white stallion," the shaman's woman replied, leering at the prospect of the promised spectacle. "Shamans give drug to horse, makes him very excited. So excited he will even mount human woman if she is held for him. Fertility of the horse is passed on to the person, enters the entire tribe."

"What happens to the woman?" Epona asked, horrified, seeing in her mind the enormous penis of a stallion.

"Woman dies, but tribe will grow. Shamans have promised. Shamans have very special woman for sacrifice."

You are the chosen sacrifice, Epona, said the voiceless voice of the spirit within.

Chapter 29

THE WOMEN LEFT HER ALONE for a time, though securely bound and with a guard at the entrance to the tent. Epona lay sweating in horror. She could not keep herself from picturing the ceremony they had described; the shameful degradation of the beautiful animal, the insult she and he would be forced to offer to the earth mother. Twisted, evil! These were not white shamans, but black, according to the beliefs of their own people. And she was powerless against them.

No. Not powerless.

She clenched her teeth hard and closed her eyes, forcing herself to concentrate. Without sleeping, and by the force of her will alone, she summoned the gray mist and the swirling, the darkness that gave way to the light. She would not be afraid of what she found there this time.

Spirits of my people, she called. *Be with me.*

Epona, said the voice.

I hear you.

But she saw nothing, only light and shadow. Nevertheless, she could sense something around her; disembodied life that was more alive than flesh and blood; life that throbbed and burned and moved. Radiant, exultant. Life.

Weak tears of joy stole from beneath her closed eyelids.

Spirits of my people, she whispered. *Help me. Help Kazhak, who is a good man.*

You owe us, came the reply.

Yes, she said, acknowledging the debt at last. *I owe you for the gift of life.*

Something brushed close to her in the swirling mist and she had one brief glimpse of a hairy distorted face, and two yellow eyes that were totally mad. She recoiled in shock, feeling the sudden strain this put on the tenuous thread connecting her with her recumbent body in the Scythian tent.

Her body leaped violently and her eyes opened. For a moment she did not know where she was; the transition was too abrupt, too painful. Then she heard the wind blowing, and the wailing of the shamans, and she knew.

The sound of a scuffle nearby caused her to try to lift up enough to see what was happening, but the bonds that held her were too tight. She whipped her head back and forth in frustration, fighting with every muscle to gain some precious slack in the ropes.

"Be still, Epona. Someone will hear." Kazhak bent over her, with a Kelti knife in his hand.

Her eyes mirrored her relief and joy at seeing him. He bathed himself briefly in their warmth, then glanced over his shoulder toward the limp body of the guard that he had dragged inside the tent. "Is not much time," he whispered. "Soon shamans will come, for you . . . for my horse."

"*Your* horse?" Her voice was weak with disuse.

"Shamans mean to take Kazhak's stallion for White Horse Sacrifice. Last year he was too dark, but gray horse gets white with age. This season . . ." He clamped his jaw on the words and did not finish. "Will not happen," was all he said.

The knife had cut the bonds on her wrists and arms and Kazhak moved down to free her ankles.

"How did you find me?"

"Strange thing happen. You were gone; Kazhak asked everywhere, no one knew. Or would say. Could not search every tent, men would not let me in. Where to go? Then Kazhak saw wolf, huge wolf, with torn face. Clear as Kazhak sees you now. Wolf looked right at me, then ran this way, into this tent. Kazhak followed. Guard tried to stop, but Kazhak had good knife, put in guard's throat before he could cry out."

She was free at last, and he helped her to her feet. The effects of the drug left her dizzy but she was fighting it off with every

373

breath she drew. "Where is the wolf now?" she managed to ask. Kazhak glanced around the tent. "Gone," he said simply.

The noise level outside was increasing. Added to the ritual cries of the shamans and the omnipresent shrieking of the wind were the shouts of men, and the clatter of bones and rare, hoarded wood being dragged into a central place for the sacrificial fire. "Must go now," Kazhak said urgently. "You ride away on my stallion, *now*, or shamans sacrifice you both."

She dug her heels into the earth and resisted his tugging hands. "I will not leave you! I want to stay here to help you, Kazhak. You must not send me away now, when you need help most."

"You can help most by leaving and taking stallion with you," Kazhak told her. "Kazhak raised that horse from a colt. Taught him everything. Has been brother to me, that horse. Shamans know this. They know if they kill that horse, they will tear out Kazhak's heart. If you are safe, stallion is safe, it will be easier for me."

"But what will you do?"

"Try to convince my brothers not to listen to shamans. Try to see Kolaxais, if he is still alive."

"They will kill you too, Kazhak. If I go, you must come with me, now. You must ride away with me so we both live."

He smiled a bitter smile. "Kelti put much store by their honor, is it so? Would not be an honorable thing for Kazhak to leave now, while father may still be alive but helpless in grip of shamans. Kazhak must stay long enough to do what he can for Kolaxais, or is not an honorable man. Is it so?"

Once more she was being pushed and shoved. She would get no chance to pit her powers against those of the shamans; she would flee the Scythian encampment like a thief, taking the gray stallion with her, and leaving a brave man behind to attempt to fulfill his own obligations to those who gave him life.

Tears burned in her eyes. She could cry now; she was a Kelt. "I cannot leave without you, Kazhak," she said. "It would . . . tear out Epona's heart."

"Is not an order. But Kazhak asks."

They met and locked eyes in a silence that had no room for anything other than their two spirits.

Epona was the first to lower her eyes. "Where will I go?" she asked in a voice so soft he could hardly hear it.

"West," he told her. "As far as you like. Dasadas will go with you; he knows the way to get you back to the Blue Mountains, if that is what you want."

"Dasadas?!" She could not believe her ears.

"He will not let anything happen to you," Kazhak said with certainty. "You are safer with him than with any other man. Kazhak had rather you live, with Dasadas, than die to give glory to shamans."

"But I am not afraid of dying, Kazhak."

The bitter smile remained. "You always argue. There is no time for arguing. You are not afraid, Epona, but Kazhak is afraid for you. What if life does not go on forever, like you think? All this"— he lifted a strand of her hair and fingered it. Kelti gold — "all of this would be gone.

"Go with Dasadas, Epona. He is waiting with my horse. If we are very careful, may be we can get to them before anyone sees us."

He caught her wrist and pulled her after him, out of the tent. As she stepped over the guard's body she saw that he lay in a pool of blood, and she was glad.

The huge fire of sacrifice was being built in the center of the encampment, and the entire tribe seemed preoccupied with it. Every able pair of hands was engaged in collecting and carrying anything that might burn, including the smashed wagons of men already dead by the shamans' order.

Tsaygas and Mitkezh were determined to light at the next sunrise a blaze that would be seen from horizon to horizon, symbolizing the birth of a new power on the Sea of Grass.

They will be very disappointed, Epona thought to herself, running behind Kazhak, bent over to be less visible in the gloom of a cloudy afternoon, dodging breathlessly between tents and wagons. *When their main sacrifices escape them, they will lose much status. The earth mother does not show pity to priests who abuse their privilege.*

A few people saw the fleeing figures, but no one raised an outcry. It was not a good time to draw attention to oneself. Kazhak and Epona succeeded in reaching the edge of the encampment without anyone's summoning the shamans.

Perhaps my brothers will stand with me after all, Kazhak thought. But he did not have a good feeling about it. Men who

375

have turned against you once are not to be trusted a second time.
As he had promised, Dasadas was waiting. He rode his new bay
stallion, a heavy pack of provisions fastened behind the saddle,
and he held the reins of Kazhak's gray. His eyes lit with relief as
he saw the two approach. "Dasadas got to stallion before shamans
came with drug," he said. "You found Epona. Is good, Kazhak.
Good. But is anyone following you?"

Kazhak glanced back. "No one follows, not yet. But soon. Is
strange thing, but none of those who have become so friendly
with shamans seem to have noticed us. Is like they were blind."

Epona glanced back the way they had come. A mist, as of water
vapor, seemed to have settled on the encampment. A very unseasonable fog, that shielded some sights from inimical eyes.

Uiska, she thought.

The smoke of cooking fires hung unusually heavy in the air,
clouding the vision, making eyes smart and burn. It was hard to
see clearly in such an atmosphere, and the Scythians groped
through their duties as if half-blinded.

Tena, Epona said to herself.

Still, there was very little time. At any moment the shamans
would return to the tent to check on the condition of their treasure; perhaps to give her additional potions to make her more
docile, even as they meant to drug the horse. If they were to
escape, they must do it now, while all the usually mounted Scythians were on foot, engaged in perparing the sacrificial bonfire.

Urged by Kazhak's demanding hands, Epona had reluctantly
mounted the gray stallion and taken the reins from Dasadas, but
now she turned for one more look at Kazhak — and that was her
undoing. His eyes met hers with a look of such loss and longing
nothing else mattered: not the fire of sacrifice, not the stallion,
not her own tribe. "Kazhak!" she cried, and threw the reins down
on the horse's neck, preparing to dismount.

"Run!" Kazhak thundered at the stallion, slamming his hand
across its haunch with all the force he possessed. The whip of
inarguable command was in his voice and the animal obeyed,
leaping forward with such a bound that Epona was nearly thrown
from the saddle. She instinctively grabbed the stallion's mane,
pulling herself back into balance, and at that moment she heard
angry cries and saw a group of men running toward her, led by
the furious shamans.

"Do not let them escape!" Tsaygas screamed, as his men scrambled for their horses.

"Come, Epona!" Dasadas yelled, grabbing the gray stallion's headstall as he galloped beside her. There was always the chance she would turn and go back, to certain death. She tried to fight him off but he dodged her desperate fist. When she tried to leap from the saddle he urged the bay in so close to Kazhak's gray that he was able to clutch the back of her clothing in his hand and hold her on the horse. "Is what Kazhak wants!" he yelled, and this time she heard him. Her struggles lessened and she sat upright in the saddle, allowing the flight to continue.

But she turned in the saddle and looked back in time to see the first of the Scythians reach his own hobbled mount, unfasten it, and vault aboard. At that moment a figure — lean and lithe, like a giant dog — darted from between two tents and launched itself straight at the throat of the Scythian horse. The animal reared with a terrible scream, the rider fighting for control. The horse crashed to the earth, its rider with it, pinned beneath the heavy body. The silver wolf attacked the helpless man then, rather than the horse, slashing his throat open and then whirling on the next Scythian who approached to aid his comrade. The speed and fury of the wolf's assault seemed to paralyze the man with fear. It hurled itself upon him, driving him to the earth, tearing him open. Even as he died the wolf left him for its next victim, and the next after that.

It seemed to be everywhere at once, snarling, slashing, its fangs savaging flesh as if with an insatiable thirst for human blood. In moments it had wrought havoc in the Scythian encampment and so panicked the hobbled saddle horses that even the best horseman could not calm one of them long enough to free it and mount.

Kazhak snatched his bow from his *gorytus* without thinking and fired a quick shot, but the arrow passed harmlessly by the wolf — or through it. That could not be; he blinked and rubbed his eyes, and in that moment the wolf turned once and looked at him, with such insane eyes that he was rooted where he stood. Yet the creature did not attack him; its primary interest seemed to be in scattering and slaughtering those who would pursue Epona. Already the area reeked with blood and rang with the cries of torn men, and the animal appeared to grow stronger with every man it killed.

No one was going to be pursuing Epona; not for quite a while.

377

But it was Kazhak's people who were being slaughtered. Though they had been turned against him, the men who were dying had once called themselves his comrades. His brothers.

He drew his Kelti sword. If Epona was right, perhaps the wolf would back away from that weapon. He could do that much; he could stand with his people against this thing, and try to keep it from sending any more Scythians into the wooden houses. Perhaps, when Epona was far enough away to be beyond all hope of catching her, the wolf would even let them alone.

If he lived through that, the battle would still not be over. The furious shamans would demand an explanation. He would tell them, "She stole my horse. Fastest horse on Sea of Grass, is it so? No one can catch woman on that horse. Dasadas helped her. Is known fact, he has looked at my woman with hungry eyes. They run away together."

The shamans might not believe him, but his brothers would see him as the injured party in Epona's escape with Dasadas, and the sympathy won by that stratagem might gain him admission to a few more tents. Perhaps he could still gather enough men to challenge the shamans . . . perhaps Kolaxais was still alive . . .

Before plunging into the fray, he looked westward one more time. He saw two horses, already far across the grassland and racing like the wind; dark miniatures silhouetted against the setting sun as it broke through heavy clouds. The baleful orange light burned Kazhak's eyes; perhaps that was what made them water.

The galloping figures were too far away to hear him, or to see the hand he raised in a last salute, but he whispered the words, just the same.

"Ride, Kelt," he called to Epona, very softly, entrusting his words to the wind. "Ride *free*."

PART THREE
Again, the Blue Mountains

Chapter 30

THEY RODE as if demons pursued them in the flesh. More than once Dasadas shouted to Epona, "Do not look back!" because he was afraid of what would happen if she did. She would turn the gray stallion and go back to Kazhak, and Dasadas would be sacrificed with her for helping her escape.

But she did not go back. She made herself lock her eyes on the western horizon and lash the horse with the ends of her reins until he found a speed within himself he had not known he had, and soon they had outdistanced even Dasadas and his strong young mount and were racing alone across the steppe.

Dasadas followed her. It was not difficult; he knew the only direction she would take. He did not allow himself to think of the coming night, when they would be alone together. He did not allow himself to think of Kazhak, facing the wrath of the shamans.

He thought of nothing at all but the running horse and the setting sun.

If a party of pursuers came after them they never knew it. Long after dark, guided only by a sliver of moon and the gray stallion's unerring instinct, Epona was still traveling west. She had at last fallen back to a trot, and she heard Dasadas calling to her from the distance.

"Epona? Are you there, Epona?"

"Here, Dasadas." She reined the gray to a halt and waited for him.

"Clouds return," the Scythian commented as he rode up. "With no moon is too dark to see ground, not safe for horses. We stop here?"

"I think we can. The last time I looked back, there was a terrible fight going on in the camp; all the men were involved in it. It was . . . the wolf, I think. It was impossible for anyone to mount a pursuit party just then, and we have come a long distance without catching sight of any followers. We might as well rest here and ride again before dawn. The shamans will surely send someone after us eventually, but our horses are swift and we have a great start; they can never catch us now."

"How far do we go?" Dasadas asked, unhesitatingly surrendering the mantle of leadership to her. To Epona, who was not like other women.

"I am going all the way to the Blue Mountains, Dasadas. Like Kazhak, I have an obligation."

He did not understand what she meant by that, but he understood danger to himself well enough. "Scyth will not be welcome in Blue Mountains," he told her.

"If you come riding that stallion you will be. The Kelti raise ponies for pulling ceremonial carts; if we breed your stallion and mine to pony mares, in the future my people will have horses large enough to be ridden. Your good bay will make you welcome, Dasadas. You bring treasure with you."

"Can do more than that," he told her. "Dasadas will show you."

They made camp in the lee of a slight rise of ground, but they did not dare light a fire, though the night was dark and cold. To eyes accustomed to the steppe, however, there was enough light to see, dimly, the things Dasadas pulled from one of his saddlebags to show Epona. An ivory comb. Gold jewelry. A copper bracelet.

"These are your things, Dasadas?" Epona asked in surprise.

"No, were sent by wives of Kazhak. For Epona to buy safety, food, whatever she needs."

She recognized the copper armband, then, that she had given Talia. She sat on the earth, holding the little hoard in her lap, and wondered if she was going to cry. Those reserved, indifferent women. They had never encouraged her to think of them as friends; they had never really allowed her behind their veils. Yet

382

they had sent all the wealth they could gather to insure her a safe journey.

I never knew them at all, she thought, her throat scorched with regret.

"When was there time to do all this, Dasadas?" she asked.

"When Kazhak found you were missing, he guessed what shamans intended. From that moment he meant to find you, send you away. He told one wife, she told others."

"I am surprised the shamans weren't guarding him as they were me. Surely they did not think he would allow them to sacrifice his woman or his horse without offering any resistance."

"Why not?" Dasadas inquired. "Order of Kolaxais, Kazhak would never disobey. So they thought. On Sea of Grass, if one man disobeys his *han*, word travels on wind. He will not find allies in other tribes; princes of other tribes would not allow. What man wants to make angry the man who rules him?"

"The power of the *han* is not only total, it can be terrible," Epona commented. "Only now, among the Royal Scythians, it has become the power of the shamans. Why are they doing this, Dasadas? Why hurt their own people for the sake of gold and livestock?"

"Is not only reason. Shamans are jealous men, Dasadas thinks. They have watched many years as *han* ruled people, made decisions. Shamans think they can do better. They want their turn. They want everything."

Epona shivered. The cold of the steppe was settling around them. Though Dasadas had brought a wide range of provisions, including her *gorytus* and ample clothing, he had found himself unwilling to touch or pack the bearskin cloak, and Epona must now satisfy herself with a Scythian cloak of sewn skins and a blanket of goats' hair.

"I do not think Tsaygas and Mitkezh are possessed by white *taltos*, Dasadas," she remarked as she sat, thinking. "I believe they contain black spirits, spirits of evil. Only such creatures would harm their own kind or use magic for selfish purposes. In time they will be punished for it, of course. The earth mother insists that all things ultimately come into balance."

Her words had no meaning for him. He was content merely to sit as close to her as he dared, smelling the aroma of her skin, thinking his own thoughts, and dreaming his own dreams.

383

"I should have stayed, Dasadas. I should have stayed to help Kazhak," she murmured, as much to herself as to him.

Dasadas said nothing. She was tormenting herself over what she perceived to be her defection, but that would pass. They had many days to ride, and sometime along that journey she would stop thinking of Kazhak.

"Be my brother now," Kazhak had said to him. "Take care of my woman as you would your own. Guard her with your life."

For that, a man must have some reward. Kazhak would not have expected it to be otherwise.

The same thought played at the edges of Epona's mind as she sat on the earth, listening to the gray stallion cropping a last few mouthfuls of grass before she signaled him to lie down beside her. A new pain twisted her as she realized what it must have cost Kazhak to send her away with Dasadas.

It should have been Kazhak who fled with her; who took her safely home. But Kazhak was a man of honor; he had stayed to try to fulfill his obligation to his father and his tribe.

And I ran. I ran, Epona thought, hating herself.

When she could bear it no longer, she had the stallion lie down and she pillowed her head on his neck and surrendered to silent, bitter tears.

Dasadas lay a few paces away, waiting.

Soon, he promised her under his breath. *Soon Dasadas will give you a reason to stop crying, Epona.*

They fell into a half-sleep, almost expecting to hear the thunder of approaching hooves.

Thisworld did not look better in the morning. If anything, it was colder, grayer, and more forbidding. Epona would have almost welcomed an attempt by Dasadas to invade her body and drag her away from her own thoughts, but the man kept his distance, watching her with the same mixture of lust and worship she had seen in his face for over a year.

"They may come after us now," he cautioned. "We must go."

"You will travel with me, then — all the way back to the village of the Kelti?"

"Kazhak ordered me to take you where you want to go," he answered.

When they had eaten a quick meal of dried meat and hard

bread, they turned the horses westward. But as they rode, Dasadas explained that this would not always be the direction they
took, though their ultimate goal was in the direction of the setting
sun. "Is very bad weather here in winter, you know that, Epona.
Dasadas thinks it is better we ride south soon, toward shore of
Black Sea. There are good roads there, trade roads, easier in this
season. There are towns where we can get supplies."

"But Kazhak avoided all settlements; almost all settlements,"
she reminded him.

"We were war party, then. Too small a number; we were careful. Now, just two people, no one will see a threat in us. Dasadas
has clothes for you, man's clothes; we will smear dirt on your face
so no one can tell who you are. We will ride as travelers only,
emissaries of some prince of the horse. Is well known Scythians
possess much gold. We may be welcomed if it is thought we bring
commissions for craftsmen. Scythians have good reputation among
craftsmen in the south."

All the way back to the Blue Mountains. It would be a very
long journey, and Epona realized that any such travels were dangerous of themselves. She might never make it to her own village;
anything could happen.

But that has always been your destination, the voice within
told her suddenly. *Go home, Epona.*

The days rolled past under the hooves of the horses, and the landscape changed and changed again as they entered new territories.
Since they were not trying to avoid those who might take them
for hostile marauders, they did not always ride across trackless
expanses. When bitter weather drove game into hiding and their
bows found no targets, Epona and Dasadas ventured into settled
communities and bartered for meat and staples, or a strengthen-
ing measure of grain for their horses.

Dasadas was determined that they avoid the tribes of "savages"
occupying the western fringes of the gréat steppe. He hoped to
follow the coast of the sea south to the Duna and across the father
river, then travel west across Moesia, avoiding the dark Carpātos

altogether. A longer route, one that would take much more time, but Dasadas was not comfortable with the prospect of facing the Carpātos again.

Disguised as a male Scyth, her bright hair darkened with mud and topped by the pointed felt cap that protected ears against bitter wind, her body encased in tunic and comfortable trousers, Epona experienced a new kind of freedom. She rode with Dasadas as a comrade, an equal, and soon he fell into the habit of talking with her as he would have with one of his brothers. There was not the closeness between them that her spirit had established with that of Kazhak, but they became comfortable with one another.

Except at night, when they were alone in the darkness, and she was as aware of his thoughts as of the horse beneath her.

No amount of dirt would disguise the fact that Epona had no beard, but the weather worked for them, providing ample reason for her to wrap a scarf around the lower part of her face. As she rode the superior horse, those they met assumed her to be a young noble and Dasadas her attendant, and while they hastened to do his bidding — spurred by dreams of Scythian gold, or fear of Scythian reprisals — they bowed deferentially to her.

Epona found she quite enjoyed their forays into the settlements.

Following Dasadas' plan, they worked their way southward toward the coast of the Black Sea. They crossed two major rivers on their journey across the Sea of Grass, rivers Dasadas identified as the Borysthenes, a large and powerful waterway, thickly settled along its southern reaches, and the Hypanis, a smaller stream, easily forded as it was surprisingly low in this season.

"Next river will be the Tyras, which is boundary between Scythian land and the territory of the Neuri," Dasadas explained. "We cross Tyras, we ride on to Duna, we are out of range of the people of the horse. From the Duna we will be safe . . . if the wolf-demon does not follow us."

The wolf seemed to be a preoccupation with Dasadas, second only to his obsession for Epona. Yet neither of them had seen the wolf since the evening they fled the winter camp of the royal tribe, in spite of the fact that for many nights they had been too cautious to build a fire. But Epona was not concerned about the wolf. She was heading back toward the Blue Mountains; she did not think it would bother them now.

Dasadas was not so sure. He kept his Kelti iron close to his hand, and when they heard distant animal sounds in the night he was instantly on his feet, staring into the darkness. "Since Dasadas drank the blood of first man he killed," he confided to Epona, "according to our custom, no enemy has escaped the bow of Dasadas for long. Except that wolf."

"It is not to your discredit that you could not kill him," Epona said as she tried to reassure Dasadas. "As Kazhak said, the silver wolf is a . . . demon."

"Have not killed him yet," Dasadas corrected her. "But someday. Someday."

The bleak reaches of the Sea of Grass lay behind them, and so far they had avoided pursuit or challenge. As they crossed the Tyras — seasoned travelers now, with many days in the saddle behind them — Dasadas looked north, upriver, and shuddered. "If we follow Tyras to land of Neuri we will be again in the Carpātos," he said. "Demon wolf waits for us there; Dasadas is sure of it. Wolf was very strong in Carpātos, Epona, remember? Remember? But we fool him; we go another way."

That night, when they camped, Dasadas cried aloud in his sleep, and it was not the groan of a man but the whimper of a frightened child, with a nightmare it could not shake.

Slowly, reluctantly, Epona raised her head and listened. The pathetic sounds continued. She got up — one step at a time, ready to go back at any moment if they ceased — and went to Dasadas, where he lay wrapped in his blanket, sobbing in his sleep. She lay down beside him as gently as the fall of snow and put her arms around him.

"It's all right, Dasadas," she whispered in his ear. "It is only a dream, the wolf no longer follows us. There is nothing to fear that you cannot handle with your bow and arrows."

She had to talk a long time before she felt him start to relax. His sleeping body burrowed against hers, seeking warmth, and she let herself mold to fit him. They lay together throughout the night with their arms around one another, and when Epona awoke at dawn his gray eyes were open.

"You are in my blanket," he said in a low voice.

"You cried out in the night."

"Dasadas never cries out in the night. You came to me; Dasadas always knew you would." His arms clamped around her.

She did not want him; she wanted no one but Kazhak; yet Kazhak was many days away. She might never see him again. He had put her in Dasadas' care, surely knowing the price the other man would demand. Indeed, for her sake Dasadas had left his own wives, his tents and wagons and people, to make the dangerous trip to the Blue Mountains, where he might well receive a hostile welcome. A debt had been incurred.

And she was sorry for Dasadas. It was not desire that rose up in her, but the vast mothering pity of a woman for a frustrated child. A child sick with longing for something it could never possess.

I am not Kazhak's wife, she thought. *I am a free woman.*

Closing her eyes so she need not see his face, Epona gave what comfort she could to Dasadas.

He knew he had been cheated. He knew it almost at once, when the excitement faded and he realized he had only possessed her body, but not the essential inner something that fueled his hunger. Still, the prize had surrendered to him at last, he thought; the quarry had been brought to earth. It was something. It would be more. Somehow, he would make it more.

They rode on, and at night, when he could bear it no longer, he came to her. Though not every night; it was too painful to lie beside her and know that her thoughts were far away. It was agony to hear her whisper Kazhak's name in her sleep.

They rode on.

As they approached the seacoast the climate became more benign, and there were times when Epona forgot her disguise and bared her head to the welcome sun.

"You must not!" Dasadas warned her, again and again. "Traders — Dacians, Ionians, Assyrians — they would take you for slavery and kill Dasadas. Or we might meet savages. The Tauri live on the seacoast; they would do terrible things to you."

But they did not encounter savages. They found themselves riding almost from village to village, following a chain of settlements that encircled the sea like the globules of amber Epona never took from her throat. For the first time, she saw some of the long-settled towns the traders had described around Touto-rix's feasting fire. Many of them were mere clusters of mud-brick houses, surrounded by fenced patches of farmland; but as they neared the mouth of the Duna the signs of man's long occupation of this region were expressed by actual cities, centers of commerce dictated by the location of good harbors for merchant ships or adequate facilities for metalworking, the preoccupation of the region.

Cities had streets paved with blocks of stone rutted by many generations of wooden wagon wheels. Cities had more people than Epona had ever seen in one place, until the winter encampment of the Scythians. Cities had noise and dirt and unfamiliar smells, and offal that stood in the streets instead of being buried in squatting pits. Cities radiated an aura of anxiety.

Cities disgusted Epona.

"You are always asking questions," Dasadas teased her. "Would you like to spend some days in city, see what is like?"

"No," she told him without hesitation.

She was more interested in the sea, that vast body of water men called Black, glimpsed across stretches of beach or between trees. "Let us ride over there, Dasadas," she implored. "I want to know what the sea looks like. I want to get off and wade in the shallows; I want to taste the water on my tongue."

"Is not good thing to do," Dasadas said. "Sea is full of monsters. You will be eaten; Kazhak will blame Dasadas."

He could not control her, however; stronger men had tried. He watched, glowering, while she satisfied her curiosity about the sea and ran back from incoming wavelets, squealing with delight. Each squeal brought his hand closer to the hilt of his shortsword, but no monster materialized to attack her.

Epona was entranced by the sea. Giant, liquid, ceaseless; it was like some incredibly large womb, gestating life in its darkness. She felt an answering within herself.

"Perhaps we should stay here until spring, Dasadas," she suggested, half-seriously. "I have a feeling this would be a good place to bear a child."

"Child? *Child!*"

She smiled, her eyes full of dreams. "Yes."

389

"Is my child?"

She hated having to kill the hope she heard in his voice. But a child must not begin with a lie. "No, Dasadas; it was sired by Kazhak, on the Sea of Grass."

"You are certain?"

She put one hand to her waist, feeling the ripeness there, surprised he had not already noticed. "Hai, Dasadas. Very certain." A child with dark eyes, and an irresistible grin, waited in her womb. Her arms shaped themselves unconsciously into a cradle to hold it. Dasadas saw the gesture and turned away.

"We go," he said. "Would not be a good place to have a child. We are strangers here. You should be with your own people."

She thought of the endless distance stretching ahead of them, the towns they must pass, the marshland, the dusty roads, the rivers to cross and hills to climb. The other great plain that still lay between her and the Blue Mountains. And the mountains themselves, rising sheerly toward the sky in almost unclimbable steps.

"I don't know if we can reach the village of the Kelti before this child is born," she told Dasadas.

"We try. Kazhak would want." He kicked the bay stallion and started forward at a trot, anxious to be moving, to lose himself in the rhythm of the horse, which he understood. He could not understand Epona. She was as incomprehensible to him as the stars. She must have known she carried Kazhak's child when she lay in his blanket with him that first time; yet she had said nothing, as if it did not matter . . . he felt betrayed, and angry for Kazhak, whom Epona had also betrayed.

It did not matter, to Epona. With Kazhak's child safe inside her, part of her, its spirit added to her own, she felt everything else become secondary. She rode as if in a dream, experiencing the wonder of being part of creation, a lifebearer. All her senses were simultaneously intensified and sweetened, so that tastes were richer, sounds clearer, sights more colorful than she had ever known. She felt a generous outpouring of herself that extended to everything she came in contact with, even while her thoughts and her concentration turned inward, to the child.

She could be kind to Dasadas, it did not matter. Kazhak's child was safe within her; he was her husband now, in truth, and the small pleasure she gave to Dasadas did not diminish Kazhak. The man was brave and loyal, a good warrior. He was just not large enough in her eyes to blot out the vision of Kazhak.

But she wanted to leave the region of cities; there was something unclean about them that must not touch her unborn child.

Now that he knew about the child, Dasadas changed. He withdrew into himself like a woman going behind her veil, and he quit talking to Epona aside from the most necessary exchanges. He did not come to her at night, with pleading hands and hungry body. He looked at her almost as if he hated her, which puzzled her. In the village of the Kelti, a woman carrying life was admired by everyone.

As they approached the estuary of the Duna, Dasadas remarked that they would need to hire a ferryman to take them across the river ahead on a flat-bottomed barge, for it was too wide to ford and too deep and swift to swim the horses. The ferryman would cost some of their gold.

"Why do we have to cross the Duna here at all?" Epona asked. "Why not follow the north bank, inland?"

"Dasadas planned to go beyond river, south, to city of Varna. Buy supplies there, maybe find some brothers who came to Thrace for horsetrading. Pick up an escort for part of journey."

"I don't want to go to Varna, Dasadas, and I need no more escort than you."

"Woman with child is helpless."

She still dressed as a Scythian man, unwilling to relinquish the comfort and convenience of her trousers. She rode as well as ever, and the day before she had brought down a fat heron with her bow. She did not feel helpless. "No escort!" she ordered. "And I want to save our gold; as we cross Thrace, we will spend it instead for good big mares."

"For why?"

"With Thracian mares in addition to our Kelti ponies, we can be breeding bigger horses sooner. We can find other ways to pay for supplies, if we need them; you can split wood for a farmer with no sons, or I can gather and sell herbs. But I mean to take some Thracian mares to the Blue Mountains, for with them, and the methods of training I learned on the Sea of Grass, I will be able to see my own kin become horsemen within this lifetime. I can mount Kazhak's son on his own horse and put the reins in his hand, Dasadas." Her eyes were shining. But the magic was not for him. Would never be for him.

Dasadas felt he had grabbed for stars and caught a handful of dust.

His voice was surly as he answered. "We two alone could never drive a band of mares all the way to your village. Why you want to try this?"

She paused a moment, thinking. "So I can go home with my head high," she said at last.

It was not difficult to find people willing to sell them good mares; they were riding through a country that prided itself on its breeding stock, and every farmer boasted of his year's crop of foals. But Epona insisted on those animals with the deepest chest and the sturdiest leg bones; good lungs and tendons not easily torn would be essential in the mountains. Soon they had spent their little hoard of gold, and the only wealth they had left for trade was the metal on their horse trappings and the amber around Epona's neck.

In return for a dun mare with powerful hindquarters Epona traded the amber necklace without regret; her belly carried a far better remembrance of Kazhak.

As Dasadas had foreseen, there were numerous difficulties for two people in trying to drive a band of mares many days across difficult terrain. The stallions Epona and Dasadas rode did not make matters easier. They constantly pranced at the very edge of control, displaying themselves for their new harem, all but forgetting the riders who cursed and struggled in an effort to keep them looking ahead and moving forward. The gray, older and better trained, gave Epona fewer difficulties than Dasadas' young and impetuous bay; but both horses obviously considered their riders secondary in importance to the mares.

The mares, the mares. Nine young mares, with untold generations in their bellies; on their backs.

The weather was less of a problem. Each night, when they camped, Epona spent a long time in concentration over the campfire they never failed to build now. She chanted invocations to the clouds and the wind; she bent low to the earth mother and murmured words of praise. She treated the fire with respect and hailed trees they passed with gestures of love.

392

They rode through a calm land and a gentle season, and Dasadas grieved in his heart for the magic he would never be able to grasp.

The woman's belly was swelling richly now, and at the end of each day there were dark circles under her eyes where exhaustion lay. "We should stop," Dasadas told her again and again. They were following the valley of the Duna northward, aware of the great mountain ranges that lay east and west. They were safely past the unhealthy marshlands of Moesia now, into the rich and fertile valley through which many generations of traders had made their way north to the Baltik. There were well-beaten roads, prosperous farms, frequent settlements. There were tribes whose names Epona knew: the Daci, the Scordisci, the Breuci. But Epona refused to break their journey and await the arrival of her infant in some comfortable haven.

"I want to go all the way," she said stubbornly, and there was no arguing with her.

To avoid seeing the pain in his eyes, she did not discuss her reasons with Dasadas until he became so insistent she had no choice. "Kazhak may have had to flee the tribe by now," she said. "The odds against him were so great, Dasadas; but I do not think he would wait meekly for the shamans to sacrifice him. He may be riding west himself. If he comes to my village I must be there first, or it could go hard with him."

"We never see Kazhak again," Dasadas told her with certainty. "We should not even say his name; to say names of dead draws their attention, they could hurt us."

"Hai, Dasadas, you know nothing," Epona said softly. "Kazhak is not dead. And the spirits of those who have made their transition are not necessarily our enemies; Kazhak would not be. But he is not dead," she repeated.

"How you know?"

She put her hand on her belly. "I know."

She thought she knew; the feeling was strong in her, but there were times of doubt, nevertheless. She lay on the earth at night and remembered the words of Uiska: "It takes much courage to look into the future, and some of the things to be seen there would scorch your eyes." But she was *drui*; she had the power. If she truly believed, she could visit the future and see if it was inhabited by a living Kazhak.

393

Remember the other words of Uiska, counseled the spirit within: *Learning to resist temptation is part of the discipline of the druii.*

Yes, Epona agreed silently. The shamans had not resisted the temptation to abuse their power and reach out with greedy hands, and only ill would come of it. Whatever pattern governed the lives of the Scythians would be damaged beyond repair, made into something warped and ugly.

But that was not her concern. Her concern was her own tribe. Her people. Her people forever; and she and her baby were going home.

The way was long and hard, but her heart was singing in her every step of it. She felt guided as if by unseen hands. She was as buoyant as though she floated on water. At last she was conforming to the pattern as it pertained to her, and all things would go smoothly now.

She was going home.

They drove the mares to a shallow backwater of the river for grazing and watering, and even as Dasadas and Epona were unsaddling their own horses, they knew they had made a mistake, but it was too late.

The war party came swarming over the crest of a wooded hill and had them surrounded almost before they could put arrows to their bows.

Chapter 31

THEY WERE DACIANS, by the looks of them: hard-muscled, fair-haired men armored with bronze corselets and carrying javelins in addition to their shortswords. Epona's first reaction was relief that they were not one of the hybrid bands of robbers that plagued the trade routes, preying on insufficiently guarded merchants.

That relief ebbed quickly. A long-jawed man wearing the plume of leadership on his bronze helmet pointed at her and yelled, "That's the one, that's the Kelti woman!" and the others ran toward her.

She and Dasadas worked frantically, fitting arrow to bow and firing as quickly as they could, accurate shots that took down a man with every singing of the bow. But they were outnumbered, and almost a score of Dacians reached Epona and Dasadas, grabbing at the bridles of their horses. They fought hard, with knife and sword now, but Epona was clumsy in her pregnancy and even Dasadas was soon overpowered, though he fought like a man possessed.

Their little herd of mares, spooked by the furor, stampeded up the road and was soon out of sight.

The leader hauled a shaken Epona off her horse. Too late, she regretted that she had not given the gray stallion the kill signal that would have set him lashing out with teeth and hooves at the enemy. It was almost as if the unborn life within her held her back from such close-quarter killing.

"This has to be the woman," the leader crowed in triumph. As two of his men held her he snatched the felt cap from her head and let her hair tumble free. "Reddish-blond and big with child," he said, with satisfaction. "She answers the description that farmer gave us."

"What farmer? What is this about?" Epona demanded to know. She would not let them see her be afraid.

"You healed the lame pony of a man who gave you food and water in return, and held some mares for you in his pen," the Dacian told her. "And that farmer talked, oh, yes, he was delighted to talk. You made quite an impression on him."

As her pregnancy advanced, her disguise as a Scythian man had became quite impossible, and Epona had recently, reluctantly, abandoned it altogether. Now it was too late for regrets, however. Someone would have spotted her anyway, she knew that as soon as the Dacian explained his reason for seeking her.

"There is a price on your head south of here, woman," he told her. "A Thracian, one Provaton, has talked of little but you for a year or more. His uncle, who is a wealthy horsebreeder, I understand, even financed a little expedition to the east in search of you but nothing came of it — except they encountered some Scythians who relieved them of their horses and their heads.

"But you are known, Kelti woman, and there is talk of you at every horse fair and trading center where stockmen meet. When it was rumored that you had been seen in this region, my men and I decided to go into business for ourselves, you might say. We will get a good price for you; you will be the most valuable slave auctioned this season, eh, men?" He glanced over his shoulder at his comrades, grinning, sharing his victory with them as he would divide the price they would get for her, and in that moment when he was distracted Epona leaped at him.

Her movement startled the two men who held her just enough to allow her to pull free of their grasp. They immediately grabbed for her again, but by this time Dasadas was waging his own small war with knife and Kelti sword, taking advantage of Epona's diversion to break free of his own guard. No one expected a pregnant woman to move so swiftly or fight so fiercely. Epona did not strike to kill, now; she only slashed and cut to get through the men surrounding her and reach the gray stallion, who miraculously had not fled after the mares, as had the bay of Dasadas.

When the men closed around her again she whistled shrilly and the horse answered her, obedient to the command. His attack was as unexpected as her own, and the men of the Daci backed away from his rearing body and flailing hooves. Epona leaped for him, feeling one of his knees strike her unintentionally in the belly, and with a desperate heave she caught him by the mane. He whirled instantly and broke through the circle of men. Epona, half-running beside him, unable to pull herself onto his back, clutched his mane and gritted her teeth. Then Dasadas was with her, shouting something, shoving against her with his shoulder, and she was draped across the stallion's back with the yelling Scythian behind her, covering her body with his own. The Dacians recovered quickly and ran after them, hurling their javelins, but afoot they could not hope to equal the speed of the horse.

Epona heard Dasadas grunt once, an anguished sound, and felt the thud of something strike his body, but he did not fall.

The gray lowered his head and pinned his ears flat against his head, running away from his attackers, running after the younger stallion who had taken off with his mares. He had remained, as he was taught, with his rider, held by an invisible chain, but now that chain was broken and nothing could restrain him. A rival had stolen his mares; that was his only thought.

He had run so far and so fast that the Dacians were mere specks in the distance before Epona was able to pull herself upright in the saddle and haul on the flying reins, and then she had to fight with all her strength to slow the stallion appreciably.

Dasadas was lying against her, his arms clutching her body, his head bobbing against her back as if he had no control over it. There was a dreadful lancing pain in her own belly and spots of light danced in front of her eyes, but she could not surrender; not yet, not until they were all safe.

They came to a wooded area with the dense underbrush resulting from centuries of alternate slash-and-burn cultivation and abandonment. Epona succeeded in fighting the stallion to a halt, then turned him aside into the woods. Still he whinnied incessantly, calling after his mares.

She slid from his back and tied him securely to a tree, then sank onto the earth, dizzy and sick. Dasadas still sprawled on the horse's back, and when the stallion fidgeted and danced, fighting his tether, the Scythian slid to the ground with a sound like that of a sack of meal falling.

Epona crawled over to him. There was an ugly bleeding wound in his side and the broken point of a javelin was embedded there. When he breathed, she could hear a rattling in his chest, and see bloody bubbles form and break in his open mouth.

"Dasadas. Dasadas!"

He opened his eyes weakly and stared up, but he did not seem to see her.

The pain in her belly was getting worse; it had spread to her back, and felt like a hand squeezing. Dasadas ran his tongue over his lips and made a sound that could have been a request for water.

Epona slumped down onto the earth mother. There was nowhere else to go; nothing to do. She was suddenly very tired, her bones limp within her flesh. She pressed her face into the earth, smelling dirt and moss and dead leaves, and waited.

And strength came back to her, a little at a time.

At last she was able to get to her hands and knees, and then, shakily, to her feet, and follow the distant sound of running water. At a tiny, icy stream she knelt and bathed her face until she felt better, then soaked the bottom of her old woolen Kelti gown with water until she had enough to carry back and squeeze into Dasadas' open mouth. When she was stronger, she would fill the one empty waterbag the stallion carried, and they would ride on in search of the other horses.

If Dasadas would be able to ride on.

You will die with blood in your mouth beside a muddy river, Kernunnos had once said.

Dasadas was badly wounded, there was no doubt of it, and the injury was not amenable to the techniques she knew. She searched for yarrow to pack his wound, but found none. She put her hands on his body and concentrated, reaching out with her spirit for help, but felt no answering flood of strength.

My gift is not for my own kind, she thought sadly. *It only works with animals.*

And then the pain came again, stabbing her so savagely she doubled over, forgetting everything else, and lost herself in swirling stars and hot, sticky darkness.

When she next opened her eyes it was twilight, and her head was in Dasadas' lap. The Scythian had recovered enough to prop his back against a dead tree, and he was gazing down at her with anguish. "We are hurt, Epona," he managed to say.

"You are wounded. I am . . . I think I am going to have the baby, Dasadas."

His eyes flared open. "Here? Now? But Dasadas cannot help you. Weak . . ." He broke off to cough, as if to prove his statement. "Dasadas does not know how to birth a child."

"It is not a thing men need to know," Epona told him.

A *gutuiter* should have been there, to hold her hands and steady her as she squatted in the birth posture, and to sing the song of welcome for the new spirit. When the birth was concluded, the *gutuiter* would have helped her lie down and put the naked, bloody newborn on its mother's belly, so the strong muscles within her could contract in acknowledgment of their completed task and be healthier for the next birth. With the aid of the *drui*, skilled in the arts of summoning life, the baby might have had a chance to live.

But there was no *drui*, no Nematona with her herbs and teas, no Uiska of the soft voice. There was only pain and dizziness, and Dasadas' useless, frightened fumbling as he fought off his own weakness.

And when it was over, Kazhak's dead son, born too soon to survive in this way, lay on the earth mother, and Epona wept over him as she had never wept in her life.

Dasadas went back to the tree against which he had lain, and buried his face in the crook of his arm. The gray stallion, nervous at the smell of blood, pawed the earth and thought about his missing mares.

They buried the child at the foot of an oak tree. Epona returned the small spark to the great fire with whispered words of transition; Dasadas commemorated its passing by slashing his arms and earlobes, losing precious blood he could not spare in his weakened condition, but Epona did not criticize him for it.

She knew that he blamed himself for this loss. Again and again, he muttered words of self-castigation. "Dasadas did not fight good enough; Dasadas has failed Epona." He would not be comforted, and though she ached to spend her own grief, she had to set that aside and try to deal with his.

Then, too, there was the matter of the Dacians. "They will be here soon," Dasadas told her. "They will track us; they mean to have you, Epona. We must go."

"You are too badly hurt to ride, Dasadas."

"What about you? But is no choice. We must somehow get on gray horse, or stay here and be captured. We could not fight free this time."

No, she agreed, they could not escape again. She found moss and sweet grass to pack her body and hold back the bleeding, and she bandaged Dasadas' side as best she could with fabric torn from her clothing. They refilled the waterbag and tried to eat something for strength, but neither had the appetite for it. They were not able to travel, but they must.

And so they did.

Crawling onto the horse was a nightmare of pain, and the fainting sensation that followed was worse, but somehow the man and the woman rode the gray horse, and turned his head northward. He was only too glad to go. His instinct, and then his ears and nose, told him where the mares and the bay stallion waited, grazing peacefully in a hidden meadow, and he set off after them with only nominal guidance from the half-unconscious woman holding his reins.

Epona looked back at the grave beneath the oak tree. It was such a little mound in sun-dappled shade. She did not even have the amber necklace to leave with her son. It had gone to pay for a horse.

All the pain was not in her body.

"Find them," she whispered to the stallion, leaning over his neck. "Find them."

The missing mares and the bay stallion of Dasadas were responsible for the fact that the Dacians had not caught Epona, though she was unaware of it as she rode through a blur of grief and discomfort, doing the impossible because there was nothing else to be done. The Dacians were a fighting unit, returning from skirmish warfare at the edge of their territory, one of the constant battles they enjoyed with the neighboring Scordisci. They were not experienced at hunting and tracking, and the confusion of hoofprints left by the fleeing mares confused them. They never noticed when the stallion's prints veered off to the west, toward the glade where Epona and Dasadas lay attempting to recover.

The Dacians had followed the mares until they realized the hopelessness of catching loose horses in open land, and then they reluctantly abandoned the quest. "We will catch up with that woman some other time," the leader promised his men. "A woman that far gone — someone will see her. Someone will mention her. And those horses will be hard to hide; big horses, they were, good Thracian stock. What do you suppose she's doing with them up here?"

The gray stallion knew where his mares were and he carried Epona and Dasadas to them unerringly. The young bay, hearing him approach, whinnied a warning to the encroaching male, but Dasadas managed to rouse himself enough from his own suffering to call a command to his horse and the bay did not attack the gray. The two animals glared at each other, necks arched and nostrils flaring, while Epona dismounted and caught Dasadas' horse, then helped him to mount.

It was obvious he could go little farther, but she was anxious to find a more sheltered, less visible place to spend the night, now that they knew they were hunted. She did not ask Dasadas if he could make it; she did not ask herself. She rode around the mares, bunching them into a tightly packed band once more, then took hold of the rope on the headstall of the lead mare and set off, the rest of the little herd following and Dasadas, drooping in his saddle, bringing up the rear.

They were very fortunate. They soon found a tributary running back from the Duna to a deep, hidden valley that showed no sign of human habitation, or even discovery. In this season there was a thin covering of snow over the exposed grass, but beneath the trees there were patches of dry ground and plenty of deadwood for building fires. In such a place they could stay long enough to recover their strength, Epona thought.

The spirits were being good to them. Perhaps the sacrifice of her child had been enough; perhaps nothing more would be asked.

I have nothing more to give, Epona thought sadly. When she closed her eyes she did not see Kazhak's face anymore. She saw a little mound over a grave dug with a Kelti knife, beneath an oak tree.

Dasadas was much the weaker of the two. Even though her own body ached for rest, Epona found herself hunting for him, setting snares to catch small game and patiently waiting for half a day, within sight of the grazing horses, for sight of some edible bird she could bring down with her bow.

But the wild creatures, aware of the presence of the intruders, avoided the area, and game was very hard to get. *We need the art of the shapechanger*, Epona thought, without even a shudder of revulsion at the thought of Kernunnos. He seemed no more than a natural part of the world, now; there were things far more unpleasant than the vulpine face of the priest.

Dasadas thought of the shapechanger, too, though differently. He dreamed at night of a huge silver wolf that tore at his flesh and sapped his strength, slowing his recovery, but when he spoke of it to Epona she brushed his words aside. "The wolf follows us no longer, Dasadas, I told you that. I give you my word on it."

But the wolf was in Dasadas' mind, and it did follow; would follow forever.

When they were able, they moved on, at a much slower pace now. If they encountered no more trouble, they might reach the valley of the Kelti . . . by sunseason.

Sunseason seemed a very long distance away.

There was trouble, of course. Dasadas' wound did not heal well, and he was in constant pain, though he refused to admit it. Though he had never been able to link Epona's spirit with his, he had somehow become infused with her own grim determination to reach the Blue Mountains; to take the horses home. He drove himself relentlessly, and every day he grew thinner, until his gray eyes stared out of a skull-like face. He did not try to touch her now; he had no strength left for anything but the journey. That had become his personal battle; the one left to him that he refused to lose.

When they reached the broad plain of Epona's earlier memory, where the Duna turned sharply westward at last, one of the mares escaped them. The mares, bred by the Thracians for many generations to have exceptional qualities of both speed and endurance, had handled the trip well, losing little flesh. Epona had particularly looked forward to seeing the colt the gray stallion would sire on one powerfully built brown mare, a splendid animal that would have been the pride of any Thracian wagonmaster. But the mare wandered away, sometime in the night, and they were never able to find her.

Dasadas blamed himself. He should have been standing watch over the herd that night, and he had fallen into an exhausted, uneasy sleep, filled with frightening dreams . . . He beat on his head with his fists, punishing himself, until Epona ordered him to stop.

They lost the second mare when the land rose at last toward the mountains again, just as Epona's heart was lifting. The horse, unused to rocky terrain, stepped into a fissure and snapped her foreleg below the knee, and neither Epona's skill nor magic could save her.

Epona wept, then; long, deep sobs that wracked her body. Some of them were for the dead horse; some for the escaped mare. Most were for the grave beneath the oak tree.

Her tears frightened Dasadas. He had come to take her strength for granted, relying on her as on a brother, and now he hovered around her helplessly until she lashed out at him and drove him away.

Go to the bottom of grief alone, said the spirit within. *Cry out all the pain, then mount your horse and go on.*

In the distance, the Blue Mountains stood free and clear, waiting for them.

That was the hardest part of the trip. Since losing the brown mare, Epona had kept the others lashed together in a long string, using thongs and strips of hide and even rope she wove from grass, and now she rode at the head of the column, leading the first mare up the rocky road, leaving Dasadas to bring up the rear. They had traveled for so long and suffered so much, and they were both thin and short of temper. The climbing was demanding, sometimes treacherous, as rocks skittered underfoot and loose earth slid. The thinning air made human and horse tire more quickly. When the pain in his back and side was almost unbearable, Dasadas would sometimes look ahead at Epona, riding on, riding, riding, and shake his head in disbelief. A woman.

She did not look much like a woman now. Since their near-capture by the Dacians, Epona had hacked off her tawny hair with her knife, and kept what remained hidden beneath a Scythian cap. Her body would fit in man's trousers again, and her face and hands were burned dark by sun and wind. She could have been a lean nomad boy, with a sword at the waist and bow and arrows in the *gorytus*.

Riding, riding.

The terrain became familiar. The trees, the stones, the light were friends, and Epona acknowledged them with mixed feelings. Her eyes had seen so much since they last saw this place; the Blue Mountains appeared to her through memories of the Sea of Grass, and all the regions between. Perhaps nothing would ever look quite the same again.

But that pine, she knew that one — and that great boulder, bone of the mother, springing free of the earth — and the scent of the air, so sweet —

She was home, in the presence of familiar spirits. She knew them all; she felt them around her and experienced a sense of being reinstated into their world.

Water. Spirits. Trees. Spirits. Stones. Spirits. They knew she moved among them. The water saw her with its shining eye. The stones felt her presence. The trees heard her passing. She was forever bound to the great communion of spirits, of which her own was a part.

She halted the gray stallion and dismounted slowly, walking to a massive stone thrusting nakedly from the hillside, its exposed surface patterned by lichen and warmed by the sun. Dasadas watched as she stood beside it, concentrating, seeking to take part in the interchange she sensed between sun and stone. Something was being given and something taken, a timeless intercourse beyond the understanding of humankind, but as necessary to the pattern of life as earth and rain.

After a time, she smiled and returned to her horse.

When she heard the sentry's voice challenging her, at first she did not recognize it as that of Vallanos. Both the voice and the accent were unfamiliar. Then the words formed themselves into patterns she recognized and she knew all at once, and truly, that she was home.

"Vallanos! It is I, Epona! Daughter of Rigantona!" She kicked the gray horse into a trot and hurried forward.

Vallanos came scrambling down from his customary rocky perch, sword in hand. He did not see Epona of the Kelti; he saw a beardless Scythian horseman, and this time he was ready. He had almost reached the gray stallion's side before he got a good look at the blue eyes laughing down at him, and then he halted in confusion.

"Epona? Is that really you?"

"Yes, Vallanos. Don't you know me?"

"No one would know you, dressed like that. Where did you come from? Where have you been, what's happened . . ."

"All in good time, Vallanos. I suppose I should speak to the elders first, and Taranis."

"Yes, they will want to see you, all right. You will have much to explain." He broke off, staring in wonder at the string of mares, and Dasadas, waiting with them. "Is *that* a Scythian, that man with you?"

"Yes, Vallanos. He is my . . . friend. If it were not for Dasadas, I would never have found my way back to you. I want him treated with all the hospitality of the Kelti, and I want the *gutuiters* to see him soon, for he was badly wounded and the wound has never properly healed. He needs their care."

"Nematona has died since you left, Epona," Vallanos said sadly.

"Nematona?" She could not believe it. "What happened?"

"She said it was her time. She lay down in the sacred grove and did not wake up again."

Daughter of the Trees. A slim brown shape moved among the trunks, rustling with the leaves, and vanished into them forever. Part of the whole.

Epona closed her eyes and bowed her head.

"You wait here, Epona," Vallanos told her, "and I will go and announce your arrival in the village. Everyone will want to come out to greet you . . . this is such an occasion! . . . wait right here, don't go away . . ." He ran off, already breathless with the news, and Epona and Dasadas exchanged amused glances.

"You are welcomed here," said the Scythian.

"And you, as much as I. I owe you a great debt, Dasadas."

The Scythian was slumped low in his saddle. "There is nothing you can do for Dasadas, Epona."

"You are mistaken. We will make you well, here; you will be strong again, and you will be honored among my people."

"Is not important." His eyes were almost lost in their dark

405

sockets and she saw how dreadfully thin he was; how much of his own life he had spent for her sake.

And in thislife there was nothing she could do to make it up to him.

Vallanos returned, aglow with delight, to lead them triumphantly into the village himself. He told Epona that news of their arrival had thrown the community into an uproar; a feasting fire was even now being prepared, oxen were being slaughtered, runners had been sent for Mahka and the warriors.

"Mahka and the warriors?"

"Okelos has put together a band of trained fighters and allowed Mahka to join them. They have built two-wheeled carts for battle and they practice each day on that small strip of level land across the lake. They plan to leave the Blue Mountains soon, in search of new land and more room for our tribe."

Epona looked at her string of horses and smiled. "There are faster, easier ways to travel than in a cart, Vallanos," she said. "Though I suppose these Thracian wagon mares could speed a light cart along very fast, with a pair of armed warriors whipping them on."

Following the strutting Vallanos, she and Dasadas rode down to the village beside the lake.

The lake was as intensely blue-green as she remembered it. The embracing mountains were as steep, as furred with pine. But the village itself had changed.

Many of the lodges boasted heads on poles, either real skulls or carved wooden heads mounted until the genuine article could be obtained. Men walked about in trousers of tartan wool, modeled on the Scythian garment. Curving animals similar to those represented in Scythian decoration were carved on the sides of wagons; sculptured in bronze and affixed to the rims of cauldrons; painted on the row of shields leaning against the sides of every lodge.

There was a heady tension in the air; the tension of people bursting with energy, on the move. The village no longer felt like a placid, prosperous community, nestled in its mountains and waiting for the world to come to its gates. It was exploding like a fire when fat pine knots are thrown into it, sparks flying out in every direction. Epona had been gone only a few seasons, but in that time the Kelti had begun thinking in new ways and looking in new directions.

The village was an exciting place to be in; she could feel it. The energy was not random now, spending itself in games. It was directed like an arrow notched to a bowstring, ready to be shot outward.

Epona leaned down from the saddle. "What caused this, Vallanos?"

"Your leaving, partly. Everyone thought the Scythians had stolen you, and Okelos got support from the other young men to prepare a war party and go after you, but then bad weather came early and they could not leave. They fretted here, and complained of being trapped in these mountains. A small band of Taurisci came after snowmelt, looking for trouble, and Okelos killed their leader in a quarrel and mounted his head on a pole. The other men liked the idea. They already had their women making two-legged skirts for them to wear; they say the garment is more convenient in the mines. Once things began to change, it happened faster and faster. Traders came and were . . . made nervous . . . by what they saw here, they bartered quickly and left, giving us more for less. Taranis was pleased, and he encouraged the young men in their aggressive behavior.

"Now there is much talk of fighting, and we all look forward to it. I may go myself."

"Is the tribe pleased with these changes?"

"Not everyone. Kernunnos has been very upset; very strange. Some say he is mad. He stays in his lodge almost all the time now, and when anyone tries to talk to him he is lying on his bedshelf in such a deep sleep he cannot be wakened. But he is not dead — just away, in otherworlds. But we do not need him as much as we once did. Since we started putting up the heads, there has been abundant game — the heads must be as powerful magic as that of the shapechanger!"

Oh, no, Vallanos, Epona thought to herself. *There is nothing to equal the magic of the shapechanger. Perhaps, if the spirits will it, there is still time for me to learn from him. Perhaps he will forgive me.*

They entered the open gates, riding through the wooden palisade, the string of mares in tow. People came running toward them from every side, calling Epona's name. The mares spooked and snorted at the onrush of humanity, but the gray stallion stood firm, and the horse of Dasadas followed his example.

Taranis emerged from his lodge and strode toward Epona, a smile spread across his face like melted marrow spread across bread for seasoning. "Sunshine on your head," he greeted her, and she had to search her memory for the appropriate response. There were so many other words in the way . . . so many other things had been said . . .

Sirona, her newest baby clinging to her legs and rubbing sleepy eyes with a grubby fist, came forward, and welcomed Epona as warmly as if she had not been Rigantona's daughter. Others crowded after her, eager to touch Epona and assure themselves it was really she. Eager to get a look at the horses she had brought, the wonderful, towering horses, the breeding stock.

"I have learned how to train horses to accept men on their backs," Epona told Taranis, and she saw excitement leap in the chief's eyes.

The elders, their numbers slightly diminished by transition, came hurrying, anxious for an accounting of Epona's nights, but Taranis suggested that might wait until they were all seated comfortably around the feasting fire, with Epona in the place of honor. "First we will prepare heated water for you to bathe, of course," he reassured her, "and you will want to see your mother."

Epona's face was calm beneath its layers of sun- and windburn. "I am in no hurry to see Rigantona," she said.

There was a flurry of discussion as to what was to be done with her, but the elders ultimately decreed she should be given the guest lodge — and Dasadas with her, if he so desired. But he nodded his head in negation.

"Dasadas will sleep outside with horses, Epona; guard you."

"I need no guard now, Dasadas. I am home."

"Outside," the Scythian repeated. He looked so thin and drawn, so gutted by his inner fires. She longed to welcome him into the lodge with her, to bathe his damaged body in heated water and comfort it with red wine, but he would have none of it. He followed, leading the mares, as she rode the gray stallion toward the guesting lodge, and the Kelti trotted at their heels, touching the horses admiringly, chattering among themselves about this miracle.

A lone figure came across the commonground, wrapped in fury. No one noticed him; all attention was fixed on the new arrivals. Kernunnos, awakened from his sleep by the shouting, since even the *gutuiters* had learned not to bother him, no matter what the news, followed the disruptive noise toward its source, vibrating with anger at being disturbed. He saw . . . two Scythians! . . . mounted on horseback, fully armed, once again invading the village of the Kelti!

It was not to be borne. His mind still clouded from the mists of the otherworlds, the priest ran forward, pulling his knife from his belt. He shoved through the astonished crowd and hurled himself with all his strength at the nearest mounted figure, dragging it from the horse. The Scythian fell heavily to the earth with surprisingly little resistance, as if too weakened to fight back, and Kernunnos plunged his knife into the nomad's heart again and again, screaming in insane triumph.

It happened too fast, Epona did not realize Dasadas was being attacked until it was over and he lay dead on the ground, gray eyes staring sightlessly upward. Something gave way in her brain then, and she shrieked her own command at the gray stallion. The war command, ingrained in the animal's disciplined spirit by Kazhak's thorough training.

Kernunnos felt the chill of a shadow looming over him and looked up just in time to see the horse rise above him, hooves pawing the air. Then the mighty legs descended and the gray stallion stamped him into the earth mother.

Trumpeting his own battle cry, the horse tore his opponent to bloody pieces, rearing and striking again and again until at last Epona recovered herself and reined him aside, where he stood trembling.

The Kelti stared down at the trampled, bloody form of the shapechanger, lying next to the man he had killed. In his final battle Dasadas had succeeded in driving an iron knife made at a Kelti forge into Kernunnos' body, a knife the Scyth had carried to the Sea of Grass and back again. But it was the hooves of the horse that had rendered the priest little more than remnants of bloody flesh and splintered bone.

Only his face had escaped the horse's attack. The yellow eyes were closed, their light extinguished. On one side of his head a hideous mass of twisted scar tissue pulled his face into a grimace, a permanent snarl extending almost to the place where an ear should have been.

Sickened, Epona slid down from her stallion and threw herself onto the bosom of the earth mother.

A hand touched her shoulder but she pulled away from it. The insistent touch was repeated, and she looked up to see Tena, She Who Summons Fire, standing beside her with old Poel.

"Is this really Epona?" Tena asked, bending forward to peer into her face.

"It was Epona," she answered, sitting up wearily. "A long time ago, when I left the Blue Mountains, this was Epona. Now I hardly know who it is."

"It is the chief priest of the Kelti," Poel announced.

Chapter 32

H IS WORDS MADE NO SENSE to her. They were like rain beating against her ears; she did not understand the language. Tena and Uiska stood on either side of her, supporting her gently, murmuring to her, and the faces of the Kelti watched them, and she understood none of it. She got up, slowly.

Kernunnos lay dead at her feet. And Dasadas . . . oh, Dasadas!

She looked around with uncomprehending eyes. "Kazhak?" she asked in a small voice, and the watching Kelti muttered in surprise to one another.

Rigantona pushed through the crowd. "My child!" she cried, flinging her arms wide to welcome Epona, but the young woman drew back.

"I am not a child," she said in a hoarse whisper. "And I am not yours." Then she understood her mother's anxiety to establish a warm relationship.

"I am told" — she said in a voice that threatened to desert her altogether at any time — "that I am . . . the chief priest."

"It is truly said," Tena agreed. "You are *drui,* and you have slain your predecessor. The honor and the responsibility are yours now, Epona. It has never come to a woman of the Kelti before."

The words still had little meaning, but she could see how much they meant to Rigantona. She could see the woman all ready to embrace her, overflowing with newly discovered maternal fondness and pride. She took a step backward and felt the solidity of the gray stallion behind her. His shoulder was a wall to which she could set her back, and feel safe.

"Go away, Rigantona," she said with infinite weariness. "Go to your house and count your treasures. I am not one of them."

The Kelti were growing insistent, and she let them do what they would with her. The bath in heated water, scented with perfumed oils from luxury-loving Etruria. Her kin standing around, anxious to serve her in any way she might suggest. Food and wine. Songs of thanksgiving to the spirits for her return, and a visit to see the horses, now securely penned and surrounded by admirers, and Epona must relate again and again the difficulties she had encountered in bringing them.

The young men were the most vocal, begging her to begin at once, teaching them how to ride.

"These are Thracian wagon mares, not saddle animals," she said. "But their foals can be trained in the way I have learned. There will be time enough then for you to sit atop a horse, and feel the wind on your teeth."

The feasting fire, and the ceremonial cup. It came first to her, now, even before Taranis and the elders. The value of the horses, and the knowledge she carried within herself, set her apart from all others.

Different. And I did not want to be different.

But in that you have no choice, said the spirit within. *This is the pattern, Epona.*

Yes.

The story had to be told, and then her kin retold it to each other, embroidering it as they went along, making it as colorful and wild as the predators savaging their prey on the felt medallions that hung from Epona's saddlecloth.

Kazhak would laugh if he could hear them, she thought.

The feasting fire burned bright and hot.

Goibban came to her. Beautiful, golden Goibban, his muscles rippling, his teeth gleaming white within his beard. "Epona," he said, and laid some elaborate piece of bronzework at her feet, but she never looked at it. She tilted her head back and looked up at the stars, which were so much more beautiful.

Sometime before dawn she slept in the guest lodge, and on the next day she requested that a burial ceremony be prepared for Dasadas the Scythian. The Kelti listened with wide, round eyes as she described the cart upon which his body was to be laid. "Take him to every house," she instructed, "and let every family gather around his body and drink a last cup with him. And I want to hear crying."

"Crying . . . for the transition of a spirit?"

"Crying. If the men cannot do it, let the women wail aloud, but there must be crying and tearing of hair for Dasadas the Scythian."

It was wonderful, the way the people hurried to do her bidding. But she would not take advantage of them. She remembered Tsaygas and Mitkezh, abusing their power, working for themselves rather than the tribe.

Their punishment would come, in thisworld or the next. At least she had that consolation. That certain knowledge. As she had other knowledge and other certainties, for with the assumption of the mantle of chief priest a kind of peace had come to Epona. She no longer questioned, and the old recklessness seemed to have burned away. She had so much to learn, but she had the patience now to listen, and be taught. And, as had been promised, she could see the pattern. See it changing, for better or worse, and understand her part in that changing.

She no longer fought, for there was nothing to fight — except the loneliness of the night, and the emptiness of her bedshelf. She was not a *gutuiter*, she was chief priest, and if she had wished for a partner she could have taken one to warm her bed and body. But she did not. Goibban came often, with little gifts, and she smiled at him and accepted them to avoid hurting his feelings, then set them aside and never looked at them again.

Behind Goibban's eyes, there was no one she knew.

The mares were bred, and Uiska prophesied they were all safely in foal. There was much excited talk of the horses to come, both from the Thracian stock and from the cross of the bay and gray Scythian horses on the little cartponies. Epona rode the stallion every day, alone, following wherever the trails led, and thought her own thoughts.

413

Sunseason flooded the mountains with clear white light, then softened into diffused gold, signaling the approach of the festival of the great fire.

Goibban met Epona just inside the palisade gate as she returned from a ride. The smith held out his latest offering, a diadem of interlaced gold wires set with blue stones for which he had traded many iron farm implements to the Illyrians.

Epona dismounted and accepted his gift graciously, though her eyes did not linger on it as Goibban had hoped they would. "Your spirit is generous," she said, starting to turn away. Then she paused. His heart leaped with hope.

She lifted her head, and her eyes filled with such radiance it hurt Goibban to look at them. It was like staring into the sunrise over the eastern mountains. But she was not looking at him. Her gaze went past him, to the palisade and the road beyond, and her face wore the intense expression of one who listens. She cocked her head slightly, a smile playing at the edges of her mouth.

Down the road from the pass, a horseman came riding.

crated to the good of the tribe, was to acquire a peculiar secondary immortality.

But the most truly influential of all the Celtic pantheon, in the long sweep of history, would be Epona herself. Goddess of the horse.

Aided by the horse, the Celts expanded into what is now northern Italy; into Switzerland, Hungary, southern Poland, Czechoslovakia, Yugoslavia, Rumania, as well as into Germany, Belgium, and France. They sacked Rome in 390 B.C. and were in Delphi a century later. As Galatians, in central Anatolia, they were the recipients of epistles from Saint Paul in the Christian era.

Their energy carried them westward as well, toward that horizon that has always lured the adventurer. They crossed the Pyrenees and entered Iberia; they crossed the channel to Albion, to shape Britain and give birth to Arthur. They dared the cold Irish Sea to set foot on green Ierne, five hundred years before Christ was born.

They carried with them complex art forms, unexcelled craftsmanship, a passion for poetry and music, and a deep reverence for nature. They passed on their vitality and fierce love of liberty to their descendants, a bequest ultimately carried by the peoples of Europe to the New World.

The Celtic contribution to western civilization has never been fully appreciated. For the countless millions who, perhaps unknowingly, carry that indomitable blood in their veins today, it is a priceless heritage.

Tracing the Celtic trail backward through time meant sifting the vast amount of information coming to light as archeologists focus more and more interest on non-Mediterranean Europeans, as well as studying Celtic mythology and folklore to find the seeds of real history from which such stories grow.

Progress often occurs in the fringe areas where two cultures clash. When Celt met Scyth, West met East, and the wily Celt profited greatly from the exchange. Herodotus, the earliest historian to write extensively of the Scythians, provided a springboard for an exploration of their culture, though his geography of the Ukraine and the steppes was flawed. However, his comments on the Scythian culture have proved to be less fanciful than we once thought, as archeologists learn more about Eastern Europe and the region from above the Black Sea to the Altai Mountains.

The preliterate history of the Celts is also manifest in their artifacts, and can be constructed, to some degree, from their own bardic tales and the imprint they left on subsequent cultures. The first to write of them were the Greeks, who called them *keltoi*, a phonetic version of their own name for themselves. Later, Julius Caesar would have ample opportunity to write of them and to study them. As Gauls and Britons they proved to be among his most formidable opponents, and he would arbitrarily divide Gaul into three parts to avoid confronting the Germanic branch of the family.

The magic of the Celtic Druids would fuel the fires of imagination in song and story for over two thousand years — and be absorbed into many other religions. The symbols of that forgotten faith remain with us to the present day, their shapes only slightly changed. And wherever the Celts went, they carried with them the stories of those who had come to be their deities, those who had done spectacular things in their own age and time. Goibban, eventually known as Goibniu, whom the Romans equated with Vulcan. Nematona, goddess of the trees. Toutorix (also known as Teutates), Taranis, and Esus, the Celtic trinity. A host of other figures who passed into mythology as Suleva and Macha, Rigantona and Vallaunus — and great Cernunnos, lord of the animals. Cernunnos would be transmogrified, in ways only a shapechanger might fully appreciate, into the fearsome werewolf of Transylvanian legend, to haunt the Carpathian mountains forever. The shapechanger, ancient practitioner of sympathetic magic, conse-

Afterward...

THE INTRODUCTION of horses suitable for riding or for pulling war chariots at speed provided unparalleled mobility, as
culturally catalytic to the early Celts of 700 B.C. as the combus-
tion engine would be to a later era. No longer restricted to tribal
territories or depleted soils, they were free to seek new horizons.
With abundant energy and superior iron weaponry they exploded
from their homeland to sweep across the face of Europe.

Epona's story is set in what is now known as Hallstatt, in the
Austrian Alps, site of some of the richest finds of early Celtic
archeology. The Celts were never, in the truest sense, a nation,
but a loose confederacy of tribes spread through the mountains
and rich river valleys of ancient Europe, developing their own
unique culture even as Troy fell and Athens rose. Theirs was the
Bronze Age, and the spectacular, history-making dawn of the Age
of Iron.

Within a century of acquiring the eastern horse and mastering
iron, the prototype of the Celtic warrior was fully developed.
Fearless, passionate, proud, poet and warrior, headhunter and
entrepreneur, the tall Celt emerged from dim prehistory to fur-
nish much of the foundation stock for modern Europe. Becoming
equestrians brought to the surface qualities that may have been
lying dormant in earlier, proto-Celtic natures: a fiery tempera-
ment, a taste for adventure, the idealism of one whose star is
always just over the horizon.